"A stubborn man David Evans is," Griffin said thoughtfully.

"Well, I don't care," Caitlin said defiantly. "I'll take a carriage from the stables and we'll ride, now, to Carfax. Surely we'll be able to find a justice willing to marry us. And then Father won't be able to do a thing about it. Not a thing!"

Griffin touched her lips with a silencing finger, then moved it slowly along the line of her jaw to her soft hair. She leaned closer and held her breath, the long lingering kiss momentarily shattering her despair.

She held him tightly as they sank to the grass. Her tears still flowed, but the bitterness soon changed to joy when she felt the weight and the heat and the magic of him. And as they shed their clothes, the embers beneath her skin fully flamed.

"Oh, Griff!" she cried, glad to banish the grief from her soul.

SEACLIFF
by Felicia Andrews
author of SILVER HUNTRESS

Also by Felicia Andrews

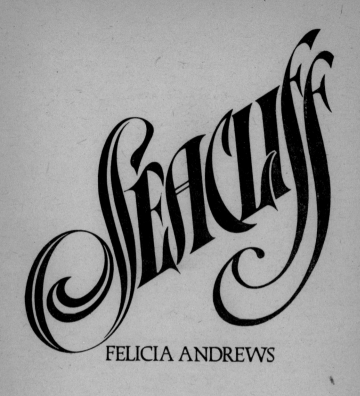

SEACLIFF

FELICIA ANDREWS

CHARTER BOOKS, NEW YORK

SEACLIFF

A Charter Book/published by arrangement with
the author

PRINTING HISTORY
Charter Original/March 1984

ISBN: 0-441-75640-9

Charter Books are published by The Berkley Publishing Group,
200 Madison Avenue, New York, N.Y. 10016.
PRINTED IN THE UNITED STATES OF AMERICA

PROLOGUE

Wales, 1771

THE GLEN was a special place, a secret place, a guardian of dreams.

Hidden in the mountains not far from the western coast, the glen was an emerald set between steep rocky slopes that protected it from all but the fiercest winter storm. The trees were tall and richly crowned, the grass in the clearing low and thick, and a stream coursed through the middle to a wide pond. Wild flowers painted the banks with splashes of every color of the rainbow, and the birds singing above in the branches made this an idyllic playground for man or beast. Occasionally a stag and its family ambled in to drink, first nervously eyeing the clearing for signs of predators that frequently included man. Eagles flew in the currents above the mountain summits in the distance, their cries soft and their wings golden in the sunlight.

It was peaceful there, the air a soft green from the ceiling of broad leaves that laced together overhead; and it was private. Those who were aware of the glen seldom told others. It was much too special to share with any but the like-minded.

A large flat-topped boulder jutted over the pond on its western side. Ringed with reeds, its sides were spotted with dark green moss. Glints of mica shone on its surface; a streak of ebony gleamed in the center.

And on it sat a young woman.

Even with her legs drawn up among the folds of her long sable skirts, it was obvious she was tall and slender, and under the gentle silk ruffles of her white shirt she had a flat stomach, a narrow waist, and full breasts that turned men's heads when they were not dazzled by her face. Her raven black hair was long and captured the afternoon sun as it fell in natural waves far below her shoulders. Her forehead was high, her eyebrows dark and thick, and her eyes obsidian. When her temper flared, they became hard; when she was at peace, they softened and glowed. Her nose gently sloped upward, her lips were full and red, and her chin was rounded and cleft.

At that moment she could easily have been taken for a portrait had not her hand risen suddenly to wipe away a tear from her cheek.

It's not fair, she thought.

"It's not fair!" she cried aloud, for the hundredth time since reaching the glen. Her hand clenched and struck her thigh once, then a second and third time while she stared blindly at the diamond-shadows of fish swimming below the pond's surface.

She knew she should not have been surprised by her father's announcement at breakfast that morning; he had been hinting for weeks. Nevertheless, when it came time, she'd been too stunned to react.

"No," David Evans said flatly. "The answer is no."

"But, Father, I want to marry him!"

"No," he repeated, regret now coloring his gravelly voice. "You may have known Griffin Radnor since you were both in swaddling, and he may now own a fair estate, but he's too wild, too full of himself to be entrusted with my daughter."

"Father," she said, "I've heard stories of your own youth, and they were not exactly tales of a saint."

"Griff Radnor is different," he declared as he walked from the room. "You may be sixteen, but I'm still master of Seacliff, and I say no!"

She sat open-mouthed when he cast a sad smile in her direction before leaving, and shortly afterward she stormed from the house and rode headlong to the glen, bemoaning all the while her father's hatefulness and Fate's apparent alliance against her wishes.

It simply was not fair!

A sound, then, distracted her, and she looked angrily over her shoulder, an oath at her lips to renew the battle if her father had followed her.

But it was not David Evans.

In the clearing was a stocky white stallion, and standing beside it a man dressed in snug brown breeches and an open-throated white shirt. His long hair was the deep color of copper, his face rugged and tanned by the sun, and his shoulders and chest broad enough to prove he wasted little time sitting behind a desk piled high with ledgers.

The moment Griffin Radnor smiled, Caitlin scrambled down

from her perch and raced into his waiting arms, weeping as she blurted out her story. He nodded and murmured softly as he stroked her back, then gently eased her away without breaking their embrace.

"A stubborn man David Evans is," he said thoughtfully.

"Well, I don't care," she said defiantly. "I'll take a carriage from the stables and we'll ride, now, to Carfax. Surely, we'll be able to find a justice willing to marry us. And then Father won't be able to do a thing about it. Not a thing! Oh, Griff—"

He touched her lips with a silencing finger, then moved it slowly along the line of her jaw to her soft hair. She leaned closer and held her breath. She could feel the sun's warmth on her back. It merged with the sudden fire in her lungs as he kissed her. It was a long lingering kiss that momentarily shattered her despair. She held him tightly as they sank to the grass. Her tears still flowed, but the bitterness soon changed to joy when her eyelids fluttered closed and she could feel his hands caress her like the cooling breeze that danced through her hair. She could feel the embers beneath her skin fully flame as they shed their clothes . . . could feel the weight and the heat and the magic of him as they joined in a centuries-long moment that temporarily banished the grief from her soul.

And afterward, clothed again and listening to the stream's crystal voice, she whispered, with a grin, "Father says you're also working with the rebels against the English."

A kiss on her cheek for an answer.

"Well? Are you?"

There was mischief in his eyes. "Would you mind?"

She didn't know if he was serious or not, but her response was grave just the same. "No. But I do not believe it. Father is . . . he is ill, and sometimes I think he sees phantoms, even in daylight." She sighed then and smiled. "No. I don't believe it."

"And why not, Cat? Don't you think I could fight those damnable English?"

"I'm sure you could," she answered hastily, "but I doubt you do. No matter what stories Father tells about you, I've known you all my life. You wouldn't deliberately put yourself in that sort of danger. Lord, if the king's men caught you, you'd be hanged!"

He said nothing, only sat up abruptly and gripped his knees

with his hands as he stared at the pond. There was no time
here in the glen. There never had been enough, but suddenly
she felt as if time had aged Griff so that he was much older
than she; so much older that she grew a little frightened.

"Caitlin, you know . . . you know how I feel about you."

She watched his back warily. "Yes." A wren sang cheerfully
in the boughs overhead. "Yes, I do."

"But your father is right," he said, after too long a time.
"I'm really not the best catch you could find." He rose then
and stood over her. "And he is your father. It would be wrong
to go against his wishes."

Before she could move, he strode up to his mount and swung
into the saddle. She called to him as she struggled to her feet,
their loving seeming to have vanished like smoke.

"Griff," she said, rushing to his side, "what Father said, all
those things aren't true! They're—"

His expression was painful: love shone clearly in his eyes,
but it was veiled by a shadow she did not understand.

"Griff, if you went there," she said desperately. "If you
went to Seacliff and talked with him, you could convince him.
I know you could."

Sadly he shook his head.

Anger, then, and hurt blended to harden her voice. "You
mean you will not fight for me?"

"Mr. Evans has spoken, Caitlin."

"I see. Yes. Yes, I see. If he gave his assent, you would
take me without question. But one word, one little word and
you fold like a leaf." She glared. "I thought I was worth fighting
for, Griffin Radnor."

He opened his mouth to speak; instead he shook his head
and wheeled his mount around. The stallion bolted into the
woods and was, in seconds, little more than a specter among
the trees. Within seconds, all she could hear was the sound of
hooves, and the flutter of leaves above her.

Why? she pleaded silently. Why, Griff, why?

Then, with a glower, she stamped her foot, forgetting the
beauty around her. "Damn you, Griff. Damn you, Griff Radnor, I hope the English take your head!"

PART ONE

Daughter

Eton, England, 1775

1

THE FALCON appeared to be little more than a speck soaring against the sky's brilliant blue. With its powerful red-tipped wings, it climbed until the gently rolling land below took on distinct patterns: squares of green pasture, silver threads of streams, gem-shaped lakes where fish leaped unnoticed and skiffs rode under canopies of gold. Great oaks blended into sculptured masses, herds of grazing cattle and an occasional solitary horse rounded out the scenery.

The bird rose higher and coasted far above the tiny village of Egham and the narrow band of the Thames. Past Runnymede, then past Englefield Green sprawled atop a low hill. To the parkland on the outskirts of the royal town of Windsor it shuddered and blinked. A soft *scree* sounded to mark a sighting, and within a fraction of a second the beast had folded its wings and plunged into a dive almost too fast for the human eye to follow. Within moments it reached some unseen, but no doubt startled, quarry below.

A woman on horseback heard the hunting cry and reined in her high-strung chestnut to a sudden halt. Her companion just behind was startled and cried out. The other woman raised her brown-gloved hand to her full red lips—a signal for silence—and the other swallowed her protest. She followed the pointing finger to where the falcon was already rising again, its long-eared prey limp in its talons. The companion shrugged.

There had been nothing novel about either the dive or the falcon; it was a sight she had seen nearly every day of her life, and being in this new country didn't make it any more savory.

Then she urged her mount alongside the chestnut. "If we don't get along, we're going to be late."

"But it's so beautiful here," the woman said, awe in her voice. Her eyes sparkled as she twisted slowly around in her saddle.

The companion shrugged again. Perhaps it was, but in her present mood all she could see was that every tree and every bush seemed to be stamped "England" in bold lettering—not her notion of beauty.

The woman noted the disapproval and sighed loudly—a rebuke not entirely intentional. "Gwen," she said, "you're really not being fair."

"Fair enough," Gwen Thomas muttered.

"But look!" she cried, gesturing so strongly that her green velvet cloak fell back over one shoulder. "Look at what they've done here. It's magnificent. It's stunning. It marks a true eye for beauty, Gwen Thomas, and you cannot deny it no matter how sour you are."

Gwen's lips pursed, and she whistled silently. Finally, under the other woman's steadily smiling gaze, she nodded her reluctant agreement and looked away, knowing her friend would suspect the lie if she added words.

Beyond was the Long Walk. It began on the low hillside to her left, a clearing of underbrush and trees across a lawn nearly one hundred yards wide. The Walk flowed down the slope in a brilliant green flood, jumped the road and the river, and continued for nearly a mile. Marking its end was a sudden rise above which rose the bannered turrets and Round Tower of Windsor Castle. Around the castle was an impressive sweep of land and an artfully planted double row of trees so that the king, if he had a mind, could look out from his chambers at night and see the green carpet that led to a statue of a mounted nobleman.

"Beautiful," the woman cried. Gwen barely contained a groan.

"Cat, if we don't move along we're going to be—"

Caitlin twisted sharply around, her eyes narrowed and lips taut. "Do not," she said quietly, with steel undertone, "call me that while we're here."

Gwen glanced up and down the road. There was nothing but a cluster of sheep grazing on the Long Walk. "But . . . but there's nobody here," she protested.

"I don't care," she said, though less sternly. "If you keep on saying it, you might slip in front of Oliver."

There was a moment's pause before Gwen decided not to argue. As much as she hated to admit it, her mistress was right. Caitlin's husband displayed a severe enough temper whenever the two women slipped unawares into their native Welsh; and to use Caitlin's familiar childhood name invariably sparked a lecture from Morgan accusing Gwen of being unseemly and trying to rise above her station. She herself did not mind, because Oliver was English and she delighted in every jab she could safely make. Unfortunately, he saved a portion of his anger for Caitlin whom he rebuked for encouraging that sort of talk. And God knew her mistress's life was hard enough as it was.

"Caitlin." A soft voice cried. "Caitlin, don't be mad. I couldn't stand it if you were mad at me."

Caitlin considered the sky gravely, and the river, the sheep, the stately arrangement of trees.

"Cat? Please?"

A grin, sly and mischievous, formed, hidden from her friend. "All right, all right, if you're going to whine like a pup."

"Whine?" Gwen's back straightened. She was shorter than Caitlin, plumper but not as voluptuous. Her hair and eyes were midnight, and her will just as strong. "Whine? Me?"

Caitlin's expression assumed a parody of sternness. "Whine," she said sharply. Then she poked her riding crop at Gwen's arm. "You must learn your place, Gwen. It's not proper for a servant to rebuke her mistress."

"Servant? You're calling *me* a servant?"

Her lips quivered in the effort to hold back a smile. "But of course, my child."

"Child?"

"Just the other day, in Eton, didn't that duke or baron or whatever the devil he was tell you he'd like to have you in his household for an evening or two? To help you come of age, as it were. Isn't that what he said?"

"Caitlin Morgan! If your father could hear you——"

But she was forestalled when Caitlin gestured a warning and began easing her mount to the side of the road. A moment later came the rhythmic sound of carriage and horses approaching behind them. Caitlin quickly adjusted her skirts and cloak, and pushed herself forward so she rode higher in the gleaming English saddle on the chestnut's back. She threw an apologetic glance to Gwen and began moving sedately along the grassy verge. It was disappointing to have to rein in their joking; it was something they had little time for when Morgan was home from one of his business trips. He always insisted on prim comportment, an attitude he felt befit the wife of Sir Oliver Morgan, retired major in His Majesty's army. He did not seem to understand— or he refused to acknowledge—that she was also, and most emphatically, Caitlin *Evans* Morgan, daughter of David Evans and mistress of Seacliff, Cardiganshire, Wales. And no matter what Oliver or any of the others might say, it was a heritage that she most profoundly cherished.

The carriage behind them slowed, and when she turned, she saw two pairs of matched grays approaching, each with a flowing white plume affixed to the leather strap between its ears. The coachman and footman were in scarlet and silver livery, and the closed, gold-trimmed vehicle looked impressively bright beneath its faint powdering of road dust. Within sat a bloated, powdered, and rather myopic old woman who had pulled aside the linen curtain and nodded a stiff, imperious greeting. The coach halted beside Caitlin.

"Lady Corning," she acknowledged, thinking that of all people she had to encounter on the road it would have to be one of the most self-important harridans she'd ever met.

"My dear," the older woman said. "Enjoying the air, I see."

"We've just come from Egham," she said. "We ordered some stained glass for my husband's home." She smiled. "Egham is such a lovely little place, don't you think? And the work there is positively superb."

"It is indeed. And how are you enjoying your stay in England, child?"

Her smile stiffened somewhat, but her response was nonetheless genuine: "Oh, lovely! I've never seen such marvelous things in my life."

From the shadowed confines of the coach came a barely stifled laugh. Lady Corning's sister, no doubt, Caitlin thought.

"But it's true," she insisted.

"Of course it is, my dear," Lady Corning said. "I hear that response from all visitors to our country. They just cannot seem to get enough of it."

Caitlin frowned in puzzlement. "But I'm not really a visitor, you know. That is, I do spend almost as much time here as I do in Wales."

A snort from the sister, and Lady Corning smiled tolerantly. "Wales, my child, is not really England."

"Well, I know that," she said, more sharply than she'd intended, "but it's been part of the country for nearly two hundred years. More, if I'm not mistaken. And certainly far longer than the place those sour-faced Scots call a country."

"Yes," Lady Corning said stiffly. "I'm sure." And at a rap against the door the coach lurched suddenly into motion, forcing Caitlin to back up quickly and turn her head away from the dust raised by the coach's large red wheels. Once the air had cleared, Caitlin stared after the departing noblewoman and wondered what she'd said to offend her. She'd only spoken the truth as she saw it, and she had certainly said nothing against the old woman herself. Gwen pulled up alongside her, and Caitlin raised an eyebrow in silent question.

"I don't know," Gwen said. "I didn't hear all you said."

"Oh, dear," she sighed. "I hope I haven't done it again."

She rode on silently, reviewing the brief conversation over and over in her mind, trying to pinpoint the moment of offense. But she could not; and the more she thought about it, the more it distressed her, pulled at her, tossing her back and forth between two convergent loyalties—her husband, and her country.

And in that moment of melancholy, and in an abrupt surge of homesickness, she saw in the June air before her the mocking visage of Griffin Radnor, his long, dark copper hair flowing behind his rugged face in some impossible breeze. Oh, Griffin, she thought in momentary desperation, why did you let me do this thing? And the instant the thought formed she scowled. Griffin Radnor was of the past. Whatever she might have felt for him was over, done with. Her father was right, had been all along. Griffin's past was too dark to brighten Seacliff's future, and whatever dreams she might still dream about him were simply the lingering fancies of a young girl, not those of a married woman. They would fade soon enough, just as the twinges of her heart would fade until the sound of his name no longer provoked her.

A sigh, whisper-soft, passed between her lips, and she looked guiltily to Gwen, who returned a quiet smile.

"You're thinking of Griff, aren't you?"

"No!" she snapped, almost shouting. Damn that girl. Always bringing up his name when it wasn't wanted. Implying this and wishing that until Caitlin thought she would scream. Wasn't it bad enough she and Oliver were locked in a marriage that was in name only? Must she always endure Gwen's sporadic reminders of what might have been?

A tear welled in one eye, and she wiped it furiously away.

And in that gesture she snapped back to a time almost four years ago, to a glen nestled in the mountains far from Seacliff's valley. She recalled a soft spring afternoon and a diamond-sparkling stream, birds of all colors weaving rainbows in the trees and deer by the dozens gamboling down to the banks to cool their thirst. She'd been told shortly before by her father that no matter how wealthy Griffin Radnor was, no matter how large his holdings or how respected, there would be no union of the Radnors and the Evanses. There were too many unpleasant rumors about Griffin's time in the army, in which he did everything from gamble to wench, and perhaps worse. And wasn't there Morag Burton's claim that Griffin was the father of her bastard child? Sowing wild oats was one thing, her father had preached, but doing so in your own back yard was something else again.

Caitlin had raged and wept, had finally fled the house and ridden into the mountains to the glen where she and Griffin often met . . . to talk, to dream, to laugh at their elders as children will do when they love those elders. And he had come to her, having heard from Gwen the story of the fight. He had taken Caitlin in his strong arms and comforted her, stroking her until she could no longer stand the anguish of their parting. She had taken his hands and placed them firmly on her breasts, wound her fingers through his hair and pulled his lips down to hers. The warmth of the sun and the salt of her tears, the caress of the cool breeze on her flesh as he disrobed her slowly, like a man at devout worship, came back to her. He said nothing, but spoke with his fingers and the fire-touch of his mouth. And then, with the grass soft beneath her and the sun filtered by the trees, she had—

"Cat? Cat, this is where we turn off."

Caitlin blinked away the images swirling around her, put a hand to her cheek and felt the flush of her memory. She nodded, not daring to speak. Without warning Gwen, she leaned hard over her mount's neck, nudging its flank with her crop and whispered into its silky ear. In no time the chestnut exploded into a gallop down a narrow lane lined with towering oaks. The foliage blurred past, the wind wove through her hair, and before long she was laughing again and listening to Gwen's shouts as she raced after her.

And Griffin, she thought then, could go straight to hell. He could have had her if he'd truly wanted her. But he hadn't even put up a fight. It was his loss. And it served him damned right! She really didn't care anyway. She'd been a lot younger then, and hadn't known her own mind.

Five minutes later, just as the trees fell away to expose Morgan's estate, she slowed her mount to a halt.

The house at the end of the circular drive was not overly large and, because it stood in the middle of sprawling lawns bordered by forestland rich and verdant, it appeared much smaller. Morgan Hall was a large-beamed Tudor structure built during the reign of Elizabeth, comfortable enough without ostentation, and near enough to its neighbors despite the woods so as not to seem unpleasantly isolated. Oliver's grandfather had purchased it after his tour in the army, and it was maintained by his father who'd been shrewd enough to invest much of his officer's pay in the mercantile business. A forest of chimneys populated the angular roof; diamond-shaped panes of leaded glass reflected the last rays of the sun. The exterior glowed because it had been freshly whitewashed, and the flowers and tall shrubs that grew around the house seemed to be waiting especially for her coming.

On the steps leading up to the front door stood a white-haired, slouch-shouldered man whose face was heavily lined and whose red and black livery seemed too large. He held Caitlin's reins wordlessly as she dismounted, and led the horses away to the small cluster of stables near the line of trees on the left. Gwen looked after him with a faint moue of distaste.

"Nasty old brute, isn't he?" she said, following Caitlin inside.

"Oh, Bradford's all right. You just don't give him a chance."

Gwen's expression was doubtful. "Has he ever smiled at you? Does he ever bid you good morning?"

Caitlin shook her head. "But he's a quiet man; that's all. He's been with Oliver's family for years." She paused. "But I do wish he didn't look as if he were eating lemons all the time."

Gwen giggled, and covered her mouth quickly.

The foyer was wide and unadorned, flowing to a sitting room on the left dominated by a ceiling-high fireplace. On the right was an ornate dining room. When neither Mrs. Thorn the cook nor Mary the sullen maid came out to greet them, Caitlin shrugged off her cloak and handed it to Gwen.

"Oliver will be home soon, I imagine," she said, heading for the fan-shaped staircase that swept to a landing beneath a round, stained-glass window. "I'd better clean up. He hates me smelling like a horse. Tell Mary I'll need plenty of hot water, will you?" Then she stopped and hurried back, planted a solid kiss on Gwen's cheek, and thanked her breathlessly. "You do help me manage, you know. You really do."

And before Gwen could respond, Caitlin was running up the steps, hurrying down the corridor to the sanctuary of her large sunny apartment overlooking the front of the house. It had a massive pair of wardrobes in scrolled walnut, a gold canopy bed raised on a dais covered with wine velvet, a canted-beamed ceiling, a crescent vanity and several mirrors, some armchairs, a chaise longue, and a fireplace much smaller than those on the ground floor. A fire was already crackling against the onset of a cool evening. She stood on the hearth and stripped off her gloves, shrugged off her jacket and sank wearily to her knees.

Her room wasn't Oliver's, and a brief wave of resentment clouded her eyes and tightened her jaw. It was all very well that she had married Oliver to provide a steady hand for Seacliff after her father's passing; and it was all very well that Oliver had been a military hero during the last battles of the French and Indian Wars; and it was even understandable that they should spend almost half of each year in Eton because England was, after all, Oliver's country. But at quiet moments like this, and after encounters with people too much like Lady Corning, she longed to gaze out the window and see the tides thundering in at the base of Seacliff's bluffs, the misty rolling hills in the distance, and the broad valley where she'd been born.

Perhaps, as her father had suggested from his sickbed, much of her problem was in her attitude, and her unrestrained tongue. Certainly the latter had caused her no end of embarrassment because, unlike the English, she did not deliver her opinions obliquely but stated them boldly. And she stated her opinions far too often, to too many of the wrong people. Thinking before speaking was, she conceded, not exactly her strongest virtue.

As for her attitude, marriage with Oliver was not even close to what she'd dreamed marriage should be. Gwen claimed the man had no sense of romance. That much was surely true, though in his fashion he *did* care for her somewhat. Nevertheless, his excuses for not coming to her bed, and his response whenever she suggested she was more than a bauble to be displayed, puzzled her. There was also the curious fact of the marriage itself—a union between a young Welsh woman and a strict, though not always uncharming, army major. All of this made her determined not to let her spirit break. She would endure for her father's sake, if for no other reason.

A hesitant knock on the door disturbed her ruminations, and Mary—thin, fox-faced, and sullen—entered with two steaming pails of water, which she emptied into a curved metal tub set against the far wall. That done, she left and returned with two more, then went out and closed the door silently behind her. Not a word was exchanged.

As soon as Caitlin understood the servant girl would not return, she disrobed quickly and tested the water with her foot. She winced and hugged herself against the room's slight chill and sprinkled lavender scent over the surface of the water. A moment later she stepped into the tub, sighing as she eased herself down into its narrow confines. She pulled her knees up to her chest and grasped them loosely.

She closed her eyes and reveled in the bath-warmed room. She had a fleeting image of Griffin, then of her sickly father, before she slipped into a doze interrupted only when Gwen knocked impatiently on the door and let herself in. Without speaking, she bustled across the room, lit all the candles in their bronze and ebony sconces, then snatched up the cotton cloths Mary had piled by the tub and gestured sharply.

"He's back," she said, "and he's in a proper foul mood."

"Oh, Lord," Caitlin sighed. She rose and allowed Gwen to dry her. Then, as she climbed into her petticoats, and let Gwen slip over her upraised arms a simple dark-blue shirt and matching multipleated skirt, she shook her head slowly. "All this stuff," she said sourly, smoothing the bodice and adjusting the high neck. "I think I'd rather be naked."

Gwen laughed, and followed her to a tall, silver-framed mirror to one side of the vanity. She picked up a pearl-handled brush and stood behind her, frowning. "You didn't pin it up again, Cat," she scolded lightly, pushing at the wet-dark ends of black hair. "When are you going to learn?"

"I didn't think of it," she said. "Besides, it's not as if I'm going to see the queen, is it? Not that I'd care."

Gwen laughed as she wielded the brush deftly. "Ah, Cat,

you do reassure me, you really do." And in answer to Caitlin's questioning reflection: "I sometimes fear you've gone English on me, you know. The way you talk sometimes, and the way you go around to all these places..."

"Gwen," she said solemnly, "there is nothing wrong with enjoying myself while I'm here. It's a lovely country, and you know that well. And there are some here who don't mind who we are and where we're from. But don't you forget, ever, that I do know who I am."

Gwen nodded. "Yes, and that's what gets you into so much trouble."

"Well, can I help it if I say the wrong thing now and again?"

Gwen rapped her skull lightly with the brush. "You must learn to think before you speak, Cat. There's just so much these people will take from us before—"

Suddenly, heavy boots pounded swiftly along the corridor and, with scarcely a pause, a fist slammed against the door.

"Caitlin, goddammit, what have you done to me now!"

2

CAITLIN LOOKED to the ceiling in a silent prayer, then waved Gwen into the corner near the door. Drawing in a deep breath, she bid her husband enter just as she folded her hands primly at her waist.

"Caitlin!"

Oliver Morgan was not much taller than she, but his iron-rod military bearing gave the illusion of height. His shoulders were square, his chest broad, and the only evidence of his high style of living was a slight paunch. But he was also much older than his twenty-year-old wife, and his own fifty years were beginning to manifest themselves in the lines inching across his face. The corners of his red-rimmed eyes were webbed from perpetually squinting, the flesh around his jawline sagged somewhat, and his thin lips were gaining a tight look about them. Because he refused to powder his own hair, his head was shaven and the flesh taut, somewhat gleaming, and darkly veined. Over his shirt and knee breeches he wore an ankle-length, velvet-lapeled dressing gown that billowed as he strode angrily into the room. He glared, and Caitlin backed away, gesturing to a tall chair by the hearth. He took it without speaking and dropped into it as if carrying a weight, then stared at the low fire with a slow shake of his head.

"You really are trying to ruin me, aren't you?" he said. His voice still sounded like a command even when kept low.

"I don't know what you mean, sir," she said in a whisper, at the same time flicking a hand behind her back to get Gwen outside. "I would do nothing deliberately to disgrace you. You know that."

He looked up, the flames' shadows darting oddly across his eyes. "I wonder, Caitlin. I really do wonder. My God, what were you thinking of?"

She spread her hands helplessly before her. "Oliver, I don't know what you're talking about."

"Don't you really?"

"Really, I don't." She moved closer, smiling. "But if you'll tell me what you heard, I'll tell you what actually happened."

He did not return the smile. "You were in Egham today. As I understand it, on the road back to Eton you met Lady Corning."

Her eyes closed briefly, and a hand fluttered weakly to her throat. She *knew* she'd done something wrong; my God, when would she learn just to smile and nod!

"Caitlin, Lady Corning was born in Edinburgh. The baron's family comes from Stirling. Have you ever heard of these places, my dear? Could you find them on a map?"

"Oh, Oliver." She felt herself blushing. "Oliver, I'd forgotten."

He nodded. "Of course you had. Just as you forgot last week that the king's family is from Hanover and you made some stupid remark about fat German women. And the week before you refused to walk in the garden with Lord Cornwallis."

"But he kept putting his hands on me," she protested.

"He's a general, you dolt! He can put his bloody hands where he bloody well wants to!"

She opened her mouth to retort, took in a slow, deep breath and turned away. The wrong was hers, and the only way to forestall a worsening of his temper was to be meek and quiet.

Though it wasn't, she thought, as if she had deliberately lied. The Scots she'd seen at court were indeed sour-faced, and the king was no more English than she was. If she were a man, of course, things would be different; but let a woman speak her mind—

"Caitlin, are you listening to me?"

She turned back and smiled sweetly. "I'm sorry, Oliver, no. I was trying to think of a way to make it up to you."

He clapped his fists to his forehead and fell back in the chair. "God save me," he muttered to the fire. Then his hands dropped into his lap, and his gaze lifted. "It's that Thomas woman," he said finally. "I knew we should have left her behind. My dear, she's not good for you. Not here in England."

Her jaw dropped in shock. "Not good for me? Oliver, how can you say that? We grew up together. She's practically my sister."

"Exactly my point," he said, rising. "She's not your sister; she's your personal maid. You have a position, Caitlin—"

"Oh, bother the position!"

"Caitlin!" He took a menacing step toward her, then abruptly softened. "My dear, you will please instruct her to mind her manners, and to remember where she is and to whose household she belongs." He waited, then brushed at his lapels. "I must go out after dinner this evening. I expect you'll be retired before I return."

She said nothing. He was always going out after dinner these days, though she knew it was necessary. Part of his agreement with her father was that he would make arrangements in England for the sale of the goods the estate produced. To this end he was constantly being invited to gentlemen's parties where brandy was plentiful and pipes blued the air and prices advantageous to them all were discussed. And he was good at it. All of the men seemed very impressed by his bearing, his tales, and his wounds—and the fact that he'd taken a Welsh wife appeared not to have hurt his dealings in the slightest.

"My dear." He was at the door, his smile meant to be reassuring. "Bradford will be serving in fifteen minutes."

And when he left, she sagged against a bedpost, almost ready to weep.

Morgan closed the door behind himself and started down the hall. But before he got far, he suddenly turned onto the rear staircase landing and reached into a dark corner, snaring

Gwen's arm. She gasped and tried to pull away, but he yanked her to his chest, his other hand gripping the back of her head. When she tried to free herself, he quickly released her arm and put his hand around her throat.

"Spying again, are we?" he rasped.

She shook her head vigorously, unable to speak.

"Welsh bitch," he sneered. "I know what you're trying to do, you know. Trying to turn the woman against me so she'll complain to her father and have him annul the marriage." He leaned closer, and her eyes widened in terror. "It won't work, gel. It bloody won't work. There's a lot more at stake than your feeble brain could manage to uncover, and I won't have you disturbing my wife with all manner of lies!"

Gwen fell against the wall when he took his hands away. She rubbed gingerly at her throat and tried to restrain herself when he suddenly plunged a hand into her square-necklined dress and roughly fondled her breast. He pinched it until she yelped, and then slapped her for making the sound.

"You're all alike," he whispered harshly. "All of you. If you're not fouling yourselves in the mines, you're pretending to be civilized in miserable stone huts. By God, if it weren't—"

He stopped suddenly and pulled away. Drawing himself erect, he glared down at her.

Gwen swallowed several times and brushed her dark hair away from her eyes.

"You will say nothing of this, of course," he told her confidently. "If you do . . . Well, you do love your mistress, I'll say that for you. And you certainly don't want anything to happen to her, do you? Of course you don't. You're almost smart, little Gwen-me-gel. Almost."

He laughed softly and stepped back into the hall. But before she could loose the tears building in her eyes he turned back to her, glaring once more over his shoulder at Caitlin's door. "Your tongue," he said. "Be sure you mind it when you go back in there. It won't be long, little one. It won't be long now."

And when he was gone, she reached out for the wall, bowing her head as she tried not to retch. She would have to bathe now, to get the stench of him off her. She was thankful he had never carried out his threats to come to her chamber while the others were sleeping. She shuddered, and coughed. Below, she could hear Mrs. Thorn and Mary bustling about the kitchen, and Bradford holding forth on some topic or other, most likely the barbarians in America who were causing so much trouble. The man never failed to equate barbarians with the Welsh either.

And when she thought she was ready, she straightened her bodice, brushed at her plain brown skirts, and wondered how long she would be able to remain silent.

Caitlin brushed her black hair over one shoulder and checked her reflection. The color contrasted nicely with her honey dress, but she couldn't help wishing she did not have to wear the high neck with its stiff collar of lace. Whenever they attended receptions and parties Oliver encouraged her to dress in the latest fashion, no matter how daring. But here at home he was curiously against it. As if, she thought, he did not wish to be overly tempted.

When Gwen returned, she sighed and laid the brush on the vanity. "Why didn't you tell me the old hag was a Scot, Gwen?" She expected a humorous reply and frowned when she saw the woman's expression. She turned and faced her friend. "He was at you, wasn't he?"

"He scolds," Gwen said, avoiding Caitlin's gaze by hurrying to the vanity to open a velvet-lined jewelry box.

He *presumes;* that's what he does," she snapped angrily. "I don't tell him how to handle that worm, Bradford, and he has no right—"

"It's all right, Cat," Gwen assured her, turning with a string of pearls in her hand. "I don't mind it."

"Well, I do!" she said, stooping slightly to allow Gwen to put the pearls around her neck. "I've only you and Davy Daniels here, you know. He wouldn't let me bring anyone else."

"It's all right," Gwen said again, more firmly.

"I should have a word with him is what I should do."

"No!"

Caitlin was astonished at the vehemence in her response, but before she could press Gwen for further information the clear sound of the dinner gong reverberated through the house. One last check in the mirror—well, she thought, he just doesn't know what he's missing—and she swept out of the room, praying that his ill humor would not be exacerbated by Mrs. Thorn's cooking.

She was surprised.

Though the meal was simple—beef, wine, and fresh bread, with fruit for dessert—Oliver did not make his usual show of displeasure at the barely adequate talents of his cook. Instead, once she realized that his mood was changing, she was able with just the right touch of innocence and interest to prompt him to brag about his conquests. And brag he did, for nearly an hour; and she laughed and exclaimed as she always did, relaxing as she saw him as he wished to be—a retired and honored major whose civilian interests permitted him to work for his country, even if they did not involve the danger and excitement to which he'd grown accustomed. Now, as he gestured and regaled her with tales of intrigue and high hilarity, she could also see the rough but elegant man who had courted her at her father's urging. A man with a purpose, a man she hadn't thought she'd mind living with.

By the time the bottle of port had been drained and Bradford had brought Oliver's walking stick and gloves, the two of them were seated beside each other at the long oaken table, he covering her hand, she eagerly listening to his snippets of court gossip.

"Sir," Bradford said, "your carriage is waiting."

Reluctantly, Caitlin followed him outside and waited on the flagstone steps as Bradford lowered the carriage steps and gave orders to the driver, Davy Daniels. Oliver entered with a flourish and a wave, but suddenly poked his head out the window and grinned. "My dear," he said, "I nearly forgot to tell you my secret."

"Secret? What secret?" She looked up at Davy, who was leaning over from his post and smiling, his white-powdered wig slightly askew. When he shrugged, she looked back to her husband. "Oliver," she said, feigning a pout.

"Well, m'dear," he said expansively, "it seems I've had a communication from . . . from . . ." He put a finger to his chin as if trying to remember. "Damn and blast, who was that woman?"

Caitlin stomped a foot and folded her arms across her breasts. "Oliver, you know full well who 'that woman' is. Please tell me, before I freeze to death out here."

The air was actually quite mild for early June, but she hugged herself tightly and rocked from side to side in mock discomfort. Oliver laughed and slapped the coach's side. "From someone named Charlotte Sophia, I believe her name is." He thumped on the coach's roof with his walking stick, then. "Is that her name, Daniels? Have I the woman's name right?"

Davy could barely contain his laughter and rolled his eyes, his dark brown tricorne waggling atop his head.

"Oliver—" She caught her breath in the middle of the warning. The name had sunk in. Her eyes widened, and she put her hands to her cheeks. "I don't believe it."

"Believe it," Oliver told her, his humor fast fading. "I do not jest about things like that."

"But Oliver, she's the queen!"

"The last time I saw the king, yes she was."

"You spoke to the queen?" Her voice rose to a shrill note, and she descended the steps. "You actually spoke with the queen?"

Oliver nodded, clearly regretting having started the game. "There's to be a gathering at Windsor the day after tomorrow. A number of the king's friends will be down from London, and we have been asked to attend." He raised an impatient hand to cut off her exclamations. "Two days to prepare yourself, my dear. And to practice holding your tongue."

He did not wait for a reply but stabbed at the roof again with his stick. Davy jumped, grabbed the reins and long whip, and cracked the four black horses into a practiced smooth motion.

The queen, Caitlin thought, nearly forgetting to wave. My God, the queen!

She turned to the house, but suddenly its dimensions seemed too small. She could not go in until she'd found a measure of calm, so she moved off at a brisk walk, following the sweep of the drive to where it banked sharply toward the Windsor road. Then she stepped onto the lawn, her hands fluttering over her skirt and the ruffles of her blouse. Pulling at a thick handful of hair, she stroked it as she would the back of a cat.

Above, the moon and the stars glowed and turned the dark heavens silver. She heard the hoot of a hunting owl, the twilling of insects in the trees. All around her the grass sparkled with early dew, and the sculptured gardens glowed with the moonlight as if touched by a wand. In the stables a horse whickered and kicked at its stall; a dog barked; and from somewhere back on the main road the evening's orchestration was enhanced by the clarion call of a horn—a long warning blast as a nobleman's coach thundered through the village. The sound lingered on the same breeze that rustled the leaves, lingered until she'd found her own place for thinking.

A hundred yards from the house, through a narrow stand of chestnut and birch, was a pond. It was meant, she'd been told, to be admired for its symmetry, and for the hundreds of goldfish swimming lazily below the surface. English ladies—she'd learned three years ago shortly after the wedding ceremony—did not remove their boots and stockings and go wading. But the temptation was always strong. It was stronger during daylight when she knew she might be caught; less so after sunset, when she did it nonetheless.

Tonight, however, she only walked to a marble bench set a yard back from the water's edge and sat, hands folded in her lap. In the pond's water, she watched the moon's reflection as the breeze drifted by.

She still felt dazed. The queen. At any other time she might have remarked caustically about the wife of the king. It was almost a national pastime in Wales, and one she had mastered so well she could set her friends laughing for hours on end. Yet now . . . she grinned at herself, shook her head slowly. The English considered the Welsh something less than human; the Welsh, with their hot tempers, lashed out at the English as frequently as they could. And here she was, Caitlin Evans Morgan, stunned as a schoolgirl over the prospect of attending a party at the castle. And not just any party. She'd been to the Hanover residence before, but the royal family had never been in attendance. But now—now!—she had a royal invitation. The likes of Lady Corning and her shriveled sister could sink into the moors for all she cared.

The water rippled and lapped quietly at the white pebbles bordering the pond.

She felt a brief surge of guilt: for all his shortcomings, and for all her frustrations, Oliver certainly knew how to ignite her excitement. Would he could do it privately as well, she thought.

The queen—and before she could banish the thought, another struck her: would Griffin be jealous if he knew where she'd be in forty-eight hours? Would . . . would he even care?

She scowled. This was no time to fall back into girlish fancies. The king and queen were ahead of her, and this would be her chance to show that the Welsh did not parade around in pelts and black-charred faces. It was a matter of honor, and it was—

With a sudden shriek of joy she yanked up her skirts and raced back toward the house, shouting Gwen's name.

3

THE ORCHESTRA's spritely pauanne was high, lilting, and sweet, and dispersed over the valley by a late spring breeze that had risen shortly after sunset. Banners and colored standards, so bright the dark could not dim them, pointed the way to the eastern horizon from poles set atop the castle's central Round Tower. The flickering of torches in elaborate ironwork brackets made the gray stone walls appear gold, and added dizzying depth to the polish of the coaches waiting patiently in the courtyard. The horses, finely curried and beribboned, were stamping anxiously now as midnight's chill approached the high walls. They shook their heads and snorted while the grooms and coachmen leaned casually against their charges and traded gossip of their families, their exploits, and their slowly dawning fear that some of them might soon be impressed into the army to fight again—not against France this time, but against people of their own kind.

The castle itself was a massive, dynamic structure begun by William the Conqueror and later added onto by subsequent generations of English monarchs. Its lower wall fronted Windsor's High Street imposingly, and across the cobblestone road were rows of taverns and inns that faced the royal residence like urchins pressing close to a rich man. And on every corner were bands of infantrymen at the ready, their red-coated uniforms gleaming with polished brass, their hats white-plumed and catching the wind. Passersby joked with them, brought them ale and fresh bread while their officers carefully looked the other way. It was going to be a long night, by all accounts, and they knew their men would stay more alert if they felt they were as important as the townspeople made them out to be.

Within the wall was a narrow courtyard lined with stables, a farrier's shop, and several deserted stalls used during the morning market. Farther up, as the hill gently ascended, was the medieval splendor of St. George's Chapel, followed by another open stretch of cobblestones and hard earth. The residence proper began at the base of the Round Tower, a structure that thrust high above the surrounding walls to give guards and visitors alike an unobstructed panorama of the valley rimmed by low hills.

And behind the tower was the warren of apartments housing the royal family. The most splendid of these rooms was directly in back. Ceiling-high windows and dark oak paneling, portraits and tapestries, a balcony for the musicians and a broad-pegged floor for those who came to see as much as to be seen and to dance. Just outside the ballroom, touched by the gay lights filtering through the French doors, was a vast garden of shrubs and flower islands, gravel paths and solitary benches—a trysting place for lovers, a thinking place for the king's ministers, a place where the king himself could walk without an onlooking populace.

Caitlin was aware of the ground on which she trod, and as she wound her way aimlessly between rosebush and privet, she felt as though she were walking on a cloud. Every few steps she would pinch the inside of her wrist and tell herself it was, in fact, the royal palace, and not a dream.

The orchestra, unseen by the people below it, could have been playing from heaven, as far as Caitlin could tell. There were candles four and five feet tall—and some no higher than a baby's reach—rising from the wall sconces or towering on marble pedestals, giving the entire room the aspect of a feverish dream. Diamonds, emeralds, and pearls in profusion; delicately painted fans; flashes of lightning from ceremonial swords and silver-encrusted gold braid. Gem-laden goblets were distributed by liveried servants to those couples or groups who preferred to sit at small round tables; crystal glasses of cognac were delivered on engraved silver trays; gallons of burgundy and port were there for the asking.

Flirtations were begun and affairs quietly ended. Gossip and envy were lost in the laughter, in the witty chatter, in the occasional spurts of impromptu singing. In a far corner, beside a platform covered in silk and velvet where King George and his consort oversaw the reception, men in severe dark clothing muttered about politics and finance, war and domestic unrest until the king, his lean face flushed with drink and his thickening waist straining his gold-trimmed jacket, ordered them silent.

Caitlin shook her head vigorously and brushed a white-gloved hand swiftly over her eyes. It really was too much— so many new people, so much splendor. When she and Oliver had first entered, she hadn't even heard their names announced because she'd been so overwhelmed. She paused for a breath, and fixed on her lips a careful smile that she hoped didn't make her look addlepated or drunk.

And before she knew it she was dancing—with a young man from the north country, with an older man from Canterbury she later discovered was a duke, with a succession of noblemen who complimented her husband while refusing to take their gaze from the powdered swell of her breasts. She did not mind. The attention was more potent than anything she might drink, and Oliver seemed pleased that she wasn't disgracing him, for a change. At one point, however, a military man whose rank she hadn't caught had questioned her rather closely about the rebels in Wales. Remembering Gwen's admonitions and Oliver's threats, she managed to turn aside his blunt inquiries with laughter, a coquettish smile, and a bland statement that salved her conscience and forced him to silence. It had been, she thought afterward, a harrowing moment, a struggle between her anger at the man's obvious condescension and her fear of what her husband would say if she let loose her tongue.

But then there was the wine. Every time she turned around someone was pressing a fresh glass into her hand.

The music filled her ears, set her blood to singing, made her feel as if it had been written especially for her.

The reflections of candlelight winked from polished mirrors.

And finally the presentation began, trumpets blaring and colorfully costumed attendants taking their places.

General Arthur Lancaster, with Oliver proudly at his side and Caitlin nervously a half-step behind, approached the royal pavilion as though marching to battle. The general diplomatically reminded the monarch of Oliver's knighthood and distinguished career, then stepped aside to introduce her—her!— while Oliver took the offered hand of the queen and bowed as low as he dared.

"Lovely," said George III, his accent not quite English.

Caitlin had curtsied perfectly, elegantly, but she did not rise because the king had not offered her his palm.

"You are from Wales, as I understand these things. Is that not correct, my dear child?"

"Yes, Your Majesty," she'd answered, her voice barely louder than a hoarse whisper. The back of her neck burned. She was positive the rest of the company was staring at her and laughing silently. She was also afraid someone had told him of her "fat German women" remark.

"A pleasant place, I'm sure."

"It is quite so, sir," she said.

She looked up then, and he was smiling.

"I understand you Welsh are rather independent-minded."

Oliver was glaring at her, she knew, but she could not see him. "We've been known to have opinions, yes, sir."

A sound she thought was a chuckle surprised her into grinning, and she didn't dare believe he'd actually winked at her. He couldn't have. Stories of his dalliances with ladies of the court came instantly to mind, but she dismissed them when finally he gave her his hand and permitted her to rise.

"Your husband is not unknown to us, Lady Morgan," he said, and his free hand lightly touched the side of his wig. "You should be pleased to be his wife."

"I am, sir. Very."

"But not too independent-minded."

"Not too, sir, no."

A pause followed, and she felt him release her hand. "We are pleased you could come."

And it was over. The corpulent Lancaster nudged her to one side where she touched hands with the queen. There was no talk here; just a look that barely acknowledged her existence. Then the general bowed to her and led her to the ballroom floor. She danced, and knew she danced well. And she also knew the general eyed her boldly. But it didn't matter, not now. The king had actually spoken to her, and she'd made clear by her tone that she was proud of who she was without calling down Oliver's wrath.

She smiled. She grinned. She glanced over her shoulder to the dancers inside. Gwen, she thought smugly, you should have seen me in there!

She walked around a shrub clipped into the shape of a peacock and found herself at one of the ballroom's closed doors. The deep velvet draperies had been drawn, and she could barely see her reflection in the glass. A step closer, an appraisal, and she could not help but admit she was living vindication of a sometimes frenzied preparation.

Her dress was of dark green silk, the low square neckline adorned with miniature bows and Spanish lace. The bodice, which came to a sharp point just below her waist, was taut and clinging, but her skirts flared below her waist where they billowed out over her pannier. The front of the skirt rippled to her ankles in shimmering folds and was gathered up slightly to expose the silk petticoat, the gold-buckled slippers, and the trim line of her calves encased in sheer white silk. Around her neck she wore a choker of fine diamonds aflame even in this dim light. More diamonds winked from the lace spilling over her long white gloves.

Beneath the dress a stiff corset chafed and made her breathing shallow, pushing upward her lightly powdered breasts—not as severely as those of the women who doggedly aped the fashions from the court of Louis XVI, but enough to leave no doubt that she could have achieved the same effect without much underpinning.

Her hair she'd wanted to leave rustling down her back, but Gwen had prevailed, warning her she would scandalize the court if she didn't curl it atop her head and loop it with strands of Belgian lace and matched baby pearls. Her hair was held in place with a dusting of fresh milk.

"I feel like a cow," she'd complained, wiping splatters of milk from her breasts. "And it's going to stink like a dairy when it dries."

"Who's going to notice?" she was asked. "Only the men have enough sense to use talc in this misbegotten country, and they're used to the smell anyway. Besides, you'll be swimming in gallons of perfume. Now hold still, Cat, before I dump the pitcher on you and we have to start the whole bloody mess over."

Oliver, with a simple grunt and a nod, apparently approved. "Caitlin."

She started, a hand to her chest as she spun around, thinking perhaps she shouldn't be standing in the shadows alone.

Oliver stepped onto the flagstone apron that separated the garden from the castle's inner wall and held out his hands. Nervously, she took them and allowed herself to be drawn close.

"I missed you inside," he said with just a faint hint of reproof.

She smelled the wine on his breath, saw the flush that crept from his cheeks toward the perfectly curled outer edges of his wig. Yet he did not seem annoyed with her, and she released a breath she hadn't realized she'd been holding. At that moment she was not altogether steady on her feet. She smiled weakly.

"A little air, Oliver," she said meekly. "It's just so . . . I've never been quite so . . ." She ducked her head. "I don't know how to say it."

His hands caressed her arms above the elbows. "I understand, my dear. But I do want you to know how proud I am of your demeanor this evening. You have certainly charmed all the gentlemen here."

Her smile broadened, and she tilted her head when he leaned forward to kiss her cheek wetly. He was not in uniform but was wearing a gold-trimmed jacket of dark brown velvet that reached mid-thigh and was adorned with ruffles and lace aplenty, like the clothing of the finest of dandies. It was important, he'd told her earlier, that people continued to know he was not living his retirement in seclusion, and without influence. Though she still did not grasp the full extent of his mercantile and government business dealings, she understood completely the necessity of maintaining a facade. The merest hint that he was in disfavor with one group or another would ruin him . . . and seclude him indeed.

Her cheek brushed the soft fabric on his shoulder, and she closed her eyes dreamily. To think she would ever be in a place like this, dressed like this, mingling with ministers and royalty—it was enough to make her think kindly of England now and again.

"I must return inside," Oliver whispered. He kissed her again. "A number of matters need to be discussed before the evening is done." His face hardened slightly—though it might have been only the shadows. "Do not stay too long, my dear. People will talk."

"Just a little while," she promised. "Just until I can put my head back to rights."

He patted her shoulder and left, his heels clicking on the flagstone, his back rigid, and his arms swinging at his sides. As she watched him turn smartly and vanish, she could not help feeling a momentary unease, as if he'd conveyed a certain distrust of her in his parting. But before she could examine it the feeling was gone, replaced by a queasy sensation in her stomach where the wine had mixed with the excitement to produce a mild burning. With her hands over her abdomen, she reentered the garden, picking her paths at random while the music and laughter ebbed and flowed about her like a relentless, uncaring tide.

The unease returned.

She scolded herself against it. It was only his manner she was reacting to, nothing more; and it was something she'd learned to live with, part of the bargain she'd made to be his wife.

A thorn caught at her gown, and she took several long seconds to extricate herself.

Bargain. The word was distasteful, but she knew that's what it was, and she knew why it had been struck.

David Evans was without a son and needed a male heir to whom he could bequeath his lands. Oliver Morgan had been traveling through Cardigan with several former military colleagues, searching out men who'd had army experience, hoping to reenlist them in the king's service for the struggles looming with the recalcitrant colonies in America and with a perpetually antagonistic France. The party had stopped at Seacliff for the evening. Evans and Morgan—despite an initial, mutual distrust based on their cultural differences—had somehow managed to strike a truce, which had developed over the next year into a curious sort of friendship. Both understood that each was using the other—Evans to acquire an heir, Morgan to gain someone to care for him in his old age. Still, they were amicable enough, and it hadn't been long before Morgan had permission to court Evans's daughter.

Caitlin had had no say in the matter. And once she'd learned through the Reverend Mr. Lynne that Griff was indeed the father of Morag's child, the pain of his betrayal almost made her fly into Oliver's arms. And curiously, her acceptance of the bargain at the time had not been terribly difficult. Oliver had been the model of a gentleman, flooding her with letters, gifts, and promises of security for herself and for Seacliff. That he was an Englishman (whose great-grandfather had, however, been Cardiff born) seemed somehow not to matter so long as her father was satisfied that he was an exception to the breed.

She looked down at her hand then, the one the king had held, and smiled. Suddenly she gasped as she collided with a woman hurrying away from the garden's low back wall.

It was Lady Corning, her coiffed gray hair slightly mussed, the age-pale thrust of her bosom flushed pink. Behind her, Caitlin spied the figure of a man vanishing behind a high shrub. She apologized profusely, but the woman would have none of it. Drawing herself up, Lady Corning snapped open her fan and glared at Caitlin over its scalloped edge.

"You make a habit of prowling, do you?"

"My lady, no, I was just—"

"Snooping around, that's the way of it."

Flustered now and feeling the wine clouding her thoughts, Caitlin shook her head vigorously. "I assure you, I was simply out for some air; that's all."

The noblewoman looked at her askance, scornfully, as if from a great height. "I really do find you people tiresome, you know, my dear. I can't for the life of me understand why these affairs must cater to just anyone."

Caitlin swallowed an acid retort. "I'm sorry if we cannot get along, my lady. If I have offended you, I apologize."

Lady Corning snorted.

In an effort to salvage something of the encounter—and in hope of preventing Oliver from learning about it later—she looked back at the ballroom. "Such beautiful music, don't you think?"

"I do."

"It's so . . . simple, so plain. It's—" She faltered when she realized the woman's face had darkened, and she groaned silently, realizing that somehow she'd managed to commit another gaffe.

"The melody you're listening to, young woman," Lady Corning said stiffly, jabbing her with the now closed fan, "was composed by my husband. It has been hailed in London and Paris as a piece marked by intricacy and sophistication—something I'm sure you Welsh wouldn't recognize if you fell over it."

There was no opportunity to protest. Lady Corning brushed past her quickly and headed directly inside. Caitlin was left open-mouthed and staring, her anger rising quickly. Then a hand tapped her shoulder. She spun around, eyes blazing, expression daring anyone to cross her.

The man she faced, however, was grinning.

"She's a right proper bitch, isn't she?" he said, jutting his chin toward the departing baroness. "You could say good morning to her, and she'd turn it into the most dreadful case of treason England has seen since Charles lost his lovely head."

4

HE WORE glittering dark silk lace at his throat. His thick brown hair was unpowdered and brushed from a high, creased forehead into a braid that rested between his shoulder blades. Several modest rings adorned his fingers, lace flared at his cuffs, and silver-gold thread was woven artfully into his waistcoat. His breeches were black, fitting snugly and ending just below the knee, and his white stockings remained unwrinkled despite his casual stance. Low-topped boots and gold buckles completed his attire which, despite the jewelry and the flash, was modest compared with that of the rest of the company.

Though a number of tall torches were set around the garden, Caitlin still found it difficult to examine the man's face as fully as she would have liked. What she could see of it, however, appeared hard-ridged, with deep-set eyes of indeterminate color and a full mouth that curled up at one corner because of a narrow scar that crossed from the side of his aquiline nose. He wore neither beard nor mustache, and from the deep shade of his skin she surmised he worked outside most of the time.

Her first impression was of carefully contained cruelty, her second of a handsome bearing that was far from refined. On any other occasion she might have excused herself immediately from his company, but his jibe at Lady Corning's expense endeared him to her—at least for the moment.

"Have I said something wrong, then?" he asked, his voice smooth and somewhat deep.

"No," she said cautiously. Then, more boldly: "Quite to the contrary, in point of fact, Mr.—" she prompted.

"Flint," he said, bowing to her with mock formality. "James Patrick Flint at your service, ma'am."

She gave him a slight inclination of her head. "Lady Caitlin Morgan," she said, groaning instantly at the coy lilt she'd added to her response. If Oliver had overheard her, he would accuse her of all types of treason.

He smiled pleasantly. "If you'll excuse me again, ma'am, I am pleased to make your acquaintance. I am acquainted with your husband, and have been for some time."

"Indeed?"

"Indeed. And he was quite right, if I may be so bold as to say so. You are without question the most beautiful creature to have come out of Wales in at least a century . . . and most likely longer."

She looked for an insult—an automatic reaction—and when she realized there was none she felt a blush rise from her chest to her cheeks. She turned away quickly to stare at a shrub she could barely make out in the half-light. Despite herself, she was wonderfully pleased. It was the first compliment she had received since arriving at the castle that was not given for Oliver's sake, or for the sake of formality. This man she felt would not bow to any convention that displeased him. There was an almost tangible aura of strength and purpose about him.

"I'm sorry, my lady," he said then, looking at her as his smile faded. "Am I disturbing you?"

Before she could stop herself she reached out to touch his arm. "No! Not at all, Mr. Flint. I'm afraid that the baroness caught me off guard, that's all. It's nothing to do with you, believe me."

He crooked an elbow toward her and, after a moment's pause, she took it and permitted him to guide her through the garden's rare treasures.

"She does that to most people," he said, keeping his voice prudently low. "I've known the old cow for a number of years, and I don't believe there's a man-jack in the country who wouldn't gladly have her heart. She has the idea, you see, that coming from that barbaric land of hers to the north gives her special privileges. The Scots are all like that, in fact. Runny noses, god-awful music, and an unshakable belief there's a divine plan afoot that will eventually hand them the English throne, move London to Edinburgh, and force men to wear

ludicrous skirts. You will notice, however, my lady, how she's
managed to purge her nasal honk of the guttural rolling *r*'s that
mark her as a northerner. A paradox. Worse—a hypocrite. I
really do believe she'll die in her bed quoting that sham, Robert
Burns."

Caitlin, fascinated by the exposition, burst into laughter at
the image of Lady Corning propped up by dozens of pillows
and attended by sniveling servants, reading at the top of her
voice the Scottish poet's most clamorous verses. Impulsively
she hugged his arm to her side in approval, and he smiled down
at her.

"I am, of course, something of a hypocrite myself," he told
her with a grin that took the confessional sting from his words.
"I am quite the opportunist in point of fact. I'll espouse any
cause, as long as it keeps the tradesmen from pounding on my
door. I'll woo any beautiful woman, any man who is rich, any
country that will have me for more than ten days at a stretch."

"Really, Mr. Flint!"

"Really, Lady Morgan."

"You shouldn't denigrate yourself so."

"My lady, I am above scruples and conscience. I leave them
to the nobility, who can afford the indulgence."

She grinned and sidestepped a bordering stone that had been
kicked out of place.

"If you think so little of Scotland, what think you of Wales?"

"A land of unsurpassed excellence, incredible mountains,
and marvelously fat sheep that somehow contrive to look like
their masters."

She could barely restrain her laughter as they reached the
far end of the garden.

The wall was no more than waist high, giving onto a drop
she estimated was easily one hundred feet to the huge boulders
below. It made her dizzy to look down so steep an incline and
she hastily lifted her gaze to the valley gently rising in front
of her. She could hear the night sounds and see the glittery
lights of nearby Windsor and Eton. The hills on the horizon
were obscured by the night, their outlines marked only by the
stars overhead. It was as magnificent a vision as she'd ever
seen, literally breathtaking in its scope. Within moments she
found herself drawn perilously close to the wall. A hand grasped
her shoulder, and she started, blinked furiously, and gulped
when she saw how far she'd been leaning over the stone barrier.

"Are you sure you're all right?" Flint asked her.

Flustered, she passed a nervous hand over her eyes. "The wine," she said, and swallowed twice.

At that moment a liveried young boy passed by with tray in hand. From it, Flint plucked two crystal goblets and handed her one of them. She almost demurred, but the smile in his eyes stayed her. And when he lifted his glass in a silent solemn toast, she knew she could not refuse without giving him offense. It was, after all, a special occasion. There could hardly be any fault in having a bit more to drink.

She emptied the glass as if quaffing ale, and put her fingers to her lips to stifle a giggle. Flint laughed and drained his own, catching the young boy on his way back so he could exchange the goblets for two more.

"No, really," she protested weakly. Her eyelids were growing heavy, and she heard her words begin to slur. A special occasion was one thing, but turning into a common drunkard was something else.

"I insist," he said gently. His smile widened. "You Welsh have a particular burden to bear when you visit the Conqueror." He straightened. "To Lady Corning. May she discover her husband abed with the queen and call it the act of a sublime patriot."

Caitlin hiccuped and giggled, nearly spilling the wine over her dress. She turned to lean back against the wall. Lifting her goblet she studied the ballroom's glow in the faceted glass. It was mesmerizing. The wine sparkled, and stars seemed to be entrapped in the liquid. She sipped, sipped again, and did not move aside when Flint stood closer to her. He gestured then to the garden, to the castle, to the valley behind them. "It's all rather lovely, isn't it?" he asked, his voice faintly rasping.

"There are no words for it," she agreed with an emphatic nod.

"I take it, then, you're enjoying yourself?"

"Oh, yes!" she exclaimed, excitement welling once again in her chest. "I don't think I ever want to leave, Mr. Flint. It's as if I've fallen asleep and found some fairyland. I . . ." She caught herself babbling, and flushed with embarrassment. My goodness, Cat, she thought, you'd think you'd never been to a party before.

He moved still closer. "I know what you mean. It's not often someone like myself finds a place in these proceedings, and I confess I find it rather hard to breathe."

"Birds of a feather," she said. "I'm not exactly a member of the English family."

An abrupt, elaborate fanfare shattered the peaceful evening, and she looked anxiously toward the castle.

"It's nothing," he assured her, a restraining hand on her arm. "The queen is leaving, that's all. She doesn't much care for these things and goes to her rooms as soon as she dares. The king will leave in an hour, unless he keeps 'tasting' his wine."

"Mr. Flint," she admonished, "that's hardly the way to talk about him, you know."

His smile grew into a sardonic grin. "My apologies—and I do seem to be doing that a lot this evening, don't I? But I had assumed, your being Welsh and all . . . Well, I'm sure you know what I mean."

"And you're right," she said, stifling a laugh. Her head felt giddy. "But there is such a thing as discretion."

"Quite." His smile softened, and his hand began to stroke the lace on her arms lightly. "You must be tired."

"A little," she admitted.

"Sir Oliver can be demanding." And to her questioning look he lowered his gaze. "I have worked with him several times over the past years. Not in the army, directly. In other things."

She frowned, trying to recall mention of James Patrick Flint, but nothing formed in her mind. Oliver never spoke of business except when he'd completed a particularly lucrative transaction. And then he spent the evening gloating, more often than not drinking himself to sleep in his hearthside chair.

Flint spoke again, his lips near her ear: "Do you see the way the light is caught in the windows? Stars, I should think, aren't nearly as fortunate. And the perfumes of these flowers, even after sunset—they reach the senses like warm wine. You can almost feel them settling into your soul."

Caitlin's eyes closed against the man's softly droning voice, and she could almost feel the course of the wine as it lit slow fires in her veins. She squirmed, without moving away from him; her shoulder shifted under the warm weight of his palm as he continued to whisper the words and gild the images. Sighing when he paused, she turned in the hope that he would continue in that lullaby voice, ignoring the warning chime in her head.

"I should hasten to add," he said suddenly, "that none of this holds a candle to you, Lady Morgan."

She smiled almost shyly. "You know how to flatter, sir." And she thought, Would that Oliver did, too.

He grinned. "I don't consider myself glib, my lady. But I do feel an obligation as a gentleman to expound upon beauty wherever and whenever I am blessed to be near it."

For a moment she thought he was mocking her, yet she could find no evidence that he was in his penetrating gaze. "As I said, sir, you flatter well." And you, she scolded herself halfheartedly, are playing coy games. She pushed herself a little farther away.

"You dislike flattery?"

"I didn't say that."

"The Welsh are direct."

"The Welsh," she said, "know the value of words."

She knew she was on the edge of drunkenness, and suspected Flint was teasing her for it. But a gust of wind chased away her renewed caution, and when she felt him lay a solicitous hand against the small of her swaying back, she found no strength to protest.

Raucous laughter rang out from the ballroom, distracting her briefly just as his face closed in on her neck. A momentary panic pushed her away, though not far enough to break off his touch. More guests had begun to wander into the garden— couples with their heads close together in shared secrets, men taking out long-stemmed clay pipes, women rapidly fanning their bosoms and necks against the heat of the ballroom and the exertions of their dancing. A guard shifted noisily at his station in a far corner. On the battlements above, two soldiers met, saluted, turned in about-face, and marched on.

The music swelled, and the night deepened.

She realized she was still holding her goblet, emptied it in four swallows, and felt nothing at all.

"My lady," Flint said, "have you done much exploring?"

She blinked slowly as she looked his way, and put a hand to his cheek to prevent his face from slipping away. He covered it quickly and, before she could stop him, turned her palm upward and placed a gentle kiss in her palm. On the inside of her wrist. And then on the inside of her elbow before her wits returned and she drew her arm away.

"Yet again I apologize," he said. But his hand remained on

her back, penetrating the layers of silk and cotton, sending warm waves along the length of her spine. "Perhaps another brandy?"

She tried and failed to wave a dismissing hand. "No," she said at last. "I'm really . . . Nothing more, thank you."

His breath caressed the side of her neck, spilling over the hollow of her throat to the swell of her breasts.

Oh, dear, she thought, and backed up against the wall. A glance behind her, and she nearly lost all the wine at the whirling sight of the valley spinning slowly under the moon.

"Lean on my shoulder," he whispered, taking the goblet from her hand and setting it on the ground. "I shouldn't want you to fall."

Fall? She had no intention of falling, yet she felt unsteady on her feet. She felt as if a feathered veil had been drawn over her senses; she could not concentrate. The brandy, the music, the laughter of the guests befuddled her and made her giddy.

"My lady, there's a bench just over here—"

She allowed herself to be led away because suddenly she felt she couldn't stand on her own.

The bench was in the shadows, away from the torchlight. Flint sat beside her, a hand on her knee, his chin brushing her shoulder.

"My husband . . ." she began, licking her lips, frantically searching for words.

"A fine man," he told her. He kissed her neck once, then drew away and waited.

"I don't think—"

"Neither of us should, not on a night like this," he said. "That's the trouble with the world these days, you see. One thinks and another disagrees, and the next thing you know they're bashing away at each other like children at a fair."

She giggled into her palm. "Mr. Flint, I don't think my husband would approve your description of battle."

"A fine man," he repeated, and kissed her neck again.

This isn't happening, she thought wildly, as panic and unnerving desire began to mingle disturbingly. Lord, I can't let this—suddenly, the world began to draw away from her, and her head began to reel. No, she cried silently; I can't faint now. Oh, God . . .

"My lady," Flint said. "Are you all right?"

She wanted to nod, but when he grasped her hand another

surge of excitement forced her to close her eyes. A moment, she decided; all I need is a moment alone.

Flint rose then, solicitous as he brushed the hair from her forehead, pulled her handkerchief from her grip and fanned her lightly. The makeshift breeze was welcome, and she leaned into it gratefully, sighing, thinking what a disgrace it would be to swoon in the king's garden, and with Oliver nearby.

"I'll fetch your husband," Flint said then. "I don't think you should be alone."

"No," she pleaded, thinking of Oliver's anger. "Not yet, please!"

"It'll be all right," he soothed. "I'll handle the explanations. You've nothing to fear."

"But Mr. Flint, please—"

"I shall detain him long enough for you to calm yourself. And then," he added softly, "I'm going to invite myself to dinner."

5

"I TELL YOU, Cat, and I tell you true—there are times when I think you should be locked away. Imagine having all that to drink and then almost disgracing yourself, right in the king's garden!" Gwen paused for a breath, her broad smile putting the lie to the sternness of her tone. "Honestly, you give the Welsh a bad name, you do. Why, what would your father think?"

They were riding slowly along the Windsor road, approaching the Eton turnoff to Caitlin's English home. Caitlin said nothing to Gwen's friendly, sometimes laugh-punctuated jibes.

"And Griff," Gwen said slyly. "Why, if he were here he'd probably have you over his knee in a trice."

Caitlin nodded to herself. Griff probably would do something like that. The man had no sense of propriety, and certainly he did not have the grace of a man like James Patrick Flint.

A muffled sound of disgust escaped her lips. How, after what he'd nearly done, could she think of him so ... so kindly? She drew her cloak more closely around her, though the twilight was anything but chilly.

"Cat? Cat, did you hear what I said? About Griff?"

"I heard," she answered sullenly, "and I'd appreciate your not mentioning him again. Or prattling on like this."

Gwen sobered instantly. "Oh. I'm sorry, Cat. I understand."

But she didn't, Caitlin thought. Gwen was under the impression that she was feeling great waves of remorse—and she wasn't, and that was what bothered her.

Three days had passed since the reception at Windsor Castle, and this was the first day she'd left the house without feeling as if every servant and villager in the country could see the guilt on her face. Oliver, fetched by Flint, had scolded her harshly all the way home and had punished her by refusing to take his meals with her. Thus isolated from everyone but Gwen, Caitlin had had plenty of time to review the incident and to thrash over her feelings. And then there had been the dreams: at one moment she was trying to lure Griff into her bed by behaving like a harlot, and at the next she was dancing with him, her gaze unwilling to leave the flashing dare in his eyes. Oliver, too, stalked her at night, smashing through her bedroom door with the butt of his musket, stripping her of her night-clothes and laying open her flesh with steady strokes of a coachwhip. Griffin laughed at her uproariously; Flint consoled her and stroked balm on her wounds; Oliver returned to open them again.

Finally, just after the midday meal, she'd had enough of her own thoughts and ordered Davy to prepare her horse despite Gwen's protest that it wasn't safe to ride so late in the day. They rode at a furious pace along the banks of the Thames until both mounts were threatening to lather. Then they walked back for over a mile before they remounted and Gwen began her attempts to bring a smile to her mistress's face.

And the worst part was that Caitlin had been unable to tell Gwen everything. She'd hinted broadly about Flint's bold advances, but covered herself with lies about her drinking and the silly reactions the wine had produced.

"Cat, did you hear that?"

Caitlin looked up quickly. She saw nothing but the columns of trees that marked the lane into which they were turning.

There was nothing but the early evening's chorus of insects. And their road sounds were muffled by the foliage overhead. The shadows writhing in the brush heightened her abrupt sense of unease, which she blamed on her friend's nerves—and her desperate need to feel guiltier than she did. She was, after all, a married woman, with obligations to a husband. No matter that the husband refused to perform his husbandly duties save once or twice every few months, when he was either elated over business, or steeped in his port. No matter. She was married and bound by duty. Yet just when she thought she had banished Griffin's ghost from her dreams forever, along came James Flint to exchange places with him.

And she didn't even know him!

"Cat," Gwen whispered, continuing to speak Welsh as she had throughout the day. "Cat, we're not alone."

The chestnut's ears were pricked up high, and Caitlin tugged lightly on the reins, cocking her head to listen.

She could only hear an owl and the faint rustle of the brush in the shadows.

Directly ahead, the narrow lane vanished into the ebony night. Not even the lights from the house were visible at this distance. A faint wind whistled through the leaves. The jangle of the harnesses, and the clop of hooves rang out.

Suddenly, something huge and black exploded from the brush to her right, and Gwen released a scream that was abruptly cut off. A hand grabbed for the chestnut's bridle, and before Caitlin had time to dig her heels into the horse's sides massive hands pulled her from the saddle, clamped hard over her mouth, and dragged her off the lane into the darkness.

She lashed out with her feet, her hands becoming claws, digging into the flesh of the hand that was nearly smothering her. A grunt, and a hard knee into the small of her back knocked the wind from her lungs. She sagged, fell, and shaded her eyes when a lantern was brought near her face. She could hear several things at once: the horses pounding down the lane toward the house, Gwen's struggles nearby, and a deep-throated chuckle from the lamp holder. She pushed herself up to her elbows and crawled backward until she came against the bole of a twisted elm.

"Who are you?" she demanded, unable to see the face beyond the glowing light. "You can't do this!"

A laugh, menacing and confident, sounded.

"You don't know who I am! My God, my husband will have you killed when he finds out."

"Speak English, bitch!" came a rough command out of the dark, and Caitlin realized that in panic she'd been speaking Welsh. "You ain't so high-and-mighty, are ye . . . m'lady." And the title was dragged out in mocking tones.

Caitlin looked wildly from side to side, seeing nothing but the contours of bushes. She wanted frantically to find Gwen, but even the sounds of her struggles were denied her now.

The lantern was lowered, and a tall form towered over her. She pushed herself hard against the bole, and cried out when two hands from behind the tree grabbed her arms and then pinned them down. The lantern holder chuckled and dropped to his knees. His face was masked with black cloth; only deep-shadowed pits marked the place where his eyes should be. She kicked out when he grabbed her calf, and gasped when his grip tightened to a vise. Her skirt rode up her leg. He snared her other leg and forced it to one side as he moved quickly between her knees.

"Ye'll not have a great pain if ye don't fight it," the man said, his voice muffled by the mask.

"Bastard!" she spat, her rage temporarily overwhelming her terror.

He laughed and pushed her skirts up to her waist, reached out and pawed at her breasts. When she screamed, he slapped her into silence. She could taste salty blood at the corners of her mouth.

"They say, y'know, that Welsh women are wild. Like animals, they are." The tone was leering and frighteningly calm. "Are ye an animal, m'lady bitch? Huh? Be ye—"

She screamed again—this time because the man suddenly let out a yell and pitched over her left leg into the dark. A second figure charged across the lantern's low beam, and the hands that pinned her vanished as though stung. Immediately, she pulled her legs to her, hugging herself and trembling violently. Though a fight raged only a few yards away, she could hear it only faintly. Blood was rushing to her ears; her heart beat wildly; and the dim light took on an unearthly red glow, neither warm nor cold.

Something told her to move. An urgency demanded she escape while she had the chance. But her legs would not obey her. There were tears in her eyes, but she didn't feel them; an icy coating of perspiration covered her face, but she didn't feel it. All there was for her was an eternity of waiting, the feel of the man's hands on her legs, the sinister hatred in his voice, the look of those eyes that had no color at all.

"My lady."

She started, whimpering, then tried to push herself to her feet.

"My lady, please."

"Go away," she pleaded. "Go away, go away!"

"My lady, it's all right. You're safe now. It's all right."

She had no idea how long it took for the words to penetrate, but suddenly the lantern was floating in the air before her, and a familiar voice was saying, "I told you I was going to invite myself to dinner."

And the last thing she saw before consciousness fled was James Flint's smile, crooked and hard.

The darkness was comforting. Several times she had left it, only to find Gwen sitting at her bedside, pale and drawn. And several times she retreated again, though each time now she grew more reluctant to return. But finally with a weary hand over her eyes to blot out a dim sun, she lay amid pillows and quilts and dared ask where she was.

"Home," Gwen said, and embraced her.

The tears flowed easily, and for nearly an hour, before Caitlin rose to a sitting position, she looked around the room as if she'd never seen it before. Then she glanced at Gwen, a questioning look on her face.

"It was Flint who saved us," Gwen told her. "He'd just arrived when the horses came hell-bent out of the trees. He . . . he saved us, Cat. He saved us."

Caitlin rubbed her face hard, pressing her knuckles into her eyes and wincing at the pain. "I thought it was a nightmare." She sniffed and took Gwen's hand. "Are you . . . all right?"

Gwen's smile turned slightly bitter. "It seems I'm not the prize. I was taken off as you were, but I was not touched. And you?"

Caitlin shook her head slowly. "I hate this place, Gwen," she said, her voice low and angry. "Every summer we come here and we stay for months on end. We put up with those asses who mock us for who we are, and assault us almost on our own doorstep." She felt tears well up in her eyes and drove them back; she would not weep. The time for weeping was past. "I'm going to tell Oliver I want to go home."

Gwen shifted uneasily on the edge of the mattress. "Cat, you're speaking Welsh."

"I don't give a damn!"

"But Sir Oliver . . ." She glanced at the door.

"Oh, my God," she said, "I'd forgotten all about him. Is he waiting? Oh, God, Gwen, let him in!"

Gwen climbed off the mattress, off the dais, and opened the door. Oliver strode in immediately, concern making his face pale and his eyes narrowing. He grabbed Caitlin's hands in his and kissed her soundly on the cheek, murmuring over and over again how sorry he was. She laid her forehead against his cheek, grateful for the solace that lasted several minutes before he drew away and faced her.

"Those men," he said.

"I never saw their faces," she told him, shuddering slightly at the image of the eyes behind the mask.

"They ran away, the cowards! Flint was superb, absolutely superb, but there were three men, and they managed to elude him." He raised a fist that trembled beside his cheek. "I can't believe it. I simply cannot believe this could happen to my wife."

"Oliver?"

His scowl softened, but his glaring eyes remained angry.

"Oliver, I want to go home."

He leaned back and stared. "Home? But you are home, my dear." Then realization struck him. "Ah. You mean, a journey to Seacliff." He patted her hand, like a father with his child. "We'll talk about it later. Right now you must rest yourself."

"Oliver . . ." Her stomach growled, making her smile. "Oh dear, I think I'm hungry."

"And well you should be, Caitlin," he said, rising from the bed to stand with hands behind his back. He smiled. "You've been sleeping for nearly a day."

"What?"

"As a matter of fact, we're dining in less than an hour. If you should feel up to it . . ."

"We?"

"Mr. Flint," he said, "has consented to stay until he is assured you have suffered no ill effects from your . . . adventure."

She wanted to argue with his choice of words, but merely

nodded noncommittally and smiled when he kissed her again before departing.

Flint, she thought as she thrust aside the covers. First he practically tries to rape me; then he saves my life. She frowned, puzzled. She couldn't stay in bed now that she knew he was downstairs, waiting. Over Gwen's protests she dressed simply, moving about the room in small steps until her equilibrium returned. And once she felt sure of herself, she descended the stairs on Gwen's arm, shaking off her unease as they reached the dining room.

Oliver expressed delight at her courage. Flint, however, merely lifted a wine glass, toasting her, and smiled.

Dinner passed as if in a dream. Oliver spoke at length about everything but the attack. Flint kept his comments to a minimum, brushing aside her thanks with a murmured "At your service, ma'am," and changing the subject. Then she noted how restless her husband was, leaving his chair, pacing a few strides, returning to pour himself another tot of brandy. Perhaps, she thought, he felt awkward in the presence of his wife's savior, but she wasn't sure. After the meal, she was relieved when Flint suggested a stroll around the grounds since the evening was so balmy. Oliver declined to join them; instead, he muttered something about attending to business and waved them on absently.

Caitlin frowned, but said nothing. She was feeling much too relaxed, and she didn't want to spoil the sensation by pressing him too hard over something he obviously considered no concern of hers. A normal state of affairs, she thought as Flint took her arm and started around the house toward the pond. Too normal by half.

Then she chided herself for being so critical. Oliver was, after all, a busy man. With a wrench of her will, she allowed all her senses to reach out to the night—to the languid scents, the lazy sounds, the feel of the soft, cooling grass underfoot. And when they reached the pond, neither having said a word, they sat on the bench and watched the silver surface of the water undulating under the currying of the breeze.

"Do they have places like this in Wales, then?" he asked, his voice gentle, his nearness warm.

She smiled without looking at him. "They do, Mr.—"

"James, please. Under the circumstances . . ."

"Yes," she said. "You're right, and James it is." She waited, but he said no more. "In the hills there are glens, waterfalls, a mist that covers everything until the snows come. And there are so many hills and glens that you never meet anyone unless you really want to. A perfect place to think a bit, to find some peace from the day."

"And is that what you wish, Lady Morgan?"

She turned to him, grinning. "Caitlin. Under the circumstances . . ." She allowed herself a small laugh. "Besides, Lady Morgan makes me sound so much older than I am."

He shifted to face her. "But surely you're not ancient."

"No, I'm not that. But sometimes I feel as if I were. Sometimes Oliver makes me feel . . ." She stopped herself, annoyed at her laxity in front of a virtual stranger. But when he pulled away the hand she'd clamped over her mouth, she admitted he didn't feel like a stranger at all. The way his eyes penetrated to the rim of her soul, the way his fingers brushed over her palm—it was as if they'd known each other for centuries, not hours.

"The pond," she said without turning away. "It's lovely."

"Beautiful," he said quietly.

She moistened her lips quickly, and swallowed, trying to ignore the hand moving up her arm. "My quiet place," she said. "Oliver doesn't like it here. Oliver thinks it's a waste of time to sit and do nothing but think. He would rather be out, Oliver would." She held her breath when she felt his hand reach her bare shoulder, but she did not shrug him away. "I often come here."

His eyes. She hadn't realized how intense was their gaze, how dark their color or how flecked with points of fire, as if reflecting some field of distant candles.

"I really can't thank you enough for what you've done," she said, barely getting the words out.

"An honor, my lady Caitlin. An honor indeed."

All she'd been taught melted away under the pleasure she felt as his voice seemed to drift over her cheeks and circle her hair. And she did not stop him, because it was the first time in a long while that someone had liked her despite her connection to Oliver instead of because of it. And she reveled in it. She didn't care what cautions crept into her mind; she didn't give a damn what her husband might think. She liked the way James Flint's hand had worked its way under her flowing hair to the back of her head. She closed her eyes slowly, tilting her head back and rolling it to one side.

"You're tense, Caitlin," he said. "Still not thinking about—"

"No," she said quickly. "No." A sigh. "You handled yourself well."

"I've known my share of men like that, my lady. Enough."

His free hand caressed the other side of her neck. The wind gusted up suddenly, then settled down to rustle the bushes. The night birds in the distance trilled softly. She winced when his massaging hand accidentally pinched her, held her breath when he saw her pain and covered the hurt with a kiss.

"James," she whispered.

He kissed her again. "An apology," he said, "for not arriving sooner."

"You're being silly." Her hands squirmed in her lap, and when she felt her balance threatened she reached out, inadvertently placing them on his thighs. Then she lowered her gaze to the hollow of his throat and saw the pulse there. "I . . . I should return to the house," she whispered, her mouth suddenly dry, the beat of her heart hard against her chest.

"Yes," he said reluctantly, though his hands remained where they were.

"Oliver will be annoyed." Her smile was sardonic. "Actually, no matter what you did, he'll be furious."

"I've seen him so on occasion."

She reached up with every intention of pushing his hands away, and found herself tracing the line of his jaw instead.

"James, we really shouldn't stay here much longer."

He smiled. "But a little while, yes?"

Before she could answer he'd covered her lips with his, his left hand cupping the back of her neck to hold her until the contact was broken and his fingers were buried in the thicket of her hair, caressing it. Watching him carefully while he watched her, she recalled the nights Oliver came to her in a stupor, or did not come at all.

He kissed her again, and this time she allowed herself to respond; she needed the tenderness, even if it was only for one moment of one evening.

His right hand slipped from her shoulder and swept tenderly over her breasts. She shuddered, almost pulling away, then without thinking shifted so he could work free the laces as he gently eased her from the bench to the soft mattress of grass. It was time to stop this madness, she told herself suddenly. But as they faced each other in the moonlight, the laces finally slipped from their ivory eyelets, and her breasts fell softly into his palms. Pressing, gently kneading, he let his mouth break free of hers and slip to her throat, to the hollow between her breasts. She gasped and tilted back her head. Listening to the rustle of her skirts as they rode toward her hips, she could feel the grass against her legs. His hands, slightly rougher now, stroked her flesh, igniting sparks too long unkindled.

She had one last heartbeat of resistance as he eased her tenderly to her back; then all resistance was gone. A gold buckle glinted in the moonlight. His chest was bare and covered with a pelt of dark hair. She reached out to slip his breeches down over his thighs, her fingers trembling, and her lips quivering.

The wind gusted, and her flesh accepted its caress.

The water lapped softly at pond's edge as she lifted herself to his face and pulled him to her. His grin faded to an expression of feral intensity when she closed her teeth over his lower lip and teased it. She moaned deep in her throat when finally he entered her and ignited the fire she craved. There was a clarity to the heavens overhead, a soughing to the wind that matched her own sighing.

And when he whispered her name in time to their rhythm, she opened her mouth and laughed through the tears that sprang to her eyes. Laughed when the tears blurred the stars into white comets. Laughed at the explosion of the sun in her loins.

6

A WEEK PASSED, and July loomed on the horizon. The temperature began climbing earlier in the day, and a heavy, ghostly mist clung to the trees long after dawn, to gather again quickly after sunset and cloy the night air. Though logs were stacked ceremoniously on the lion-faced andirons, the fires remained unlit; the house remained reasonably cool during the daylight hours, and neither would the night necessitate the striking of a match.

Yet despite the heat, Caitlin spent as little time as she could inside. Most often, between meals, she would wander about the estate, a parasol in her hand and her gaze fixed on nothing in particular. And more often than not she found herself at the pond, standing beneath the high boughs of a stately pine whose needles had carpeted the ground and whose shade was like the touch of a cool autumn breeze. She would stand and she would stare at the glass-smooth surface of the water bleached of color as the sun grew white. And at the bench she knew would be almost too hot to touch until Davy roused himself and brought its canopy from storage. And finally she'd stare, after a great deal of stalling, at the patch of ground where James had made love to her.

For the first two days she had suffered an intense bout of guilt, refusing to meet Oliver's eyes. Ignoring his drinking she prayed he would not notice the seemingly perpetual blush on her cheeks. But on the third morning she had caught sight of herself unexpectedly in a mirror and realized with a sardonic smile that no adulteress's mark had been branded into her forehead, no devil's horns had sprouted from her head. At that moment she had taken to the pond to think, to wonder if in fact she really felt guilty. She knew there was no question about Oliver's conjugal disinterest—either over her physical or her emotional needs. And while she would not have given herself to just any man, James Flint had happened along at just the right time. His words, his manner, his carefully tender caresses had all struck complementary sparks within her, inflaming her senses.

Gwen still knew nothing definite. There had been several questioning looks, a few almost comical hints, but Caitlin had had the sense not to broadcast the affair. Besides, she knew what her friend would say, that she'd known all along Oliver was making her miserable, and if that was the case why didn't Caitlin hie herself back into Griff Radnor's arms?

Caitlin smiled and leaned against the pine bole, encircling the tree with one arm as she lowered the parasol to the ground.

Dear, wonderful Gwen, she thought. Sometimes she was so marvelously predictable. And so maddeningly stubborn. As if Caitlin really wanted Griff anymore, as if there were anything to go back to even if she did. She suspected that Gwen's eagerness was partly due to her father's urgings in spite of his disapproval of Griffin, and partly due to Gwen's own growing feeling for Davy Daniels. Caitlin's smile grew. No silly dreams of princes and kings for level-headed Gwen Thomas. No, she would content herself with a solid young man whose future was ensured and who loved her in turn. That much was obvious. Davy, whenever he was able, followed Gwen around like a puppy—as Caitlin herself had done when first smitten by Griff.

"Damn Griffin!" she said suddenly, an exorcism to drive the man from her mind. Lord, Gwen managed to have her thinking about him even when she wasn't around.

She moved to the other side of the tree and watched as a pair of blinding white geese swept out of the pale blue sky and landed with barely a ripple on the water. They swam about for several minutes, tested the bottom with their beaks, and were gone in a diamond shower of sunlight and droplets. And in watching them depart—fading from white to black as they shrank to motes against the blue sky—she thought of her father. For a reason she'd never been able to fathom, geese were his favorite birds; probably, she thought wryly, because they were so cantankerous, like him.

Like him, she reminded herself, when he was younger and in good health.

She sighed, and gnawed absently at her lower lip. It had been several weeks since his last letter, and she was beginning to worry. When they'd left in early April he was still abed, coughing and aching, and insisting at the top of his baritone voice that he was perfectly all right, thank you very much, and would she please stop fussing over him as if he were a child? But he *was* a child now, or almost so. The coughing produced blood, though he hadn't wanted her to know that; and his sleeplessness was extending further and further into the night. She made no attempt to deceive herself; she knew he was dying—by slow stages that sapped his strength and taxed his will. He was slipping away from her, and only his temper and Oliver's importuning had persuaded her to leave Wales for another stay at Eton.

The lack of word from him bothered her.

Flint had left Eton before she'd arisen the day after their assignation—a messageless departure that was only now beginning to rankle. On top of that, she was concerned about her father, and slowly she grew determined to ask Oliver for permission to return to Seacliff soon, just to see for herself how her Welsh father was doing.

She closed the parasol and turned abruptly into the grove. As long as she was thinking about it, she might as well do it. Oliver had stayed close to home these past seven days, pacing through the house like a caged lion. It was possible he, too, was growing restless, and she might not have a better opportunity to talk him into leaving Eton, if only for a month. His activities seemed to have ground to a temporary halt, and better they—or she—be on the road before he started to wreak his ill humor on her.

She walked slowly, reluctant to leave the shadows, and so was able to see the rider before she stepped out into the open.

He was astride a large black horse whose sides she could tell even at this distance were lathered. Its head drooped, and its mouth kept opening as if gulping for air. An old mount, she thought, not used to hard traveling.

The horseman himself was of great height, she could tell, and even in the midday warmth was wearing a long brown cloak that nearly covered the black's haunches. The rider's hat was plain and wide-brimmed, and as he scanned the house with an air of clear disdain she squinted and caught a glimpse of his face—ruddy, scarred, with a ragged white patch set over his left eye. She shivered, instinctively moving farther back into the shadows behind a thick maple. She didn't feel at all ashamed.

He waited in the sun for several moments, the horse pawing at the drive, its tail slapping lazily at flies. The man's lips moved, and he cocked his head. His right hand slapped hard against his chest as he spoke with someone Caitlin couldn't see. Before he had finished talking Oliver stepped into view. His hands were firm on his hips, and he was scowling. He listened, interrupted the man two or three times, then reached into his jacket and pulled out a leather pouch. The horseman stared at it. Oliver jerked a thumb over his shoulder, but the man shook his head, clearly adamant about remaining where he was.

Oliver brandished the pouch; the rider spat on the ground.

Caitlin felt herself leaning forward, as if the extra few inches would help her hear their voices. Though she suspected strongly that this was another one of those transactions Oliver had labeled none of her wifely business, she was fascinated. The rider's hard demeanor and almost ragged appearance contrasted starkly with her husband's scarlet jacket and military posture.

That two such dissimilar men should have dealings with each other intrigued her, so much so that she almost broke her cover to rush over and join their tête-à-tête. She did not, however. Caution, and an eerie feeling she couldn't put her finger on, stayed her.

Suddenly, the rider reached into a dusty saddlebag and withdrew a packet of papers bound together with ribbons. He leaned over and handed them to Oliver, who held them close to his eyes and leafed through them. When he was apparently satisfied, he tossed the pouch negligently toward the rider who teetered dangerously in his saddle as he tried to snatch it. A second, briefer exchange followed, and Oliver stepped hastily back as the rider wheeled the black around and thundered down the drive toward the Windsor road. It did not take him long to vanish into the lane, and when Caitlin looked back, Oliver was gone.

She had an abrupt sinking sensation. Her husband's mood had rather rudely darkened in front of her. If he was going to permit her to return to Wales now, she would have to be more than politic in her asking. And certainly she would have to wait until he'd taken some of his favorite port. In the meantime, she would talk to Gwen and the other servants, to see if they had overheard any of the conversation. Though she knew Bradford and the others would say nothing to her, it was entirely possible they might let something slip in front of Davy or Gwen. Gwen should know enough to at least keep her ears open.

As she stepped swiftly across the lawn toward the mansion's entrance, Caitlin thought again of how different her life would have been had Oliver been willing to take her into his confidence. It would not only have alleviated much of the uncertainty with which she lived, but it also would have eliminated the need to find things out by going through the staff.

Of course, she told herself, if she weren't so nosy, if she comported herself as a good English wife should and tended only to the affairs of the house, she wouldn't feel this way. On the other hand, she was neither English nor a proper wife, when she thought about it. Oliver's view of marriage had taken care of that quite readily. For another she wasn't content to sit prettily by the hearth and light up the room with charm and beauty. More and more during the past three years she had come to learn that she was just as good, if not better, than most of the stuffy men she'd encountered; and she would be damned if she was going to spend the rest of her days pretending her mind was filled with thoughts of flowers and little else, her hands working automatically on whatever projects women were supposed to engage in. That, she thought as she stepped into the cool kitchen, was about as insulting to her as anything she could think of.

And the more the notion took hold of her mind, the greater grew her agitation and sense of injustice. By the time she'd tracked Gwen down, curiosity had transformed itself into an obsession, and even Gwen was taken aback by the sudden determination in her voice, the falsely bright smile that replaced her grim expression.

Davy Daniels was more bone than meat, more height than solid weight. His slick black hair was curly, and one lock was forever slipping down over his right eye. His clothes, even when he was seated, seemed rumpled and ill-fitting. Aside from acting as coachman to the Morgans, his duties included seeing that the horses were properly shod, expertly curried, and exercised. And he coddled them when they felt poorly. He had very little schooling, other than what Gwen and Caitlin had given him, but his quick wit had stood him in good enough stead over the years to keep him in high favor in the Evans household.

But that, he thought sourly as he walked through the stables, was before Sir Oliver-damned-Morgan had come into his life. The old man disliked him. Davy knew that, and he knew why. Alone among those who worked for the major, he had seen instantly through the man's facade, knew him exactly for what he was.

And Davy hated him.

He hated the evening trips to the taverns in Windsor, the waiting outside no matter the weather while the major cavorted within with old cronies and prostitutes. More than once he'd had to drag the fool away from a fight with men twenty years younger than he, or away from a heavily painted woman who demanded payment for her services. And more than once he'd been forced to leave gold sovereigns behind to silence those who might make life in higher circles difficult, if not impossible, for the major.

Yet he did not do it for the man; Davy did it for his mistress. If she should ever discover what her husband actually did during those evenings when he was supposed to be out dining with gentlemen, her heart would break. He was sure of it. Gwen had told him dozens of times how miserable Lady Morgan really was, in spite of the happy face she put on in public. Miserable. And justifiably so, he thought, moving into a stall and picking up a straw brush. Justifiably damned so.

He stroked a dapple gray's flanks and whispered to it soothingly, patting its neck and scratching it hard between the ears. Then he began working with the brush and a handful of straw, currying, whistling, thinking about how Griff Radnor would better appreciate a handsome beast such as this more than Sir Oliver ever would. Now there was a man, he thought, a real man who knew how to treat women, and whose life had been filled with enough excitement and adventure for twenty men. Davy envied him, and he'd been dismayed when he'd learned Caitlin wasn't going to marry him after all. It had been assumed she would. And he himself had assumed that old Evans would give no credence to the rumors of Griff's past. But, surprisingly, he had. And the next thing anyone knew, Morgan was there, and when he left, Caitlin went with him.

The gray snorted, and Davy stepped back to examine his work. Satisfied, he nodded and turned around, stopping in his tracks. The major was standing in the doorway.

"Boy," Morgan said, "you seem to be in a hurry."

Davy glanced rapidly from side to side as if searching for escape. "I do my best, sir," he said softly, his young man's voice rather high.

Morgan stomped across the wide planks and inspected each of the horses, touching them with one finger as though expecting to come away with a smear of dust. He grunted. He looked back to Davy, who kept his face averted.

"Not bad," the major judged when he was done. "Not bad at all—for a Welshman, that is." He laughed harshly, his hands on his hips.

Davy said nothing. It was unhealthy to rouse the man's temper; he knew that from many a beating taken behind the stable wall.

"Now then, come here, lad."

Davy shambled over, his shoulders shrugged forward to diminish his height. His long arms brushed the sides of his baggy trousers. His throat had gone dry, and a lead stone weighed heavily in the pit of his stomach. When the major grabbed his arm roughly, Davy nearly cried out.

"Now listen, lad," Morgan said, the words hissing between clenched teeth, "we'll be heading back to Wales in a bit, and there's a few things you and I must have clear before then."

Davy caught himself before he smiled. Wales. They were going home earlier than usual. For a moment he wondered why Gwen hadn't said anything to him about it, but he decided to let the question pass when he saw the feral look in Morgan's squinting eyes.

"Lad," the major said, "I can read your mind, you know. I can do that. I can see deep down in that curdled porridge you call a brain that you're just itching to say a few things to your mistress about what we've done—paying visitations on the elegant ladies of Windsor and all." He chuckled, and tightened his grip on the coachman's arm.

Davy winced, and would have kept his gaze on the floor had not Morgan grabbed his jaw with one powerful hand and wrenched his face around.

"But you will say nothing to her, will you, Davy Daniels? You'll not say a single word to your mistress, isn't that right?"

Davy shook his head as best he could, his skin breaking out in goose flesh and his blood turning cold.

"Because you know what's happening now, don't you, Davy? You're a clever lad, aren't you? You know I shall be sharing the task of running Seacliff. Perhaps I'll be more in command of that miserable hovel than you suspect. And being in charge, Davy, well . . ." He leaned closer, Davy's face still hard in his grip. "Well, that means I'll have a few things to say about how your brother and father will prosper, won't I? Oh, yes, Davy, I will, I will."

Davy broke away suddenly, falling against the wall. A harness slipped from its peg, and dust rose from the flooring where it fell.

Morgan straightened. His eyes narrowed, and his lips pursed. "You do understand, don't you, Davy? Tell me you understand so I don't have to worry."

The epithet erupted before Davy could stop it: "Bastard!"

Morgan only grinned.

They stood for a long moment in the dim light, dust rising about them as the horses sensed fear and anger and began stamping their hooves on the straw beds of their stalls. Then, without warning, Morgan closed the space between them, lifted an arm and, after a telling hesitation, flashed the flat of his hand across the young man's cheek. Davy was thrown along the wall, arms flailing for balance until he reached the narrow doorway and stumbled outside. He would have been all right, but a half-buried stone caught his left foot and he sprawled face down, rolling onto his back to look up just as Morgan exited the stable. He fully expected to feel a boot in his side, or to see the man withdraw a whip and lay a few lashes across his chest. But he didn't. Instead, Morgan clasped his hands behind his back and rocked several times on the heels of his polished black boots.

"You should eat better, Davy Daniels," Morgan said, his eyes scanning the ground, the trees, the few clouds in the sky. "You should eat better, and perhaps you wouldn't fall about like that."

Davy said nothing. In that instant he would rather have been struck than to have heard the winter's cold of the man's voice. A deep winter's cold that took all the warmth from the sun and made him shiver in spite of himself.

Morgan placed a finger to his lips to caution silence; then he nodded and walked away.

Davy remained on the ground. His cheek ached from the blow, and the fall had left a wide scrape along his leg, but he did not make a move to comfort himself. Instead, he tried to find consolation in the thought of returning to Seacliff, but the major had taken even that cheer from him.

Caitlin stepped out of her room and walked quickly down the corridor, passing the stairwell and opening the door to what would have been the nursery. She had been coming here often since their return to Eton this year, stepping across the bare floor, imagining the places where the chest would have been, the cradle, the nursing bed . . . all of it now a mere specter in her mind. The room was empty. Slanting shafts of sunlight placed squares of gold on the floor, and the faint odor of disuse pinched her nostrils.

The next room down the side hall was Oliver's den. There he spent most of his days working on projects that would presumably, if he handled them properly, bring more work to the people of Seacliff's valley, and more gold into the coffers of the estate's manor. She was not permitted to enter there, but if she stood near the wall of the nursery she could faintly hear Oliver pacing up and down, or exploding in an oath—neither of which indicated anything but what his mood would be that evening.

Just a short while ago he'd stormed into the house, made straight for the den, and slammed the door behind him. It hadn't taken her long to decide to eavesdrop, to gauge his possible reaction to her request to return to Wales.

And as she listened to him, her ear close against the wall, her eyes opened in astonishment.

Oliver was singing.

His rough-edged voice rose and fell in the peculiar cadence of a military song, and she could almost imagine him marching about the room.

She stepped to the doorway and into the hall, and had almost knocked on his door when Mrs. Thorn appeared on the landing.

"Yes?" Caitlin said, distracted and sounding distant.

"Dinner, m'lady," the tall, precariously thin woman said in a high nasal voice. "There'll be but the two of ye? I'd ask Mr. Bradford, but he's not to be found."

"Of course," Caitlin said. "Who else would there be?"

Mrs. Thorn buried her hands in a soiled apron. "Well, m'lady, I just thought since there was others for luncheon . . ."

Caitlin wrenched herself away from staring at Oliver's door, her gaze hard on the cook's face. Though it was true she'd been eating at odd hours for the past week, she was sure no one else had been with Oliver while she'd strolled around the gardens. No one could have been. She'd not been out all that long . . . unless her daydreaming had completely thrown her sense of time off kilter.

"Others?" she said finally.

Mrs. Thorn flinched as if she'd been slapped. "Yes'm."

"Who?"

"Why, Mr. Flint, m'lady," she said.

"What?" Caitlin came around to the stairs and hurried down to the landing. "Mr. Flint? Mr. James Flint's been here in this house?"

The cook shied away, realizing she'd said more than she should have. "Yes, m'lady. Twice this week. He's . . . he's not comin' for dinner then?"

Twice, Caitlin thought. Twice!

She dismissed the woman with a brusque wave and turned to stare up through the balustrade at the door to her husband's den. In defiance of all of Oliver's rules he'd met with someone here at the house, the rider with the white patch; and James Flint had been here twice, and neither time had he attempted to speak with her. Since he was definitely not the sort of man who would cringe at or shy away from a husband's wrath, he had another reason—and as she made her way slowly, thoughtfully, downstairs she wondered if she had a reason to feel used.

7

THE SITTING room was dominated by a massive fieldstone fireplace that extended the entire length of one wall. Two armchairs and a low, scalloped couch embroidered with gold, silver, and spring green designs were arranged before it. Similar settings were placed throughout the room to take advantage of the large bay window overlooking the sweep of the front lawn, or the relative peace of the far corner where conversation was held to a minimum. Here were the only shelves Oliver had in the house, the books being kept for occasional reading. The rest of the walls were taken up by hunting tapestries and oil portraits of the Morgans, including one of Oliver himself in full major's regalia over the mantel.

As Caitlin sat in a fireplace armchair, Mary hurried in with a long taper to light the candles in their ebony sconces. The girl said nothing, but Caitlin noticed she'd been weeping. Curious, she thought, but no more curious than the rest of the day's events and discoveries. She'd been waiting for nearly two hours, keeping her hand on a book of French poetry while her gaze flitted often to the foyer. She hoped Oliver would come down long enough before dinner so she could ask him the dozen questions that were swirling through her mind. Her temper had surged and calmed as she considered Flint, and Oliver's annoying restlessness, and when she found herself reading the same verse repeatedly, without understanding a word, she closed the book and laid it on the small round table near her left hand.

At that moment Gwen entered the room. She paused a moment, her hands buried in the ample folds of her simple brown skirt. Then she stalked across the floor to stand behind the couch. Her eyes were ablaze with rage, and her chin trembled with the effort to keep from shouting. Her cheeks flushed, and she swallowed several times while she avoided Caitlin's astonished, concerned look.

"That . . . man," Gwen finally managed, her voice tight and harsh, her eyes softening now as tears welled. Quickly, she swiped the back of a hand over them, dried the hand on her square-necked blouse. "He's impossible!"

Between Gwen and the couch was a long, narrow walnut table upon which lay an engraved silver tray with several crystal wine glasses and a decanter of dark brandy. Gwen's right hand closed around the neck of the decanter, and for a moment Caitlin thought she was going to yank out the stopper and pour herself a drink.

"Gwen," she said softly, and the hand fell away.

Gwen looked at her—fury and sorrow twisting her lovely round face into something close to hideous while her throat worked to force out the words.

"Gwen, what happened?" Though she wanted to rise and take her friend in her arms, she sensed that a single movement on her part would send Gwen racing from the room. It was all she could do to keep herself still.

"He beat him!" Gwen said loudly, turning toward the window and glaring at the dying light. "He . . . the monster beat him!"

Caitlin did rise then, and came around the couch to the table. After a moment's hesitation she poured a measure of brandy into a glass and handed it to Gwen. When Gwen shrugged the offer away, Caitlin grabbed her arm.

"Beat him," Gwen whispered. "Beat him like he was some kind of street dog. I can't believe he'd really do that to him." A tear shimmered, and fell untouched.

Caitlin gently forced the glass into her hand, then led her back to sit on the couch. Gwen stared at the brandy as if it were something totally alien to her, looking to Caitlin who nodded and then drank it as if it were water. She choked, and Caitlin poured another, a more generous portion. Then she sat on the couch beside her.

"Who?" she said. "Who beat whom?"

Gwen held her glass in two hands and stared blindly at the

hearth. "Sir goddamned bloody Oliver beat Davy, that's who!" she spat out the words as though Morgan's name were an obscenity. "For no reason at all he beat the poor boy around the stableyard. Kicked him! Thrashed him!" She turned to Caitlin suddenly, the tears flowing freely. "Why? Davy's a good boy, Cat, you know that for a fact. He'd never . . ." She swallowed and turned away quickly. "He never would, you know. He's a good boy. He's a good boy."

Caitlin pulled a handkerchief from her sleeve and daubed at the tears until Gwen freed one hand from her glass and took the handkerchief herself.

"Are you sure Oliver beat Davy?" she said, trying mightily to keep her voice calm. She knew enmity between Daniels and her husband existed, but though she loved Davy dearly she would not put it past him to make up such a story to cover a wrong.

Gwen nodded vigorously and blew her nose. "He was in the stable, curryin', Davy was. Without so much as a by-your-leave, the major comes in and starts knocking him about, pushing him to the ground and—and . . ." She drained the glass and took a long, deep breath.

Caitlin put a hand on her friend's arm, stroked it while Gwen struggled for speech. "Gwen," she said, "I hate to say this, but you know how Davy is at times. And you know how he'd like nothing more than to have you fuss a bit over him. A fall, perhaps, and he—"

Gwen snatched her arm away and stood glaring. "David Daniels does not lie to me, Cat! If he says Sir Oliver thrashed him, then that's what happened." A pause, and Gwen's face drained. "I don't believe you're actually defending him, Cat. How could you? How could you after what he's done?"

Caitlin cursed herself roundly for not thinking before speaking, and tried to appear as contrite as she could. "I am not defending him, Gwen. If he did indeed lay a hand on Davy—"

"Dammit, Cat, he did! I just told you he did!" Her hands clenched into fists at her waist, and her foot slammed on the floor twice. "He did!"

Caitlin leaned back and stared at Gwen's swollen red eyes, her quivering lips, and felt her own expression harden. "You say he kicked him. Several times? Once? Did Davy say anything? You know how my husband is, Gwen. Did Davy say anything to him?"

Gwen hesitated, her gaze wandering about the room like that of a small animal searching furtively for an escape. She lifted a trembling hand, dropped it wearily, and stared into the glass she suddenly realized was still in her hand. Her lower lip quivered; there was a faint tic under her right eye.

"Gwen?"

In a soft voice, reluctantly: "He didn't . . . well, he didn't actually put a boot to Davy, no. Not a boot, anyway. But that—"

"How many times did Davy say he'd been struck?"

"Cat, I don't—"

"Answer me," she demanded as kindly and sternly as she could, rising swiftly to take the woman's arm in a gentle grip. "Gwen, how many times was Davy struck?"

The young woman swallowed heavily, but still refused to meet her probing stare. "All right. Once," she finally admitted. But she added, quickly and desperately, "But he didn't have to hit him, Cat. He didn't! All Davy said to him—" She stopped guiltily, and Caitlin gave her a soft, encouraging smile that almost brought a smile in return.

"Yes?"

"Well . . ."

A caution: "Gwen."

Gwen looked to the floor. "Davy says he called the major a bastard."

Caitlin groaned and closed her eyes, opened them and raised her eyebrows in mild exasperation. "Why? Why would Davy do a stupid, reckless thing like that?"

A helpless shrug, and Gwen looked up. "I don't know. I really don't know. And Davy . . . he wouldn't say. He told me some things, but he didn't tell me all of it."

Caitlin lowered her arms and moved heavily to the hearth, looking blindly at the fresh logs and the gleam of the brass andirons. Her hand pushed through her hair, and came to rest on her shoulder. "Davy knows better than that," she said, almost to herself. "I can see how he is around Oliver. And," she added flatly and turned quickly, "I can see how you are around Davy, you know."

Gwen's mouth opened in astonishment, then closed tightly while she fought to regain control of her temper. Then, abruptly, she went on the defensive. "But the man hates us, Cat! Why . . . why, he couldn't hate us more if we were the French."

She looked past Gwen to the front hall, feeling the tension

make a wooden mask of her face, and an icy flow of her veins.

"It doesn't matter that he dislikes you," she said sternly. "Though God knows you've given him little chance to feel anything different."

"Cat, please—"

"And," she said, her voice rising, "it does not matter to me what Davy said to him. I do not approve, mind, but I know the lad well, and he must have been provoked or he would not have said something so completely, so terribly wrong." Her eyes narrowed then, and Gwen backed away from her. "It was wrong; you must understand that, Gwen. It was wrong, what Davy said."

Gwen nodded quickly.

"And it was equally wrong for my husband to strike him. He has no right. Provoked or not, he should not have raised a hand." A fist pressed hard to her chest. "He has no right!"

In the face of Caitlin's anger Gwen seemed abruptly ill at ease, regretting that she had said anything at all. Her lips moved soundlessly, and her expression lost its combination of rage and sadness, twisting instead into fearful concern.

"Cat, he mustn't know what I've told you. He mustn't know I've said anything at all."

"What?" she snapped, the obsidian eyes turned to glaring stone.

"If . . . if you say something to him, he'll only take it out on poor Davy again. Or on me. It'll only be worse, Cat, believe me. I'm . . ." She put a trembling hand to her forehead. "I'm sorry I said anything at all."

"No," Caitlin told her sharply, striding purposefully off the hearth and taking her friend's hands in her own. "My God, no, Gwen, you must never think that. Never. You must tell me everything. Do you hear me? I'm not permitted to discipline Bradford or the others, and by God I don't care what Oliver thinks, he is not permitted to take such charge of my people. My own people!"

She took a trembling deep breath to say more, to bring some small comfort to ease the pain Gwen was feeling, but in the midst of her pause she could hear the clatter of heavy footsteps descending from the gallery.

"Listen, Gwen," she said quickly, her gaze on the doorway. "You must promise me something."

"Cat—"

She lowered her voice almost to a hissing. "There's no time! You must promise me something."

Gwen, confused, nodded rapidly.

"If this ever happens again, or if anything like it comes to your ken, you must come to me at once, do you understand?"

"I . . . yes."

"You swear to me, Gwen?"

Gwen put a hand over her heart. "I swear."

The footsteps paused, their echoes in the hall swiftly fading.

"All right, then. Get along now, before he finds you here. I'll speak to him, believe me. This won't happen again."

Gwen opened her mouth as though she were anxious to say something more, but the renewed hard crack of boot heels against stone sent her racing from the room, through a narrow door in the paneled back wall. Caitlin waited with hands at her sides until Oliver stood framed in the doorway. He wore his black silk dressing gown open as if it had been flung on in haste, and his shirt was unfastened halfway down his chest; the disarray took her aback until her mind's ear heard again the distress in Gwen's voice.

"Oliver, I must talk to you."

Oliver nodded once, but said nothing. He walked calmly to the brandy and poured himself a portion much larger than he usually took so soon before dinner. He stared at the glass for several long moments, and her own tempered anger prevented her from seeing immediately that his face seemed abruptly older, more lined, and that the flesh on his scalp appeared as fragile as parchment.

"Oliver?"

He lowered the glass without sipping the brandy and crossed to her side to lead her to the couch.

"Oliver, what is it?"

He cleared his throat, obviously uncomfortable. "This afternoon," he began.

"Yes," she said sharply. "I want to talk with you about that. I would like to know by what right you have struck one of my people."

Oliver looked at her stupidly, blinking rapidly until he was able to comprehend what she was saying. Then he pulled away slightly without releasing his grip. "You have heard."

"I have."

"It was necessary."

"Oliver"—she lowered her voice—"I cannot see the necessity of striking anyone who is part of the staff. And especially someone who is my friend."

"Caitlin, this is not a proper topic for discussion in my household."

She reacted as if she had been slapped. Hot blood rushed to her cheeks. "How . . . how dare you!" she said. "How dare you speak to me this way! David Daniels, may I remind you, sir, is a member of my household. I would not presume to take a switch to that sniveling child, Mary, just because she mutters about me behind my back—though I would take pleasure in doing so, I assure you—and I fail to see how—"

"The lad was insubordinate," Oliver said, his tone oddly muted.

"Oh, Oliver, for heaven's sake, this isn't the army, and these are not your soldiers we're talking about."

"Caitlin," he said firmly, "this is not what I wished to speak with you about."

Her mouth opened, closed, his words finally soaking in. Was he going to tell her why James Flint had been in the house without her knowledge? And in thinking his name, Caitlin wondered if Flint hadn't, for some reason, told Oliver about their tryst. The idea of it chilled her, but she was relieved when she sensed her husband was not the slightest bit angry.

"Very well," she said, when she understood he'd been expecting some sort of response. "We will discuss it later. What is it you want?"

His fingers kneaded the backs of her hands, and suddenly she was filled with the most uncanny feeling of dread.

"Oliver, tell me."

He inhaled slowly, deeply, then let the air whistle out between his teeth before he spoke again. "This afternoon, while you were out walking, I received a visitor."

She held herself quite still, not wanting him to know she had in fact seen him talking to the man.

"He brought me a packet of letters. They were all quite dated, I'm afraid. Somehow they had been sent on to London, because Bradford mistakenly assumed I would be traveling there this past week. A perfectly natural error. But I have spoken to him rather sharply about it to be sure it will not happen again."

"I don't recall messengers coming here, Oliver," she said,

the dread now working to drive a chill through her bones.

"You have been walking quite a bit lately," he told her in mild reproof. "I barely see you at meals, much less during the evening."

Not trusting herself to say anything in response, Caitlin only nodded and hoped he would take it for an apology.

"Be that as it may, there was a note in the packet from Reverend Ellis Lynne. It was addressed to me."

Her eyes closed slowly, and she felt a wave of dizziness wash over her. A hand took her shoulder and pressed her gently to the couch. Her tongue moistened her lips, but try as she might she couldn't swallow away a sour lump lodged in her throat.

Reverend Ellis Lynne was the Anglican clergyman in Seacliff's valley. He was not universally liked, being as he was a transplanted Englishman and harshly prim. He believed it was his duty to pry into the lives of all his parishioners whether they liked it or nor. Her father thought him a small man in both stature and character, and had once told her he believed the cleric was involved with the English. But since he had no proof, he could do nothing except speculate and complain.

Caitlin had no feelings toward the man one way or the other. But a letter to Oliver, not to her, could mean only one thing.

"Caitlin?"

"Oliver, please, say it quickly and be done with it." But she would not open her eyes.

"Shortly after we left, my dear, it seems your father took a turn for the worse. According to the good reverend, Evans insisted on his afternoon walks along the cliffs, and though he was always accompanied by a member of the staff, on this particular afternoon he wanted to go alone, to see some tree or other. I don't understand the significance of that, but it's what the reverend reported."

"My mother," she said weakly, feeling a slow burning in her eyes. "There's a great pine near the end of the wall, the only one there. When I was seven, she died during the winter and though she's buried in the churchyard, Father always went to the tree when he wanted to . . . to talk to her. He proposed to her there, you see; I suppose he'd be considered a sentimental old fool."

Oliver went on, his voice droning. But because there was a roaring in her ears, Caitlin caught only a few words and phrases. They were sufficient for her to know her father had obviously guessed he would not last out the year and was making his peace with himself the best way he knew how. When a sudden squall swept in from the Irish Sea across Cardigan Bay, the staff raced out to bring him back. They didn't find him until just before sunset, lying at the base of the cliffs. The wind, it seemed, had overpowered him.

There was a long silence punctuated only by her attempts to catch her breath before she broke into sobs. Tears coursed down her cheeks, and she made no move to brush them away. And when she opened her eyes, Oliver was staring at her intently.

"We have to go," she said.

Oliver nodded without hesitation.

"We have to go now."

PART TWO

Wife

Seacliff, Wales, 1775

8

IT WAS early afternoon when Caitlin stood impatiently by the first of two polished black coaches, drawing her pale gold shawl more snugly around her shoulders. Her hair had been spun into a loose knot at the nape of her neck. But the haste with which she had performed the task now permitted the silken strands to free themselves in the softly cool west wind coasting down the slopes of the low mountains on the horizon. A vast armada of storm clouds swept grandly overhead, alternately blocking and releasing the sun. Their shadows rippled eerily over the rolling landscape. Caitlin shuddered involuntarily as one passed over her, but she did not move to climb inside the coach and take her seat. Instead, she let her gaze drift over the country she'd been traveling through for the last several days.

Despite the storm that had hounded the solemn, fast-moving procession for nearly a week, the land was a brilliant, gem-encrusted green. Flocks of black- and white-faced sheep roamed the low hills; Welsh ponies with hardy shoulders and thick manes trotted down the cobblestone road, effortlessly pulling flimsy carts and heavy wagons loaded with produce. The villages she had encountered since leaving England were, for the most part, small, their cottages carved from native stone. They hugged the sides of the narrow roads behind waist-high walls constructed long before the time of the Romans. There were lush orchards and verdant forests, white-running streams and shallow rivers, pastureland and tilled land that strongly evoked Eden.

Whenever they approached a cluster of homes it seemed to be a signal for work and play to halt. Young children lined the road laughing and whistling, their round faces ruddy, their traditional dark clothes billowing behind them in the wind. Older men fresh from the mines that scarred the slopes glanced

71

up at the commotion, coal dust streaking their pallid foreheads and cheeks. They doffed floppy wool caps when they realized the status of the travelers. Women curtsied halfheartedly; their hair was bound in scarves and their skirts were hidden behind aprons. The Welsh emphasis on education was marked by the large numbers of schoolhouses set on well-kept plots of their own. The steeples of a number of churches loomed above each community like sentinels, the largest of them buttressed and towered and forbidding.

There were ruins of ancient castles, of fortresses, of Roman baths, overgrown now, reclaimed by the land.

Caitlin sighed loudly and laid a heavy hand on the brass latch. The coach was large and richly appointed, bearing Morgan's crest on each of the doors. On the driver's bench, Davy was dressed in scarlet and black livery, his neck chafed by a stiff, high collar. His tricorne had settled near the back of his head, and from it waved a thick white plume, blown about by the wind. She glanced up at him, caught his gaze, and smiled wanly.

He nodded once toward the mountains. "By sunset, mistress, if I reckon it right."

"I know," she said, and sighed again. Her stomach lurched lightly, and she pursed her lips against a faint taste of bile. She'd eaten quickly in order to get the household moving again, but Oliver had insisted on changing his clothes in a place where he was assured of some small comfort. The inn was not large, but at least, he said, it was far better than changing under some fool tree or other.

She wore dark brown, as she had since they'd left Eton.

"It be fine, mistress," Davy said then, quietly. "He'd want you to feel right about comin' home again. He really would. I know that for a fact."

She started, amazed that Davy had divined her conflict so readily—and dismayed that it showed so openly in her face. But she made no response because she did not trust her voice. On the one hand, her mourning was still deep, still churning in her breast. Yet she had also realized by the second day away from Eton that she'd already reconciled herself to his passing. Not that the shock of knowledge had lessened, nor was the guilt she felt at not being with him when he died any weaker; but her grief was now tempered by the sure understanding that he was, after all these years of waiting, at last with her mother, the only woman he'd ever wanted or loved.

So, then, her excitement was unbidden but muted. Once they'd crossed into Wales and had made their way northwest toward Cardigan Bay on the west coast, she'd felt an electric thrill that prompted her to shift from one window to the other. Like a child would point at a flock of thin-coated sheep or at an arm of forestland stretching down a hillside and cry "Look!" Every tiny house, every stone-embedded road set her heart to racing in spite of herself. Her eyes sparkled with sad and joyous tears. It was as if she'd been gone for a dozen years and returned to discover something new, something more grand than she had noticed before.

Then a glance would catch at the black arm band on her dress and she would turn sober, sit back, and fall into gentle memory.

But the closer they came to Seacliff, the more somber she grew; and that morning she'd awakened in a nervous, short-tempered mood. Gwen was of no help. She traveled in the more Spartan coach with Bradford and Mary behind theirs. They'd barely passed a dozen words over the past two days, and though on her own part Caitlin put it down to mourning, she knew something else was bothering the woman.

"Sunset," Davy said, his voice rising in pitch. Then he took off his hat and wiped a sleeve over his brow. "Before, maybe." He sniffed, and clucked patience to the team of blacks he was handling. "Mistress?"

She looked up, blinking.

"It's not your doin', y'know." He looked pained, as if he had no right to say what he wanted to say. He drew in a sudden deep breath, and seemed to change his mind. "Was Bradford's fault fer not givin' you the letter, that's what it was. 'Sides, the master didn't hold fer buryin' anyway. He says t' me once, 'Davy me lad, outta the house and into the churchyard where I can be with the Missus. Don't you dare let that girl of mine make a pageant of my goin'.' I . . .." He stopped abruptly and looked away, clucking again at the horses, which were already in their traces and anxious to be moving.

After a long moment Caitlin said, "I know, Davy. But still . . ." It was hard. Not being by his side when he died, and not being there for the funeral. She knew Davy was right about what her father had wanted, but she could not help thinking that her absence would drive another wedge between herself

and her people. It was one thing for Oliver to keep her away
for most of each year; it was quite another for her to miss the
passing of her own father. Though word of Bradford's error
would soon spread among the villagers, she knew they'd have
their own thoughts about why she'd not come.

Nevertheless, she was grateful for Davy's attempts to comfort her. Now if only Oliver would finish his dressing so they—

"Cor," Davy muttered then, "will you look at that, now."

She turned quickly, just as the front door of the inn opened,
and Oliver stepped out.

He was wearing a scarlet-jacketed uniform embroidered with
gold thread. A triple row of silver buttons marched steadfastly
down his chest to the cutaway waist. Behind him the material
stiffened and flared, and was edged with white and silver piping
that trapped the fleeting sunlight and threw it back in lances.
His white wig was perfectly curled, and over it he wore a wide-
brimmed black felt hat adorned with a ruby-studded band and
a massive black plume. His black boots were mirror-polished,
their gold buckles almost too large to hold in one hand. There
was no question but that he cut a dashing, even imposing figure.
And despite her annoyance, Caitlin could not disguise a soft
smile as the innkeeper's children followed him silently, awed
by his impressive presence.

When he reached her he stopped and bowed slightly. "Are
you ready, madam?"

"I am," she said. "You're making me seem rather plain,
I'm afraid."

He preened, barely raising a hand. "The best way I could
devise to pay tribute to your father. And there is nothing here
that could throw a shadow on your loveliness." He glanced
around the yard, ignoring the children and the innkeeper at the
door. "However, I think it best we begin the last leg, my dear.
I'm sure the household is waiting for us."

He opened the coach door for her, and gestured impatiently
to Davy to remain where he was while he unfolded the steps
himself.

Caitlin, however, suddenly balked and shook her head.

"My dear?"

"Oliver, I can't. I . . . I can't stay inside there one more
minute." Ashamed, she lowered her eyes and sighed. "I need
the air, Oliver, please don't make me ride inside."

She gauged his reactions carefully, knowing he would be

thinking about her weeping all over his uniform, or worse—
losing her luncheon. But what she'd told him was true. She
did need to ride topside today. She needed to see the valley
unfold before her; she needed to feel the wind in her face and
her hair, needed to smell Cardigan Bay, hear the thunder of
the surf as it smashed relentlessly against the rocks. She needed
the time, and the memories . . . and most of all, she needed to
see Seacliff before Oliver did.

"Please, Oliver, indulge me just this once."

He reached into his side pocket with a white-gloved hand
and withdrew a handful of coppers. He tossed them carelessly
to the children. When their squealing laughter filled the air as
they scrambled through the mud for the money, he looked down
at her and smiled as if her needs always came first.

"Very well, my dear. I understand how you feel. Your
country, your land . . . Believe me, I understand." He leaned
over and kissed her cheek. "But do remember where I am
should you need a shoulder."

She thanked him in a small voice and looked back to the
second coach. Gwen's face was not visible, and she stifled an
impulse to run back and join her there; if Gwen had something
on her mind, sooner or later it would surface, and they would
talk. Meanwhile she took a deep breath and accepted Davy's
hand to the bench. The four blacks tossed their heads as they
sensed movement in the air, their harnesses rattling like so
many ill-tuned bells. Davy sighed loudly.

"We're on, mistress," he said at last.

"Then on it is," she told him solemnly.

The long whip curled through the air and cracked just over
the heads of the lead horses. They started, pulled, and within
moments clattered through the narrow yard gates and onto the
roadbed of crushed stone by now driven hard into the earth by
a thousand hooves. The wheels creaked, the blacks stepped
high and proudly, and the wind carried the sound of a ragged
child's cheer as they left the village behind and set off across
the lowlands toward the slopes of the mountains.

*David Evans stood before the great front doors of Seacliff
and with a grand gesture indicated the entire valley at Caitlin's
feet. He was a short man, swarthy, with ice-blue eyes that were
darkened now with concealed pain.*

"Darlin'," he said, "this will be yours, you know, when

I've gone to your mother." A glance back, then over his shoul-
der. "He's a fair man, your husband is, but I don't think he
knows the land the way you do. Inside," and he thumped at
his chest, "inside, where it counts."

"But Father, the law says—"

"Be damned with the law!" he snapped, nearly shouting.
"The major can wave about all the papers and hire all the
solicitors he wants, but it doesn't change the fact that this land
will never be his the way it will be yours. You must work with
him then, child, be with him to explain and to help. When I'm
gone—"

"Father, please, I don't like you talking like that."

His smile was gentle, his expression melancholy. "Darlin',
there's no other way to talk, now. It's comin' and I feel it. I've
seen sixty winters, and that's considerably more than most men
see. I can't be greedy now, can I? It's time, but I'm leaving
all this to you. Don't forget that, child, when you're away with
him and the heathens, don't forget that."

With the heathens.

Caitlin smiled to herself. Her father had said that the day
she and Oliver left for their first stay in Eton. It would be nearly
ten months before they returned, and by then David Evans had
finally succumbed to the ravages of his illness and was in his
bed. For three years he'd clung to life, praying aloud for a
grandson and not understanding why his daughter hadn't yet
given birth.

It's Oliver, she'd told him once; he says he's too old to
nurture children, that I'll still be young enough to bear children
for another when he's gone.

Evans had scoffed. He reminded her he was just over forty
when she was born, and Morgan seemed to him a fit enough
man to bear the responsibilities of family.

No argument flared. He'd fallen into a deep sleep, and he
never brought up the subject again.

And now, she thought as she gripped the edge of the seat
tightly, they'd have no conversations about anything anymore.

Then, with sudden vehemence, she shook herself, realizing
they were almost upon the valley's remarkable entrance.

To either side the land rose abruptly. Huge, magnificent
boulders jutted out from the hillsides, narrowing the road into
a shadowy gap and creating sharp echoes of the coach's passing. The sun was temporarily blotted out, the shade cool and

welcome. One hundred feet and more the rocks climbed the perpendicular slopes, and she remembered more than one after-noon spent climbing to the summit and pelting passersby below with eggs stolen from a nearby farm. And it was especially daring, and exciting, when the riders were English soldiers.

The road curved to the right. The rock faces blurred into a wall of gray streaked through with deep reds, pale whites, and here and there a fleeting, mossy green. The boulders and the road looked like a tunnel without a roof, she thought as Davy maneuvered through the gap expertly. He called to the horses to calm them of their nervousness.

And then they were on the other side.

"Slow, Davy," she said over the sound of the wind.

He looked at her questioningly, then nodded his understand-ing and clucked to the blacks. They slowed instantly, and the road finished its banking, straightened, and the rocks fell away as if crushed by the fists of an angry giant.

"Ah, Davy," she sighed. Lifting her hands to her head, she combed them through her wind-tangled hair and wished pro-foundly her homecoming had not been occasioned by grief.

"Aye, mistress," he said somberly. "Aye."

The mountains' western slopes were gentle and thickly for-ested. In the valley below, the land was a series of varishaded green and gold squares marking the tenant farmers' fields. Herds of cattle wandered behind low walls; a flock of sheep followed tinkling bells across the pastureland to the south. A stream that was little more than a ribbon of glittering silver meandered lazily from north to south. It threaded past individ-ual cottages two stories high, homes of stone and earth, barns and stables and outbuildings beyond number. The air was cot-ton-soft and even at this distance smelled of the brine of the sea.

She managed to draw a deep breath and hold it until her lungs felt near to bursting. Then she released it with a rush that left her feeling dizzy but deeply content.

Several miles ahead, in the center of the steep valley, the houses of the village lay like carelessly tossed diamonds on a swatch of green velvet. Chimneys and a church spire pointed toward the heavens; gardens blossomed in profusion; and though no more than four dozen large families provided Seacliff with staples, their homes sprawled in such a way that they seemed ten times that number.

She looked to her left as the road swept downward, to the

hills that separated the valley from the rest of the shire. She knew that a trip of less than a hundred miles would take her to the great boiling waters of Bristol Channel, the arm of the Irish Sea that divided Cornwall from Wales.

Then, with a visible effort, she glanced to her right.

In the far distance the hills rose into rugged mountains whose peaks were cloaked in everlasting mist, whose glens offered refuge, and where even now a handful of men took to hiding to avoid impressment into the English army. They were out-laws, but only in the eyes of men like Oliver Morgan. To the Welsh they were, at the very least, prudent, and at the most, romantic heroes.

And on the slope of the hills, less than a mile from where she rode, she could see through the small groves of venerable pine and oak to a sprawling stone house. Its thick walls glittered with mica, its multipitched roof made a cheerful red amid the gables and chimney pots. A gated low wall surrounded it, and the wall in turn was flanked by towering trees that broke the wind before it reached the front door. Behind the house was the forest; ahead, a vast downward sweep of land that reached almost to the valley floor. It encompassed several small farms, a foundry, and at the base, on land claimed by no one, the ruins of an ancient Druid place of worship—a dozen ringstones that mocked distance by their size, and time by the preternatural power of their past.

Aside from the Evans estate, this was the largest, most prosperous holding in this portion of the shire.

It was Falconrest, and it was the home of Griffin Radnor.

As it swept by her in a blur of foliage, Caitlin suddenly could not recall ever feeling quite so lonely.

"It's been a bit of a while," Davy said to her.

She looked to him, ready to frown before she understood he was referring to how long it had been since they'd shifted households to Eton.

"It has," she agreed.

Then he nodded toward Falconrest. "Would he have been there, do you think, mistress? At the funeral, I mean. He should have done, considering his position, but I wonder if he was."

"I wouldn't know," she said distantly. And then, when she realized she'd sounded almost wistful, she added, "What the man does is none of my concern."

Chagrined, Davy returned his attention to the horses.

"Nor," she added sternly, "is what that . . . that man does any of yours, Davy Daniels. As far as we are concerned, he is just someone else who lives in our valley. And that is the way it should be. You mind me, Daniels. That is the way it should be."

He was stung by her rebuke and its curious ferocity and concentrated on his driving, his hands working the reins, his left foot nudging at the brake to keep the coach from sliding on the still rain-slicked roadbed of crushed stone and gravel. He'd been hoping for some sort of sign, anything that would tell him what Gwen suspected was true—that his mistress still carried feelings for the Falconrest master. But evidently it wasn't true, which meant there would be no one to save her from Sir Oliver once he got his hands on Seacliff. No one. And gloom descended over him like a stifling cloak. He began muttering to himself about the injustice of the English and the perverse ways of women.

Caitlin heard the mumbling and bit her lower lip. She'd offended the young man, she knew it, and instinctively reached out to apologize. But an abrupt rush of tears blinded her, and she wiped at them angrily with her handkerchief. She commanded herself to stifle the tears; later, when you're inside and alone. You can't cry now. The village is too close.

Then Davy inhaled sharply and she stared at him, saw him gazing fearfully off to the right and turned to see what had startled him. A hand fluttered to her throat, and her eyes widened.

My God, she thought; my God, how did he know?

9

As THE road wound down into the valley it dipped below an embankment of new grass and soft gold and blue wildflowers. The embankment rose steeply to a stone wall that held at bay the encroachment of brambles and the dangling thick branches of overhanging trees. In a gap between two immense oaks stood a great white stallion, its mane, forelock, and tail of such a stormy gray that they appeared black. As Davy inadvertently slowed the coach in astonishment, the stallion snorted and tossed its sculptured head. The man astride it, as if on cue, leaned forward anxiously.

Oh, God, Caitlin thought, who told him? Who told him I was coming?

He was tall—like a giant on his proud perch above the sinking roadbed. His shoulders and chest were the imposing breadth of a man used to working long hours at hard labor. His narrow waist and hips were those of a man who refuses to spend his time lolling about a sumptuous table. Unrestrained by either cap or headband, his deep copper hair was swept to one side by a breeze blowing languidly from the bay. It caught the sun's light in streaks of dark, smoldering fire. His face was touched by a light tan that darkened his heavy eyebrows and underscored the nightshade of his deep-set eyes. An aquiline nose, high cheekbones, and squared chin cast him as rugged, but also as a member of the gentry who had neither abandoned nor forgotten his origins.

Caitlin caught her breath despite herself.

Her unrelenting daydreams had not been exaggerations: her memories had not added to the man's natural glamour. He was handsome, and she could not deny it. But it was a description he would never apply to himself. He carried himself even now on his stallion in such a way that dared others to label him as anything else but a man who took the world on its own terms, and who laughed when it conflicted with his own. Unlike James Flint, she thought, who adapted himself to get what he wanted.

Well, Gwen, she said silently, hoping the woman could read her thoughts, I hope you're satisfied. I trust his appearance has made you happy.

The coach slowed down even more then, and Caitlin suddenly remembered Oliver sitting below. She looked wide-eyed at Davy, saw his grin, and became alarmed. "What are you doing?" she whispered frantically. "Move on, Davy, move on!" And she had to restrain herself from grabbing hold of the whip and cracking it wildly over the team's bobbing heads.

When Davy hesitated, she repeated her command and he obeyed instantly—though his grin was replaced by a disturbed, perplexed frown. Caitlin laid her hands in her lap, clasping them until her fingers ached, swallowing her panic until the coach drew abreast of the stallion, and she turned to stare as boldly as she could.

Griffin Radnor smiled sadly and raised a hand in greeting.

She nodded once and looked straight ahead, ignoring whatever signals he might be tempted to send her. Part of her was dismayed that she'd seen him at all; the rest of her mind spun in sullen anger that he'd dare show himself to her on a day like this. As if the three years since she'd last seen him had not passed at all. But that was like him, she thought; exactly like him. He'd taken her in the glen on the day her engagement was announced, and then he had abandoned her. Not a word, not a message, not even a gift for the wedding.

And now, suddenly, he had shown up without warning, in all likelihood confident she would smile her forgiveness. As if she could forgive his silence, or his consorting with that swinish Morag Burton. My God, he must think her a complete fool! Did he really think she had such a low opinion of herself that she would fulfill his expectations in return for a smile and a wave?

She seethed, scowling so fiercely that Davy was reluctant to halt the coach when Oliver began pounding on the roof with his walking stick. Nevertheless, he pulled back on the reins and eased the brake forward with his left foot. Caitlin glared at him and pulled away from his extended hand when Oliver demanded she ride the rest of the way home inside. And not once as she made her way from the bench to Oliver did she glance back along the road to see if Griffin was still watching. He could crawl on his hands and knees for all the thought she would waste on him. She suddenly caught herself hoping she'd never see him again.

How stupid she was! All those fancies she'd had while staying in England, struggling to rid herself of his memory when all she had to do was glimpse at the serene arrogance in his face, the self-assured confidence of his gaze, to understand that she meant no more to him than she meant to . . . to James Flint.

She resettled herself with a thump that made Oliver frown, but he said nothing to her, made no sign that he too had seen Griffin waiting by the roadside.

The passage through the village was made at a solemn, almost stately pace. Word had already spread through the town, and dozens of people had come to their cottage doors, to shop stoops, to the edge of the community green to watch the coaches clatter by and to catch a glimpse of Seacliff's new owner. There were a few tentative waves with handkerchiefs, and men pulled off their caps and hats in respect, but Caitlin saw little save the blur of ruddy faces.

Oliver held her left hand and sat forward to be sure his profile could be seen through the window—sturdy, strong, eyes unblinking and gaze unwavering.

On the other side of the green and past the last cottage, they approached the gray stone church. Its steeple was a thin spire, and a high iron fence enclosed its graveyard.

"My dear," he said to her quietly, "do you wish to . . ." and he nodded toward a mausoleum in the far corner, elegant in its simplicity. The bronze doors were closed, and the yard was littered with the remains of flowers long since dead and turned brown.

David Evans had died the night Caitlin danced at Windsor; he had been buried three days later.

"No," she said, patting the hand that touched hers. She could feel eyes boring through the coach's rear wall, could hear whispers rising from the village. "This isn't . . . It's not the time, Oliver."

"You will be all right," he said, mechanically, without emotion.

She nodded, knowing she would. Knowing, too, that to stop now, with all the baggage, the coaches, the people in them, would seem to the others to be making a pageant of her bereavement. When she went to her father's graveside she would go alone.

She gave a soft, shuddering sigh. Despite all her rationalizations that he'd been dying for a long time, she could not help a stinging at her eyes, a burning in her chest. Her hands chafed each other dryly, and she forced herself to release them to look again out the window, to the gently rising land, to the large farms with their rich pastures and fields, the groves of oak and ash, the boulders larger than many cottages dotting the landscape. Then, before she could stop herself, she leaned her head out the window and saw her ancestral home, stark and warm against the soft, post-storm blue: Seacliff. Waiting for her. Waiting in she knew not what state.

It stood on a broad stretch of flatland bordered by wind-

bent trees and remnants of stone walls. In front was a yard
green and recently cut, and sweeping like an emerald river
around the mansion to the back where, less than two hundred
yards away, it stopped at a three-foot fieldstone wall built by
her grandfather. Beyond that could be seen the flat tops of
cracked boulders and a few straggly shrubs that marked the
hundred-foot drop to Cardigan Bay. It was a vast and turbulent
body of water reaching west to St. George's Channel—the arm
of the Irish Sea that spilled into the Atlantic. It was still rough
now after the recent storms. The west wind raised whitecaps
on the billowing waves, sending sprays up the cliffside almost
to the top.

The carriage pulled over the last step of the rise, and Caitlin
pounded her hand suddenly on the ceiling. When Oliver looked
up in astonishment, she said nothing, only waited until the
vehicle came to a halt. Then she climbed out quickly.

"I must walk," she told her husband.

He nodded once, sharply, and called out to Davy to proceed
without delay.

She stood to one side on the embankment. The second coach
swept by, and she could feel Gwen's questioning look and
Bradford's disapproving glare. Then she was alone, facing what
was hers.

Seacliff had been constructed of stone of various colors. It
rose two stories to a slate pitched roof pierced by a dozen
chimneys whose broad mouths seemed continually to spout
gray and black smoke. All the leaded windows were high and
arched, their broad sills cushioned for seating. The double doors
of native oak were handsomely carved. The bands of polished
iron and knobs of brass were cleaned four times a day. The
doors rose twelve feet above the threshold and required two
men to open them once the latch had been lifted. At either end,
squared towers protruded out to form, from the sun's vantage
point, a massive *I* pointing north and south. Their arched windows were narrower and considerably more imposing. In the
south tower, quarters were reserved for the staff; the north
tower had been rearranged to provide apartments for visitors
who intended to stay for more than an evening.

The ancient structure was massive; it was solid; and despite
the stone and slate, Seacliff possessed an aura of comfort and
warmth generally reserved for the most luxurious wayside inn.
Less a mansion than a home; less a fortress than a dwelling.

She walked slowly toward it, taking it in slowly as if she'd never seen it before, and as if she knew every stone, every curve, every tiny crack in its walls. And as the sun began its slow descent over the bay, she noted the flames of candles appearing in the windows. She stopped, then, in the center of the road. The wind had chilled, the house's shadow crept toward her. In the distance the muted thunder of massive waves pummeled the cliffs. She glanced to her left and saw the collection of stables and barns, the farrier's workshop and the carpentry shed, and the group of small cottages where the married staff lived. The coaches were already at the stables, Davy and a handful of men scurried about them, unharnessing the teams and unloading the trunks.

She could hear the cry of a disturbed ewe, and the lowing of a cow long past its milking time.

She walked forward again, slowly, unable to believe her father would no longer stand at the cliffs and rant at the bay— as he was prone to do—or climb with Davy to repair damaged shingles. Everything he had done was now consigned to the past, and she wept silently, knowing she was feeling more sorry for herself and her loss than she was for her father. And that was all right. He would understand because he'd known her so well, and the thought made her smile as she cried, wiping at the tears with both her puffed sleeves.

Then she stopped a second time and stared at the doors.
Something . . .
A faint nagging sensation began nibbling at her mind.
Something . . .
She closed her eyes for a moment, opened them suddenly as if the snap would bring into focus what was bothering her now. But nothing happened. The feeling, she decided, was a product of the mixed emotions that had accompanied her home. And if it was important, it would come to her eventually. Nevertheless she found herself walking off the lane and across the lawn toward the north tower on her right. Her teeth gnawed thoughtfully at the inside of her lower lip. Her left hand reached up absently to rub the side of her neck. In all the haste to uproot herself from Eton, to rush back to Wales, something had been mentioned that gnawed at her now.

Something about her father.
About his dying.
She had almost reached the corner when she heard someone call her name. A step farther, and she turned around to see

Davy running toward her from the stables. He had discarded his wig and replaced it with his ever present blue cap. His long legs seemed rubbery, and the combination of livery and cap was so incongruous she couldn't help grinning. She started back to meet him just as a movement at the corner of her eyes told her someone had opened one of the front doors.

"Mistress," Davy said breathlessly, skidding to a halt on the lane that was inlaid with brick. "Mistress . . ." and he glanced toward the house.

Caitlin waited patiently, but his puffing cheeks and that silly cap made her giggle before she could put a hand to her mouth.

"Mistress," he said, puzzled and not knowing if he was being made fun of or not.

"It's all right," she said, waving a hand. It must be the homecoming, the funeral and . . . she smiled again, shaking her head slowly and wishing she could get hold of whatever was bent on keeping her giddy. "What is it, Davy?"

The door opened farther, and though they heard the hinges creaking neither of them turned.

"In the stable," he said, half turning to point. Then he wiped a hand over his face, then through his hair.

"Davy? I don't understand. What about the stable?" Concern stiffened her. "Is somebody hurt? Did somebody—"

"No, no," he assured her quickly. "Ain't nothin' like that, mistress. "I was just in there, doin' the horses, see, and I look—"

Footsteps sounded on the path. Both of them spun around. Bradford was moving rigidly toward them, his chin high, his expression that of a man trying to avoid smelling a supremely noxious odor. Caitlin told herself Oliver would have to speak with the man, because an attitude like that was definitely not going to endear him to Seacliff's less formal staff.

"M'lady," he said with a slight bow.

"What is it, Bradford?"

With a barely discernible sniff he looked to Davy. "Daniels, Sir Oliver wishes you to wipe down the coaches before you retire for the evening. He does not wish this sea air to ruin the brass."

Davy rolled his eyes heavenward. "Lor', I got brains enough t' know that."

"Just see that it's done." And by looking to Caitlin, Bradford dismissed Davy.

Davy hesitated, and Caitlin understood his reluctance to

leave immediately. Not only was there something he wanted to tell her, but he was home now, and by rights his mistress was the only one who could give him commands. Another problem to resolve, she thought wearily.

"It's all right, Davy," she said, smiling and hoping he would see the apology in her eyes. "I'll speak with you later. I should visit your father, in any case, to see how he's faring."

"Yes'm," he said, and put a finger to his forehead; he glared once at Bradford's blind side and rushed off.

"Bradford," she said sternly, "I think you'll find it easier if you remember where you are now. This is not England, and this is not Eton. You've been here often enough to know the household isn't run like Sir Oliver's."

"Yes, m'lady," he answered tonelessly.

"And you have something for me?"

Bradford kept his gaze carefully focused on the valley spread behind her. "Sir Oliver wishes to see you at once, in the drawing room, if you will. The staff is assembled and waiting to greet you."

She looked back toward the north tower. Nothing, however, of her previous uneasiness returned, and she could not recall what specifically had drawn her to the corner. Then she blinked as she realized the butler was speaking to her.

"I'm sorry," she said with the trace of a stiff smile.

"I said, m'lady, that I'd taken the liberty of placing the visitors in their apartments in the tower. I understand they will join you for dinner."

"Visitors?" She frowned. "What visitors?"

"I believe Sir Oliver wishes to tell you himself."

Her right hand bunched into a helpless fist, buried in the folds of her skirt. "For heaven's sake, Bradford," she said impatiently, "stop playing these silly games, will you? You act as though . . ." She stopped when his pale eyes hardened and his jaw stiffened. Oh, God, she thought, you've done it again. "All right," she said, resigned, though not apologetic. "I'll be there in a moment."

"With respect, m'lady, Sir Oliver asked that I escort you in at once."

She clamped her lips together before she went too far and provoked Bradford into speaking to her husband. As it was, the old servant would take out what he obviously thought was an insult on Gwen and the others. She would have to think of some way to make it up to them. Meanwhile, Oliver apparently had a surprise up his well-tailored sleeve, and she had no choice but to follow his lead until he decided to spring it on her. As she followed Bradford into the house, however, she hoped there would be some way she could convey to Oliver her displeasure. The timing, if nothing else, was not exactly opportune.

And she wondered, too, what it was Davy had thought so important.

Puzzles and puzzles. And suddenly she was too weary to think. Her loss had acted as a numbing agent on her mind, and it might very well be that none of this was worth thinking about at all. She didn't know. She just didn't know.

Bradford, who had reached the doorway, turned to look at her questioningly. She managed a weak smile and lifted a hand to indicate she was coming. She only hoped that the sound of her husband's grumbling voice drifting out toward her did not mean another conflict lay ahead, or another jolt to her already weary system.

"All right," she muttered when Bradford beckoned stiffly. "All right, all right."

10

THE CENTRAL hallway ran directly to the rear of the mansion and soared to the rafters above. The corridor was lined with elaborately designed standards hanging from brass pikes fifteen feet above the polished wooden flooring. Hanging below them were exquisitely colorful tapestries, most of them woven by village women depicting heroic Welshmen embattled by lions, fierce Norsemen, and fantastic beasts that had, in their own terrible way, a fascinating beauty. Hard against the left and right walls were staircases leading to the gallery above, off of which extended corridors leading to the family's living quarters. There was wood everywhere, replacing the cold stone of the original structure wherever possible and bringing a warmth that was more than mere illusion.

Caitlin paused for a moment, then turned to her left and stepped into a large room filled with armchairs and round tables. They were centered on the rear wall by an enormous fieldstone fireplace. Its hearthside had served for generations as the place for conversation, board and card games, and David Evans's most ardent passion—reading. This explained the shelves lining the walls between family portraits and tapestries, jammed with bound folios, books, ledgers, journals, and every writing implement imaginable.

Oliver stood on the raised brick hearth, his back to a low fire. Before him were arrayed a series of high-backed scrolled chairs and a low, thickly upholstered couch upon which sat Gwen and Mary. From the Seacliff household were Elaine Courder and her sister, Alice, neither of whose duties had ever been explicitly defined. Thus, at any given moment either one could be found fussing in the bedchambers with linens and dustbroom, or fussing in the living quarters with rags and polishing oil. They were gray-haired and stout, a decade apart in age and yet looked as much alike as any set of twins. When they heard Caitlin's entrance they rose as one, their red, chapped hands twisting at their aprons, eyes puffed and complexions pallid.

She paused, then strode quickly across the room to greet them with a silent, long embrace and a loving kiss.

Oliver, still in his finery and with hands clasped behind his back, cleared his throat gently. "I was explaining to the staff, my dear, how deeply we feel their loss."

She turned slowly. "And mine," she reminded him. "And mine."

"But naturally. And I have taken it upon myself to speak to the men while you were alone with your thoughts. They will not bother you during your mourning. And these magnificent ladies will attend you as they've not done before."

She sensed a subtle change in his tone she could not quite identify. She set the thought aside when he dismissed the women with a wave of his hand and assisted her to the couch.

"Are you well, Caitlin?" he asked, his eyes sympathetic. "You have been weeping."

"It's so big," she whispered, looking around the room. "It's all so big."

"That is my worry, my dear, not yours. It is, after all, what a husband is for."

A log split, and a rainbow of sparks showered toward the chimney. She felt tears again, and Oliver quickly placed a cloth into her palm, sitting back until the weeping had passed.

"He was a fine man," he said. "I was proud to know him."

It was the grief, she told herself, and the sudden sense of being overwhelmed by all that was now hers. But she couldn't help feeling his words were somehow perfunctory, almost parroted. But before she could dwell on it, and before in the same moment she could query him about the guests, he suggested she visit the staff in their rooms.

"They would appreciate your presence for a minute or two," he said. "And in point of fact, I've already told them you'd be there."

"Oliver!"

"Duty, my dear," he said with a brief smile. "You must get used to it." He stood and took her hands to assist her to her feet. "I have directed Mrs. Courder the elder to serve us in here when you return. I shall be waiting."

Her lips parted to protest his organizing her return, but she saw the wisdom of his actions and decided not to press the issue. With a grateful nod, she moved around the hearth, slid open a pair of paneled doors, and walked down a narrow corridor dimly lit by tapers in silver sconces. Ahead was a similar doorway, leading into a slightly smaller sitting room overlooking the rear yard and the bay. With a glance to her right she turned in the opposite direction and made her way along the carpeted hallway, passing the library and the family dining room before reaching the end. Here, set deep into the wall, was the entrance to the south tower and the ground-floor warren of staff quarters.

She waited for a long moment, gathering strength. Without exception they had been deeply devoted to her father—many of them shielded by him since birth—and though she knew they loved her as well, it was a matter of grave conjecture how they were responding to Oliver.

Finally she lifted the latch and stepped through into a brightly lit corridor filled with aromas and odors—not of polish and age-old tapestries—but of sweat, honest toil, homespun fabrics, and unperfumed tallow. Above her, on the second floor at the back was her own spacious apartment from which, as a child, she'd made many a clandestine excursion to mingle with Gwen, Davy, and the others.

This, however, was different.

Now she was Seacliff's mistress, and she felt curiously alien as she made her way to the common room ahead. There were voices, none speaking in English and none raised louder than a reverent whisper. But as soon as she stepped in there was silence.

She smiled broadly, and the silence was broken.

The room was twenty feet long, the furniture designed for temporary respite only—hard chairs, a battered couch, several open closets containing stoneware and glasses. A half-dozen narrow doorways led to the staff kitchen, bedrooms for the single servants, two-room suites for married couples without an outside cottage. And all the servants seemed to have assembled here for the moment. They babbled at her respectfully until Elaine Courder bulled her way through and took her traditional position.

"Mistress," she said in English, "we all be so pleased you come home."

"I wish the circumstances had been better," she said, wondering at the choice of language.

"He was a fine man," a deep voice boomed from the back of the group.

She nodded agreement. "Indeed, Orin Daniels, and this house will never be shed of him." Then Alice Courder burst into tears and was led away to a chair. When the others seemed upset, Caitlin shook her head and spoke deliberately in Welsh: "There's no shame in it. Let her be. And Mrs. Courder, I don't know what my husband has ordered for dinner, but I trust it's suitably substantial." She rubbed a hand over her stomach. "The English are preoccupied with starving the barbarians."

A heartbeat passed before the men chuckled their approval and the women hid their laughter behind cupped hands. Then she passed among them, speaking softly, accepting their condolences, feeling the love washing over her gently. Within ten minutes, however, she was at the side door and out, having decided there was one more visit she had to make before dining. She said nothing, but Orin Daniels was suddenly at her side, and they crossed together to the cottages backed against the south wall of the main structure.

Orin, unlike his younger brother, was short, sturdily built and bearded. He was the estate's farrier, and his brawny arms and thick waist attested to the vigor he threw into his work. His face was round, perpetually sullen, and his left eyebrow was a fire-scorched scar that paled when he lost his temper.

"How is he?" she asked.

"Not good, mistress," he said bluntly. In Welsh. "He coughs blood these days, and he sleeps poorly."

She sighed and followed him into the first home to one of two rooms curtained off at the back on either side of the hearth. She headed directly to the lefthand cubicle and pulled aside the worn woolen hanging. A man lay on a cot beneath a slotted window, covered to his pointed chin by a sheepskin stained with food and spilled drink. His hair was streaked an unpleasant gray, his dark eyes lusterless as they glanced from the windowpane to her face. His mouth was small, the smile he gave her weak.

"Mistress," he croaked, and broke into harsh coughing.

She knelt by the bedside and stroked his hand. "You're a trial to me, Les Daniels," she scolded softly. "A genuine trial." She glanced over her shoulder, and Orin shook his head.

"Mistress."

A groping for her hand, and she let the old man take it.

"I be so powerfully glad you think to come to me 'ouse."

"I missed you, silly."

"No. No, you didn't, really."

"Father!"

"It's all right, Orin. He's been at me all my life, and I'd be afraid for him if he changed now." She grinned at the old man, then, and leaned over to kiss his sunken cheek. "If you need anything, you'll send a son?"

"Nothin' can 'elp me now, mistress."

"Bosh," she said as cheerfully as she could while rising. "You just eat Mrs. Courder's food, and you'll be right as rain in no time."

Daniels could only hack loudly into a dark-stained cloth, as she left the cottage quickly, Orin beside her with a lantern in his hand.

"Not the winter, mistress," he said.

"I know. And that man taught me more about horses than anyone. And the stories at night, all those terrible things about creatures that creep into your bed and feed on your blood . . ." She shivered in remembered delight. "A good man he is."

"A fool," Orin grumbled. "Ain't never wanted t' see no doctor. Says he can manage his own dyin', thankee very much."

They walked in silence to the tower entrance, but when he made to open the door for her she laid a hand on his arm. He hesitated and frowned, suddenly ill at ease.

"Orin, why . . . why were they all speaking English in there when I went in?"

Daniels looked to his boots and sniffed, then at the hand that wiped at his shirt.

"Orin," she warned.

He sniffed and wiped a hand over his mouth, muttering at the same time.

"What?"

"Orders," he said then. "I said, it was orders."

She stepped away a pace and stared at him perplexed. "Orders? What orders? Not to speak the language?"

"In the house, mistress," he said, his gravelly voice unnaturally quiet. "We're not to say anything in the house unless it's in the English tongue."

"I'll be damned. Who told you a fool thing like that? Bradford? My God, I'll have the man's own tongue for this. Who does he think he—"

"No, mistress," Orin said. "'Twas Sir Oliver what told us. His man brung us a letter what the vicar had to read to us."

Caitlin put a hand to her forehead, to her neck, bunched it into a fist that finally dropped to her side. "I don't believe it, Orin. This is impossible. What man? Tell me what man brought this letter."

"Don't know, mistress. I never saw him. Mrs. Courder gets it and since Gwen be with you, she takes it down to the vicar who reads it to her. She told us."

"I'll be . . ." She started for the door, the chilly sea wind now cooling a simmering rage. But as her hand took the latch she realized there was something Orin hadn't told her. She turned; his face was averted from the lantern's weak glow, as if he couldn't bear the sight of the accusation written on her face. "Orin?"

"Mistress, it be late."

"Orin!"

The big man pulled in upon himself like a child expecting a stiff blow.

Caitlin, however, was in no mood to draw him out by inches.

Her scowl deepened, and she took a short step toward him. She stopped short when he recognized the faint twinges of fear that belied his size. "Tell me," she urged.

"You're not to . . . Mrs. Courder, she tells us—"

Her foot stamped on the ground so suddenly that he jumped. "Orin Daniels, you stop this ridiculous nonsense instantly and talk to me, do you hear? Straight out now, Orin. What else did the letter say?"

He inhaled deeply. The feeling that he would turn and run was suddenly so strong that she almost reached for his arm.

"We're to speak the tongue, mistress." He swallowed, and looked fearfully at the tower wall. "And if we don't, we're to get the sack."

Stunned, Caitlin could neither move nor look away. Her glare was so intense that Orin finally lowered his eyes, muttering to himself as if he were casting a spell to ward off her rage. The lantern wavered in his grip, and the light flickering over the ground finally galvanized her. With a grunt of utter disgust, she whirled around and yanked open the heavy oak door. She opened it so quickly and powerfully that it flew out of her hand and slammed against the outer wall. Those still milling around in the servants' common room jumped to their feet and gaped as she charged through without seeing them. She barged through the next door with the palm of her hand and fairly raced down the corridor. She paid no heed to the voices raised in astonishment behind her; all she could think of was the talk, the very long and informative talk she was going to have with her husband about the conduct of Seacliff's affairs.

"Fool!" she whispered as she stormed toward the south tower's entrance. "The blithering, bloody fool!"

It was one thing—and in a sense perfectly understandable—to take over command of the staff without so much as pretending to consult with her; it was, however, very much another to command that same staff to speak a language not even its own. Why, she wasn't even sure everyone knew English, except perhaps to hear and understand it. Old Les, the perfect example, would rather die on the spot than let a single word coined in London pass his withered lips.

"Fool. Idiot!"

She exploded into the main house, pausing only long enough to slam the door behind her with a rattle that brought a humorless grin to her lips. Then, with her hands in white-knuckled fists at her sides, she headed directly for the drawing room, talking fiercely to herself and punctuating her monologue with sharp tosses of her head. Her breath came in short, heated bursts, and her stomach, feeling light, threatened to make her queasy. She slowed, then, and finally came to a halt at the doors of the main room, her lips drawn between her teeth, her chin raised defiantly.

Driving back an impulse to kick the door aside, she closed her eyes tightly and winced at the spinning lights that whirled behind her lids.

This will not do, she thought, licking her lips and swallowing hard several times. You can't go in screaming at him, or he'll not listen to a single word. He'll march off and leave you there looking like a simpleton. Besides, you're a lady, remember? You must act the part, be his wife, and for God's sake stay reasonable.

But how could she possibly be anything approaching reasonable in the face of what she'd just learned? And what manner of unholy demon was it that drove the man to issue such a self-defeating, high-handed, impossible command? It was as though he thought her no more important than the scullery maids, with no more brains and no more wit than a patch of rotting moss on a dull rock. It was absolutely unthinkable that he could—

Her temper began flashing again, clouding her ability to think. She squeezed her eyes more tightly shut and struggled to restore a fragile calm. Her chest swelled as she inhaled deeply, quickly, hoping to cool the dangerous fires of her indignant rage before they consumed her.

Damn the man for his incredible impertinence!

She swayed, and reached out a hand for the wall. The coolness of the panel reached her almost instantly and triggered another spell of breathlessness. She swallowed the sour gorge that had risen in her throat. Her free hand pressed against her stomach. One heel tapped unevenly on the floor.

All right, she thought when control seemed hers once again; all right, I'm fine.

Her hand dropped slowly from the wall, covered the other, and she was amazed at how cold her skin felt. She felt as if she'd been hollowed out and filled with fire, yet there was a dampness to her flesh that made her think of autumn fog. With a start, then, she buried her fingers in her skirt and opened her eyes, relieved that she could see without the dim red veil spread over her vision of a few moments before.

Oh, Oliver; and this time the name was thought not in rage but in helpless melancholy. Oh, Oliver, why did you have to do something like this now? She looked to the ceiling, to the floor, to the doors. Her father was dead. Was Oliver so blind that he couldn't see how in her state she could be easily perturbed?

She held her hands in front of her and willed them to cease their violent trembling. Several minutes later they did, at least enough for her to take hold of the knob without rattling it. But she didn't wrench it open. The moment her fingers touched the cool brass she realized that throughout the process of calming herself she had been unconsciously listening to a dialogue inside the dining room. She moved closer to the door. Who . . .? With a glance in both directions to make sure she was alone, she leaned her head closer.

"No," she heard, the identity of the speaker impossible to determine. "I say you're dead wrong, Oliver. You could not be more wrong if you tried."

"Well, m'boy, as usual, you have misjudged the situation and mistimed the event. It bothers me not in the least, however. I am confident as ever we shall have no troubles at all. In fact, I would wager this house on it."

"Thanks to me, I trust you understand."

"But of course, my dear friend. Though I expect you've already been amply rewarded, eh?"

The dialogue became a muttering as the two men walked to the far side of the room. Then a word was spoken loudly in sharp disagreement. Another in swift, smooth conciliation. A moment later they returned, and Caitlin pressed even closer.

"I should think, Oliver, you could have been more discreet."

"I was as careful as I thought proper, and we will be done with that sort of talk in my house, do you understand, sir? We are not at court any longer, if you take my meaning."

"I was only attempting—"

"You attempt much, friend, but you must remember to whom you belong, now and forever."

"And to whom, *friend,* does Caitlin belong?"

"She is my wife, sir. And I suggest you remember that."

Caitlin knew she was courting disaster by standing in the hall for so long, obviously eavesdropping. Should Bradford

happen by, she had no doubt the matter would be brought to
Oliver's attention at the first opportunity. So, before she was
discovered, she straightened up, took hold of her skirts, and
with a determined smile on her face pushed aside one door to
step cheerily into the room.

"Oliver, my love," she began . . . and stopped.

Oliver smiled. "Caitlin, I was beginning to worry about
you."

"Good evening, my lady. I, too, was beginning to wonder."

She maintained her composure only because she was too
unnerved for anything else.

"Good evening, Mr. Flint," she said tightly. "What brings
you to Seacliff?"

11

A SMALL, dark pine table occupied the center of
the room. It was arranged with two settings, between which
an eight-branched candelabrum of engraved silver had been
set. The tapers on the walls had been lit, and despite the gloom
in the corners of the room, the atmosphere was cheery enough
for a quiet meal. Caitlin, however, saw only Flint's gentle,
welcoming smile—and the slight hint of arrogance in his eyes.
He wore a green velvet cutaway jacket and a pearl gray waistcoat. His dark hair flowed loosely and settled perfectly around
his shoulders.

"What brings me to Seacliff," he mused in echo of her
startled question. He lifted a faceted crystal glass from the table
and held it to the light as if examining the wine within.

Oliver, who was standing behind his chair, waved her impatiently to her place. "Mr. Flint," he said heartily, "is, as you
know, an employee of mine. In fact . . . in very fact, he has
been watching out for our interests here while we've been in
England."

Caitlin allowed Flint to hold her chair while she sat down. She nodded when he snapped open the linen napkin and laid it with a flourish in her lap. The nearness of him bothered her; it was both annoying and exciting, and the brush of his arm against hers made her hands clench tightly in her lap. She looked steadily at Oliver and said, "It's very kind of him, I'm sure."

Oliver laughed. "Kindness has nothing to do with it, my dear. He's being paid, and paid well, for his time."

She was unable to conceal a puzzled frown, one that deepened when Flint pulled a chair to the table and took a place to her left.

"Sir Oliver," he said, gently chiding, "I do think you might have explained to your lovely wife the circumstance of my employment. She might well take it badly otherwise."

Oliver's smile grew, while Caitlin, confused, nearly scowled. Keeping her gaze on her husband, she could not avoid seeing Flint at the corner of her vision, watching her boldly, as if reminding her that the curves beneath her traveling gown were well known to him—and would be again. She almost blushed.

"Well, my love," Oliver said as he scrutinized the display of foods Mrs. Courder had prepared, "during the time we've been in England your father—God rest his soul—was in no condition to see to the running of the estate, as you well know. It was my duty as your husband, and as his son-in-law and ranking member of the family, to see that his and my investments were protected while you and I were absent. And to do that, I was fully prepared to call upon the best assistance I could muster."

Her right hand crumpled the napkin as she finally blotted out Flint's stare and fought instead to control her temper. "There are men at Seacliff who are quite capable of that, Oliver."

"Oh, I agree completely, my dear. I quite agree."

"Do you? Then why did you have to bring Mr. Flint here?"

Oliver's eyelids fluttered a moment as if in exasperation, but he drew in a calming breath while forking a large portion of cold meat onto his plate. He took a bite and savored it elaborately, sipped his wine and touched his lips with a napkin.

Caitlin watched the ceremony with a stony stare, swallowing the impulse to scream out his name.

"If you'll permit me," Flint said quickly, his hands cupped about his glass.

"Please," Caitlin said, with a shade too much relief. "I wish someone would explain this."

"It's really rather simple," he said, flashing her a smile so warm that she smiled back. "The men here are capable indeed, and more than that, I assure you, my lady. Your father trained them well, and his father before him. However, Sir Oliver has, as you're no doubt aware, other interests as well, and this increasing nonsense with the American colonies has taken up a considerable amount of his time."

"Doing what?" she demanded.

"Therefore," he said, smoothly brushing aside the query, "he needed someone he could trust to travel between Eton and Seacliff, not only to deliver his instructions as to the running of the estate, but also to keep him apprised of potential problems."

"Did those problems," she said, suddenly remembering, "have anything to do with ordering the servants to speak English at the risk of losing their positions?"

Oliver cleared his throat, but Flint paid him no heed. "That was . . . unfortunate," he said. "A misunderstanding on the part of the vicar in translating the message. There was no threat intended."

"Caitlin," Oliver said before she could respond, "whether there was a threat or not is beyond our consideration now. The order stands."

"But Oliver—"

"It stands," he insisted. "I do not speak enough of the language myself, nor does Mr. Flint. Therefore, to be sure my instructions are obeyed, English will be spoken."

"Even by me?" she said, her voice dangerously low.

He smiled. "My dear, as mistress of the house you may do as you please."

At the risk of my extreme displeasure, his tone implied, and Caitlin decided there was no point in continuing the argument; at least, she would not engage her husband in front of his hired man. She sensed the conversation had gone on too long as it was, but she still suspected Oliver of taking advantage of her mourning for reasons she'd not yet determined.

"You mentioned problems," she pressed on then. "Were there any?"

"None that should concern you," Flint said.

"Caitlin," Oliver scolded lightly, pulling a shred of meat

from between his teeth, "this is all rather silly."

"I hardly think so," she snapped. "After all, we are talking about family property, aren't we? *My* family."

Oliver's face darkened, and he laid his hands hard on either side of his plate. "My dear, I consulted your father every step of the way, and whenever he disagreed with my suggestions, I deferred to him at once."

"I should hope so," she muttered.

"Caitlin!"

Suddenly, Flint's hand covered hers, and she was drawn to his compassionate gaze. "Sir Oliver," he said, without taking his eyes from her face, "perhaps this is not a good time to discuss such matters. After all, the homecoming has been less pleasant than it might have been. I can see that Lady Morgan, despite her courage, is rather distressed." His hand drew away, and she wanted abruptly to snatch it back.

"Ah, yes," Oliver said guiltily. "Yes."

With the tension thus defused, Caitlin took the opportunity to rise. "Oliver, I think I will retire now." She smiled at Flint gratefully, and moved to her husband's side. He kissed her hand and nodded his understanding. "Good night," she whispered and hurried from the room, taking the near staircase to the gallery and, when she was positive no one was watching, broke into a run down the rear corridor toward her south tower rooms.

"I'm sorry," Flint said, not very apologetically. "She would have thrown something if I hadn't stepped in. I'm sorry, too, she had to find out like this."

"I shouldn't worry about it if I were you," Morgan told him. "She's had rather a bad time of it lately, I suppose. I'm only sorry we had to return so soon, but that fool brought the letters back too quickly. I would rather you'd had more time, as it were."

Flint dismissed his statement with a shrug. "It can't be helped now, can it? What's done is done. I still see no great obstacles."

"Neither do I," Morgan agreed, attacking his meal and nodding for Flint to take Caitlin's plate. "But it is a bother."

"Maybe," Flint told him. "Maybe not. We shall see in about a month's time, won't we?"

Several minutes passed in silence. Morgan ate heartily, and Flint refilled his glass twice. Bradford came in once, to light the fire at the hearth and bring at Flint's command a fresh decanter of brandy. None of the other staff came near the dining room, and the only sounds in the room were the muted voice of the sea and the humming of the chilled wind that set the tapestries to fluttering.

Then Morgan pushed away from the table and stared at Flint, his eyes narrowing and his jaw setting. "Have you spoken with Radnor?"

"I can't get near the bastard," Flint said in disgust. "He has these great bloody dogs..."

"He'll prove even more difficult if he's not approached."

Flint tossed his napkin down angrily. "Approached with what, Major? He's in no need of money, and he'll only laugh at threats. What can we do?"

"We can keep Caitlin away from him, for one thing."

"Easier said than done, Major."

Morgan smiled mirthlessly. "But if the Americans keep up, or if the French start again, there's always the army."

"He'll never stand for that. He'll run first."

The smile became feral. "Then he'll be an outlaw, won't he?"

Flint lifted his glass in a silent toast. "You're rather amazing. You know that, don't you?"

"I know," Morgan told him. "And my friend, don't you ever forget that." He rose heavily, his knuckles pressed to the table. "I have never yet failed to get what I wanted. And no man is indispensable to me. No man, James. Not even you."

The moon seemed to unroll a silver carpet over the valley, deepening the shadows and transforming the streams into ribbons of metal. The white stallion paused at the bank of one and dipped its head to drink. It was patient, and it switched its dark tail lazily, as if it had all the time in the world.

Griffin Radnor, however, could not shake the feeling that time was fast running out for him. He'd been bitterly disappointed when Caitlin had not bothered to greet him on the road, and he'd spent the rest of the day trying to convince himself it was because of her husband. She could hardly wave while he was there. But by the time he'd finished his late supper, restlessness had driven him to the stable and to his mount. And before he'd ridden a mile he knew the truth: Caitlin would never come to him of her own free will.

He was tempted to forget her, as he'd been trying to do for

the past three years; but that, too, was a failure. No sooner was the resolution made than her face floated in front of him out of the leaves, the streams, the shadowy patches beneath the boulders, taunting him, promising him more anguish.

He looked across the valley to Seacliff, and slapped his thigh.

Ten times the fool he might well be, but he would prowl the fields and the groves until he saw her alone. Sooner or later she would have to leave that place, and when she did he would be there. Waiting. Demanding to know why she'd never written, why she'd never answered any of his letters.

And if she turned him away, then he would be done with her. He was not a man to crawl after a woman like a beaten, sniveling beast. He would be done with her, and live the rest of his life as if she did not exist.

The first room of Caitlin's apartment extended the width of the south tower, but was only fifteen feet deep. It was a cluttered, comfortable, draped and curtained room where she spent most of her quiet time when she was not walking the bluffs. Beyond that was a vanity and wardrobe room where the walls, when not covered with gay fringed hangings, were lined by tall clothing chests in which her dresses and gowns hung in colorful profusion. There were not so many of them now, most of them remaining in Eton, but she had brought enough to give her a sense of permanence nevertheless.

The last and largest room contained a massive four-poster bed set on a stone and ebony platform, a circle of chairs around the hearth, a scrolled secretary for writing, an armchair for reading, and at the back a ceiling-high window opening onto a balcony. The balcony overlooked the bay. She stood on it, brushing the tears from her cheeks. Though she couldn't see the water she could feel the waves rising toward her. In the distance she could hear the rise and fall of a coast schooner's horn.

England. Oh, Lord, how she missed it tonight!

Caitlin, a voice scolded silently.

But it was true. From the moment she'd entered Wales she'd been aware of forces buffeting her about, confusing her much more than could be blamed on simple bereavement. Oliver's high-handedness, Flint's sudden appearance, the villagers backing away from the coach as it passed. It didn't make sense. Nothing added up.

She left the balcony and undressed, shivering and hugging herself against the cold. Then, for a moment, she felt James's arms around her, his lips on her lips, and suddenly, fiercely, she willed him into the room with her. He would explain; she knew he would. She'd seen the looks he'd passed her at dinner, felt the touch of his hand; she'd wronged him by thinking he'd used her. She had wronged him indeed. Damn, she thought; if only she were in England with the time to sort things out . . .

She kicked at her dress and petticoats, which were piled at her feet, and kicked again. Then a third and fourth time until she started laughing and dropped onto the mahogany chest at the foot of her bed.

Fool, she told herself. All this worry, yet she was forgetting the most important thing: she was not in exile, she was in *her* country and Oliver was just going to have to learn that as well.

A knock at the outer door sounded, and Gwen entered timidly. Caitlin rose and walked toward her, taking a fur-trimmed robe from its wall peg to cover herself. She held out her arms, and they embraced, sobbing, as the loss they'd suffered came home in full measure. And when it was done she took Gwen's hands and squeezed them tightly.

"Gwen," she said quietly, "as long as I'm here you know you've nothing to fear for your homes or positions. And I've seen the papers, my father's will, and there's no doubt that Seacliff is *mine*." She lifted a quick hand to silence the maid's objection. "I know what Sir Oliver says, but there are things Stanbrooke the solicitor calls holes, through which the clever Welsh can make sure matters do not change simply because London wills it. This place is mine, Gwen, all of it. And you be sure the others know it, too."

Despite Gwen's smile, Caitlin could see the doubts glow in her eyes, but there was nothing more to say. She had her misgivings but it wasn't the time to air them. Instead, she exchanged one last embrace before Gwen left, stared blindly at the door, and returned to the bed where she slipped beneath the embroidered quilt. Dancing shadows on the ceiling weighted her eyelids and deepened her breathing.

Yours, she thought. Remember that. Seacliff is yours. Don't let them take it away.

But the last image she saw was of James Flint, smiling seductively at her. And she couldn't remember if she followed his beckoning.

12

THE MAUSOLEUM had been constructed of soft gray marble streaked by soft white. The bronze doors were taller than a man and unadorned. They were solid and heavy yet hinged in such a way that when the bolt was thrown aside they could be parted with little effort. Above the structure spread an ancient birch whose crown had been shaped in its earlier years to shade the marble and resist the strong winds that blew in from the west.

Caitlin stood just inside the threshold, her hands clasped loosely at her waist, the raven black of her hair cascading down her back. She was wearing a simple shepherdess dress, with a black silk tie around her throat, and a red ribbon wound through the lace at the neckline, which was just low enough to expose the tops of her breasts.

Ahead of her in the gloom barely retreating from the spilling sunlight was the back wall, where several bronze plaques marked the sealed drawers beneath them. Most of them had darkened with time, but one still gleamed, its mortar still freshly white. She stared at it for nearly an hour, allowing her mind to sort through childhood scenes dominated by her father's presence: the winter nights when he protected her from the spirits walking the mansion, the light summer days when he stood at the base of the cliff and watched her wade into the water at tide's ebb. She could not imagine him lying in the crypt alone. At one point she was grateful her last memory of him was when he was still alive, grumbling and laughing in spite of his monstrous illness.

And when, at another moment, she felt hurt and angered that he had left her on her own, she reminded herself that he was with her mother now, and Caitlin Morgan was a grown woman who could, if she'd a mind to, take care of herself.

Her weeping was done. There remained a quiet, empty space

in her heart that she knew would never be filled, one tinged with loss and love. And with a smile that blended joy and sorrow she promised her father silently she would use the old pine tree as he had himself, to draw consolation and to reacquaint herself with what and who she was when necessary. Then she murmured, "I love you, Father," and in the center of the floor laid a single rose she had taken from the garden.

A backward step, and she pushed the doors closed and threw the bolt. She touched the cool bronze in one final gesture, and her eyes blinked rapidly as she walked away from the mausoleum, noting without really seeing the headstones that marked the history of the village.

And she stopped, suddenly.

There in the distance, in the middle of a brilliantly green field, was a man on a massive white horse. It took her no time at all to recognize him, and her left hand clenched into a fist at her side. She realized Griffin Radnor had followed her, and he looked like a blinding white ghost in the middle of the day. There was no thought of permitting him to catch up with her. The ghost, she thought, was a good way to think of him—a specter from her past that could touch her only faintly like a childhood memory.

She glared, hoping his keen perception might note her displeasure. Then she made her way quickly along the gravel path through the cemetery. Davy was waiting on the road for her with a pony and trap. She glanced up as she neared the low iron gates and saw him wipe a voluminous sleeve under his nose hastily. She smiled, as much at his sorrow as in relief that he had not seen Radnor prowling the fields. That would have been too much. Davy had never kept secret his admiration for the master of Falconrest, and she did not wish to endure his clumsy reminiscences now.

The smile almost faltered, however, when the young man's expression altered suddenly, and his back straightened as if he'd been prodded with a knife. Following his gaze, she turned her head to the right and saw a scrawny man leaving the front of the narrow gray stone church. The temptation to hurry on was stifled instantly. Sooner or later, once an appropriate period of solitary mourning had passed, the villagers would make their way to Seacliff to express their condolences. Tradition dictated they do so. There was no way she could avoid the painful procession of visitors, and she knew she might as well greet the first of them now. Especially since this one would probably be the least enjoyable.

Once through the gate, then, she swerved and walked along the grassy verge until she came to a break in the wall that ran parallel to the road. There she stopped, hands at her waist, her face composed while she waited for the vicar.

Ellis Lynne was a scrawny man, blinkingly myopic, with flyaway brown hair he was forever spitting back into place. His frock coat was too long, his breeches too loose, his white cotton stockings bunched at knees and ankles. Though his demeanor was properly solemn on virtually every occasion, he had a habit of making a sound distressingly like a chuckle whenever he asked a question. To those who were used to it, it passed by unnoticed; to others it made him appear the perfect fool. Caitlin, however, knew the latter was distressingly far from the truth.

"My dear, I am truly sorry for your loss," he said as he came to the gate, his voice a high-pitched monotone. His hands felt clammy as he grasped hers and wrung them in sympathy. "Truly, truly sorry."

She lowered her eyes, accepting the condolence, and as quickly as she dared she retrieved her hands.

"But," the vicar said, clapping his hands once, "we shall never forget him, will we?" He prattled on for several minutes, Caitlin wondering if they were mourning the same man—so effusive was his praise. "However," he said with a ferretlike smile, "it's a new life to which you're accustomed, is it not, Lady Morgan? I do believe the valley is in good hands."

"We will do our best, sir," she said politely. "At least for the time being."

Lynne frowned, his spiked eyebrows meeting in a tangle over the top of his nose. "I'm afraid I don't quite understand, m'lady."

"Well," she said airily, "what I meant was—"

"You mean, you have no intention of remaining at Seacliff?"

"Why, of course I'll be here, vicar," she said, puzzled at the sharp intensity of the question.

He relaxed visibly.

"For the better part of the year."

He lifted his pointed chin and stared around the churchyard. "I see."

"Well, no, not really, you don't," she said, increasingly

sorry she'd stopped to see him at all. "Sir Oliver, as you well know, does have his family estate back in England, and he certainly cannot leave it forever. Quite naturally, we'll be traveling back and forth to see both places." She forced a laugh she hoped sounded rueful. "I have a feeling I shall be run ragged in a year's time, don't you think?"

He said nothing for a moment, simply clearing his throat. Then: "So you will not, as I've been given to understand, stay the year round."

"For heaven's sake, who told you that?"

"I thought it was common knowledge."

She glanced up and down the road, then nodded slightly to Davy, hoping he would see her and ride the trap up.

"A pity," Lynne said absently. "A pity."

"Well, I won't be gone as long as before," she told him, checking her tone so it sounded natural. "And we do have Mr. Flint."

"Ah, yes," he said, smiling. "Mr. Flint, indeed. He has kept the machinery oiled, as the new phrase has it. There's no doubt about that."

She lifted her hands with a smile just as Davy pulled up behind her. "Then there's no problem, is there?"

The vicar plunged a hand into his rumpled waistcoat and pulled out a dull gold watch, thumbed over the plain cover and held the face close to his eyes before squinting hard at the sun. "Ah," he said with an apologetic smile, "I have an appointment with Master Randall in his shop."

"And I must be getting home."

"A pleasure, Lady Morgan," he said as she climbed into the back of the tiny cart and adjusted herself on the seat. "Do keep yourself from becoming a stranger."

"I'll do that," she promised, and grabbed the sides as Davy clucked the pony into motion. She waved and turned away from the vicar, expelling a deep breath and rolling her eyes heavenward. The man was a human rat rooting for gossip, and she'd no doubt her plans would be all over the village before midafternoon. She didn't mind, since the news would have come from the household anyway sooner or later, but she wished she had been more politic in her pronouncement. She had a terrible sinking feeling that Lynne would make it appear as if she couldn't wait to leave. And there was her father, not yet cold in his grave.

A few yards from the church stood Lynne's thatched cottage, and a hundred yards from that, toward Seacliff, was a thick grove of tall oaks whose foliage was confined by weather and growth to the top branches. She was trying to force her mind onto more pressing matters than Reverend Lynne's sensibilities when, out of the corner of her eye, she caught a shadow that did not belong.

"Davy, stop a moment," she said.

The trap rattled to a halt, and she shaded her eyes to see into the grove more clearly. And when she did she gasped. "My God, Davy!"

Davy turned quickly, saw where she was looking and peered after her. Setting his whip suddenly on the seat beside him, he vaulted to the ground.

"Davy, no!"

He ignored her. The wall here had long since crumbled into small stones and dust, and he hurried across the grass to the first gray bole, where he leaned and stared. From a smaller, gnarled tree protruded a thick branch that held no leaves, no buds, not a hint of twigs. A thick rope had been tied around its thick arm, and from the end of the rope dangled the body of a man. His clothes were in rags, his face blackened, his hands swollen, but his disfigurement in death was not sufficiently severe to prevent Davy from recognizing him.

With a gasp he turned around and lurched back to the cart, leaned hard against the pony and shuddered as he breathed as deeply as he could. Caitlin instantly climbed out and, deliberately avoiding a glance into the grove, put her arm around his shoulders.

"You know him, Davy?" she asked, whispering.

He nodded shakily and gulped several times before he could find his voice. "Lam," he said, and swallowed again. "Lam Johns. He were the lad what worked for the vicar after you and the major went to England the first time. He..." Davy suddenly whirled around, forcing Caitlin back. He reached under the seat and grabbed a long knife. "I got to cut him down, mistress," he said loudly, and raced off into the grove.

Caitlin, weak with shock and horror, struggled back into the cart. By the time she'd sat down, Davy was back, sweating profusely and trembling.

"Not by his own hand?" she asked as the trap jumped into motion.

Davy shook his head. "He was hauled up, mistress. He was hanged."

A hanging. Not since her grandfather's time had anyone in the valley been sentenced to hang. The most severe punishment her father had ever doled out was ostracism, which inevitably led to self-banishment. Either the villagers had taken justice into their own hands for whatever offense Lam Johns had committed, or . . .

Impatiently she waited until the trap pulled to a stop in front of the house. Then she jumped to the ground, shoved her way through the unlatched door, and marched down the central corridor until she reached the glass-paned doors at the back. Oliver was sitting at a white wrought-iron table on the lawn, glass in hand, port by his side. She pushed through the door and strode toward him, not bothering to return his smile when he glanced over his shoulder.

"My dear," he said, rising, "I—Caitlin, is something wrong?"

She stood behind the chair opposite him, and grabbed the back until her knuckles whitened. "Wrong? What could be wrong? I paid my respects to my father, spoke with the vicar, and saw a dead man in the grove. What could possibly be wrong?"

"Oh," he said, and resumed his seat. "Oh."

"Oh," she said, bitterly mocking him. "Oh. And is that something else you've decided to take care of without consulting me, Oliver?"

He met her enraged stare evenly. "That is not something to concern a woman, Caitlin."

"If it concerns Seacliff, it concerns me. My people—"

"Well," he interrupted, "one of *your* people, my dear, viciously attacked a king's soldier several months ago. He escaped into the hills and was captured only a day or two before we returned. There was, in this case, no alternative."

She paused for a few seconds, fighting for calm. "And who gave the order of execution? Who carried it out? How was it—"

"I gave the order," he said stiffly. "I issued instructions, and Mr. Flint carried them out. As to the person who informed us, I have asked Mr. Flint to keep the name to himself. The others would not, to put it mildly, take it kindly if they knew one of their own—"

"All right," she said sharply. "I've heard enough."

"I suspected as much."

She spun on him suddenly, startling him into leaning away from her glare. "You suspected as much? Oliver, you push me too far."

Slowly he unfolded himself from his chair and rose, his face florid, his lips taut and bloodless. For a moment she feared he would strike her. The rage passed, however, and he took careful hold of her arms, shaking his head in shared sorrow. "Caitlin, Caitlin," he whispered, "can you ever forgive me?"

She eyed him warily. "For what?"

"For forgetting my place." He stepped to her side and kept hold of one elbow, guiding her toward the wall just off the cliffs. "I am only trying to spare you until you're able to shoulder your share of the responsibilities. And in this case, my dear, I do know the law. If this man had been freed— which you must admit you might have been moved to do your-self—a dangerous precedent would have been set. You do see that, don't you?"

She nodded her agreement, but not before he caught a flurry of doubt in her eyes. He stepped away and bowed rigidly before turning and heading for the house. She wanted to follow, yet she couldn't think of anything to say. She shivered when she recalled the offhand way he had spoken of the execution, and worse—he had said that someone in the village had actually taken the English side and played the traitor.

She leaned over the wall to stare at the water below. The breakers tumbled furiously over boulders laid bare by the tide. Oliver was right: she never would have ordered a hanging in this instance. Some weeks in a cell, hard labor in the fields . . . but never a death just for striking a soldier.

She stumbled along the wall blindly, not looking up until she realized she'd reached the twisted bare pine that marked the wall's corner. She stopped. It was here her father had come for peace, and it was here that he had died. Before she could stop herself, she peered down the sheer face of the cliff. The stony beach below was flooded, the place where her father had been discovered was now tumultuous surf. She sighed and turned around, and the wind tangled her hair in front of her eyes, so she couldn't see.

She brushed it away, and suddenly something became clear in her mind.

The wind. That was what she'd been trying to recall—the wind! Oliver had said her father was out here in a squall, and in his weakened condition had toppled over the wall. But how could he have? The wind would have been blowing in the wrong direction.

No. She shook her head feverishly, rejecting the horror that crept into her mind. "No," she said aloud, "no!" And a hand took her shoulder. She spun around, heart leaping into her throat, her palms clasping her chest. James Flint snatched back his hand as if he'd been burned.

"My lady," he said, "I'm sorry. I didn't mean to startle you."

"You didn't," she snapped. "No, you did. But I wasn't talking to you. I was . . ." She sputtered to an awkward halt.

"I do apologize, Caitlin," he said more softly. "But Oliver has been noting the approach of a storm, and he did not wish you to be caught out here." He looked pointedly at the tree and the wall. "Especially . . ."

She nodded curtly, but she realized he didn't understand her mood. Rather than explain, she allowed him to take her arm and start leading her away.

A fierce gust of wind suddenly slapped debris against her back, and she turned to face it, her eyes narrowed. The pine was straining under the gale, disappearing into the darkened shadows and taking on the unpleasant appearance of some desolate grave marker. She shuddered once, violently, and commanded herself to stop thinking. It was the argument with Oliver; it was visiting her father's resting place; it was Lynne's perfunctory sympathies; it was all of these things . . .

And yet she couldn't shake the feeling. The wind had been blowing in the wrong direction.

13

LATER THAT EVENING, after hours that seemed years long, Caitlin stood before an oak-framed, full-length mirror and examined herself from all angles as she drew a brush thoughtfully through her hair. Downstairs in the front parlor, Reverend Lynne was talking to Oliver—his official greeting to the master of the house. The rest of the village would soon follow, taking up much of her time and energy. And though she did not wish to dwell overly long on her father's demise, she was grateful for the opportunity to sense the village's re-action to her, and to keep her mind on the proprieties of grief and away from the terrifying images that had been assaulting her since morning.

Several times in the last hour she had drifted out to the balcony and stared down at the pine tree in the wall's far corner. And several times she found herself recreating the elder Evans's struggle against the squall. Finally, when the wind grew too strong and drove her back inside, she realized the accident could indeed have happened the way she'd been told. The wind took many directions once it reached the shore—barreling in-land like howling banshees, or swirling around the ground in violent eddies that broke through the crevices in the cliff and wall. It could very well have happened. It could have. And when she had almost blurted out her suspicions to Gwen, she also realized how incredibly farfetched they sounded, like the ravings of a woman who'd lost her senses to grief.

The outer door opened, then, and Gwen entered with a damp cloth. Despite the storm's approach it was stifling inside, and the cloth was for wiping the perspiration from Caitlin's cheeks.

"The vicar'll end up staying for dinner," Gwen said sourly.

Caitlin grinned. "You object to a cleric in the house?"

"To a toad sitting on chairs I have to clean, yes. I swear,

that Mary's less than useless around here. Like a weasel she is."

Caitlin laughed and adjusted her neckline, smoothed her skirt.

"You could always swoon, y'know," Gwen suggested as they headed for the door. "That's proper, ain't it?"

"It wouldn't stop them from coming back," she said. "And the sooner I get it over with, the sooner I can get to work."

"Cat!"

Caitlin frowned. "I didn't mean it badly, Gwen."

"I know, but you'd best not say that to them. They don't know you as well as I."

She remembered the unfortunate conversation with the vicar, and sighed. Sympathies she knew she could handle, but sensibilities were another matter entirely. Patience, she knew, was not her strongest virtue.

Patience that shortened as July passed near to August, and the summer's heat began taking its yearly toll on the land. The villagers came and were polite enough, but she was aware from the outset of a distinct reserve that made her uncomfortable. Neither did Oliver assist her through the ordeal. His patience vanished entirely, and he muttered that the villagers seemed ready to turn her father into a damned local saint.

"Were it not for you," he said one morning, "I'd be back to England in a trice."

She said nothing. She'd known it would be difficult for him to take her father's place, but he also had a duty he was leaving all to her. And that bewildered her. One day he was telling her to mind her place and her tongue, the next he seemed ready to leave it all and flee to Eton. As a result she had no idea where she stood, and she felt emotionally drained in face of his temper swings.

Griff Radnor helped her not at all.

Each day, during her riding, he was there, in the distance. Shadowing her, watching her, staying in the distance.

And then there was James Flint.

For the most part he managed to keep to himself. He'd been granted apartments in the north tower, and he was seldom seen out of them. Once or twice a week he came to dinner, but he held his silence save for polite responses to direct questions, and gave her no signs of encouragement she could catch. Yet she had to talk with him. Still convinced he hadn't used her, convinced he was keeping his distance to avoid Oliver's jealousy, she found herself haunting the corridor by the tower until, one afternoon, he appeared, dusty and hot, and red in the face from exertion.

"James, please, just a minute," she said, a hand on his arm to detain him.

He stopped and took a long moment before turning. "My lady?"

She smiled coyly. "What happened to *Caitlin?*"

"I have been trying to remember my station here."

"I see."

His expression hinted he didn't think she did. "I told you once he was a hard man."

"I know," she said softly. "To me as well."

Suddenly he truly smiled, and relief flooded her; she hadn't been wrong. James Flint cared.

Then: "Caitlin, I would talk if I could, but Sir Oliver is waiting and I must change. But perhaps," he added more quietly, "you might enjoy a stroll after dinner this evening. The air is wonderfully cool. It would clear your head for sleeping."

She watched his departure with a heart wildly beating. But once dinner had been cleared away, and Bradford had taken the brandy into the sitting room, she excused herself and fetched a shawl from her room. Once outside she was lost in the calming influence of the night's cool air; the moon's silver carpet across the gently rolling water; the call of the night birds in the groves.

She walked slowly, her eyes half closed; she did not see him until they'd nearly collided. Then she was taken into the shadow of her father's pine.

"James—"

The rest was smothered by a long, ardent kiss, his hands pressing her close. When he finally broke away, she sighed and took several deep breaths.

"I believe," he said, "the proper expression is 'How dare you, sir!'"

She giggled and turned to the wall; he stepped closer and slipped his hands around her slim waist. She leaned her head back against his chest.

"He doesn't treat you as he should, you know. He doesn't know what he has."

"Oh, he does," she said sadly. "He really does."

"I didn't mean having Seacliff," he scolded lightly.

Her smile broadened. "Are we back to flattery again?"

He seemed to relax.

She felt herself drifting on a cloud, and realized the danger he was putting himself in by holding her thus; she was right to trust him. A moment, another, and suddenly, quietly, she unburdened herself of her suspicions about the manner of her father's death, pulling out of the embrace once to indicate the tree and the height of the wall. He listened intently, grunting several times, and finally turned her back to the water filled with night whispers and diamonds.

"I can understand your concern," he said, pulling her gently until she was once again leaning against him. "Were I in your position, I would leave no question unanswered until I'd uncovered the truth. But tell me . . . why haven't you asked Sir Oliver about this?"

She shook her head in slow dismay. "He would only laugh. Or worse, he would lecture me and tell me I was being a foolish, grief-stricken woman. I would gain no satisfaction from confiding."

She felt his nod of agreement.

"Do you have anyone in mind?" he asked then. "A culprit?"

"No. Lord, no, James."

"What about Mr. Radnor."

She stiffened, unable to prevent herself from wondering if Flint knew what she'd once felt for Falconrest's master. But when she did not respond immediately, she knew he'd taken her silence for—if not a negative answer—then at least one that did not instantly condemn Griff.

"He's an odd one," Flint said after a few moments.

"Is he now?"

"He is." She hesitated, and frowned until he cleared his throat softly. "There's word, you know, that he's in league with the mountain outlaws."

"No," she said, almost too quickly. "There's a great deal about the man that infuriates me, James, but I doubt he would deliberately flout the law."

"Are you sure?" Flint asked her, his voice velvety, his thumbs shifting to brush the underside of her breasts. "Are you really sure? I haven't seen him here. A curious breach of courtesy, don't you think? An important personage such as he does not, it seems to me, ignore the proprieties. Especially not in a case like this. I find it, in fact, rather reprehensible."

Caitlin nearly nodded, checked herself, and held her tongue. She did not tell James of Griffin's distant pursuit of her, nor did she admit that she'd lied. It would, in fact, take little energy to imagine Griffin assisting the outlaws in the mountains. It would be exactly like him, since most of them were fleeing from English sentences passed down by English judges on rather arbitrary English laws.

To agree, however, would place her stamp of approval on Flint's obvious dislike of the man, and that she was oddly reluctant to do.

And she certainly could not condone the implication that Griffin had been involved in her father's death.

"Still," he said, so quietly she'd almost missed his voice, "the winds here are rather impish, don't you think? This way and that, and there's no telling what they might do if they'd a mind."

"Do you really think so, James?" A desperation colored her voice, and he hugged her, slowly taking the breath from her lungs. Then he kissed the side of her neck, the slope of her shoulders, and she made no move to stop his hands from cupping and squeezing her breasts. Instead, she closed her eyes and allowed the soft fires of his caresses to warm her, to soothe her, while the heat of his lips branded her flesh.

"James," she whispered.

"I dare not remain for very long," he told her breathlessly. "Despite Sir Oliver's arrogance, he is no fool."

"James, please." She tried to turn in the circle of his arms, to see his face, but he would not permit it. "James, you can't—"

"Caitlin," and he buried his face in the coils of her raven-colored tresses, his hands slipping away from her breasts and leaving her with only a sigh of regret. "There is a great deal to be done these next few weeks."

Her eyes widened, and this time she wrenched away from him, stumbling back against the wall. "What do you mean?"

His face was in shadow. "It will be difficult to see you again."

"My God, James, we live in the same house."

"Which puts us continents apart, as you must realize."

She wanted to reach out to him, to touch him, but her breath was still ragged from his teasing fondling.

"You must trust me," he said then. "You must trust me enough to believe that I do not make a habit of dallying with women who are not free." A hand snaked out of the darkness and swept the gentle slope of one of her shoulders. "Trust me, Caitlin. Trust me enough to believe that I know what I am doing."

She attempted a lighthearted smile. "I suppose I have no choice, Mr. Flint."

"No, my lady," he said. "You have no choice at all."

"And what am I to do in the meantime?"

"That is entirely up to you. Were I you, however, I would be Lady Morgan. You do it well, you know. You do it very well indeed."

His boots crunched on the needles carpeting the ground as he rose; but before he had reached the far edge of the tree's shadow he stopped and turned back.

"And I would think about Mr. Radnor, too, if I were you, my lady. Though I share your doubt of his guilt in abetting the outlaws, there are a great many stories wandering the village and elsewhere. Smoke and fire, my lady. Smoke and fire."

Smoke and fire.

She recalled his parting words several times during the next few days, trying to decide if Flint was truly concerned over Griffin Radnor's apparently growing reputation as a clandestine supporter of the outlaws, or if he was trying to tell her something else, something that carried greater weight. But nothing came to her, and before long even the villagers, who had completed their visitations, left her alone.

Like Flint.

True to his caution he stayed at a distance. When he dined with her and Oliver, he made no attempt at all to signal her of his desire to speak with her, or more. Rather, he was achingly formal, emotionally cold, until she felt both angered and depressed, and cut herself off from husband and staff alike. She knew she was behaving irrationally, yet she was unable to prevent herself from haunting the corridors and rooms of Seacliff in hope of catching at least a glimpse of the man. Several times she tried to enter the north tower on flimsy pretexts that even a blind man could decipher, but on each occasion she was stymied by the door's being bolted on the other side.

And then, one morning just after the first day of August, she found herself standing outside the narrow door that led to her father's den. Without thinking, she took hold of the knob and let herself in—and there, waiting patiently for her, was the answer to her distraction.

14

THE DEN was much narrower than any others in the house. Its casement window was covered with a soothing wine-colored drapery, its flooring was hidden beneath a faded and worn Persian carpet. As soon as she crossed the threshold she realized with a start, and a grin, why she had been avoiding the room since the day she'd arrived. It was laden with memories of the way she would crawl unashamedly into her father's lap as a child, demanding he put aside the musty old books and read something to her. Or of the way he would take her out to old Daniels's so she could be frightened by the ghost tales and cling to his strong frame, or just walk on the rock beach when the tide was out.

With good-humored grumbling, he would talk about his falling empire, but he would take her hand and lead her away; he was concerned about cloaking her with guilt, because he adored her so very much.

And there were the aromas, too: the tobacco clinging to his clothes, the scents he used after bathing, the damp wool in the rainy weather, the leather of his chairs, and the bindings of his books.

She had not thought herself prepared for any of this, but with Flint avoiding her, with Oliver stomping around the house like a petulant child, and with the villagers staring at her as if she'd suddenly developed an unpleasant likeness to the English queen, she discovered this morning she had no other choice.

She closed the door behind her, hesitated as the room and its memories took her by gentle storm. She then wandered from the wall shelves to the rosewood desk to the window overlooking the lawn and village. At the desk she looked over the ledgers and letters and took a deep breath.

This, she thought, is where Seacliff's mistress belongs.

She studied the estate's workings intently, meticulously, unaware of the days and weeks that flew by. It fascinated her, consumed her, finally sending her one afternoon across the corridor into the sitting room where she dropped into a thickly upholstered armchair with an explosive, satisfied sigh. A moment later, Oliver walked in.

"Damn, but it's hot," he complained. "God's blood, it's worse than Eton!"

"Oliver, please," she said wearily.

He glowered while scratching at his red, naked scalp. "You've been at the books again," he said accusingly.

She lowered her hands from her eyes and smiled. "Naturally."

"Why naturally? It's not something for you to fuss over."

"Of course it is," she said. "I have to know what's going on, don't I?"

"I don't see why," he said with a shrug. "James and I are doing rather well, I should think."

"Oh, Oliver," she sighed, "I don't mean I don't trust you. But this is my property, and I'm not so thick-skulled I can't grasp its working."

He swiveled about abruptly and paced to the open balcony door to stare at the lawn. His hands were clasped behind his back, tucked beneath the brown frock coat he wore when riding. "Caitlin, I do wish you would cease reminding me who has the legal rights to—"

"Oliver, that's unfair!"

"But may I also remind you," he continued stiffly, "of who rides out there every damned day, dealing with those people and their petty little problems. 'Sar, if ye'll pardon me, that ain't the way Master Evans done it, sar.' 'Sar, the milk's gone dry, sar.' My God, Caitlin, it's a wonder they don't still live in caves." A pause, and a heavy deep breath. "There have also been sightings the past few days. Damned outlaws. Word is they're snooping about."

"What for?" she said, reaching for an orange in the fruit bowl by her side. "What would they want here?" and suddenly she recalled Flint's accusations about Griffin.

"Food, weapons, a head or two of livestock." He slashed the air sharply. "I'll have their bloody heads if they come near me," he said. "And the head of anyone who helps them."

The memory of Lam Johns hanging in the grove passed through her mind unbidden. "Oliver," she cautioned.

"Well, dammit, they're criminals, Caitlin. Now don't tell me you've decided to take their side as well."

"As well as what?" she wanted to know, wishing she had gone directly to her rooms.

"As well as trying to make me feel incompetent."

She sputtered and half rose, then dropped back into the chair and took a glass of water to refresh herself.

"I am not trying to make you feel incompetent, Oliver," she said slowly, measuring each word so she would not be misheard.

He looked to the table, at the peeled and partly eaten orange. "You should finish that, you know. They say it keeps you healthy."

"Oliver, we're not talking about my health."

"Well, you are rather pale, my dear. You should eat better, and get out more often."

"I . . . have . . . been . . . busy!"

"So I've noticed," he said disgustedly.

"Oliver, when you're like this, you're not the man I married at all."

"Oh really?" He leaned away from her and raised an eyebrow. "I was under the impression we were still man and wife—unless, of course, you've found some marvelous Welsh law that changes that, too."

Strangling the impulse to strike him, she rose, then suddenly swayed and had to grab hold of the back of the chair. Dizziness swept over her and made her gasp in surprise. Oliver hurried to her side at once, murmuring his concern, but within moments she was able to wave him off and continue on to her rooms.

There she swung open the French doors to the balcony and stepped outside, closing her eyes to the sea's gentle breeze and the warmth of the sun, which was not nearly as intense here as it was below. The balcony itself was less than six feet deep and eight feet long. The wall was chest-high and gap-toothed, and as she stood near one of the openings she felt as if she were riding a cloud. She felt soothed, and she was reminded of how many hours she'd been in the study, poring over the ledgers and reconstructing a life she hadn't known existed. It was exciting. It was so much a challenge she could easily understand why Oliver lived for his own business and let all else fall by the wayside.

And she was wondering what it would be like to have the reins completely in her hands, when she heard over the whispering of the breeze someone approaching from behind. She turned, and grinned when she saw Gwen's stare.

"Fresh air," she said.

Gwen looked doubtfully at the balcony, and the drop beyond, and glanced away. "You could do with more than a stand," she said. "You could do with a ride."

Caitlin, to Gwen's horror, leaned back against the wall. "I don't know. I suppose."

"I was in the village this morning and saw the seamstress."

Caitlin's brow furrowed as she tried to recall the woman's name. "Sharnac? Grace Sharnac?"

"Susan," Gwen corrected flatly. "You don't remember."

"For heaven's sake, Gwen, it's been so long!"

"It has that," Gwen said. "Mistress Sharnac thought you'd gone back to England."

"Ridiculous."

Gwen put a hand to her forehead and sighed loudly. "Cat, you're not getting the message. They think you've gone. You stay in here all day, every day, and all they see is Sir Oliver and that man of his riding about like he owns the earth."

Caitlin stepped inside quickly, combing her fingers through her tangled hair. "Gwen, we've already been through—"

"I know. But I thought you should hear what's being said."

Caitlin glanced to the bed then and saw her green riding habit and boots waiting. A grin pulled at her lips, and she threw up her hands in surrender. It would be a good idea to get away, she thought, and leave it to Gwen to play mother again. And as she dressed, she asked for gossip, any news that would prevent her from saying something she shouldn't.

"Well," Gwen said, fussing with the ruffled gold blouse and shaking her head in despair at having to hide Caitlin's sumptuous figure, "seems Quinn Broary and Orin aren't to be married. They was going to ask your father, but they're afraid now of Sir Oliver. You know Broary? They say she's fey, what with all that red hair and that round face. I heard tell that Williams, the cobbler, he's got gold under his flooring. 'Course they always says that. They think he has little people working for him, too. Then . . ."

Caitlin turned at the sudden silence and sat on the mattress, waiting for Gwen to slip on the boots. "Well?"

"I don't know, Cat," Gwen said, kneeling and averting her gaze. "It's talk."

"Having elves make boots isn't talk?" she laughed.

"It's not elves, Cat. It's . . . men. No more than a handful, so I'm told, but they come to the village now and again and snoop about. They say sometimes Mr. Flint is with them." She glanced up without raising her head.

"I wouldn't know," Caitlin said. "I haven't seen Mr. Flint for days, and even then it's only when he's riding off on some errand or other." She waited. "What do these men do?"

"Snoop, like I said. Come into a shop and stand round like they was waiting for something. They come to the Stag's Head for a pint just after sundown, have themselves their own little corner, they do. Like they was royalty or something."

"Funny I wasn't told about this," she said, and interrupted Gwen's muttering by standing and stamping her feet. "I shall have to send for Davy, to tell him—"

Gwen grinned. "The roan's already at the door."

"Oh, it is, is it? And do you by any chance have my itinerary prepared?"

Gwen shrugged. "I can't read your mind, Cat. You go where you please."

"I wonder," she said, only half in jest. "I wonder." But she did not elaborate when Gwen questioned her, only made her way quickly downstairs and out the front door. Davy stood beside a curried and braided roan mare whose bridle was of green and gold felt, and from whose mane fluttered several red ribbons.

"Lord, Davy, I'm not on parade, you know."

"It's a lovely day, mistress," he said, doffing his cap and taking her elbow. "'Twas to make you smile."

"I am," she said, only then breaking out in a smile. She settled herself in the saddle, took the reins in hand and glanced once more at the house before wheeling about and cantering down the lane toward the road.

The farmland was still a bright green in spite of the continuing heat, and she sighed her contentment at the sparkling of the broad stream and its myriad narrow arms, and the trees and their nesting birds filling the air with lazy song. Above her a hawk shadowed the roan, swerved sharply off toward the misted mountains with a cry that made her smile until she thought her cheeks would crack. A shaggy red dog yelped at her mount's heels until an old man shambled out of a stone hut with a cane and brandished it wildly to drive the mongrel off. She called her thanks to him, and he bowed stiffly. Though she'd hoped he would offer water from his well, she was surprised when he turned and retreated back inside.

Old grump, she thought with a giggle, and turned onto a side path much narrower than the road—scarcely wide enough between low, thick hedging for a single cart. For over a mile she rode beneath a tangled overhang of trees that lowered the temperature and colored the air with a soft green tint. Bright-winged birds flashed out of hiding, scolding and whistling; a vixen and her kits ducked into a burrow beneath the exposed roots of a towering ash; a kingfisher darted from its rock when Caitlin splashed through the cold-running stream.

And as she rode her weariness slipped away; her resentment of Oliver vanished in the sunbath and dissolved under the cobalt sky. She was alone, and she reveled in it. Here she could say nothing to offend anyone. Here she could forget the pressures of Seacliff, the hidden but palpable presence of James Flint; she could concentrate on simply breathing the richness and beauty of life. It was, simply, luxury.

Up and over a low rise, she found herself at a sprawling collection of ringstones, most of which had been toppled centuries ago. The immense area was overgrown with leafy shrubs and grass. There was no visible evidence that the prehistoric site had been visited by anyone within the past decade. As the roan picked its way through a natural path toward the center, she examined the fallen monoliths, and the four still standing to loom ten feet above her, blocking the sun. Most of the villagers avoided the area completely.

"It's not a fine place," Gwen had told her once. "There are too many things felt in the ground. It's not that I believe the tales, mind, but I'd just the same not sit on rocks where folks have been murdered in heathen rites."

Caitlin, however, had never felt such intimidation; indeed,

she relished the peace and the solitude, and guarded it jealously.

A swift glance to check for intruders, and she slipped from the saddle lightly, drew the reins over the horse's head to keep it from roaming, and perched on the center horizontal stone, pulling her knees to her chest where she grasped them tightly.

A cool breeze tickled her chin. There was a scurrying in the brush. And she allowed her eyelids to droop sleepily while she thought how she should have done this ages ago, when Oliver first brought tears of rage and hurt to her eyes by a single word. She should have come here to think it all through, to decide the best way to approach the problem without bringing his wrath down on her. Hiding herself in her father's books was no solution; she'd learned that only this morning.

Oliver hadn't changed. And it wasn't until she'd found the ringstones that she'd realized, with an abrupt awakening of her dormant mind, that he was doing more than simply taking charge of the estate: he was taking it over. And taking her with it.

The roan snorted and tossed its head.

She glanced up to scold it, and saw on the nearby slope a rider coming toward her swiftly.

She stiffened, looked around, and suddenly recognized her location.

But though she slipped off the monolith with every intention of leaving, she knew it was too late. She had been seen, and there was nothing to do but face a most awkward encounter.

15

THE TALL sleek stallion seemed on parade as it expertly picked its way through the tangle of underbrush to the ancient ringstones. And once inside them, Griffin Radnor dismounted with a flourish and allowed his mount to wander off to graze.

He had not changed, Caitlin thought as she recalled him

waiting for her by the road to Seacliff. Perhaps his eyes were
a little more black than blue, and more mocking as they examined her without shame. And perhaps his hair was a little
darker, his one-sided smile more bitterly sardonic than she
remembered, but he was still a powerful-looking man, and the
way he strode toward her with his thumbs hooked in his waistband proved he had lost none of his swaggering arrogance.

He stopped a few feet from her and shifted his hands to his
hips. His head tilted slightly to one side, and his smile grew
wider.

"Well," he said. "Well, well, well."

"Well yourself, Griffin Radnor," she snapped, and instantly
regretted it. A bolt of anger flared in his gaze, subsided as she
warned herself to be the lady of Seacliff, not a simpering little
waif who couldn't keep her wits about her in the presence of
a man. She looked deliberately away, toward the sprawling
house on the hillside, wondering how she'd missed it while
she'd been riding. She must have been blind.

"Indeed," he said, his voice deep and melodic, carrying a
lilt that promised at any moment to break into song.

She nodded toward Falconrest. "You seem to be prosper-
ing."

"I have had my share of good fortune," he admitted without
modesty. "At least I don't tremble each time the king's col-
lectors come round. They go off happy, and I still get some."

She grunted meaninglessly and, after a moment's struggle
with indecision, returned to the altar stone to resume her place—
though this time she did not draw up her legs. The roan had
edged back toward the lane. She followed its movements carefully, but she did not call it to her. Griff would have laughed
at her.

"It's been time, hasn't it?" she said into a silence she could
not abide; and the instant the words left her lips she groaned
silently, cursing herself. She could not understand why she was
guarded so suddenly, why she didn't release all the things she'd
been dwelling on since leaving Eton. Where was her temper
now that she needed it to bolster her courage?

"It has," he acknowledged solemnly, his hands dropping to
his sides. He cleared his throat. "I grieve for your father, my
lady."

"Thank you."

So formal, she thought; good Lord, we're being so formal!

"I'm pleased you've returned."

She thought of him stalking her, riding the fields and lanes, keeping just out of reach of her call. "Are you?"

He glared at her, and from the corner of her eye she caught a flare of sunlight from the copper in his hair.

"Your husband is well, I take it." He changed the topic.

She glanced at him briefly, then turned away to look at the ground. There was no expression on his face either of jealousy or interest. "He's well."

"England has been good to you, then."

"Well enough." She paused as her throat constricted with a tension that swelled from her chest. Then: "There's plenty to do there, naturally, and we go to London and Windsor now and again." Her hands wrestled mindlessly in her lap, and she forced them to be still lest Griff misinterpret her apparent nervousness. "I . . . that is, we were presented, you know. To the king and queen."

"Oh, really?" he said in a mocking tone. "And did you tell him what you thought of him?"

"I told him," she said primly, "I was independent-minded, but I wasn't a fool."

"I see."

Do you? she wondered, or do you think I've capitulated to English rule like Oliver's family? And it bothered her disturbingly that she should care what he thought.

The sun had crawled past its meridian, and the westward-reaching shadows slipped darkly, cooly, over the stones. The sea breeze faded. Insects droned on in the cover of the underbrush. A slant of perspiration slid down her chest, and she tried not to wriggle away from the icy, tickling sensation, showing her discomfort.

"Your Mr. Flint," Griff said, then broke off abruptly and rubbed a hand over his face.

She wanted to tell him James Flint wasn't hers at all, but she only said, "Yes?" and saw the hard look return to his eyes. "Yes, what about him?"

Griff shook himself slightly, as if coming to a decision he still didn't trust. "I should tell you he's not making himself very popular in the valley, Caitlin. It was bad enough, what was done to Lam Johns, but Flint and his fine friends seem to think they own everything in sight." She sensed rather than saw his wry smile. "They've even tried to come at me, but they've a fear of my darlin' pets, it seems." His smile faded as if it had never been. "It's a bad business there, Caitlin. I know the types. Soldiers out of service for one reason or other. Mercenaries, for want of a better word. Like the Hessians Germany exports for our wars. Hardly the type a true master would use to oversee his charges."

She stared silently in Seacliff's direction. The men he was talking about were under Flint's stewardship. Oliver had explained that they helped James with his duties. She had never seen or attempted to see any of them. They kept to themselves in their quarters in the north tower, and none had ever tried to approach her. She didn't like the idea, and Oliver had not volunteered any further information about them; nevertheless, before she could stop herself, she heard her voice telling Griffin what her husband had said about the law and its enforcement.

Griff's eyes narrowed in disbelief. "You disappoint me, Caitlin. All these years I thought you knew the difference between the law and justice. I thought your father had taught you more."

"My father," she said tightly, "taught me a great number of things. Among them, to be wary of those with whom I share my company."

He almost laughed. "You've not changed as much as I heard, thank God. You still have a biting tongue, and you still know how to use it."

"Is that supposed to be a compliment?"

"You may accept it as such, if you please," he said.

"I do not please," she told him.

"As you will."

"Absolutely." She fought to keep from slapping him, so great was her disappointment. Was this the only reason he'd followed her to this place? To voice his doubts about Flint, about her husband? To warn her of possible trouble, in unsubtle terms? Is this all there was going to be?

"This Flint—"

"Oh . . . damn Mr. Flint! Are you trying to tell me that one man has turned you all into cowards afraid of your shadows? Are these the men my father protected all his life? One little spot of trouble and you run like sheep?"

"Lam Johns was not a 'spot of trouble,'" he said.

She looked at him warily. "There've been more?"

He shook his head, she thought too reluctantly.

"Then I suggest you make your peace with Oliver, and things will be right as rain again."

She would have said more, but the sound of her strident voice silenced her, and the words she'd shouted across the small clearing shocked her into a heated flush. She pressed one hand to her cheek. Had her father been alive he would have switched her without thinking twice, and by the glower of Griff's face he, too, had a similar reaction. Damn him, she thought; how dare he confuse me like this, make me say such awful things about my own people.

Griffin apparently noted her distress. His expression softened somewhat and, after a brief shuffling of his boots, he made motions to sit beside her on the stone. She shifted away. He took hold of her arm, and she closed her eyes briefly against his touch. But when she tried to free herself, his grip tightened.

"Griffin, I'll thank you to—"

"Dammit, Caitlin! Dammit!"

Control was gone; the tide of her emotions flooded over the dam, and she found herself shouting. "Dammit yourself!" she cried. "How dare you come to me, sneaking around like this, talking to me like this, saying all those terrible things about me when . . . three years, Griffin Radnor! Three bloody years and not a single damned word out of you. For all I knew you were dead."

"You're married now," he said, maddeningly calm.

"God in heaven," she cried, "what does that have to do with . . . with . . ." She wrenched her head away and stared at the nearest tree, her eyes blinking rapidly, tears welling and stinging them. "You could have been dead. You *were* dead."

"Cat," he said quietly, but harshly, "I do what I want to do because no man holds me. But I do not make a habit of paying unwanted calls on married women. Especially titled women. Especially . . . especially you."

Her hands were clenched so tightly that her wrists began to ache. This was not the proper way to behave, and she knew it; and where was all the anger? Where was all that righteous, self-pitying anger?

"Besides," he added coldly, "your husband is not exactly the sort of man who appreciates men like me."

She nodded quickly. "Oh, you're right about that, Griff,"

she said bitterly. "You're so very right about that."

The dam broke, and she was helpless.

"Why?" she pleaded weakly. "Why didn't you fight for me, Griff? I don't understand. Why did you let Father believe all those horrid stories?"

"You believe them," he said simply.

She looked at him squarely. "I believe most of them because I know you," she countered. "There's too much in you for you to be still for too long." She paused, and considered. "I think Father envied you in some way, too. I don't know quite how or why."

"He was not a meek man, Caitlin," Griff said. "I would suspect if you spoke with old Les or Marty Randall, you'd find your father was not in his youth what he expected you to be in yours."

"Like you," she said.

He shrugged.

"But you never denied anything," she said plaintively. "You just let them all talk about you, and you never denied a thing!"

Griff straightened. "I never had to deny to those who really cared."

"You—" The words were lost as she gasped.

"You had only to ask, Caitlin."

She pushed at him angrily. "What chance did you give me? What chance was there?"

The truth of her accusations forced him to look away. They both fell into a shocked, despairing silence. Then he seemed struck by an idea, and searched her face, quizzically. "What else do you believe, Caitlin?"

Stunned by the turn of the conversation, she could only shake her head in rueful sorrow. "You know, you could have found some way, surely, to tell me Morag's child was . . . was . . ." The words caught like hooks in her throat, and she could not dislodge them. Frustration overwhelmed her. Before she knew what she was doing she had raised her arm and, while Griffin's eyes widened in astonishment and disbelief, she brought the flat of her hand as hard as she could across his cheek.

The crack was like a gunshot.

Both horses stirred, their bridles rattled as they sidled away; a flurry of wings from the foliage indicated a flock of blackbirds had taken flight, and Caitlin put the offending hand to her own cheek, the burning on her palm feeling as though fire had scorched it.

Griffin's eyes turned to flint, but he did not touch the slightly reddened spot. Instead, he grabbed her wrist and held it, squeezing until a strangled cry broke from her lips. Then he yanked her against him, his free hand cradling her back and keeping her from escaping. He searched her face intently, and grunted as if he'd seen in her eyes no more than what he'd expected. And before she could twist out of his painful grasp he crushed his lips to hers, burying his hand in her hair.

She resisted. Not by struggling, but by remaining immobile. Her lips did not soften; her eyes did not close. She glared at him instead and waited until he could see his effect. Her chest rose and fell shallowly, a dim ache spreading from the base of her spine. Waited. Until quite involuntarily she attempted to pull away and take a breath. But he would not permit it. His grip tightened on her wrists and head, and his eyes remained stubbornly closed. Time and vision blurred. The warm scent of his face, the heat from his hair, the feel of his soft shirt all worked to undermine her determination to remain unaffected.

Her left hand fluttered over the stone; her right hand lay motionless in her lap.

He shifted, pressed harder.

She wanted to protest, but she knew if she tried twisting away again he would renew his patience and hold her prisoner until she relented.

Her left hand convulsed, and her right finally moved to his shoulders in an effort to push him away. She had to have air. She had to breathe. And she had to dispel the disturbing images now gathering about her: the glen, his touch, their eventual union which she'd almost come to believe never happened. The way he spoke to her—softly, gently, never doubting her intelligence, praising her beauty, never assuming she was anything less than she was; the way he looked at her—searching, idolizing, eyes sparkling with quiet laughter because of the silent communion they shared with no others.

Her resolve weakened. Her hands stopped their pressing, and her lips began to soften.

And immediately he released her with such rapidity that she nearly fell backward.

She gasped for air, confused, frightened, and angry. Her

mouth opened to demand explanations, but his stony face buried her words before they were born. An anguished heat then swept from her chest to her face, and with a despairing, unbelieving cry she leaped from the stone and ran for her horse. Tears drenched her cheeks. The world tilted and she stumbled into a shrub. With a foul oath, she kicked at it, yanked her skirts free of the barbs and spun around in a tight circle, trying to locate her mount before Griffin came after her.

It was too late.

Just as she found the roan less than a yard away and reached for the reins, he was at her side, grabbing her shoulders in a viselike grip she could not shake off.

"Bastard!" she hissed, and kicked at his shins.

He pushed her away, but refused to free her.

Fury blocked her senses. She shrieked at him, lashed out with her nails and boots, and as her blows landed she could hear him grunt in pain. Her head swung from side to side, her breasts felt weighed down, but she kept on filling the air with curses and trying to claw at his face until, at last, she lifted her face to him, and through her tears begged him to release her without saying a word.

He drew her closer, but did not embrace her. Her arms felt like lead, hanging uselessly at her sides. A thin line of blood trickled down his temple to the line of his jaw, and his damp hair was plastered darkly over his forehead. He was panting as well, as if he, and not Caitlin, had been struggling fiercely.

"Please," she implored. "Griffin, please."

"You love me still," he said simply, no doubt in his tone.

A brief wave of anger welled in her, and she slapped away his hands. "Don't be a fool," she said venomously.

And suddenly his wry smile returned, the flint gone from his eyes. "I need to know, Cat," he said, shaking his head and turning away toward the white stallion. Before she could deny his incredible presumption, he was in the saddle, his hair brushed away from his eyes. "I needed to know you didn't love that man."

Speechless, she could only gape at him.

"And something else," he added as the stallion wheeled about, prancing. "I've heard the tales Morag's been telling. I've heard the rumors." His smile twitched. "I've even been the object of one of the vicar's marvelous sermons." The smile vanished. "I've not said a word until now, Cat, because I don't care what people say. You know that. I've a life to live, and I will not be governed by the small minds of small folks. But you remember this, Caitlin Evans: Morag's little bastard is no child of mine."

He effortlessly released a whistle, and the white steed exploded through the brush to the fields sweeping up to Falconrest. Caitlin had no strength to do anything but stare after him, his final words clinging like burrs to her sore body.

Slowly, dreamlike, she lifted her hand to her lips. After a moment she dropped it to her chest where it stayed until the stallion and its rider vanished into shadow.

It wasn't until the roan nuzzled her arm and snorted softly that she broke from her trance. With a start, she looked about her as though she had a no idea where she was or what she was doing there. Uttering a weak sob she pressed the palm of her hand to her forehead. A tear glistened at the corner of her eye, and without awareness, she blinked it away slowly. The roan nudged her again, and blindly she struggled into the saddle, trusting the animal to carry her safely back to the country lane.

She was numb. She felt neither the pull of her muscles as her mount cantered down the lane nor the sun's heat nor the dust that rose from the ground as they passed. A large portion of her mind had gone into fearful hiding, and all she could do now was pray she'd be able to get inside the house without anyone noticing her agitation. All she needed now was Oliver ranting and raving, hurling questions at her like stones, of Gwen fussing over her like a mother hen.

Across the land rolling to the main road the roan trotted easily, and before long Caitlin was facing the mansion. The shadow-darkened windows stared out at her sightlessly, and the towers loomed against the deepening blue sky. Curious and faint sounds were carried to her on the light breeze, but she dismissed them as nothing as she finally allowed herself to sort out her emotions. But once up the slope and on level ground, she could hear the sounds more clearly; they came rhythmically, and it did not take her long to recognize their nature: the harsh bites of a whip engaged in a lashing.

She shook her head violently, driving Griffin and their strange encounter temporarily out of mind, and cocking her head until she located the sounds. After a moment's indecision, she dug her heels hard into the roan's side and galloped around the south tower's base, skidding to a halt and sliding from the saddle in one fluid motion when she saw the tableau unfolding off to the side.

A tall wooden stake had been pounded into a worn patch of grass, and a crossbar had been lashed to it at just below shoulder height. Oliver, oddly dressed in his major's uniform, was standing several yards away, his hands clasped firmly behind his back and his chin jutting squarely away from his chest. He was bewigged and enwrapped in a gleaming black sash that hung over his chest. Behind him stood the household staff, the women pressed close to the men, the men glaring straight ahead, not moving at all.

Caitlin's eyes roamed the tiny crowd until she found Gwen, but when their gazes locked, Gwen looked away.

She took a step forward, and was stopped by a vicious attack of nausea in her stomach.

Flint was standing at the edge of the worn ground, his legs carelessly apart and his coat folded neatly on the grass. His white shirt was stained with perspiration down the length of his spine, and though his back faced her she could tell that his breathing was scarcely labored. He had flung his left arm outward to one side for balance, and in his right hand he held the grooved grip of a long-tailed whip. By he way he looked at Oliver, it was obvious he was waiting for instructions to continue.

Caitlin began walking; no one paid her any mind.

With arms outspread and secured by thongs around the crossbar, with his shirt torn to ribbons, with the flesh of his back exposed to the air, and with the dark blood running freely, young Davy Daniels slumped, his knees buckled and his cheek pressed against the pole.

16

FAR OVERHEAD a flock of gulls flew in a great circle, their cries carried by the sea breeze and their shadows pocking the ground. They swarmed into a cloud, dispersed and swarmed again, and each time they converged they dropped a little lower until their black skull caps could be seen, and the black tips of their wings slashed the air like razor-sharp knives. It wasn't until they were less than twenty feet from the land that they suddenly scattered in shrill abandon, and they did not regroup until they were no more than pale specks against the sky.

Oliver, oblivious to the chaos above him, cleared his throat impatiently. "Do you in fact repent, Mr. Daniels?"

Davy groaned deep in his chest, and his mouth was misshapen by his agony.

"Mr. Daniels, I am required to ask you again. Do you hear me? Do you repent?"

Caitlin felt as if the air had hardened above her to prevent her fighting her way toward Davy. It was as though she were swimming, a leaded weight placed on her chest, making her gasp for breath. But she did move, and she was aware that faces were now turning slowly toward her, that somewhere in the crowd a hand was raised in her direction, though whether in warning or in threat she could not tell. Mouths opened, yet she could hear nothing but the fierce thunder of her own blood in her temples, the frantic race of her heart struggling to power her steps forward. And for a moment she could have sworn the earth shuddered under the impact of the breakers against the cliffs.

Flint seemed unaware of her approach. Casually, almost absently, he coiled the whip in his left hand, then released the tail and snapped his right wrist so that the obscenely serpentine leather uncoiled on the grass behind him, waiting. Once more he looked to Morgan, who had taken a lace-edged handkerchief from his sleeve and was daubing the beads of perspiration from the corner of his mouth, the ridges of his brow.

Davy took the respite to attempt standing, but his pain-weakened legs would not hold him. He sagged, and the strain on his arms brought a whimper from lips which were lined with froth and dried blood.

Morgan shook his head in weary regret. "Mr. Daniels, you really are making this extraordinarily difficult on yourself. You know that, don't you? You do know that, don't you?"

To Caitlin, his voice carried the disdain of an adder for its helpless prey.

"All you have to do is nod, Mr. Daniels, and it will be all over, I promise you. Nod, Mr. Daniels, and you will have cool water to drink and a balm for your wounds. Come, Mr. Daniels, don't prolong this any further."

Davy's tongue poked through his lips; it was dark and swollen.

"Very well," Oliver said, and sniffed. "Carry on, Mr. Flint."

After a moment's pause Flint rolled his shoulders, stretched his neck, and flung back his right arm; the whip writhed on the grass. Then he took a deep breath and, for the first time since Caitlin rounded the tower, he looked to Davy. It was apparent he was coolly measuring the distance between them, to the place on the boy's back where the lash would sting the most. His biceps flexed in anticipation beneath the smooth shirt, and Davy groaned again.

"Come, Mr. Flint," Morgan said, glancing toward the horizon. "I see no sense in dragging the lad over the coals."

Flint leaned back slightly, and the air stilled, the gulls were silenced—but as his arm began its journey forward, Caitlin snared his wrist with one hand and snatched the whip with the other. He whirled around with a snarl, fists raised, eyes flashing blackly, the scar from nose to lips pulsing in rage. His oath was muffled by the startled gasp of the assembled staff, but Caitlin refused to back down before either his language or the murderous glare in his eyes.

They faced off in black rancor, Caitlin just as intense as he.

"Touch the boy again, Mr. Flint," she said at last, the words smoldering in acid, "and I'll use this foul thing on you myself."

"Lady Morgan!" Oliver commanded, his astonishment strangling his cry.

She ignored him.

Flint wrestled visibly for self-control. Then he drew himself up and bowed to her rigidly before stepping to one side, well out of her reach. Immediately, she turned around to face the staff, searching for Orin. When she spotted him, she beckoned to him, her free hand pointing to the farrier's brother in unmistaken instruction. There was no hesitation. Several of the women scurried instantly forward to assist the farrier, their faces avoiding Morgan, who was flushed with fury. The others broke ranks and hurried back to their quarters. Only Gwen remained behind, standing alone, neither smiling nor moving.

"Lady *Morgan!*" Oliver growled again.

But Caitlin refused to acknowledge him. She waited until she was certain Davy had been freed from the post and was still breathing; only then did she cast the whip aside and march up to face Oliver.

"Lady Morgan," he said, his voice rising, "you have overstepped your bounds."

"Husband," she retorted, "I will see to Davy. When I am finished, I will see to you. And this time you will not talk to me of what the law demands. This time you will satisfy me."

And before his enraged astonishment, she whirled and strode into the staff's common room. She was capable of neither thought nor speech, so she gave her directions in a flurry of ragged arm and head movements. The long table was cleared of its clutter, and Alice Courder brought a pail of warm water from the kitchen. By the time clean rags had been assembled, Orin and two others had brought Davy inside and laid him gently on his stomach. Alice produced a carving knife, which Caitlin took without asking and used to cut away the blood-clotted fabric from his body. Though Davy flinched at the contact, he made no sound; he was unconscious and his head was cradled on his forearms. She worked swiftly, expertly, and silently. And as each reddened and bloody stripe was exposed, Alice commenced a gentle laving of the skin with her well-scrubbed but stubby, liver-spotted hands.

When the shirt was finally off Davy's back, and Elaine Courder had appeared at the table's head with a ceramic crock of balm, Caitlin backed away. She barely felt Orin slip the knife from her fingers. Gwen was standing in the doorway, watching the ministrations with trembling lips; but she shook her head vigorously when Mary sidled up to her and whispered a question. She only had eyes for Caitlin.

He's your husband; this is your doing, her expression accused.

You cannot blame me for this horror, Caitlin stared back.

Gwen leaned hard against the jamb, and Orin was at her side immediately, wrapping an arm around her waist while she buried her face in his shoulder. There were whispers now, instructions and oaths, and pity for the young man who could not hear them.

Caitlin watched as long as she could. When it was evident, however, that she was no longer needed she turned on her heels and strode down the corridor, through the door, and into the mansion where she headed directly for the rear drawing room. The room was deserted, the only sign of anyone having been there all day a woven shallow basket of oranges and a decanter of brandy on the table. She grabbed an orange automatically, tore at the rind, and bit into it savagely, consuming more than half before grimacing at the sourness and tossing the remains out the door. To wash away the taste, she poured herself some brandy, and drained the glass in several burning gulps. Her eyes stung and watered, her throat felt lined with a fire that no water could quench. She stood at the French doors and stared out blindly over the lawn, refusing to permit herself to think about the insidious horror she'd just witnessed.

Five minutes passed, and she poured herself another glass.

Two months ago, she thought, she'd been determined not to disgrace her father by admitting to a failed marriage; she had vowed to make it work despite the obstacles, while simultaneously refusing to surrender even one small portion of the land she loved more than any other.

Two months ago she had almost convinced herself she was happy—or at least content with the dizzying circumstances of her life.

But now . . .

This time . . . this time she knew beyond doubt that she was in the right and that Oliver was dreadfully, horribly wrong. Nothing short of outright murder should have brought such a punishment down on Davy's back. There was, this time, no conceivable way Oliver could justify his actions.

Five minutes more, and her glass was empty yet again.

Footsteps approached and stopped just outside the open door. She waited patiently, knowing Oliver could not disregard her wishes now. She had defied him in front of the entire staff, and he would have to make a stand or lose all his control. Not even Flint would respect him if he gave ground.

But her vision was growing slightly blurred, and as she put a hand to her brow and rubbed it gently, the room seemed to grow warm. She reached behind her and opened the French doors, sighed as the tangy breeze caressed her hair and shoulders. For the second time that afternoon she thought she felt the earth move as the surf pounded the cliffs. Then she frowned, puzzled, and glanced over her shoulder. Curious, but she would have sworn the tide would not be in until dusk. No matter. She must be mistaken; the two quick glasses of brandy were befuddling her perceptions.

Fifteen minutes became twenty, but she would not give him the satisfaction of launching a harridan's hunt. He would come to her; there could be no other alternative.

And if there was one thing she had more of than Sir Oliver Morgan, it was patience. She would wait right here all night if she had to. All night. But he would come.

And he did.

One moment she was staring into the empty corridor, the next he was framed by the doorway, still dressed as she had seen him earlier in the day. At first she thought him an apparition so swiftly and silently did he come into view; but when he folded his arms imperiously over his chest and lifted his chin to gaze down at her, she knew her mind was not playing tricks.

But she could not speak.

Try as she might she was unable to find the means to voice her outrage. Instead, she stammered and gestured with her empty glass. He only grunted, and nodded. Not now, she thought desperately; my God, don't fail now! Yet no matter how hard she tried, all she could do at the last minute was stumble across the room to her chair and sink dismally into it. The glass clinked harshly on the table beside her.

There was something wrong.

She blamed it at first on the brandy. But when she thought about it, two rations no matter how swiftly downed had never affected her like this before. Then she experienced the queasy sensation she'd felt earlier in the day, though this time it was not confined to her stomach. Her vision softened again, and a chill raced along her arms bringing goose flesh that would not subside no matter what she tried. Her throat was dry, her legs, numb.

Something was . . . wrong.

"My dear?"

Solicitous. Oh, so solicitous; you would think Davy's lashing had never occurred. But why does he just stand there? Doesn't he know there's something wrong with me? Can't he see I'm not . . . I'm not well?

"Caitlin, you wished to speak to me?"

About the weather, Oliver, of course. I want to talk to you about the weather. About how terribly hot it is and couldn't we go back to England where I have my pond and can cool my feet in the middle of the day? Of course I want to talk with you, Oliver. Of course, I do! But there's something wrong, I can't get my tongue to move.

Her head nodded slightly forward, and she had to sit up as best she could to drive off the sleep overcoming her.

She frowned severely then: sleep? At this hour?

A shadow engulfed her, and with great effort she managed to look up. Oliver was standing in front of her, his arms unfolded and his face creased with what she supposed was concern. He leaned so closely that she could smell the tobacco and wine on his breath. Where had he been? Smoking a pipe and savoring his port in the front room while she sat waiting for him? And he *knew* she'd been waiting for him.

"Caitlin, can you hear me, my dear?"

All she could do was blink once.

He yanked off his wig and tossed it into the chair, then kneeling he touched her cheek gently, her brow, her hair. She wanted to tell him to stop staring at her as if he expected her to die at any moment. But his gaze never left her face as he relaxed his grip on the nape of her neck and scrutinized her closely. He finally turned his head and pressed his ear to her bosom.

"Oh, really, Oliver! You're carrying this a bit too far, don't you think?"

Yet though she heard her voice quite clearly—even the sarcasm and the disgust—she sensed that none of it reached his ears. It was as if she'd suddenly been struck mute.

And her panic began to climb.

Her breathing increased rapidly, shallowly, and her hands gripped the grooved armrests tightly.

Another shadow appeared over her—this one more distant. Was he tall? Could it be Flint? She couldn't see him, nor could she guess his identity from his stride. And the idea that she had glimpsed a white patch over one eye was too absurd to consider. Something was afflicting and distorting her eyesight, so that solid objects twisted and swam, separated and joined before her. A faint throaty whimper broke the silence. She realized it had come from her own throat.

"Caitlin . . ." Oliver rose and backed off. "Bradford," he said in his best command voice, "you will fetch Mrs. Courder at once. Then you will send a man to the village for that Broary woman. I understand she has some knowledge of medicines. Immediately afterward you will send the man on to Llewfanon at the valley's southern end where there's a physician. Bring him here instantly. And I mean instantly!"

She heard a murmuring behind her head, but she could not decipher the words.

"Wait!" Oliver cried. "The Thomas woman. Find her and bring her here at once. She might know something of immediate help."

Again the murmur of assent.

The chill returned, and with it the sensation of a dozen small fires breaking out along her spine to the base of her skull. Nothing made sense anymore. She could no longer hear Oliver speaking, could no longer see without having the room spin before her eyes. She closed them quickly, before the brandy found its way from her stomach, and felt a pressure on her left hand. Oliver was holding it. She wanted to smile at him, to signal him not to worry . . . but she couldn't believe any of this. What she did believe was that some foul humor had taken hold of her and was poisoning her system, wrenching it, tainting her senses until she could no longer use them.

She was flying, then.

The air around her swarmed like feathers over her arms and breasts, and in the distance, through a muddy cloud that drifted from side to side as if blown by a demon wind, she could see Griffin. He was riding his stallion, laughing and pointing at the cloud, showing the woman riding behind him how curious and wonderful the world looked. The woman had hair the shade of wheat, a round pale face, and a figure lithe and supple. Griffin twisted around and kissed her. Morag Burton kissed him back.

Suddenly Caitlin landed on a pile of feathers laced with ice, coated with fire.

Water trickled between her lips; she gagged.

Her clothes were stripped from her, and she felt that given half a chance she would float over Seacliff and see herself as the gulls and falcons and eagles do before they dive for prey.

"Gwen?"

She was amazed. It was her own voice. She heard it clear as a Sunday bell.

"Gwen?" she repeated.

But the question was so weak, like a child's, she wasn't sure Gwen had heard it.

A cold finger touched her chin.

"I'm here, Cat, it's all right," a voice said in Welsh, not in English. "Sir Oliver is down in the kitchen, checking all the stores. He thinks there may be something rotten Mrs. Courder didn't catch."

But all she could reply was, "Gwen?"

And her own voice was the last thing she heard before the muddy cloud of her senses exploded and engulfed her in flaming silence.

17

THE STALLION'S name was Whitefire. And as he paced slowly across the wide expanse of the crescent-shaped clearing he shook his great head and lowered it to the dew-laden grass on which he nibbled. His moon-cast shadow vanished into the darkness of the hill's forest. The hour was well past midnight, and the only sounds heard were the muted tinkling and creaking of the stallion's equipage, and the occasional soft hoot of an owl in the branches overhead. He snorted, and swished his tail lazily from side to side. And every so often he turned his head to look for his master, as if to be sure he hadn't been forgotten.

The clearing was a natural pause in the woodland that covered the eastern range. There were no shrubs or saplings, no burrows or debris from nesting birds. And where the grass ended an outcropping of brown rock began, leading to a drop of nearly three hundred feet. At its base the trees began again, and stopped only when they reached the ancient stones of Falconrest.

Griffin Radnor squatted on his haunches in the shallow depression of a boulder, and folded his arms across his thighs. A thin woolen cloak was draped carelessly over his shoulders. From behind, he could have been mistaken for just another rock, until his head suddenly swung guardedly to one side. The view was hypnotizing, and every few minutes he was forced to look away.

The valley below seemed to be lightly coated with snow, and glimmered silver. The cottages, long since gone dark, looked like toys, the vast ocean of stars mocked the bay and the channel and the ocean below, and the bulk of Seacliff, even at this distance, loomed like a protective sentinel at land's end.

Unless it was preparing to become a tomb, he thought morbidly.

It was the end of August. The air had been cleansed twice of its cloying humidity by swiftly moving storms—one charging in from Cardigan Bay on the heels of blinding lighting, the other creeping over the hills from England, dropping three days of torrential rains and thunder on the valley. The first had appeared a fortnight before; the last had ended only two mornings before; and after the two storms Griffin had had a visitor. Gwen Thomas had come to his gates and demanded she be admitted. His man, Richard Jones, knew her and brought her to him, and it was then he'd learned of Caitlin Morgan's illness.

"The fever takes her and leaves her, takes her and leaves her," Gwen had said, her hands trembling so hard she could barely hold her mug of cold water. "That old sod from Llewfanon has given her every potion devised since God created the world, but all she does is shake like an autumn leaf."

"Does she speak?"

Gwen shrugged. "Of a way, of a way. She makes no sense, none at all." She choked back a sob, wiped a hand over her pale, drawn face and took a deep unsteady breath.

Griffin put a hand on her shoulder but said nothing more. He did not know how to comfort this woman, though he admired her for staying long enough on her feet to make the journey to Falconrest. At the Stag's Head, he'd heard of Davy Daniels's lashing and that Seacliff's mistress had been too late and not forceful enough to save the boy from being permanently crippled. But when he'd broached the subject gingerly, Gwen had grown heated, her dark eyes flashing with indignation.

"Lies!" she'd cried. "Cat came round that tower like an archangel ready for battle. She took the whip from the English bastard's hand and beat him down with a look. She cut off Davy's shirt herself, she did. And when blood was all over her, she never batted an eye. Who told you this? Who'd dare tell such a foul lie?"

He'd backed away quickly, though he didn't physically move an inch, and asked her instead about Caitlin's ravings.

Gwen subsided instantly, shrinking into an upholstered chair next to Griffin's hearth until he thought she'd disappeared. "I don't know. She...there's talk about geese and birds, and once or twice she blathers about that silly pond of hers back in Eton. The rest is pure raving; I can't make head nor tail of it." She sipped from the mug. "One time she was in the middle of a story, and I didn't recognize it until I remembered it came from some old tale Les used to tell. Then the next thing I know there's Bradford telling me I have to get on with my work and the mistress needs her rest and"—her voice rose to a keening wail—"and don't he think I know that I've work to do, but I can't do it, because she's lying there wasting away with nothing to be done for it? Don't he know that?"

He kept his face impassive, waiting for Gwen's anguish to pass.

"A white patch," she'd said after a while.

"What?"

"A white patch. I don't know what she meant. Twice, I think, she sits up with her eyes all wide and staring, talking about a great bloody giant what wears a white patch over his eye. I had all I could do to keep her from leaping off the bed! All I could do. All...I could do."

It was then that Griffin rose from his chair and pulled Gwen to her feet and embraced her. He held her until her sobbing was over and insisted she should get back to the house before

Bradford discovered where she'd gone. He'd had Jones take her as near to Seacliff as possible in a cart, and had immediately begun a vigil that lasted all day and night until he could no longer keep his eyes open. When he slept, it was badly. When he ate, it was quickly. He let Richard see to the running of his estate, collect the rents and arrears, and take the goods to the market in Llewfanon.

And each evening toward dusk he rode with grim purpose up the road and through the village, determined not to stop until he reached the doors of Seacliff.

But on those lonely rides he would draw up abreast of the grove where Davy had discovered the body of Lam Johns. And though he was afraid of no man—and especially not of Sir Oliver Morgan and his henchmen—he was reminded of Morgan's ruthlessness. If, as the master of Falconrest, he paid a call on the mistress of Seacliff to ask after her health, which he'd heard was frail, he might make Caitlin's life more difficult than it was now.

So each evening he turned back at the grove and used the side roads to avoid passing through the village again. He didn't want to set tongues wagging, tongues that could be loosened more by Morgan's money.

Oliver Morgan already had ample reason to be furious with Griffin. Several times over the past three years James Flint and his cronies had carried messages from Morgan, offering to purchase Falconrest and all its surrounding holdings for a sum that Griffin found difficult to believe a retired major of His Majesty's army could have amassed. He refused, more bluntly each time, and it wasn't long before he began to hear complaints from his farmers and foundry workers about damage. The incidents were minor to be sure: fences knocked down, livestock badly injured, highwaymen swooping past cottages at night laughing maniacally and shouting obscenities, unnerving his people more than frightening them.

But this last spring, the incidents had grown worse. A fire had destroyed a newly restored barn and silo; a prime bull had been found in the field with its throat slit; a well near the foundry had been poisoned, and several men had taken seriously ill.

Lam Johns had worked for that moldy creature the village called a vicar. His family had lived on Radnor land since the time of the English King Henry VIII. The tragedy of his murder had been doubled the same day when his ailing mother, despite attempts to conceal the news from her, heard of it anyway, and was dead within forty-eight hours of her son's hanging.

It had been, Griffin believed, murder twice over.

The sharp scrape of a shod hoof over a rock jolted him out of his reverie, and with infinite caution he rose from his perch above Seacliff. His joints protested their sudden call to action, and Griffin groaned to himself as he stepped backward away from the edge of the drop. Though his legs tingled, he felt steady enough. Snapping his fingers once, he saw Whitefire respond, leaving his grazing patch not far away; the stallion was at his side in a few moments. In a single leap Griffin was in the saddle, and moments later he'd left the deserted clearing behind him.

Except for the furtive sounds of someone moving through the brush, and the sounds of Whitefire thundering down the forest path, the night was quiet.

Three evenings later, having heard no further word from Gwen on Caitlin's condition, he asked Jones to take charge of the house in his absence and he went outside. It was a clear, cool night, and a nearby stream sang as he strode toward the tall iron gates set into Falconrest's surrounding wall. He had to walk. He was much too restless, too anxious to sit for any length of time, and he'd reach his destination too quickly if he mounted Whitefire and rode to it.

He decided to cut across the countryside first and stop at the Stag's Head for a pint and some companionship. The villagers, though they liked him well enough and trusted him, had taken to shying away from him. Their reticence came as no surprise. He knew that Flint's men were threatening detention if not physical harm to anyone who was too friendly with the master of Falconrest. In the beginning this had amused Griffin. He had never considered himself a dangerous man, and that Oliver Morgan believed his exaggerated reputation was proof enough the major was a fool.

After downing the pint, he would take the road to Seacliff, but this time he'd go straight to Orin Daniels. And if the farrier was well disposed to his visitor, he might be convinced to admit Griffin into the south tower. The back steps led up to Caitlin's room.

It was a foolish notion, perhaps, but one that promised a

wickedly delightful evening. He grinned broadly to himself as he closed the gates behind him and set off across the pastureland on the opposite side of the road.

With his long strides he covered the distance easily, his night vision picking out with no trouble the burrows, the stump holes, the cavities where boulders had been removed to make way for plows. He whistled. To see Caitlin was only part of the joy; to be in Morgan's house, to creep in right under the man's red-veined nose and visit his wife in her bedchamber . . . that was an irony he could not resist.

He forded a stream in a single leap.

A small herd of black-masked sheep skittered away at his approach, a few of the ewes bleating in fear though the rams refrained from challenging the stranger.

A watchdog from a cottage barked a fierce warning into the night, and Griffin was hard-pressed to resist finding it and taking it with him.

As he neared the village, he found himself on a lane that led directly to the main road. Branches formed a canopy over his head, and on the dry ground the moonlight lay in puddles that rippled when the night wind gusted down from the hills. His heels struck the ground reassuringly; his cloak flapped about his calves; his soft-brimmed hat was set at a rakish angle on his head, and his hair was worn in a braid that bounced lightly between his shoulders.

Griffin was so entranced by the evening's promise—the image of Morgan's face bloated with anger—that he almost missed the sound of a snapping twig off to his left. He sensed it came from a thicket of brier and laurel to his left.

Not pausing or giving any sign he had heard, he continued on. But he strained his ears through the muted night sounds for another sign that he was not alone.

Another came, this time from a hickory grove to his right. Could a single man move so quickly? No, there had to be more than one.

Nodding slightly, he pushed his cloak back as casually as possible to allow his arms free movement. He carried no weapon in his waistband, and he scolded himself for the oversight. Knowing it would not be long before he was the object of some harassment, he should have made it a habit to carry at least a stunted club. But he hadn't, and there was no sense wasting time or energy lamenting the fact. Now he had to determine the size of the band closing in around him. Three or four, by his guess. He might still do well by himself if he confronted them boldly, driving them off and getting only a few bruises himself. But since they were probably carrying weapons, it would certainly be more prudent to take to his heels. The village was not far ahead, and he was just one hundred yards from the main road; a right turn, and he would be less than half the distance to the first village house. The Stag's Head was the last building before the commons.

Finishing his quick mental notes, he slowed and scanned the woods on either side, hoping he would be able to see in the shadows a fallen dead branch or a loose rock he could use as a weapon. There was nothing. Only his carefully controlled breathing and the sound of boots clomping boldly on the lane behind him.

His brief smile was one-sided. There was no question they were a confident bunch. Cheeky, besides, to come right out in the open like that, without so much as a blow to stun him before the kill. He swallowed hard to keep from laughing aloud, and to remind himself he was not, after all, immortal, even though his luck had managed to keep him alive thus far.

A thud sounded: someone had jumped from the thicket to the road.

Three of them were back there now, he guessed. None of them very heavy. And they weren't closing on him; they were maintaining their distance, walking steadily in step with him like troops behind a sergeant.

His palms itched to move.

He wondered whose idea this was, Flint's or Morgan's? The possibility that his pursuers might be simply highwaymen looking for a lone mark and some easy coppers had surfaced and been dismissed; bandits in this valley were virtually unknown. David Evans had developed a reputation for dealing harshly with such criminals. No, it had to be Flint's men, perhaps with Flint himself at the head.

The skin grew taut over his shoulders, and the muscles tightened across his stomach. His heart sped up, and the muscles in his arms began an unconscious flexing, ready to power him when he needed to move quickly.

Then he slowed. As the trees thinned ahead, the shadows began to separate from the boles. Three men glided into the center of the lane and formed a barrier, their hands in front of them, clubs in their grips.

He stopped, and the footsteps behind him stopped.

They'd grown to six in number. Quite a conspiracy. He looked quickly to either side: trees to his right and a thick undergrowth of brier; a copse to his left that led to an unused field abutting the central road. The verge slanted upward for five or six feet before leveling out, but because the grass at this time of night was wet with fresh dew, it would be slippery going. Even if he could make it to the top and bolt across the open land, the three ahead of him would be able to cut him off without much effort. And there might be others waiting for him at the top. You never knew how well planned these things were.

"Well, gentlemen," he said suddenly, and loudly, "I expect you'll want my purse. Any time soon?"

A silence greeted his mocking question.

"No?" He took a step forward, and the trio narrowed the gap between them further by taking the same number of steps closer to Griffin. "Well, surely my rags have no value to men of your obvious gentility and refinement?" He plucked dramatically at his billowing white shirt, at his snug breeches, at his polished black belt, which he tugged again, loosening the buckle in a movement too quick to catch. "Don't you have tongues, then?"

Someone shifted behind him. He smiled, wryly. He'd thought by their stance they were trained in great patience, waiting for him to make the first move. For once he was pleased to learn that his first impression was wrong.

He shook his head slowly, and clucked his tongue. "My friends, unless you deign to speak with me, how can I read your desires, eh?" He spread his arms wide. "I am not one of your fey Welshmen, you know. I cannot read the spirits that ride the night, not like some I could name. You'll have to tell me what it is you're after."

He knew, however, they were working on his nerves, hoping by their dark clothes and masked faces to frighten him into submission. But this time they had misjudged their opponent.

He put his hands on his hips. "Gentlemen, I do not have all night. Either you discuss this with me man to man or you carry on with your bloody cowardly English ways and come

at me." A shuffling noise sounded again from behind. "Great
stupid English swine," he said, virtually bellowing the last
word. "It's bad enough you wage war on old women and young
boys, isn't it? Now you haven't the common courage to face
me as men. You have to hide like little gels behind pretty little
masks to hide your great, fat, ugly faces!"

He spat in disgust.

But his provocation worked. He spun around just as one of
the attackers vented his anger with a muffled yell and rushed
at him, swinging his club high over his head. There was a
shout of dismayed rage, but it was too late. Griffin caught the
man's wrist and twisted it back, his other hand grasped the
club easily as the wrist broke with a snap. The man screamed
and fell to his knees, then rolled to his side in pain. Griff,
however, had already forgotten him. With club in hand he ran
at the assailant's two companions, ramming the smooth-bored
club into one's stomach and dancing away from a blow that
was aimed at his forehead.

There was no thought of running now. That had died when
he'd decided to confront them.

A second blow aimed for his head missed by a hair's breadth,
and he lunged at the man before he could regain his balance.
He gripped the other's throat and forced him backward, first
hooking his leg around a knee and shoving. The man sank to
the ground. Before he could roll away, Griffin kicked his boot
into the man's ribs and grinned in satisfaction at the cry of
pain that ripped through the mask into the night air.

Then he turned around and waited, legs spread and club
held at the ready in front of him. The remaining three were
already lunging in full charge, one on each of the lane's shoulders, the third coming directly up the center. Griff watched
them in the few seconds before they reached him, trying to
decide which he should take first, which would give him the
best advantage. He completely ignored the three men groaning
at his feet; they would be out of action for the time he needed
to rid himself of the other pests.

His smile was taunting, and he braced himself to lunge at
the center man, trusting his own weight to knock the man
backward.

He feinted, and the middle man stalled slightly. It was all
Griff needed. With a yell of delight he charged, dodging under

the club's wild swing and putting his shoulder into the man's chest. There was a cry of pain, but the man miraculously did not lose his balance; instead, he dropped his weapon and flung his arms around Griff, grappling with him and pinning his elbows momentarily to his sides. The move was enough of a surprise to widen Griffin's eyes and make him wonder for a split second how he had gone wrong, before their feet were entangled and they fell. The attacker tried to roll with the fall, but Griffin had enough presence of mind to twist in the opposite direction and land squarely on the man's chest, knocking the air harshly from his lungs and loosening the man's hug just enough to allow him to wriggle free.

A boot came at his head. He rolled away and scrambled to his knees.

A club whistled out of the dark, and he barely managed to lift his own to block the blow. The collision was sharp, and both weapons split down the grain. His hand stung from the impact, and he yelped, skuttled back, and was only just able to brace himself before the third man leaped from the verge and landed on his back. He let himself be shoved forward while his hands reached up to snare two fistfuls of hair; he pulled, and there was a scream before he came away with a cap, a mask, and a patch of scalp in one hand.

He struggled to rise, cursing his foul luck, but a steel-shod foot grazed his shin, and his leg buckled. When he fell, his shoulder struck a rock in the lane. Fire raced along his arm, making his fingers tingle painfully. He gasped when a club glanced across the middle of his back, gasped again when another finally hit its mark on his side. He tried to roll away, and found himself leaning against the slanted verge facing two men swinging at him while, at the corner of his eye, he saw two more regaining their feet.

It was a second, perhaps two, before he made his last move, but in that time, which was all the time in the world, he understood this was no object lesson being given here. This was not one of Morgan's messages, subtle but to the point. This was not a warning; these men were trying to kill him.

And when the time came he threw himself away from the clubs speeding toward his skull, in the same motion using his good left hand to pull his belt from his waist and wrap the leather around his forearm. At the back of the gold buckle was a grip; and the edges of the buckle had been filed to a sharpness that was only partially decoration. With one leg braced behind him, he watched as the two men repositioned themselves and renewed their attack—silently, using hand signals to direct each other's movements. The second pair had finally wavered to their feet; Griffin had to move now, or he'd not have a second chance.

He shoved off with his foot, holding up his right shoulder to intercept the descending weapon before it reached its full killing power. When it landed he bit down on the inside of his cheek to prevent a cry from escaping, and instantly tasted blood; but his left hand was already in motion, slashing across the man's face and wringing an astonished, burning scream from his throat. He stumbled backward, and Griffin planted a boot in his abdomen, let the belt slip from his forearm and swung it like a short whip at the second man's face. He backed away, and the buckle hissed. Griff swung again, lower, throwing the man's timing off. The buckle creased his throat; the scream this time was muffled.

"'Sblood," he heard one of the survivors cry. "The man's not human!"

But Griffin was unable to hear the reply. Just as he was about to advance on the pair in the road, something struck him sharply across the back of his skull. He didn't fall immediately; he swayed, his neck muscles straining as he fought to stay on his feet. But the strength was no longer there. There were too many pits of flame opening on his back, his head, along his arms; there were too many voices whispering, pleading, begging him to come with them into darkness.

He had no idea if he was going to live or die; he only knew that fighting well this time had not been good enough.

He fell, spinning as he did to land on his back.

The stars blurred and were hidden by shadows, and he was astonished to see that one of the shadows seemed to be wearing what looked like a white eye patch.

18

THE DREAMS did not swarm as thickly as they once had. In the beginning, however long ago that was, Caitlin was goaded beyond the brink of endurance by the phantasms that assaulted her from the darker reaches of her soul, by the voices whispering like ghouls in her ears, by the fires crawling like lice over her skin. If she slept, she felt no healing effects. If she ate, she did not taste the food that passed between her lips. All she knew, all that touched her awareness was a constant sullen ache in her limbs, the malicious bite of the fever in her skull, and the incredible weakness that would not permit her even to raise her head.

But the dreams passed, and they passed for the most part unremembered. Many she was certain were pleasant ones, for they left her smiling gently long after the images and scenes passed from memory; and many more were nightmares, red and black clouds of nightmares that left her gasping for breath, screaming silently in vast caverns, sitting up in her bed and reaching for comfort from people who she sensed were there but who remained unseen.

The fever broke, and the dreams finally passed.

It happened late one evening, long after the candles had sputtered out and the others had slipped into dreams of their own: suddenly, the air wafting over her felt unusually calm, wonderfully cool, and though she remained conscious for only a few precious seconds she knew the ordeal was finished at last, that whatever had besieged her had admitted defeat and was beginning a slow retreat.

The following morning an errant spear of sunlight breaking through a gap in the curtains pierced her eyes. She frowned her annoyance. She twisted her head weakly away from the intrusion. And as she did so she heard someone in the room release a sharp, grateful cry. A slow, deep inhalation, and she opened her eyes.

It was indeed her room, but she believed for a split second it had been visited by angels.

Flowers were everywhere. There were flowers arranged on every flat surface, in vases perched on stone and wooden pedestals, and in large clay bowls fairly glaring with color; there were blossoms of every imaginable hue to rival the purest rainbow, and their scents mingled with the morning breeze, creating a perfume that by rights should have been reserved for the gods: greenery and prisms, sprigs and whole plants, and her standing mirror by the door entwined with mystical mistletoe.

She sighed with relief, and smiled when a damp cloth was pressed tenderly to her forehead.

"Cat?"

It was Gwen's voice, not daring yet to exult.

Though her vision was still rather befuddled by fever and sleep, Caitlin could discern with some effort the young woman's anxious stare, and the disturbing purple and gray pouches under her eyes. Her cheeks were sallow, and her black hair seemed to have lost its natural shine.

"Cat, are you back, then? Are you really back?"

She nodded and closed her eyes again. The strain required to complete such a simple gesture had been great, but she felt no frustration. She had no idea how long she had been bedridden, but she knew by the way her arms lay limply outside the coverlet that most of her strength had been sapped by something far more serious than a passing summer ague. When she tried to talk, however, when she tried to ask the dozens of questions that suddenly jumbled into her mind, she panicked; her throat closed and her tongue felt three times its normal size. When she tried to force the words anyway, all she could hear, dimly, was a series of strangled animallike cries.

"It's all right, Cat," Gwen said without bothering to hide her excitement. "It's all right." She leaped from her place on the edge of the mattress and spun around once, her hands clasped to her chest. "It's all right. Don't try to talk. I'll get you..." She bounded to a side table littered with goblets, a pitcher, vials, and bottles, and poured out a large measure of fresh, cold water. When she returned to the bed, she slipped a hand under Caitlin's head and lifted it slowly, holding the goblet to her lips and letting only the slightest bit of moisture slip into her mouth. "Easy, mistress, easy. You daren't take too much or it'll come back on you. A little at a time does it. Just a little. You'll be fine."

Caitlin knew Gwen was right, but now that she had sure proof that she was back among the living she could feel the welcome stirrings of impatience at her condition.

Another sip, and she moaned her delight at such a simple pleasure as satisfying thirst. A glance to the window, to the shaft of light between the curtains, and she realized she had had no idea how beautiful the morning sun could be. And the flowers! And the water! And . . . and Gwen! A tear slipped from the corner of her eye, and Gwen quickly wiped it away.

"Am I hurting you?" she asked nervously.

Caitlin shook her head and managed a weak smile. The words were still trapped inside, but her friend understood. She sat on the bed and alternately mopped Caitlin's brow and gave her water. An hour passed before the goblet was empty, but to Caitlin it was the most joyous hour she'd ever known, and the water had such an exquisite bouquet that she didn't mind at all when sleep pulled at her gently. She didn't mind because this time she knew she would awaken again, and this time she knew Gwen would be waiting.

The dreams again came.

She was a falcon, coasting above the rolling landscape to the rugged, misted mountains; sweeping under narrow waterfalls without a drop touching her wings; darting under elaborate bridges; playing unrestrained aerial games with a massive golden eagle whose face was Griffin Radnor's.

Then she was a cloud, drifting over the bay and watching dolphins sport below her; trailing a storm and watching lightning give way to thunder; warmed by the sun as it broke out and watching her shadow caress the land.

She was herself, and she was in bed, and a fever had taken hold of her, forcing her to stare at the four walls; night and day flickered like shadows over the ceiling; people came and went like specters in a dream—and for one long instant she saw James Flint come through the door, alone, smiling, leaning over her and brushing his lips across her cheek, laying his hands on her breasts and promising her heaven if she would recover and be his.

She tried to get away from him by tossing her head from side to side, but he refused to leave. His caresses roughened, and his teeth nipped at her chin. She groaned and threw up a hand, felt the wrist ensnared and would have cried out if her eyes hadn't opened and seen Oliver standing there.

"A nightmare, my dear," he said, placing her hand at her side. He was wearing his riding clothes, and across his lap lay his crop. The smell of perspiration and dust was on him, and for an instant she almost wept, wishing she could ride with him. "And how are you feeling? Is everything satisfactory?"

She swallowed, and nodded. But when her lips quivered in an attempt to speak he placed a finger over them and shook his head.

"Don't try, my dear. There's plenty of time for all of that when you've finally returned to us fully."

He smiled, lifted her hand to kiss it, and rose. Bowing once, he turned and crossed the room to the door through which he disappeared. Within moments Gwen had joined her, babbling cheerfully about her recovery, giving her the good wishes and love of everyone on the staff. Caitlin had no idea how long she'd slept this time, but the effect on her friend was nothing short of miraculous—the pouches under her eyes were virtually gone, her cheeks had filled out, and her hair had regained much of its luster. She sang as she pulled the dead flowers from the vases, sang as she threw open the windows and French doors to let in the sparkling air, sang as she fed Caitlin a steaming bowl of nourishing broth.

Her happiness was infectious.

By the end of the day Caitlin was humming to herself; by the end of the third day she had pillows propped under her back and was sitting up, brushing her own hair and scowling with good humor at the diminishing ravages of the illness still left in her complexion.

And she felt heartened.

She'd learned she had been abed for the full month of August, that she had awakened to coherence for the first time on the fourth day of September. Yet Gwen insisted no one had ever given her up as lost; they knew she was in the dark country battling stubbornly and demanding her right to a long and full life. They weren't worried, she was told; they weren't worried at all.

The gentle lie pleased Caitlin immensely. And it gave her

food for thought. Until she'd been stricken, she had taken altogether too much of her life for granted. First her father took care of her, then Oliver saw to her needs; there was Eton and there was Seacliff; there was England and there was Wales. All of it somehow carried her along despite her fumbling tongue and the scrapes she managed to get into. Life had been slipping through her fingers as if it were water, with no attempt on her part to taste of it fully, to understand how it flowed, to see if by her will she might somehow direct it. She had been, she thought, like a feather carried on a gentle wind, traveling with it to places exciting and wondrous, letting it guide her because she was content. If only, she thought then with a grin, a feather had the brains to change its own course.

But that part of her life was over.

Lying in the dark and seeing the sparks of fever gnaw at her mind and waste her body had been sufficient warning. Unless she stopped being that feather, unless she did something about the flowing water, it would all end as it had begun—without any mark of hers left to show she'd been there. And she was astonished to realize that this thought was not entirely new to her; somehow this regret for things unfulfilled and incomplete had reached her even as she'd worked on her father's ledgers. It was, then, more than dedication to the man's memory, and more than a familial obligation to the people who depended on Seacliff for their livelihood. It was something buried deep within her trying to break out. It was, she decided, nothing less than her own life.

And it was definitely not too late to do something about it.

A week passed in which she was determined to feed herself well enough to be able to get out of bed.

A second week passed with Gwen holding her waist tightly while she walked about the room in halting, short steps. Gwen swore mighty oaths reminiscent of Orin Daniels, and Caitlin's laughter soon lost its sickly, hollow sound. Oliver came in at least once a day, took a chair by the hearth and watched the lumbering parade with a mixture of bemusement and concerned resignation. He'd tried more than once to keep her under the covers until she was further into her lengthy recuperation, but Caitlin would have none of it.

"If I stay one more hour there," she'd said, pointing dramatically at the bed, "I'll become part of it, don't you see?

I'm not going to walk automatically, husband. I have to practice at it, keep at it, feed myself like a suckling pig and get my powers back."

"Your powers of speech haven't suffered for it," he muttered.

"You should be grateful for the weeks of silence." She smiled, allowing Gwen to help her to a chair into which she sank with a loud, grinning sigh. A spate of giggling followed, for no reason at all, and she sobered when Gwen left to fetch her dinner tray. "Oliver?"

He scowled and rose, stood with his back to the room, facing the balcony, though the French doors were closed. "You ask me every day, my dear, and every day I tell you the same bloody thing: The fruit was tainted, and the nostrums you were given did not contribute to your illness. They flushed the foul bile from your blood, but it took time. Time, Caitlin. It would have been the same for anyone."

"But I don't understand—"

He turned on his heels, a military about-face. "Neither do I, but it was done. I can only assume Mrs. Courder allowed the fruit to remain too long in her larder. She has been spoken to, I can assure you."

She shook her head to indicate that she still didn't understand but she refrained from saying more. And when it was clear that she was drained of protests, Oliver bade her a good evening and left. She stared at the hearth and wondered. Despite all the resolutions to remodel her life, she knew that Oliver was the one element she could not change. Once she'd gotten on her feet again, his concern had become perfunctory, and nothing anyone could tell her would convince her that he cared about her. It would be difficult, this new thing she was trying; by the same token, she had never gone quite so far as to convince herself it would be easy, either.

When Gwen returned with beef broth and vegetables, and a small goblet of wine, Caitlin asked her to stay awhile, and Gwen readily agreed, dropping to her knees to light the fire. She smiled mischievously as she dragged Oliver's chair closer to the hearth. A silence comfortable and gentle filled the room, and it was broken only after Caitlin had sponged the last of the gravy from her plate with fresh bread and had licked her fingers to capture every last drop. Releasing a sated sigh, she lowered the tray to the floor, her silk robe rustling as she pulled her legs under her and turned to face Gwen.

"Now," she said with a decisive nod, "you'll not put it off any longer, my dear."

"Oh, Caitlin . . ."

"For heaven's sake," she said, with a hint of exasperation, "where is it written that I must be shielded from the world for the rest of my life? Each time I ask you a question, if it's good news you bubble it all over me, and if it's bad, you pull a dreadfully sour face and tell me I must rest. Well!" She thumped her hands in her lap. "Well, I'm fed, and I'm rested, and I'm not feeling the least bit tired. So tell me, Gwen. Tell me about Davy, and what you've heard of Griff."

"Must I?"

"If you don't, I'll see to it you give Bradford his monthly bath for the next twenty years."

Gwen's feigned horror set them both laughing for nearly ten minutes, but when it was over Caitlin reminded her she'd not forgotten her question.

"Well . . . Davy is fine now, mistress. He sometimes feels the rain a bit, the weather, but he's good as new otherwise. Fact is, he'd be right pleased if you'd see him for a minute or two. When you're up to visitors, that is. He'll want to thank you for what you did."

Caitlin experienced a moment's embarrassment as she waved the thanks away. Davy had once again crossed words with Oliver, and her husband had decided it was more than high time he be made an example before the rest of the staff. Oliver had claimed the servants were growing rebellious, and this was the best way he could think of to bring them back in line. A few ill-chosen words, and a young man nearly lost his life.

"And Griff?" she said, wanting to change the subject so her temper would not rise. "Word?"

Gwen had told her of her trips to Falconrest to bring Griffin news of her illness, and she'd told her, too, of the mysterious attack on him toward the end of the month. Griffin would say little about it save that he gave as much as he got, but she'd seen the bruises and the gashes, the pained way he hobbled about the room while he asked about Cat, and she knew there was more in the telling than she'd been able to grasp.

"But this past fortnight I've heard nothing, mistress. I've not been able to go over, but I seen Master Randall who does work for him now and again, and he tells me the place is dark at night, and Jones isn't seen around neither."

"Perhaps," she said, "he's taken time off for one of his adventures."

"La," Gwen said, lifting her gaze to the ceiling. "He's adventures aplenty around here without going off and looking for them, if you ask me."

Another silence, this one weighted and hanging heavily between them.

Finally, Cat yawned in spite of herself, stretched and suggested she take to bed early. "I'll want to be out tomorrow," she said shyly, waiting for the storm of protests to begin. "I think it's time I stop playing hermit and let people know I'm still alive."

But there were no objections from Gwen, and that surprised her. She lowered her bare feet to the floor and leaned forward, staring at Gwen to try to read her face.

"What is it?"

"Tomorrow there's a hearing," Gwen told her. "It . . . it will be the second one since you took ill."

"What?" She jumped to her feet, shaking her head at the dizziness that had her grabbing for the back of the chair. "What? You mean to tell me, Gwen Thomas, that Sir Oliver has already presided over one hearing without me?"

"You . . . you were ill, Cat," Gwen pointed out, cringing into the chair away from Caitlin's outburst. "You were dying!"

"I was nothing of the sort," she cried. "And he should have waited. He should have waited!"

The hearing was an institution created by her great-grandfather to oversee legal disputes among the villagers. At least once during each two-month period the people of the valley would gather at Seacliff to present grievances against neighbors, ask permission to marry or to sell parcels of land; new families were introduced, births celebrated, levies collected, and fines assessed; and those who had committed crimes not covered by the master's domain were remaindered in a specially built cottage near the stables until the circuit judge arrived.

Under Caitlin's harsh questioning, Gwen revealed that Oliver had managed everything rather brusquely, with the estate's steward, James Flint, carrying out his orders with his band of retired soldiers. Oliver had also given a short speech on the need for soldiers in the king's army, since war had broken out in the American colonies; and if there was war in America, there was sure to be some fighting against the French who were Britain's age-old enemy and who would eventually side with the colonies. No one had come forward, but Oliver had continued to send messages into the village, and he was confident that sooner or later he would have a small troop ready for the king.

"He never said a word," Caitlin muttered, stumbling away from the fireplace to her bed. "He never said a word about a hearing. And he knows—he *knows*, Gwen!—that I must be there for his authority to be legal." She slumped to the mattress, feeling suddenly bone-weary. "What else?" she said, more to herself than to Gwen, who had followed her and was turning back the quilt. "What else has he taken from me while I've been in this damned place?"

Gwen's brow furrowed in concern. "You'd best not think about it now, Cat, really. You're not as strong as you think."

"My God!" she said. "That's all Oliver ever says. Take it easy, Caitlin; relax, Caitlin; marshall your strength, my dear, so we can have you well again." She raised a fist to the ceiling and brandished it fiercely. "Well, damn his eyes, I *am* . . . I am . . ."

Her eyes widened in mute panic as chills washed over her, and she drew up her legs, her teeth chattering, to keep warm.

"My . . . God," she whispered, and looked to Gwen, pleading. "My . . . Gwen, please! No, it can't be. It can't be, not again."

Gwen hustled her under the covers and pulled them up to her chin. "It's not," she said softly. "You're worked into a tizzy, and now you're paying the price. You rest, mistress. You just rest, and tomorrow you'll be right as rain again."

"Yes," Caitlin said. "Yes, yes I will."

She fell back to the pillows and clenched her teeth to keep them still. Gwen fetched the tray from the floor and tucked it under her arm. She glanced around the room, and she moved to each of the candles in their sconces and pinched them out until only the firelight was left. As a shadow, then, Gwen drifted out of Caitlin's vision, humming a lullaby and smiling, blowing her a kiss and closing the door softly behind her.

A hearing, she thought, alone in the half-light. He's taken over everything now, everything I own.

And though a cautionary voice told her it was only until she was well and mobile again, she could not help the tears she shed through the night.

19

SHE HEARD voices through the deep black fog that engulfed her; she wanted to speak, to scream, but she felt as though a gag had been stuffed into her mouth, and her eyelids seemed glued to the rise of her cheekbones—blinding her, though she knew her vision was still perfect. It was frustrating, it was horrifying, and the worst of it was that no one paid attention to her moaning.

". . . too much at once. I told you that, Major. Another reversal like this could very well prove fatal. You'll have to heed my prescriptions, and do that very carefully."

"I understand that, Doctor."

"I certainly hope you do."

"Well, you're certainly being forward for someone so deeply in my debt. Remember, sir, I have an estate to run—one of considerable size, lest your feeble brain fail to comprehend that fact. I cannot be in a hundred places at once."

"Nevertheless, you should have been more cautious. Now we'll have to do it right. Therefore, please see to it that Lady Morgan rests. Rests, Sir Oliver! There is no other cure for it in my experience."

"Can I take it you mean a great deal of rest, Doctor?"

"You may be sure of that, sir. You may be absolutely sure of that indeed."

"Then—"

"Then you will continue as you have done. And you'd best instruct whoever nurses this woman that on no account must she be permitted to leave her bed until—*until*, sir—I have given my permission."

"You have my word, Doctor."

"See to it you keep it. You don't want another body on your hands."

"Cat? Cat, can you hear me? Oh, God, Cat, please nod your head or something and let me know you can hear me. He'll be coming soon, and I must be quick. The cobbler, Tommy Williams, was brought before the hearing last week, and they said he's been hoarding gold under his hearth instead of paying his debts. He said nay, but Flint claims to have seen it. Sir Oliver took less than a minute to tell the cobbler he must repay his obligations within a fortnight or forfeit his home. He said nay again, but no one was listening. They dared not speak up for him, Cat. None of them dared speak up for him. It was terrible, but it isn't the end of it.

"Oh, God, can you hear me, Cat?

"Last night, it was gone midnight and Quinn Broary was out back of her place with Randall. You don't ask, and I won't tell. But they heard strange sounds from the Williams cottage that's right down the lane a bit, off the main road. They didn't do nothing about it, but they remembered it this morning, and they asked around the Stag's Head and places to see what's known. But there was nothing to be heard. Then Randall took himself to the cottage and the next thing you know the vicar was right by him, yelling and swearing and getting on his horse and riding right here to Mr. Flint.

"'Twas his duty, the reverend says. I suppose it was, but he didn't have to ride like the Brits were on his heels.

"The thing is, Cat, that Williams is gone! Wife, children, everyone gone from the whole place! Broary must've heard them packing it all together, I imagine. But it's odd they didn't hear the wagon moving out, isn't it? I mean, I would think you'd hear something of a loaded wagon on that miserable excuse for a road, wouldn't you?

"It's not good, Cat. It's not good at all.

"They've declared Williams an outlaw, and they've put gold on his head."

"What *are* you talking about, Bradford? This is Gwen Thomas here, not one of your whimpering underlings, like Mary."

"I will ignore that, woman."

"I wouldn't bet on it."

"Hold your tongue! Now, you will see to it she is bathed every other day, turned every four hours, and—"

"You bitten sod! Who the hell are you to tell me how to take care of my mistress, eh? You pomp around this house like it was your own, and do you once come up here to see how she's doing? Oh, no! Not the great and mighty Emmanuel Bradford, not you. You—"

"That is enough, woman."

"I am indeed woman enough for you, you old fart. More than enough. Now get the hell out of here before I take your hide to the fire!"

"The master will hear about this, I can assure you."

"The great and bloody master hears the damned crickets pissing, he does."

"You're in trouble, woman!"

"Fie, I've been in worse trouble from worse men than you."

She heard the voices and the comings and goings, but she could not feel heartened by her improving condition. While she did not seem to be suffering the same sort of fever as before, she was still enveloped in an invisible shroud of cotton, blinding her, gagging her, making her finally pray for the nightmares because at least they gave her movement.

"Good Lord, Mary, what d'you call this slop here?"

"Be broth, Thomas, be broth."

"Oh, my, aren't we feeling our oats today. I'm Thomas to you now? Like hell I am! You mind your place, girl, or I'll give you the kind of scars Davy has on his back."

"Not a muscle moves, Mr. Flint, as you can well see."

"A woman so lovely shouldn't be in such a condition, Sir Oliver."

"A noble sentiment, but wasted, I'm afraid. She neither sees nor hears us, Mr. Flint. She keeps her color because that Thomas bitch keeps the air on her, washes her like she was a baby, and feeds her with a spoon. Caitlin swallows readily enough, though I suspect she doesn't keep it all down."

"It isn't very good color."

"It isn't the color of death, either, Mr. Flint."

"It may as well be."

"It shan't be, Mr. Flint. It shan't be."

"When will she recover?"

"Soon. Soon."

"Radnor is back."

"Ah?"

"He was in London, doing a bit of snooping around."

"I see."

"He's not like the cobbler and his gold, Oliver. We have to be careful."

"Later, Mr. Flint. This is neither the time nor especially the place. Later. In my study."

Had she the wealth she would have ordered a cathedral built to rival Canterbury's the day she was able to discern shadows in her vision. A subtle separation of dark and light increased as time passed, sharpened as the sun strengthened, and burst into full, glorious color on an afternoon that tinged the room a curious gold.

And it was the same again when Gwen noticed her blinking. This time, however, Caitlin heeded the instructions given her, swallowed her water slowly, her food in small portions, and ordered Gwen not to tell anyone that she had regained her awareness.

Contrary to Oliver's belief and Gwen's fears, Caitlin did not attribute the conversations she had overheard to the fancies of bitter dreams. She recalled every word, every nuance, every sneered and sworn phrase, until she was ready to sort it out into meaning.

"Danger?" Gwen said, leaning away from the word Caitlin had uttered moments before as if it were an asp coiling to strike.

Caitlin nodded as she nibbled on a freshly cooked slice of mutton. "Danger. I am a healthy woman, Gwen, and don't you dare look at me as if I've gone 'round the bend. I am fully aware of what I'm saying. So mark me, Gwen, and mark me well: I am a healthy woman. If I fall ill, whether it be from tainted fruit or too much excitement, I do not fall abed like old Les with his ailments. I sleep, I heal, and I am myself again.

"This"—and she pounded a fist on the mattress—"is not natural. It is not right."

Gwen shook her head in confusion. She knew very well what Caitlin was implying, but the enormity of it threatened to engulf her in terror. Nevertheless, she listened carefully, and with increasing horror, as Caitlin related her husband's mutterings and gave her the interpretations.

"Now tell me this," she said, an impatient hand raised to keep Gwen from interrupting. "You brought me food and drink?"

Gwen nodded, frowning perplexedly.

"Mrs. Courder prepared it?"

Gwen nodded again.

"All of it? All the time? And you brought it directly here, right from the kitchen?"

Gwen started to nod a third time and caught herself. Her eyes narrowed, then widened as she touched her fingers to her lips thoughtfully.

"Well?"

"Well, I couldn't really bring it up all the time, Cat. I had to attend to my other duties as well." She scowled. "Sometimes Mary would do it for me, not that she really wanted to. But she did. She always made a hell of a mess giving you the broth. 'Twas all you'd swallow, but she managed to get more than half down your front, sure as I'm standing here."

Caitlin sank back against the pillows with a sigh. There'd always been that one glimmer of hope she was wrong, that what she feared was merely a figment of her dreams. But all it took was a few sips of broth, just a few drops, and Oliver would have his invalid right where he wanted her.

She would have wept had she not been so furious.

"But what could something like that be?" Gwen protested, still refusing to believe it.

"Oh, Lord, Gwen," she said wearily, "a bit of this and a bit of that. Powdered hawthorn, hollyhock, mistletoe ... so many things to keep me alive and dead at the same time." She went on, but by the time she was finished and Gwen convinced, the sun had slipped below the horizon, and a chill had crept into the shadowy room. Gwen, trembling, set the fire and lit the tapers nearest the bed. When warmth returned, Caitlin plumped the pillows and folded her arms over her chest.

"He doesn't want to kill me, of course," she said, wondering how she could make it all sound so ordinary, "but as long as I'm stuck up here, he can do what he wishes and tell others his decisions are made with my concurrence. Just as he claimed that everything before the illness was done with my father's consent. And if he's lying about this, then he lied fully about that."

She closed her eyes briefly. It had to be said, and Gwen had to hear it.

"My father . . ." She swallowed, and ordered herself not to lose courage now. Once articulated, the accusation could be dealt with; kept inside her, it would eat through her system like a worm through soil. "Gwen, I've no proof of what I'm about to say, but I am as sure of its truth as I am of being in this room. He was murdered, Gwen. My father was murdered that night in the storm!"

Gwen denied the words with a violent gesture that had her halfway across the room before Caitlin's harsh command stopped her and brought her reluctantly back. Then she explained about the storm's direction, the probable direction of the wind, and the height of the outer wall. The suspicion had taken root the day after she'd arrived back from Eton, but until now too much had interfered with the realization that her father had been murdered.

"But Cat," Gwen protested weakly, "you've been ill! Your mind . . . you said yourself that your mind hasn't been right for a long time. For a while you weren't sure what was real and what wasn't."

"There's nothing wrong with my thinking now, Gwen. There's nothing wrong with it at all. Look . . . I came here on the last day of June. Before a month passed, and just before the first hearing was scheduled, I was taken so ill I could not function until it was over. And just before another hearing came a-calling, I was back in bed again. Gwen, for God's sake, it's well into October! You can smell the season changing; you can smell the snow on the mountaintops. The harvesting has begun, and before long the valley will close down for the winter. I guarantee you I will not suffer again until spring. Until the land is ready to bring us gold and silver again."

"I . . ." Gwen covered her face with her hands, then dropped them and looked helplessly about the room. "I . . . but it's monstrous!"

"Yes," Caitlin said, with more restraint than she'd thought she could summon. "Yes, my dear, it's quite monstrous."

"But we must do something!"

"And so I think, too. But what? What can we do?"

It was a question she'd been thinking—dreaming—for months, tossing and turning in both her worst and her best dreams. But she still had no answers. There were scores of factors to consider, even—and she bridled each time the thought came to her unbidden—the possibility that she was entirely wrong,—that she was permitting Oliver's emotional indifference to her to affect her reason. What she required was what she'd found in Gwen—a devil's advocate. Gwen was incapable of comprehending a nebulous scheme in which the stakes were so high they would endanger the life of her mistress; and in attempting to grapple with it, she laid at Caitlin's feet any number of frivolous, cogent, and penetrating objections. One by one Caitlin dealt with them, either through outright recall of specific conversations, or with her instincts.

The debate ebbed, surged, at times became teary and at times sent them into gales of weary laughter until, at last, Caitlin's physical debility proved greater than her determination.

It seemed like hours before sleep found her after Gwen had left, hours more for the turmoil to subside in her mind; it took virtually all her strength—and more courage than she thought she possessed—to endure Oliver's daily visits, all the while studying his glances, his words, the tilt of his head for a clue to his real purpose; and by the end of the month she realized that unless something happened—unless she made something happen—her very sanity would retreat in the belief that it had all been a horrid dream.

She was walking outside again.

She had discovered early on that the residual effects of her illness proved immensely effective in getting for herself the privacy she craved. Oliver maintained a respectful, wary distance, seeing her only at meals and perhaps for a few minutes before she retired for the evening. He was solicitous and kind, but he diverted her queries about the running of the estate with a promise to keep her informed and to review with her all his actions "as soon as she was her old self again." At the same time she saw James Flint only at brief intervals and from afar. She sensed some small friction between the appointed steward and her husband, but she could learn nothing about it and wondered if her suspicions were beginning to affect her judgment. Not once did Flint attempt to approach her; not once did he offer her his sympathies, such as they were.

It was just as well.

Because as each day passed and the end of the month grew nearer, her self-doubts increased and Flint's mocking, cold presence might spark her into a rage.

Griffin Radnor did not come to her. Though she'd finally received word through Davy via the Stag's Head that lights once again burned at Falconrest, she'd heard that no one had approached the hillside mansion and no one had been seen leaving its gates. The massive black dogs Griffin kept as guardians frightened most potential visitors away, and those who persisted were politely but firmly turned aside by the cadaverous Richard Jones, Griffin's steward.

Three times since she had gathered her wits she had sent written messages to Griffin, but she had received no response whatsoever, though Davy had seen Jones slip the notes into his pocket. Worry had become feigned indifference, which in turn churned into righteous anger. The last time she had seen Griffin, he had pried from her an unspoken admission that her feelings toward him had not changed; but what of his feelings for her? If he was in love with her, if he cared a whit for her well-being, why hadn't he tried to contact her? At one point she'd riled herself into such a state that she'd ordered the roan saddled, but long before she reached the village she realized that her recovery had not yet extended to journeying on horseback. She felt humiliated, and that feeling fueled her anger further. And finally she decided that if this was the way he treated women, then Morag Burton was welcome to him for all she cared. She would carry on alone, and the hell with such damned arrogance.

A pricking sense of betrayal darkened her mood and made her temper volatile.

She took to avoiding even Gwen. Often she would throw on a heavy woolen cloak of deep blue and storm out to the cliff wall where she paced above the shore and ranted at the wind, then suffered silently as the tears welled in her eyes. Straightening up, she reminded herself she was no longer a child.

And so the last day of the month finally arrived.

She had eaten the largest breakfast served her in several

weeks, and she knew as she faced the rolling surf that she was finally healthy once more. The taste of the salty air, the feel of Seacliff's stone beneath her hands . . . it all felt as it should, and it gave her a sense of power she'd forgotten she possessed.

A sense of power and of justice.

In this strange, elated mood she was not dismayed when she saw Oliver striding hurriedly toward her, one hand holding his elegant military cape close to him, the other adjusting a plumed tricorne over his wig. He called to her, and she turned, pulling up her hood to keep the wind from her neck.

"My dear," he said, puffing as if he'd just run from the village, "I've just had word from friends in London. It seems those damned fools in the colonies have . . ." He blustered meaninglessly on for several seconds, until she laid a placating hand on his chest, frowning because she'd never seen him quite so solemn and excited at the same time.

"What?" she asked. "There've been some troubles, so you've told me, but it was nothing to worry about, you said."

"I was wrong," he admitted, pulling himself up. "Those idiots have actually fired upon the king's infantry again—near that Boston seaport place this time. Generals Howe and Burgoyne have been instructed to put the matter to rights immediately, but that means troops have to be raised. I have been asked to assist in preparing them, and to make ready in case the idiot French decide to commit suicide again."

She must have blanched, because he took her arms and smiled to reassure her.

"You're not to concern yourself, Caitlin, about such things. We will most certainly not be invaded, and I expect that it will all be over and done before next summer. Once the winter storms have cleared the seas, those fools will face the full might of His Majesty's battalions. They cannot win. And they will not win."

"But you—"

"As I've already said, if you'd only listen, I've got to see that men are recruited for the army. To that end, I shall be gone for some little while, though I expect to return before year's end. In my absence, James has been given my full consent and authority. You will see to it, please, that his wishes are as my own."

He leaned forward to kiss her cheek, and she had already offered it in some confusion before the import of his declaration reached home. Then she pushed herself away sharply.

"You said what to Mr. Flint?"

"My dear," Oliver said impatiently, "I have no intention of arguing with you. I have neither the time nor the inclination. You will do as you are told, and I *will* be kept informed of it. Make no mistake about that."

A stiff and swift bow followed, a half-salute with gloved hand, and then he marched across the lawn toward the stables, bellowing for Bradford, for Davy, and not turning once to wave her a farewell.

She stared after him, taking a single step in pursuit before in helplessness she stopped and wrung her hands anxiously. It wasn't possible things had progressed this far. Surely she hadn't abdicated. As boldly as a harlot in Petticoat Lane, Oliver had simply taken control, using first her grief and then her illness as a cover for his actions. And now...now all her plans to make Seacliff hers once again were dashed at her feet, shattered like a crystal chalice and ground to dust beneath his heel. With James in control, and without Griffin for support, it was hopeless. Entirely, completely, desperately hopeless.

A footstep sounded behind her, but she did not turn.

"My lady," Flint said, standing at her left shoulder and watching Oliver vanish around the corner of the south tower. "It appears your husband has a higher calling now."

She would not deign to look at him. Her voice was as cold as the wind from the sea. "I know what is happening, Mr. Flint."

"Mr. Flint?" he said, seemingly surprised. "And what happened to James, my lady?"

"James died months ago," she told him. "In fact, I don't believe he ever lived."

"A pity. He seemed such a bonny fellow."

"You bastard."

"Be careful, my lady. You heard the man. I'm to take charge."

He moved to stand beside her, but she started walking toward the house to keep him behind her. "There are those who have not yet given up on me, Mr. Flint. I don't know what you have in mind, but you will not have me quite so easily as you once did, and you'll not control me as you obviously do Oliver."

He followed her in silence for a moment, then reached out

suddenly and grabbed her shoulder. She squirmed under his grip, but he did not release her. Turning her roughly, he smiled as if they'd merely clasped hands.

"You speak of friends, my lady. I trust you don't mean the master of Falconrest."

With an effort she kept her expression severe. "I do."

"But, my lady, I thought your little Welsh spies would have told you by now." A finger to his chin, and he looked up at the mansion. "Ah, but I imagine it's rather too soon even for such lovely gossip."

"What are you talking about, Flint?" she demanded.

"Why, Griffin Radnor, my lady. He's been declared an outlaw, a scalawag with a bounty on his head."

She wanted to laugh, but her lips parted soundlessly.

Flint nodded. "Yes, you've heard me right, Caitlin Morgan. The man, as of dawn this morning, is an outlaw."

"But what's he done?" she cried.

"Done?" Flint laughed, a harsh barking sound. "Done? Why, my lady, he's a killer. He's wanted for murder."

20

THE SOFT touch of October's chill had hardened, become brittle, then turned into the dead cold of winter. Caitlin found her limbs locked in place, her throat constricted, her eyes glazed against the afternoon's dying light. Her first reaction was a vehement denial. Griffin might be many things, but a murderer he was not. Flint, however, had left her immediately after he'd offered the news that obviously delighted him, and she was unable to question him when her thunderstruck speech returned. Then, whirling around, she wondered bitterly what sort of trouble he'd gotten himself into this time: a brawl at the Stag's Head, perhaps, or something similar during his prolonged stay in London? His Welsh arrogance was such that she would not put it past him to use his fists to defend his country's honor, the result of which might very well be the accidental death of his opponent.

But murder? That implied a premeditated deed, and Radnor, for all his disdain for the trappings of wealth and the opinions of others, would never purposely take a life. Never.

She glanced around helplessly, fighting her panic. Then, as her concern for his safety galvanized her, she broke into a headlong run toward the stables, her cloak billowing and rippling behind her, her hood catching the wind and slipping from her head. As she raced over the grass she cried out for Davy, and sobbed her relief when he poked his head out the stable door. He gaped at the sight of her and reached inside for a large, sharp rake, holding it to his chest while he searched her wake for the culprit in pursuit.

"My horse!" she called as she neared him. "Saddle my horse instantly, Davy!"

He hesitated. He remembered clearly the last time she'd attempted riding before she was ready, and he wanted no responsibility for another near accident. Especially now that the master was gone and the demon Flint was left ruling in his place.

Caitlin would not be denied. She shoved past him when he didn't move from her path, fairly pushing him inside and reaching for the bridle hanging on the wall. Sputtering complaints all the while, hurrying as fast as he could with his back half-bent, he brought the roan from its stall. Before the animal was fully out, Caitlin was palming the bit between its teeth, simultaneously snapping at Davy to fetch the saddle, or did she have to do everything herself?

Moments later she was in the stableyard, sawing at the reins to keep her mount from rearing. "Get inside," she instructed, "and tell Gwen to be in my rooms when I return. Then . . ." She cut herself short and frowned. Behind her in the carriage house, there was an empty space where the first coach should have been. "Why aren't you with Sir Oliver?" she demanded.

Davy, who had already braced himself to sprint to the tower, almost stumbled in an effort to turn around in the same move. "He says he don't need me, mistress. He had one of Mr. Flint's lads take the bench for him."

There was no time for speculation. She merely jerked her

head to send him on his way, then kicked at the roan's flank. The horse reared in surprise, then bolted across the grass, nearly throwing Caitlin from its back. Leaning forward to minimize the effects of the wind, she squinted as she guided the animal onto the lane and down over the rise. There had been a flicker of movement at the front doors, but she didn't look back. Whether it was Bradford or Flint watching made no difference to her. Neither one would come after her.

Wall and trees swam into a single colorless blur as she sped toward the village; dead leaves already littering the roadway swirled under the horse's hooves in small dervishes. The ice-tinged air snapped red into her cheeks, penetrated her ruffled blouse and made her shiver. Her hair spun over her back, its color a perfect complement to the autumn shades that swept over the valley in breathtaking abandon. A whiff of burning leaves and twigs, the sharp aroma of cider fermenting in someone's yard still, the cutting scent of the sea as it cooled down toward winter—all of fall's delights were lost on her as she galloped past the church and ignored a startled wave from Reverend Lynne.

Around the commons she raced until she reached the village proper.

Martin Randall, standing in front of his tin- and goldsmith's shop, reached up to doff his cap out of respect for her but he wasn't fast enough. She was there and gone, and he wondered if she was trying to catch up with her husband's coach, which had also barreled through the village as if the devil himself were prodding the horses' rumps. He shrugged. 'Twas no concern of his these days, and maybe it would be better if she did catch him, and not return. Though he was sorry for her being sickly these past weeks, he felt nothing more than he would have if his own dog had fallen ill. After all, at the last hearing the major had refused his petition to wed Quinn Broary, the reason being that the army would be through soon to pick up new recruits, and the major in his kindness did not wish Mistress Broary to wed now and find herself a widow in a year's time. And in Martin's view—as in the views of many others— what the major thought, so did the mistress. Which was a pitying shame. She had been such a fine young woman before the marriage had changed her.

Similar thoughts passed sadly through the mind of Susan

Sharnac, the seamstress, when Caitlin flew past her cottage. She'd been working on a terribly fancy new uniform for that horrid Mr. Flint when she'd heard the frantic hoofbeats and thought someone was being chased by a ghost through the village. Peering through her window, however, and seeing who it was, she only snorted, turned and took out her sudden ill temper on the girls sewing in the dim light of the parlor, cursing Caitlin Morgan for making her remember how it once was.

Ellis Lynne, wringing his hands and frowning, watched as Caitlin reached the last of the houses and began the rough climb toward the gap in the barrier hills. And when she turned off onto the lane to Falconrest, his frown deepened. What did she know? he asked himself worriedly, and did Mr. Flint know where she was going? He vacillated, torn between the urge to follow—at a discreet distance, of course—and the temptation to hurry up to Seacliff with the news of Caitlin's flight. But by the time the dust had settled on the road it was too late. And just as well. He'd already done enough for the estate's steward over the past few months, and he thought he could afford to let this item pass. Besides, it wouldn't do for him to be seen at the ancient castle so soon after the previous night. People might talk. People might put their heads together, do some figuring on their fingers, and come up with four. And that, beyond doubt, would never do at all.

A woman's voice called his name petulantly.

He glanced toward the rectory and away again. He wasn't exactly ready for her again, not now, and he was beginning to doubt, too, the high value he'd placed on that bit of Flint's largesse. The idea of taking in a young woman, unmarried and with a child, had increased his standing in the village, and his reputation as a true Christian. After all, the Reverend Lynne was known for his piety, sobriety, and chastity. What safer place for Morag Burton than in his keeping? He grinned, and quickly released a grateful prayer that the child had spared him the honor of having any of his features.

Caitlin was aware of none of the faces looking on as she rode from the commons to the high road; she concentrated only on keeping her seat on the roan as it took the sharp turn into Radnor's Lane, slid heart-stoppingly, and burst forward straight out again. She was sitting taller now, trying to spot movement around Falconrest as she approached it. But it had been so long since she'd been there that she'd forgotten what was normal, and she 'slowed when the towering trees about the wall blocked her view.

The sun had dipped lower. Shadows crossed the lane to huddle at the wall's base. A long chain hung from a hole in a wooden box near the gate, and without dismounting she grabbed and yanked it. In the distance she could hear the tolling of a deep bell. She pulled the chain again and maneuvered the roan so that she was framed in the gateway. A hand quickly combed through her hair and pulled the cloak more snugly across her chest.

She waited.

She wondered at the lack of fierce barking that should have accompanied her summons.

The feeling that someone was watching her became overpowering, and she looked up and down the lane, half expecting to see Flint coming toward her, insolently, confidently, and at his own pace. But there was no one. The lane was deserted, and Falconrest looked on indifferently.

She pulled the bell chain again, and the deep ringing had barely been caught by the breeze when she saw Jones striding across the grass from the side of the mansion. He was wearing a black frock coat, a puffed black ascot, black breeches, and stockings. Never a garrulous man, he seemed to intend by his dress and demeanor to cow people into leaving before he'd spoken a word. She saw him falter as soon as he recognized her, and she raised a hand to beckon him should he decide not to admit her.

He came on, however, stopping only ten feet from the gates.

"Richard," she said anxiously, "I've just heard about Griffin. I must talk with him."

Jones, with lean face and sparse black hair seemingly set in plaster, blinked once.

"Richard, for God's sake, you know who I am!"

"I do, m'lady," he said, his voice matching his funereal appearance, somber and humorless. "Master Griffin is unavailable."

Her hand clenched in front of her tightly. "Dammit, Richard . . ." She put the fist to her lips and forced herself to think. "You are positive he will not receive me."

Jones nodded, without expression.

"Will you give him a message?"

The steward nodded again.

"Tell him—" She knew what she was about to say was irrevocable, but if he was goaded to come to her so she could learn the truth, she was willing to take the chance. "Tell him I recall our conversation at the ringstones. He told me something then; you need not know what it was. Tell him he was right. Tell him I must talk with him before he does something stu—before he acts on the ridiculous accusation made by his enemies. Do you have that, Richard?"

Jones nodded a third time and, neither bowing nor a waving, he turned and began walking away.

"Richard!" she called after him frantically. "I will wait at Seacliff for his answer."

The bay had turned a deep gray-green, and the swells heaved laboriously as the tide moved into shore. Gulls and terns skimmed low over the water, heading for the coves south of the valley where the wharves were receiving the fish-laden trawlers. The horizon was blurred with a faint gray mist, and through it the cyclopean red glare of the sun spread sullen fire over the surface.

Caitlin retreated from the balcony reluctantly, closing the door softly behind her and leaning back against it with a sigh. Her cloak was draped over the back of Oliver's chair; her blouse was unlaced to expose a fair portion of her breasts. Her hand toyed idly with the tip of one lace, the other hand slapped impatiently at the side of her skirt. Against her back the panes felt cold, but she only straightened her shoulders; she did not move away.

He hadn't come.

Somehow, during the long ride back, during the interminable dinner, she'd thought Griffin would be right behind her, pounding on the doors before she'd done with her fruit. But everything had remained quiet. Not even Flint had left his apartments to distract her with his acerbic commentary.

And Gwen . . . Despite Caitlin's instructions she was not in the house, and no one seemed to know where she had gone.

With a shudder, then, she pushed away from the French doors and took a lighted taper from its sconce over the mantel. Cupping the fragile flame with the palm of her hand she knelt to light the kindling, and with a series of gentle puffs she set the logs to blazing. She blew out the taper and set it down beside her, held her hands to the dancing fire and felt the warmth flow comfortably up her arms.

The sunset's red glow shifted to black night.

The heat of the fire brought a flush to her cheeks and forehead, made her open her blouse even farther. A vagrant thought told her to move back, but she remained seated in place; a cramp in her calves made her grimace, but she remained; and when the silence of the great house grew too heavy for her, she finally pushed herself to her feet and turned to make her way downstairs.

But Griffin was standing in the doorway.

"You asked for me," he said.

Not all the candles had been lighted, but the flames behind her bronzed his face and flicked shadows across his chest. He was cloaked and booted, and from one hand dangled a bulging canvas rucksack.

Recovering swiftly from the shock of seeing him, she lifted a hand to cover her exposed breasts. "I wanted to know," she said softly, her throat dry, her tongue moistening her lips. "I was told—"

He dropped the rucksack and with an arched brow crossed to stand before her. "You were told I've been branded an outlaw. Perhaps you were told I was granted this honor because I killed a man."

She nodded once, quickly, aware of his penetrating gaze and the tiny reflection of flame in his dark eyes.

His smile was sour as he stood beside her to watch the fire. "Do you believe this of me, too?"

She would not turn away; she faced him squarely. "You would never murder, Griffin Radnor. I don't care what anyone says, you would never murder a man."

His voice was soft, almost tender. "Thank you, Cat. But a man died last night."

She closed her eyes, drew her lips between her teeth and bit down.

"I knew you were well," he continued quietly, head down, one hand massaging the back of his neck. "Lovely Gwen could have been lashed like Davy, but she let me know how you were in spite of the danger. I sent messages, but you were too ill to receive them. I did send messages—just as I sent you letters in Eton."

I never heard them, or read them, she thought in dismay; I never received any of them at all. But she kept her silence.

"And one time . . . well, one time I even tried to come to you for a moment, but I was . . . detained, as it were." He grunted at the memory. "They should have killed me, but they didn't. I don't know why."

"Flint."

"Yes, and your husband."

She turned to him, startled, then laid a hand to his arm. "Oliver? But why? Why you? I knew, I suspected he wanted Falconrest, but to go to such lengths!" She shook her head in disbelief.

"There's more, Cat, much more." His hand stole to hers and pressed it to his arm. "Shortly afterward, I went to London. Oliver is not the only one who knows men not exactly eager to meet the king. I made some inquiries, heard some talk and—" His move was swift. Before she knew what had happened he was holding her shoulders, peering at her intently as if searching for a lie, hoping for a truth. "Surely you must know."

"I know nothing, Griffin," she said. "It is hard enough to imagine that Oliver brought me down himself, with some sort of potion, and in that time . . ." Her face twisted, and her lips quivered. "While I was ill, Seacliff was taken from me. Oh, it was my fault, too. I was more than ready to let him take over the responsibilities, much as he did when Father died. I wanted all the fun, Griffin, the way it used to be. But by the time I realized that most of the fun came from Father's hard work, it was too late."

He nodded. "There aren't many who would believe that, you know, but I do. Most of them in their little huts would rather continue in their belief that you've gone English. And I feared so, too," he admitted in shame. "Then you were ill, and I was attacked, and in London and elsewhere I learned about some of Morgan's underhanded dealings."

"What?" she demanded. "What more can there be?"

"An army," he said. "A troop, actually. A hundred men or so."

"Well, I already know about that," she told him. "He's been summoned to London to raise an army for the fighting."

Griffin laughed shortly and shook his head as he would to

a child who insisted on believing a fancy. "Cat, you will never learn, will you? It's all there before you, and you'll never learn at all."

"Learn what, for heaven's sake?"

"Sir Oliver went to London, yes. But not to raise an army. He means to bring together those men himself . . . and to bring them back here."

"I don't . . . that's impossible! It's not sensible."

"Sensible, sane, I don't care what you say it isn't, but it's true. Why he's doing it, I don't know yet. I was hoping to find out more last night. I was at the Stag's Head, hoping to buy a few gins for a man of Flint's and let him babble. But I was a fool to think it would be so easy. He led me outside for a wee talk, and I was done at again. This time a man died, and Flint's men were witnesses against me."

She saw then the ugly bruises at his temple, and the deep scratches that ran like claw marks along his neck. She touched them with a finger, and he covered her hand tightly.

"I didn't kill him, Cat. I never touched him. There was a man, a great skeleton of a man—"

"With a white patch," she whispered, and told him quickly where she'd seen him first, then listened as he explained how the others had pinned him down while they claimed he'd been the one to murder the man. A lucky lunge, however, freed him, and he returned to Falconrest.

"And I must leave that, too," he said, his regret couched in anger. "The king's men will be here within a few days, and since Flint's the steward here and no villager's willing to speak up for fear of his life . . . I must leave. For a while I must leave."

She tossed doubt and caution aside. Fear and loneliness overcame her as she cried out and flung her arms around him, burying her face against his chest. He could not leave her, not now when she needed him most. With Griff gone, who would fight for Seacliff with her? What powers of her own could she bring forward against a man who thought her nothing more than a dead flower to be uprooted and cast aside?

She wept while he stroked her back and glared at the fire; she sobbed as his hands slipped into the nest of her hair and warmed themselves there; she lapsed into a mournful silence while she felt his lips press against her forehead.

"Where . . . where will you go?" she asked, already knowing the answer.

His voice carried a brave attempt at a smile: "Where do all good Welsh outlaws go, Cat?"

The mountains. So often a precious setting for her dreams, now grown forbidding as they beckoned Griff Radnor. He would not return. She knew he wouldn't. The men who fled there were condemned to fighting for survival, every so often creeping down to a village for foodstuffs or news, then fleeing again into the mountains as sentries of the king's army made their haphazard way through the land. And the danger was doubled by those who, for a few silver coins, betrayed the outlaws' presence to a steward or a nobleman anxious to keep on the good side of his sovereign.

No, he was as good as dead. At this very moment she was embracing a dead man.

He softly touched her chin, lifting it and locking gazes with her while he traced the lines of her face, the fullness of her lips, the velvet course of her throat with his finger.

"Griff," she said huskily as he bent down to kiss her, "take me with you."

"Yes," said James Flint from the doorway. "Why don't you do that, Mr. Radnor? Why don't you do that, and add kidnapping to the charges."

Caitlin spun out of Griffin's embrace before she knew what she was doing, marched up to Flint, and faced him with her fists at her hips. She paid no heed to the two men who flanked the steward; she saw only the spark in Flint's eyes, and she wanted to snuff it out.

"Get out," she hissed. "Get out of my quarters."

"You presume too much, my lady," he answered, his gaze shifting to Griffin. "You are harboring a criminal here, and it's my duty—"

"Your duty be damned!" she cried, and slapped him as hard as she could. When he recovered after a few startled seconds, he attempted to snare her hand, but Caitlin ducked agilely under his arm and butted her head into his stomach. Taken unawares, Flint was driven back into his men. He lost his balance and toppled to the floor. Caitlin threw herself on top of him, forming her hands into talons that raked his face while her feet kicked blindly at his shins and calves. He bellowed, while the others were too astounded to do anything but gawk. And their hesitation was their undoing. As soon as Caitlin had slapped Flint, Griffin exploded into a dead run that had him leaping over the sprawled bodies into the outer rooms, slamming doors behind him as he headed for the ground floor and a safe exit.

Before long, Flint grabbed her wrists and pulled her away, then lumbered awkwardly to his feet while shouting orders for the pair of guards to begin the chase without him.

When they were alone, disheveled and panting, he flung her hands away as if they were contaminated.

"You will not get away with this, my lady," he vowed.

"I have," she told him with more courage than she felt.

"No," he said. "You may think so now, but I can tell you it's not true." He brushed at his jacket, at his shirt, then straightened his hair. Releasing a sniff, he began walking away. But as if having second thoughts, he reached the corridor doorway and looked back at her over his shoulder. "Look outside, my lady, look outside. It's coming winter, in case you hadn't noticed. And once I am done with you, you'll be wishing I would be as merciful to you as I was to your father. He died swiftly. You shall not be so lucky."

And as he closed the door softly behind him, he was smiling.

PART THREE

Captive

Seacliff, Wales, 1775–1776

21

LIKE THE almighty fists of an enraged God rising out of the netherworld, stormclouds appeared over the horizon. They came as black, gray, vivid streaks of white, dull flashes of blue-white that struck like swords in manic fury; titanic monsters crying for prey. Soaring over the water that churned below, they dragged dark veils of rain beneath them, gusting wind that tore at the treetops, turned piles of dead leaves and fallen twigs into maelstroms of ghostlike creatures. The flocks headed instantly for their pens; the herds lumbered toward their barns. Horses reared in their stalls, pawing at the air, their eyes widened in fear; birds huddled in their nests, chickens and hogs scrambled for their shelters; and hearths throughout the valley steadily moaned as the wind took grip of even the chimneytops.

Martin Randall reached through his casement windows and drew the heavy shutters closed. Locking them, he lowered the windows to cut off the drafts that stabbed ice at his bare arms. He was stripped to the waist in spite of the deadly cold, the fires of his forges giving him heat enough to withstand almost any freezing weather. His back muscles rippled as he bent over to lift an iron-banded chest from the floor, and as he turned to carry its dead weight into the back room, the firelight caught the shadow of a mark. It reached up over his waistband at his spine—a wing, an iridescent wing that his forges had scorched dark over the years since he'd had the figure tatooed in southern Spain. None in the village had ever heard of such bodily defilement before, and after his return he'd been castigated and made fun of until his great strength in wrestling had subdued most of his detractors.

The women, on the other hand, found the design intriguing, and more than once he'd been able to lure them into his bed on the promise that they'd see the image in all its wickedness. He grinned mirthlessly as he thought of the way Quinn Broary had traced its outline with her hands, then grinned more widely as he kicked open the door and saw her start from his pallet. He nodded toward the back, and holding a sheet to her naked figure she unlatched the door. Wind immediately invaded the cottage, but Randall ignored it. He had no idea if his contribution, and that of a few others, would be picked up on such a night; on the other hand, it was on just such nights that they came down from the mountains to replenish themselves. He knew it was a risk. Only last week a farmer who worked land at Falconrest had been flogged to death for spreading rumors that Griff Radnor had bested Flint in a fight somewhere in Seacliff.

No one cared if it was true or not; just the thought of Radnor strolling into the lion's den, den of English thieves, was sufficient to bring a secret smile to most men's lips.

Randall lugged the heavy chest to a copse at the rear of the house, shoved it far out of sight and dusted his hands on his thighs. His skin prickled at the rapidly approaching storm, and he tasted snow in the air. And finally he felt the cold. The image of Quinn's arms, then, her red hair and round, ruddy face sent him hurrying back inside. When she embraced him he was shivering, and she knew without asking that it was not just the cold.

Orin Daniels knelt by his father's side. The old man had lapsed into sleep three days before, and when appeals to the major had fallen on deaf ears, he had finally summoned the vicar. Lynne was standing in the shadows, a handkerchief to his nose and his sweating brow creased against the stench of dying. The heat of the fire burned fiercely in the small room.

"Well?" Orin demanded without turning around.

"I have said the prayers, Master Daniels," the vicar replied primly. "There is nothing more I can do. We must commend his soul to heaven."

Orin turned on his knees, his face dark with sorrow. "But don't ye have a potion or somethin'? Can't ye do somethin' for him?"

"My prayers—"

Orin made a loud, disgusted noise that made Lynne look away. Then he rose and snatched a worn brown cloak and floppy-brimmed hat from their pegs. "Ye'll stay here, if you please, Reverend."

Lynne seemed suddenly frantic. "But, Mr. Daniels, I—"

"I must fetch the mistress and Davy. I be returnin' within the hour."

He was gone before Lynne could protest further, and the vicar backed as far away from the sickbed as he could. Old Les was virtually a corpse already, and the vicar could feel his skin crawl at the thought of staying very long in the presence of a dead man. Thank God, he thought, for the gold hidden in his mattress. As soon as spring arrived he would pack Morag and his clothes and leave this accursed village, this valley, and if possible the entire country. Now that Lady Morgan seemed to have relinquished all control of Seacliff to her husband and his steward, the vicar's spying role was over. And he did not like the way Flint had been looking at him lately.

Night fell early when the storm finally covered the sky. The bay had turned white and was pounding at the cliffs, the trees were bent almost to the ground, the windows rattled in their frames. Within the walls of Seacliff, nature's fury was muted, but Caitlin could feel the power of the storm in spite of the near silence.

She sat alone in the dining room on the right side of the central hall. The vast, long oak table gleamed in the candlelight, and reflected the glint of silver and gold. A plate of mutton, gravy, and greens had been set before her, but though she was hungry she picked at it as if she were already sated. She was stalling. The longer she was able to remain at the table, the less time she would have to spend in her rooms. Over the weeks since Griffin had fled the mansion and Oliver had returned, she could not help feeling that the place where she had been born had turned fiendishly into her prison.

Though neither Flint nor Oliver had ever mentioned that fateful night's episode, from the following morning she was followed everywhere. When she left the house, the man with the white patch—whose name she'd discovered was Nate Birwyn—would appear somewhere behind her, keeping his distance but making no bones about the instructions he'd been given. Inside, either Oliver or Flint contrived to remain either in the same room with her or in an adjoining one. And when she was in her apartments, there was Gwen to contend with.

Gwen had finally broken down one evening in hysterical weeping and, at Caitlin's tender urging, had told her of all the abuse, physical and otherwise, she'd suffered at Oliver's hands. And worse; the day Caitlin had gone to warn Griffin, Gwen had been with Flint. He'd taken her away from staff quarters on a pretext, practically dragging her into his own rooms, where he raped her. Repeatedly. Then he threatened her life if she ever told a soul, and did not release her until he learned there was a man in Caitlin's room.

"Yesterday's ken." That's what her father had called the ability to understand an event long after it had happened. And now she felt she also had been raped by Mr. Flint. In Eton. Oliver must have known about that, encouraged it even, in order to bewilder and confuse her; just as he had known of Flint's murdering her father. From the very moment he had ridden into the valley years ago, the retired major had known Seacliff was the perfect prize to make good his dreams of grandeur.

And he was supported not by an army, as Griffin had predicted, but by a large band of mercenaries modeled after the Prussians, available for hire to anyone who had the gold. English, French, it made no difference to him. All those so-called business meetings were actually spent in enlisting rapacious, soulless men whose loyalty to him would remain unquestioned; and Flint had been given the task of arming them.

The valley, then, was their goal: enclosed, small, guarded by cliffs and mountains, hidden away on the west coast beyond the truly effective reach of London's law; David Evans, usually canny and this time gullible, had seen in the major only what the major wanted him to see; and Seacliff was for him nothing more than a continuous source of revenue until his band was ready to be launched.

For Caitlin the truth had struck home when, just after the first of December, she had seen him arriving at the head of a column of motley carts and wagons. They were transporting his troops. At first unbelieving, she ranted and despaired, but she had no means of resistance when, with a stern glance and a venomous smile, Morgan had laid down the law. His law. Morgan's Law.

What gratitude she could find was reserved for his ceasing to maintain the sham of their marriage. Since the day he paraded in with his troops, she appeared at dinners when required or in front of visitors when summoned, and she played the role of hostess perfectly. To do otherwise would mean an "accident" like her father's, and though she had wished for such an escape during those first dismal days, something happened to change her mind. It was neither dramatic nor, in the eyes of others, very important. But its significance to the salvation of a resolution nearly forgotten was incalculable.

Gwen had come to her one morning with news that a dozen of Morgan's men had been spotted reveling near the ringstones. They'd been drinking, and before order could be restored by one of the self-proclaimed sergeants, the remaining standing monoliths had been toppled from their places. Two had shattered into chunks; the rest had been vandalized—desecrated, Gwen had called it.

Of all the relics in the valley, the stones of the Druids were the oldest. They had withstood the test of time and armies and had been a great source of pride to the villagers in spite of their superstitious avoidance of the area. Now even the sanctity of the ringstones had been sullied.

Caitlin was determined not to give in to despair.

She stared at her plate and forced herself to eat. Languishing would not give her strength, and she needed food to maintain her energy. And when she was done she pushed away from the table, gathered the folds of her skirts in her hands and walked toward the gallery with every intention of going to bed. The storm had worsened, but she tried to ignore the thrashing and thundering; by dwelling on them she only worried about how Griffin was faring and whether he was safe, warmly clothed, living in someplace other than a dank cave.

She had almost reached the first step when Mrs. Courder bustled out of the side corridor and gave her Orin's message. Immediately, Caitlin followed, accepting a hooded cloak in the common room and allowing the burly farrier to take her arm and guide her through the screaming wind to the cottage. She did not look back. Nate Birwyn would be out there somewhere, and she prayed fervently he would freeze to death before she returned.

"My goodness," she gasped as Orin wrestled the door shut against the storm. "I nearly lost—" She stopped when she saw the vicar smiling wanly at her from the hearth. He was pale and perspiring heavily, and he held his Bible as if it were made of lead. She nodded to him brusquely and crossed immediately to Les. Davy was standing at the foot of the bed, cap crushed in his hands, eyes red though not tearing. She took his hands briefly, then turned to the old man.

At first she thought he was already dead, but when Orin leaned over and whispered something in his ear, the parchment eyelids fluttered open, and he stared at her without blinking.

"Mistress?"

"Here, Les," she whispered, taking Orin's place beside him and laying a hand on his chest. "I'm here, you old fool."

"It be the time, y'know," he said, the words rattling in his throat.

Her eyes burned. "You wouldn't dare leave me before spring."

"I canna hold any longer, mistress." He coughed loudly, and she wiped his mouth with a corner of her cloak. "But I did want t'have a word wi' you before I be gone."

"M'lady," Lynne protested from his place by the fire, "I really think it'd best for him if he were permitted to—"

"Ah, close your trap, y'bloody English swine," Les hawked as loudly as he could. "I be doin' my own affairs in my own house, if you please."

"Well!" the vicar huffed, and held his hands out to the fire, glancing fearfully out the window every few moments as the wind shrieked through the eaves.

"Les," Caitlin soothed, "you mustn't permit yourself such excitement. I've told you I won't allow—" She stopped when his bony hand touched her arm for silence.

"Mistress," he said, "I knew your father when we was both lads, and I held ye not long after you was born. I built your cradle, and I sewed your saddle, and afore I took this sickness I . . ." He gestured with his free hand, and Davy reached inside a grimy closet and pulled out something covered with a sooty sheet. At a nod from his father, he pulled the sheet off. It was a handsome cradle, carved out of driftwood and walnut. Its rockers were black oak inlaid with carved hawthorn.

Caitlin was not ashamed to feel the tears on her cheeks, and as the vicar gasped and Orin swallowed what might have been a sob, she leaned over and kissed him hard on both cheeks.

"I'll not see your babes," he wheezed, "but when they come, you must have a party for 'em. A grand thing it will be, and you must invite us for the christenin'."

"Oh, Les . . ."

She stopped then, nearly frightened when his clawlike grip suddenly tightened.

"I hear things," he whispered, his strength visibly failing.

She leaned over the bed and tilted her head near his mouth.

"Them boys of mine, they talk here at nights. I'm dyin', mistress, but I know what's goin' on. And I know ye be thinkin' how to . . ." His eyes darted to the vicar, who was struggling into his cloak and hat, muttering to himself. The old man spoke more rapidly, and Caitlin couldn't catch all his words. ". . . to Marty Randall, he'll know how to reach . . . Not alone, mistress. Don't try it alone or . . . damned light's so dim . . . way to save a tree is cut off the limb and . . . give the babe a party, I'll come m'self, I swear it. You give . . . cut off the . . ."

He choked, and Caitlin leaned back, still holding her hand near his chin. Then his chest suddenly expanded and his eyes opened wide, his jaw dropped, his hands grabbed for the tattered blanket. A moment later, his chest sank, his lips shut, and the lids of his eyes finally closed.

She kissed his forehead and rose unsteadily, shaking off Davy's helping hand. She barked a name, and the vicar spun around at the door. "You are to give this man a funeral the valley will never forget, do you understand me, Reverend? The children will sing, there will be flowers—I don't care where you get them—and you will give the best sermon you have ever preached in your life. Do you hear me, Reverend Lynne?"

The vicar's head bobbed up. "I will let the major know—"

"Lynne," she said, the name lashing out like a whip, "you do know who I am, don't you?"

"M'lady—"

"Exactly," she said. "And you needn't concern yourself about Sir Oliver. I will tell him myself."

"As you wish," he said unctuously, and was out the door before anyone could stop him.

"Orin," she said then, "I would be grateful if you would take me home now." But as she adjusted the cloak snugly around her throat she stared at him firmly. "I meant it, Orin Daniels. I meant every word I've just said."

"Yes, m'lady," he muttered, a hand quickly at his brow.

"And one more thing. If I hear one more word of English spoken at Seacliff, *I* will have you sacked, do you understand?"

Orin grinned. "Yes, m'lady."

She softened at the smile and took hold of his shoulder. "Small things, Orin Daniels, and I know that full well. But there are starts and there are standings, and we'll never get anywhere by simply standing about and moaning. You tell the others. I may have to stand beside my husband, but I do not stand with him. You know that; the others do not. They may not believe you now, but they'll remember you told them."

She looked back at the bed and sighed. "He gave me a great deal, Orin. And tonight he gave me something more precious than anything in my life."

He frowned his lack of comprehension, but she dared not tell him what had sprung full-blown to her mind while she'd been ordering the vicar around. It was an idea so daring, so foolhardy, she tried every imaginable way to dismiss it. But every time she found an argument, its absolute magnificence made her cheeks ache with a broad smile.

She hurried then to the house, only vaguely aware snow had begun falling, and returned the cloak with breathless thanks. The next twenty minutes she spent hunting for Oliver.

He was in the back drawing room. A full score of candles were burning, making the room illuminated to the point of near daylight. At her entrance, Oliver looked up from his chair where he'd been reading the open book on his lap. It was clear he was expecting an outburst of a sort, but his puzzlement grew when she only wandered about the room humming to herself and lightly dusting the pine panels.

"Caitlin?" he asked as if unsure it was her.

"Yes, Oliver?"

"Is there something you wish to discuss?"

"No, but . . . oh, Oliver, I've just been to the Daniels's cottage. I'm sorry to tell you that old Les has died." She managed a sorrowful expression. "The vicar was there, too. I've asked him to prepare the funeral; I hope you don't mind."

Suspicion narrowed his eyes, and she feared she'd gone too far. But she found her apprehension was unfounded; he nodded his approval, then leaned back to wait for more.

She took a deep breath and decided it was time to oblige him.

"Oliver, in three days it will be January, you know."

He grunted.

"And being with Daniels at his end has made me think." She had finally reached her chair and dropped into it gravely.

Perching on the edge of the cushion, she stared at him with a small, shy smile. "January, as you know, is the month of my birthday."

"I know that," he said, barely restraining his impatience.

"I don't like dying, Oliver," she told him in such a flat tone his squint vanished and his suspicion returned. "And that's what I've been doing since you returned, you know. Dying."

"My dear—"

"Oliver, please, this is not the easiest task I've carried out in my lifetime."

She held her breath; he searched her face, her eyes, for signs of betrayal, of chicanery, of manipulation for some secret end. But all he saw was contrition and he pushed himself straighter in his chair, allowing the book to slide to the floor. Magnanimous, she thought; he's ready to grant a boon.

"Neither of us is a fool, Oliver. I have a fair notion of what you've been doing, and what you wish to do. I know why you need Seacliff. And I know, too, that to prevent open rebellion against you, you must have me on display at least once in a while."

Suddenly, he appeared uncomfortable. As if, somehow, he had lost the advantage of intimidation.

"Oh, I'm not blind, Oliver. I know my life is yours for a whim, and please don't interrupt; this is most difficult already. My life is quite literally in your hands, and I've no means to escape. But I don't *want* to die, Oliver. I *refuse* to die. If you could have seen that dirty old man..." She gave a fierce shudder and hugged herself. "It was horrid."

"You shouldn't have gone, then."

"I had to. It was my duty to be there."

Stern approval in his expression almost made her laugh, but she held on to the brief silence just long enough for him to gesture for her to continue.

"My birthday, then."

"You have a special gift you wish?" he asked.

"Yes, as a matter of fact, Oliver, I do."

"And...?"

"A party."

It was clearly not what he'd been expecting, and this time she did laugh.

"Yes, a party." Her gaze swept to the windows now covered in green velvet. "Winter has finally come, and nothing would please me more than to warm the season with a party. A grand party, Oliver." She rose and began pacing. "Everyone in the village shall come. They will see I'm not dying, and they will work all the harder because of it. They will see you as the perfect host, and while they won't love you—and I can't pretend they will, because we both know it's not true—they will see that you're at least human."

Then, in a sweeping move she dropped to his feet and took his startled hands in hers.

"A party, Oliver. A ball! Think of it. In the middle of dreary winter, all that light and music . . . a ball, Oliver! A ball!"

She waited, smiling while her hands gripped his and she tried not to scream, tried not to tear her eyes away from his. But if her plan was to work, she must have patience and his cooperation. For without the latter, she had no hope at all.

"Oliver?"

And when he gave her a faraway smile, calculated and cool, it was all she could do not to laugh aloud and spoil the mood she'd woven.

22

"I DON'T believe it! You're absolutely mad," Gwen exclaimed, dropping onto the footboard chest, her expression incredulous. "I can't imagine that you'd try something as foolish as this, Cat."

Caitlin stood in front of the full-length mirror and turned slowly, checking her gown from every possible angle. "I don't see why I shouldn't," she said as if she were discussing the purchase of a new carriage. "It makes perfect sense to me."

Gwen closed her eyes in annoyance, but Caitlin was still wearing the same half-smile she'd had for the past hour. "You haven't been thinking, that's what it is. You just haven't been thinking," Gwen said.

Caitlin stared at the other woman's reflection. "I have been doing nothing else, Gwen Thomas, and I'll not be discouraged. I mean to leave Seacliff tonight or my name isn't—"

"Dead," Gwen said angrily. "You'll be dead before the sun rises."

Caitlin had had enough of arguing. She sliced the air with her hand, indicating silence and examined herself more closely. Her gown was of pale gold and emerald green, the plunging neckline and cuffs lined with braided silver thread. Her hair had been swept back into a dizzying series of loops and curls into which baby pearls had been nestled. Around her neck glittered a double strand of diamonds from which a teardrop diamond dangled into the cleft of her breasts. The scent of rose and lilac lingered about her like a cloud, creating a delicate comingling of temptations which, she sincerely hoped, would draw the men into staring at her figure and not at the tension she was sure ran across her face. When she moved, her skirts and petticoats whispered; when she laughed, the swell of her breasts rippled distractingly; when she held her arms demurely at her sides and buried her white-gloved hands in her gown, every curve was accentuated, every inch of hidden flesh was a promise.

It was a daring, consciously licentious costume she'd chosen for the evening, but it was essential to her plan. She must seduce all of the males in the mansion, befuddle their senses and thwart their suspicion. To do anything less would mean she'd spend the rest of her life a prisoner in her own home, just waiting for the day when Oliver tired of her and saw to it that she met with an "accident."

Gwen shook her head firmly. "No. No, Cat, I will not permit it."

Caitlin spun on her, her eyes bright with months of suppressed rage. "*You* will not permit it? You?" She covered the distance between them in half a dozen strides and grabbed the woman's shoulders. "You have no choice, my dear. It's all been arranged, and there's nothing you can do about it now."

Tears sprang into Gwen's eyes, and she rubbed at them fiercely with her knuckles. "You could have at least told me, Cat. I would have helped you, you know. Or tried to dissuade you from such suicide."

Caitlin softened somewhat and leaned closer to kiss her friend on the cheek. She shook her head sadly. "It would have been wrong, Gwen."

"Wrong? How could my wanting to help you be wrong?"

"Because of Flint," she said, knowing nothing more needed to be said. Since Flint's assault on Gwen the night Griffin fled the valley, Gwen had been afraid that the overseer would summon her again and demand to know what conversations had taken place in her mistress's apartments. And worse—she knew that under threat of her life, and of Davy's life as well, she might well have broken. Caitlin was thus reduced to planning her escape on her own. She had set up dozens of schemes and probed them for their weaknesses and strengths. But it had been Les Daniels's suggestion of a party that had made the notion more than a fantasy. After only a brief word with Orin that afternoon, she felt her chances were good, but only the evening's climax would tell.

"But why tonight?" Gwen asked in an almost whining voice. "Why must it be tonight of all nights?"

"For that very reason, Gwen," she said, turning to the vanity table and critically examining a vase of winter roses sent in from Eton: Oliver's gift to her on her twenty-first birthday. "I am supposed to be celebrating. There will be dozens of people here. Before, I had only shadows—Flint, my husband, that horrid Birwyn. Now there'll be drink, there'll be food, there'll be entertainment, and before the evening is out there'll be so many distractions that I'll be able to slip away to the valley before anyone discovers that I'm gone."

"Do . . . do you really think so?" Gwen said, wanting desperately to hope, but not daring to give her wishes full rein.

"I have no choice but to believe," Caitlin said. She plucked a rose from the vase and deftly stemmed it before tucking the vivid red blossom into a curl over her left ear. She examined herself in the mirror and winced. All she needed now was a little rouge on her cheeks and she'd be able to ply the trade in Whitehall with the best of them.

"The snow?"

She covered her face momentarily, lowered her hands and pointed at Gwen's reflection. "I have been through all this myself a hundred times over, Gwen. It hasn't snowed for three days. The roads are clear all the way to Cardiff." She adjusted the strand of diamonds around her neck. "It should be no trouble booking passage to London with one of these stones. And once there I'll be able to find Lord Carrington or Lord Devon. They'll remember me from Eton, and they'll be very interested to know what Sir Oliver is planning for this little valley of mine. Very interested indeed. It shouldn't be long before I return. And when I do . . ." She clapped her hands once, loudly.

Gwen came up behind her and put an arm around her waist, her cheek on Caitlin's shoulder. "I'm afraid."

"As am I," she said softly. "But I can't bear it any longer. And the longer I wait, the more powerful Oliver becomes. And as soon as someone in the village discovers his real purpose there'll be bloodshed. I think . . . I think some, like Randall, have already guessed, but they're afraid to speak out because of what might . . . what *will* happen."

Silence hung between them as Gwen pulled gently away and Caitlin thought of the "soldiers" quartered throughout the village. The word had been spread that they were preparing to embark on a naval frigate on its way down from Glascow, a frigate Caitlin was positive did not exist. She pulled at her neckline absently. She was forced to admit a certain reluctant admiration for Oliver's machinations, and for the patience required to bring all the disparate threads together. It had been literally years in the making, this plan of his, perhaps even begun when he realized his days in the army were numbered. It was a dark, malign vision, but a vision nevertheless and—

Gwen cleared her throat, and Caitlin was startled into the present. She turned, thinking someone had overheard their conversation or that Flint or Oliver had come to claim her. But Gwen was simply standing there, her hands clasped behind her back, a small and melancholy grin on her face.

"Was going to wait until after," she said quietly, lifting her chin suddenly as if determined not to weep. "But you won't be here, God willing." She brought her hands around to the front, to show a small package wrapped in gaily colored paper and tied with a large gold bow.

Caitlin covered her mouth with one hand while the other accepted the gift. Gwen urged her with a nod to open it, and as she did so, her fingers trembling, her eyes blinked away tears that matched the diamond gleam at her throat. Inside the package was an ornately embroidered lace handkerchief, blinding white in color and bordered with gold thread.

"I been working on it awhile," Gwen whispered. "I'm not as good as Sharnac, but—"

Caitlin dropped the package and embraced her. She wept freely as she buried her face in her friend's shoulder. Then, her arms still around Gwen's waist, she leaned back.

"The most beautiful thing I've ever seen," she cried.

Gwen blushed, and Caitlin laughed.

"And what," she said with feigned severity, "makes you think I would be leaving you?"

Gwen's puzzled look furrowed her brow. "But you said—"

"I said I'd be gone by midnight. I did not say I would be leaving alone."

"But . . . I don't . . ." Flustered, Gwen reached for the gift, looked to one side, and finally understood. "Me? I'm to go with you? Me?"

"Gwen, not only does someone of my station need a personal maid while traveling, but I certainly wouldn't leave you here alone, without me. I'm no fool, no matter what you think. I know what Flint would do if I left you behind." She grinned knowingly. "I expect that at this moment Orin has your bag ready. With Davy's help, of course."

"Davy? Is he . . . I mean, have you—"

"No," Caitlin said sadly. "He would not. He said he must stay, for his own reasons. I respect him, and I agreed."

Gwen rose and took her arm. "But how could you? He'll be killed the first minute they know . . ." Her expression hardened. "I can't go, Cat. I can't leave him—"

"You will go because he wishes it," she said sternly. "And you will go because you're my friend. Davy knows what he's doing, and what he's doing is right. If he's here, he'll be able to get word to us about Oliver, especially if something happens we should know about. Oliver and Flint will not wait until spring to see what I've done, Gwen. They'll have to move if they fail to catch us during our escape. And when they move, Davy will be right behind us with the news."

She would brook no further protest. She grabbed Gwen's shoulders and propelled her gently from the room, grinning at the woman's muttering as she closed the door behind her. But Caitlin's grin faded when she was alone again and staring at the mirror. Death, she thought; Gwen was instantly ready to face death at Flint's hands just to stay with her lover. And . . . she clenched her teeth and swallowed. And here am I . . .

She glared.

And here am I about to prove to Oliver that I am neither the fool nor the weakling he believes me to be.

It had been almost impossibly hard to maintain the fiction of docility over the past three weeks, but she had managed. Whether it fooled Flint did not concern her, not as long as Oliver was still in charge. And though she'd noticed a slight increase in tension between the two men—an old tension apparently, for why else would Oliver find it necessary continually to remind Flint of his obligations to his employer?—she had no doubts who still held command.

She stepped away from the mirror and whirled around once on her silver-buckled, satin shoes. Gwen had left the corridor door slightly ajar, and the strains of music, soft chatter, and an occasional restrained laugh on the ground floor wafted up to her. Oliver had insisted she remain in her rooms until most of the guests had arrived; an entrance, he maintained, was essential to an effective evening, and he wanted the villagers properly entranced—an added touch of legerdemain, she suspected, to keep them off balance.

"Marvelous," a voice said in genuine admiration. "Absolutely and unquestionably enchanting."

Oliver stood framed in the doorway. He wore a black velvet cutaway coat with silver buttons reminiscent of the military; his jabot was laced and spilled in ruffled waves from his neck; his cuffs, too, were made of lace; and his ebony walking stick was topped with an ivory head carved in the shape of an imperial stallion. Oliver was a study, she thought, in black and white, save for the flush that spread lightly over his cheeks and forehead. He bowed to her stiffly, to which she returned a curtsy. One last look at the precarious balance of her coiffure and she moved to join him.

They did not touch. It was as if a barrier of stone had been erected between them, high enough for them to look over but thick enough to keep them distant. She smiled—a mask only, the substance had long since evaporated—and walked with him along the gallery to the head of the staircase. The music was louder now, gaily playing various folk themes the guests knew very well; many of them were singing, stumbling over the words, and many more had decided to add harmony to the already lilting tunes. The atmosphere felt very much like the reunion of many families and, she thought sadly, this would have been one in better times. But she was compelled to admit that Oliver had done his homework well. The Courders and the rest of the staff had been cooking for days, preparing special foods and delicacies for the unsophisticated palates of the valley folk, who didn't know what they were eating. And the results were already evident. From what she could hear as they approached the staircase, the partygoers' spirits were high and lively, no small part of which was probably due to the large quantities of wine and fine northern ale laid out for the occasion.

"Caitlin," Oliver said in a low voice, "I trust you will do nothing foolish this evening."

She held her breath, suddenly fearful he'd guessed her intentions, or had somehow learned through Orin or Davy the true reason she had begged him to hold this affair. But she managed to keep panic from her eyes as she looked up to him questioningly.

"You do not take wine well," he said. "And you are not yet the woman you were last summer." He raised a cautionary finger and wagged it solicitously. "Moderation, Caitlin. In all things."

There it was! she thought. A warning: *Mind your tongue, woman, or you'll be the worse for it; watch who you talk to and watch what you say. Remember, Caitlin Morgan, you'll still be here when they have all gone for the evening.*

She looked down the staircase at the center hall, and Oliver placed her left hand on his right arm.

"Shall we?" he said.

She nodded, partly to avoid talking to him as she was made breathless by the sight below. She had been in her rooms the entire day, bathing, dressing, letting Gwen natter about as she did her hair, and she hadn't seen the decorations set into place. She'd only told her husband she wanted this to be a day the village would never forget.

And by the looks of things—her own escapade notwithstanding—her request had been met.

In the center of the hall a massive candle tree of oak fashioned into the shape of an evergreen had been erected, and on each branch a dozen candles burned brightly. With at least two dozen branches, it put forth a glare of soft white light that resembled a miniature sunrise, and its luster bathed the standards and portraits, the tapestries and paneling until they were transformed magically into shimmering jewels. There were flowers, too, in great eye-catching bouquets set on tables around the room; some were lashed to the banister and rose all the way to the gallery. She reached out to caress the blossoms as she descended, and fixed her gaze on the flaming tree, her heart thudding excitedly in her chest. She found herself grabbing Oliver's arm with both hands and just as they reached the bottom step, the Reverend Lynne stepped out of the sitting room and looked up.

He gestured violently to the others as his face creased into a welcoming smile. Within moments all chatter had ceased, and the music faded into silence.

Caitlin faltered.

Oliver took another step, paused and glanced at her. "Are you well, my dear?"

She wanted to return the smile, but her lips would not hold it. "I . . . it's all so grand!"

Self-satisfied, Oliver nodded. "It is that, and it is more, Caitlin." He looked down at the vicar, anxiously shifting from one foot to the other. "Come, my dear."

She did not know if she could do it. All this grandeur, all this work done by people who could have slit Oliver's throat without blinking, and she was planning to ruin it. At least, that's how it would look until Orin managed to explain what had really happened. But what if he never got the chance? What if she herself failed, was caught before she left the house? Or worse, just as she was nearing her goal? Why didn't she think Flint would send a dozen, a score, a hundred men after her? Why did she believe she would be able to outrun them all and make it safely down the coast to Cardiff?

Oliver grew impatient. He smiled placatingly at the vicar, then tugged lightly on her hands. "Caitlin, this is not the way to behave in front of your guests."

She wanted to yank her hands away, to grab her skirts and race back to her room. Her plan was impossible. She saw that now. She was a fool for thinking any of it would work. Oliver couldn't be duped by something so daring and treasonous; he would see through her the moment she stepped into the room and was faced with the earnest greetings of all those people. He would see the desperation in her eyes, feel the trembling in her arms. He would know, and he would kill her for it.

"Caitlin—"

She made her gasp sound like a coughing spell.

James Flint had come from the dining room, and was smiling up at her. Like Oliver he wore black velvet and silver; unlike her husband, his hair was still his own. He had brushed it

straight back from his forehead and caught it in a narrow black
ribbon at the nape of his neck. He carried a goblet in one hand,
and raised it to her in a silent, mocking toast. Then he swerved
around the candle tree and crossed to the vicar, leaned over
and whispered a few words into his ear. Lynne seemed startled
for a moment, nodded once, and disappeared into the edges of
the crowd that was forming near the doorway.

Flint looked up again, his smile never wavering. "Is there
something I can do, Sir Oliver?"

Oliver shook his head and scowled. "Caitlin, I really must
insist."

Stall, she ordered herself; stall until you can find all the
courage you've stored away in such abundance.

She glanced down at her bosom and crossed a hand over
its exposed swells. "Oliver, I think I have made a terrible
mistake."

"Caitlin, what in heaven's name are you talking about?"

She let her hands flutter down over the bodice to the skirts
and back again. "This . . . this gown. It's not right; it's too
French. I know you disapprove of such things, and I should
have—"

He yanked her down to his step and held her left hand so
tightly she nearly cried out in pain. "Christ, Caitlin, this is
foolishness. I kept a close eye on that witch, Sharnac, all the
while she was making this bewitching extravagance. Had I
disapproved I would have instructed her to make the proper
alterations. If it's your vanity you're concerned about, forget
it. I have never denied your beauty, and I shall not do so now.
You are lovely, the gown is lovely, and nothing would lead
me to say otherwise."

"Thank you, Oliver," she said, lowering her gaze.

"Don't thank me," he said. "Just let's be on with it. Were
it not for you, I would not choose to be with these . . . these
peasants this evening, and I certainly do not intend to do so
on my own. In other words, Caitlin, I have no intention of
making excuses for you. This is your birthday, and this is your
party, and, may I remind you, this is your idea. Have I made
myself clear? Caitlin, am I getting through to you?"

But she had stopped listening.

Flint had turned around to greet a woman who had left the
sitting room, a woman dressed in a gown whose neckline exposed the tips of her rouged nipples; whose bosom was so

whitely powdered that tiny flakes floated to the bodice of her gown when she moved quickly. The woman's hair was so ridiculously entwined around what looked from Caitlin's view to be a small cage of some kind that she seemed ready to tip over from the weight of it. It was so blatantly a copy of the French queen's style, and so glaringly out of place—and would have been even in London—that Caitlin almost laughed.

The woman was Morag Burton, and Flint's ogling was so coarse and false that Caitlin thought she would choke.

"Caitlin!"

"I hear you, Oliver," she said stiffly.

Peasants and whores, she thought. It was just what she needed to draw herself up, lift her chin, and take Oliver's offered arm. And as if she'd needed further goading, she spotted Nate Birwyn standing just out of sight from the gallery, down the corridor toward the back. He was well dressed, but unlike the other men he had tucked a brace of pistols in his waistband. If Birwyn was armed, she knew there were others with weapons, also.

Suddenly the evening's pleasure took on an entirely different hue.

23

SHE WALKED into a fairyland.

On the far wall great pine logs had been piled on the andirons and their blaze climbed high beyond view into the chimney. Most of the tapestries had been taken down for the evening to protect them from candle smoke and wax, and from the excesses of the guests. In their places tall mirrors had been hung, framed in filigree-carved walnut and covered with gleaming gold leaf. They were all the same shape—thin and rectangular—and their reflections multiplied the tapers in their candelabra and in their polished pewter sconces by the hundreds. It was as if she had walked into a cavern of tiny flames, each

of them fragile and imbued with gemlike beauty. They softened, too, the faces of her guests, enshrouding their winter-
harsh countenances in a delicate mask of transparent silk.

The guests applauded when they saw her.

It came as a rippling sound from the front of the crowd as
she walked with Oliver through the doorway. Then, as the
quartet of musicians—violins and flutes—struck up a touching, original fanfare, the applause spread and expanded its
volume until the walls and mirrors trembled at their moorings.
Then came the easiest gesture she'd had to make that day—a
genuine, heartfelt smile, and as Oliver led her into the room
and the crowd parted, still applauding, she inclined her head
regally to everyone whose gaze she caught, winking at some
and flashing a warm smile at others.

The furniture had been moved to another room; nothing
remained but a long table before the hearth upon which several
large silver bowls of fruited punch laced with brandy had been
set; vases of flowers in wild profusion nearly blocked the fire,
and in the center a tall, beautifully wrapped package drew all
eyes.

The applause died to an excited silence.

Caitlin found herself free of Oliver's grip as she moved to
the table, reached out and touched the silken wrapping. She
turned to face her well-wishers. They maintained a respectful
distance, but she could sense the pressure as they reached out
without motion to touch her, reassure her—or was it, she
thought suddenly, merely gratitude for relieving the dreary
winter? The notion fled at once. The truth lay most likely
somewhere in between, but she was not going to spend the
evening uncovering the true feelings of all present. What mattered was that they had come. In spite of everything, they had
come And she was hard put to keep the lump in her throat
from exploding into tears.

Orin Daniels shouldered his way through the front line. He
looked awkward in frock coat and breeches. His hair was plastered down, and his already ruddy complexion was even more
red from a harsh scrubbing. He took the center of the crescent-
shaped clearing and cleared his throat, causing a faint titter to
rise and fall behind him. Oliver merely rearranged his expression into one of benign tolerance.

"Mistress," Orin said, "everything is ready."

Caitlin held her smile.

"We've the music, and the feast, and that there on the table behind ye is a measure of our . . . our . . ." He frowned at the loss of the word. Then he smiled. "Our esteem." He bowed quickly and pushed his way back to his place, one hand mopping perspiration from his brow.

Caitlin blew him a kiss. There was laughter from the villagers, and a brief scowl from her husband.

"So? We gonna stand 'ere all night?" a voice called from the back of the room.

More laughter followed, and Caitlin gladly joined in as she turned to the package and stared at it. It was so lovely she didn't want to spoil the vision of its silvered purity, but rather than wait too long and insult her guests she took a deep breath and grabbed hold of a red string girdled about its center. She pulled, and the rustling of the silk was the only sound in the room; she gasped and put her hands to her cheeks; when she turned, she found there was no need for words. They saw the tears that gave her eyes an ethereal shine.

Oliver was transfixed. His eyes darted from the gift to Caitlin's face, and a tic throbbed at the corner of his eye. His hands, which had been folded over the top of his walking stick, were white from the pressure, but he did not turn his head nor did he utter a sound.

Quinn Broary, short and looking even shorter in a forest of beige ruffles, took a timid step forward. "'Twas from the stones, m'lady," she said, her voice throaty. "After the accident, a small block was brung t'me. I did the best I could."

She spoke in Welsh, and Caitlin could not resist looking at her husband and translating. When he nodded, once, she said to Quinn Broary, "It's the most magnificent gift I've ever received. I don't know how to thank you."

"Not me, m'lady," Quinn demurred quickly as she moved back to her place. "'Twas all our doin'."

She scanned the crowd of nearly two hundred and found she was no longer in control of her voice. She looked away quickly, back to the table where a small bust sat on a base of mirrorlike oak. To her it seemed a perfect likeness: the laughing eyes, the one-sided smile, the hair that curled slightly down around the brow and ears. She could almost hear him speak. It was her father, David Evans.

"I will treasure it always," she said softly, and in Welsh.

And as though her words were a prearranged signal, the

musicians broke into a rapid melody that scattered the guests
reluctantly. Some went to the dining room across the hall where
the foodstuffs had been laid out amid a great deal of pomp,
some to the hall where the air was cooler, the rest to the walls
around the dancing floor. Talk filled the room, boots beat time
on the floor, and Caitlin recalled that evening in Windsor Castle
and wondered how she could have ever thought it was so
wonderfully grand. She may indeed have met King George and
his queen, but upon reflection she realized that the guests there
had been engaged in posturing and ceremony, that the entire
night had been a facade, with no underlying substance.

She brushed a tender hand over the bust of her father and
felt Oliver's presence beside her. "It's grand, don't you think?"

"It's an insult," he said, keeping his voice low.

"They loved him." Her tone was neutral. "I shall keep it in
my room, if that pleases you."

"It would please me not to have it in the house. But under
the circumstances, yes, you may keep it in the tower."

Flint joined them unexpectedly and stood on her right. He
grunted and shrugged when he saw the sculpture.

"You should be circulating," Oliver said without looking at
him.

"I am, I am," Flint told him.

"Then don't you think—"

"I do what is required, Sir Oliver," he interrupted coldly.
"My men—"

"*My* men," Oliver corrected.

"As you wish. Your men have been fed, and those who
don't seem too disreputable are in their places. Nate is following
orders."

Caitlin listened to the bickering over her head as long as
she could. When their voices began to rise, however, she turned
abruptly and faced the three circles of dancing. "Do you mind?"
she said, though she kept her smile. "Do you bloody well mind
keeping your little intrigues to yourself?"

She walked off before either of them could respond, then
flashed a smile at Martin Randall when he broke from the
sidelines and offered her his hand. She curtsied before him,
and one of the circles made way for them as they joined in a
Welsh dance of spinning, graceful figure eights, and a great
deal of laughter. The women, their gowns much simpler than

hers but no less colorful, were less restrained in their harmless
flirtations and abandoned dancing; the men saw no harm in
suddenly throwing their hands high over their heads or setting
them on their hips and expressing their delight in quick, sharp
yells. Spontaneity was rampant, though they observed the circles that were the reel's convention, and before long Caitlin
was able to put aside her worries and let the music carry her
away.

And so the evening passed.

Reverend Lynne spent most of his time wandering between
the food table and a long sideboard that held flagons of foaming
ale. Morag was nowhere in sight, but as long as his stomach
was not complaining, he didn't mind. Sooner or later she would
turn up. The later the better.

Randall danced as long as his legs would hold him, then
walked with Quinn Broary outside for a few minutes to clear
his head and catch his breath. Snow lay untrammeled on the
ground—a blanket of ghostly white covered by a thin coat of
ice to rival the river-sweep of stars that formed a diamond
canopy over the valley. Twice he wished aloud that Griffin
Radnor could have been at the celebration, and twice Quinn
dug at his ribs with her elbow, nodding in silence to the dark
figures around the estate, men in shadowy army uniforms. Save
for a handful of minor incidents, the worst of which had been
the partial destruction of the ringstones, they'd kept to themselves. Quiet in the homes where they'd been quartered, they
stayed away from the villagers for the most part; nevertheless,
they were a sinister force, all the more so for their silent,
secretive ways.

Orin Daniels watched Randall and Broary leave the house.
Though he'd reconciled himself to the fact of their not marrying, he'd hoped to keep Quinn as a lover. When the goldsmith
claimed her attention, however, Orin in his usual taciturn manner had stepped aside. There were no recriminations; the village
was too small. Besides, helping his mistress with her plan was
a more satisfying way of striking back at the major. He emptied
his goblet, refused an offer from Sharnac to join her in a dance,
and made his way along the side corridor toward the south
tower. He wanted to check one more time on the roan, on the
clothes Davy had packed with Alice Courder's help, and then
he wanted to see Gwen. She'd been as nervous as a cat since

she'd come downstairs. He had to be sure she wouldn't show herself to the guests, or to Flint. One look, and it would all be over.

Flint watched the burly farrier leave the hall. Then he turned his grim attention to Birwyn, who was still at his station at the rear of the building. There was someone with him, and it didn't take Flint more than a half-dozen steps to realize the person was Morag, shoving herself against him while his hands worked their way around her buttocks and squeezed tightly. He swore harshly under his breath and lengthened his stride, deliberately coming down hard on his heels to send Nate a warning. It worked. Suddenly, Birwyn pushed Morag to one side, and she smothered her protests when she saw Flint approaching. Quickly, she tidied her hair and gown and gave him a sickly sweet smile before heading back to the ale.

"You're impossible, Nate," Flint said, standing with his back to the hall.

"She done asked for it," Birwyn replied without apology.

"Aye, that's the truth." He paused. "Morgan is getting drunk."

"So I've noticed."

"Shouldn't take me long to get him into the study. You remember what to do?"

Birwyn winked with his good eye, then squirmed uncomfortably in the tight-fitting jacket he'd been required to wear. One hand rested casually on the butt of a pistol.

"See that you do," Flint cautioned. He faced the hall slowly, brushing at his cuffs. "The major hasn't gotten this far by being an idiot. Unless we do it right, he'll suspect the truth."

"He won't," Birwyn assured him.

"And the men?"

"They know who pays 'em, Flint. And the few what have complaints will have to answer t'me. Personally." His grin was brief and diabolical. "You just do your part, and I'll do mine. Quick as pie we be masters, don't you worry."

But Flint did worry. Too many things could go wrong, including a sudden appearance by the rebels who were hiding in the mountains. For weeks he'd been hearing rumors of restlessness, and he knew the source of the problem was Griffin Radnor. Damn him! he thought. He should have killed the cur when he had the chance. Birwyn did not make many mistakes, but when he did they were colossal ones; and now that Radnor was still at large, and with men at his command, there was no telling what might happen. Thank God for the winter storms. The valley would be effectively cut off from the swelling rabble until spring, and by then——

He smiled.

Nate Birwyn suddenly found the toes of his boots fascinating. He had no idea what was running through Flint's mind, but when that devil's grin crossed the man's face Nate couldn't help but shudder. And he couldn't help but feel somewhat sorry for Sir Oliver Morgan.

Shortly before midnight the party subsided. Energies were flagging, and the drinking had caught up with most of the guests. The music had shifted into a low background melody, soft and pleasing, and a few of the villagers had already paid their respects to their hosts and left for home. But not before Oliver stunned the assemblage and his wife with a brief speech thanking them all for attending Caitlin's birthday celebration. Then, with Bradford's solemn assistance, he passed around to each family a tiny package which, when opened, was found to contain three gold sovereigns. The gasps, muffled cries of joy, expressions of disbelief—both astounded and suspicious—filled the halls of Seacliff for the better part of an hour.

Oliver reveled in the attention. He accepted gratitude and a few women's tears with magnanimous bows, brushed aside perfunctory protests, and totally ignored Caitlin's amazement. Where he'd amassed all that gold she did not know, but she was positive it had not been from any legitimate dealing. And she was sure his magnanimity was an unabashed ploy to garner loyalty and incur debts. To her dismay, in many cases it was working.

But his gesture also produced the precise moment she'd been waiting for. With all the commotion, the renewed toasts to Oliver's health and hers, she realized she would have no better time than now. A sharp pain pierced her breast as she made her decision. What she was doing was irrevocable, and to postpone it further would be lethal. She made her way through the groups of dancers and talkers as quickly as she dared without seeming in a hurry. Catching Orin's eye, she gave him a brief, significant nod. He disappeared. Then she checked on Birwyn and found him talking with one of his men at the back of the center hall; Flint was nowhere to be seen, and Oliver, she saw as she left the room, was leaning toward Bradford and listening intently to him.

Her heart drummed, and she felt beads of perspiration begin to form on her brow. Her smile stiffened falsely, and when she suggested that the musicians play something more lively, she thought the quaver in her voice would betray her in an instant. But no one seemed to notice anything amiss. They took her hands and shook them, kissed her cheeks, complimented her on her gown and coif, and left her alone.

In the hall she remembered her gift. She caught Bradford on his way to the dining room and told him to take the bust immediately to her apartments. When he balked, she snapped the order again, stood there not caring how insulted he felt, and watched as he picked up the sculpture in his arms. When he returned, she nodded, but she did not take her eyes from him as he made his way up the stairs. She wouldn't have been surprised if he'd contrived to stumble and drop the piece.

A draft from the front door chilled her ankles and made her shiver.

Morag Burton swept past her on the arm of a farmer who was too drunk to notice anything but Morag's exposed breasts.

"Are you all right, m'lady?" Reverend Lynne asked solicitously, his hair disheveled and his cheeks flushed with drink. "May I get you something?"

She did not look at him. A cold serpent was making its way through her, and no matter how hard she pressed her gloved hands to her stomach she could not still its effects.

"M'lady?"

"I'm fine," she said quickly. "It's all this excitement, that's all." Again she was positive her smile was too rigid. "A moment of quiet and I'll be right as rain again."

"I'm sure," the vicar said. "Well . . . I believe I shall try a taste of your cellar's marvelous brandy. I'm told it's quite elegant."

She nodded, said nothing, then released a long-held breath when he walked unsteadily away into the dining room.

It isn't going to work, she told herself. I just know it's not going to work.

A brief scuffle sounded somewhere, followed by the raising of a few angry voices. The music played on. The glow from the candle tree blurred and shimmered. People passed her without speaking, and it was some time before she understood they weren't even seeing her. The gold sovereigns, the food, and the drink had combined to render her virtually invisible.

It isn't going to work, she thought again.

Orin stepped out of the side corridor, brushed a hand wearily through his hair and vanished again.

Bradford returned from her rooms emptyhanded.

My God, she thought; my God, it's now or never.

A slow and steady inhalation, a holding, a prayer, and she started down the hall, exaggerating her nervousness in hopes anyone passing would think her slightly under the weather. From drink or her illnesses, she didn't care which. Those who noted would remember her heading for the staircase, looking rather lost and somewhat befuddled.

At the juncture of hallways she paused. Behind her the party seemed to have gained its second wind; ahead, Nate Birwyn was not at his post. She searched the length of the hall, peering into the shadows beneath the standards and alongside the staircases on either wall, but no one was lurking about. Flint was still missing, and her husband had apparently responded to Bradford's message, as planned.

She uttered a short prayer then, and with a hand to her diamond necklace she darted into the side corridor and hurried toward the south tower. As if a heavy door had been closed the revelry faded in her wake, and she could hear nothing but the rasp of her breath between her lips, the soft fall of her slippers on the carpeting, and the screams in her mind every time a stray draft flickered a candle.

The south tower entrance loomed directly ahead.

Beyond it, Gwen would be waiting with her change of clothes and a cloth sack containing her belongings. They would wear men's clothes, making riding easier and providing a night-time disguise. At the exit she would find Orin. He would take them across the snow-covered lawn to the stables, pretending to escort two staff members who'd taken too much brandy. Once there they would mount and be gone. With luck, the alarm would not be raised for at least two hours, and by that time they would be through the hills' gap, heading south toward Bristol Bay and Cardiff.

Cardiff, and freedom.

She was several feet beyond her father's study door before she realized it stood ajar. After glancing over her shoulder, she slowed reluctantly. A lamp glowed within. Who...? She stopped, looked to the tower and could not contain her curiosity. Slowly, walking on her toes, she made her way back and listened. There was no sound from inside. With one hand trembling she pushed the door open and stepped over the threshold. It took several moments for her eyes to adjust to the dim light, several moments more before she saw the figure lying on the floor on the other side of her father's desk.

Voices suddenly sounded from the corridor.

Without thinking she slammed the door behind her and hurried over to the figure.

Her hands covered her mouth barely in time to smother a scream.

It was Oliver. He was on his stomach, his legs akimbo and his arms thrown over his head. One stocking had been pulled down to his calf, and his jacket was spread open in a black velvet puddle. The wig, which he treated with more care than he had for her feelings, was lying on its side like some beaten, white-furred animal. And from between his shoulder blades rose the ebony-handled knife her father had used to break the seals on his correspondence.

If there was blood, it had blended long ago into the dark of his clothing.

"Oliver?" she whispered, dropping to her knees. She reached out tentatively toward his back, withdrew her hand suddenly, and reached out again. She shook him.

"Oliver?"

She shook him again, felt a softness and turned her palm to the light. Blood stained her glove.

Oliver Morgan was obviously dead.

"Oh, my God, Oliver!"

"Pity, isn't it?"

She cried out and whirled around, hands spread on the floor to keep her balance. From the shadows in the room's far corner James Flint emerged, smiling. At the same moment the door was flung open and Nate Birwyn strode in, Ellis Lynne right behind him.

"Told you," Birwyn said. "Heard some shoutin', and there you are."

The vicar nodded as if the man with the white patch had been talking about two children brawling in the schoolyard.

Caitlin's eyes widened and looked haunted, as all she could

do was gape. Lips quivering violently, she reached out in a pleading gesture.

"My dear," Flint told her, "it seems to me you have a problem."

24

As DIZZINESS swept over her and all sensation was lost in a distant buzzing filling her ears, she sagged back onto her haunches and prepared to give herself up to the welcome darkness. But just as she was slipping over the brink she felt someone take gentle hold of her arms. She resisted. She wanted to flee, and this was the best way she knew how. The hands were insistent. And when the spiraling, hypnotic lights that had invaded her mind faded to painful starpoints, she allowed herself to be lifted to her feet, where she swayed until an arm slipped around her waist and guided her to the high-backed desk chair. She sat with her head back and her eyes closed, concentrating now on not losing consciousness. Though she'd not heard a threat, she knew instinctively that she was in danger.

From behind her closed eyelids, she could hear a sharp snapping sound, a rattling, and the flutter of a heavy cloth in the air before the cacophony settled. A grunt of satisfaction sounded, and footsteps crossed the floor.

Her eyelids danced, then lifted, and when she looked over her right shoulder she saw that Oliver's body had been covered by a panel of velvet drapery yanked down from the window. Outside, though the fogged windowpanes, she could see the waning moonlight glimmering off the snow. And shadows. Movement. Horses snorting white breath, carts trundling along the lane, the glint of lantern light off bridle and harness.

A glass was pressed into her hand. She stared at it dumbly until she recognized the amber liquid. She took a slow, cautious sip and shuddered at the languid fire snaking down toward her stomach. She coughed and sipped again. The glass shook, and she held its fragile stem in both hands.

By the time the brandy was more than half gone the room had returned to focus, and she looked up to see Flint lounging against the opposite wall, examining the backs of his hands. ". . . a little early, but no mind," he was saying to Birwyn and the vicar. "It'll work out if we don't rush it."

"What . . . ?" The word struggled through a guttural strangling, and she cleared her throat harshly. Flint took his time meeting her questioning look. "What will work out?" she demanded weakly. Then she nodded toward Oliver's body without actually seeing it. "You'll not get away with this, you know, James Flint. This is one thing you'll not—"

"Oh, belt up," Birwyn snarled. "We don't need your talk just now."

"Shame," Flint scolded lightly. "But he's quite correct, Caitlin. What you're going to do now is listen very carefully. And if you're as smart as I know you are, you may walk out of this room alive." He smiled and turned to Lynne. "In a moment you'll have to see the rest of them start leaving. Apologize to Lady Morgan. You know what I mean. As for this, well, I think we won't really bother to break the news until morning." A look at Birwyn, who had closed the door softly behind him and pulled one of his pistols out to caress the long barrel. "Have you picked someone yet?"

Birwyn nodded.

Flint pursed his lips, and Caitlin choked back the urge to scream. They were handling all of this so calmly, so matter-of-factly that it might have been a nightmare she'd fallen into on her way to . . . Her eyes widened, but she sensed no knowledge of her impending escape in Flint's hard expression. Dared she hope he hadn't caught wind of it?

"Caitlin," he said then, "it appears you have two choices here, as doubtful as that may seem to you now."

"Do I?" she said. Her laugh was bitter, and short. "Do I really?"

"Indeed," he told her. "The first is, of course, the least pleasant. It appears to all of us in this room that your husband has been murdered. What must be uncovered is the name of the culprit." He leaned toward her accusingly. "Was it you?"

"Don't be an ass," she snapped, and pressed herself against the chair's high back, feeling rather than seeing the body lying behind her. Nausea rose, subsided, and it took no great feat of logic to understand that more than one life was in jeopardy in this study.

"Of course it wasn't," Flint said soothingly. "We all know that, don't we, gentlemen?"

Lynne nodded vigorously, but Birwyn only grunted.

"But neither is your innocence in stone," Flint continued. "Dear Nate, as you doubtless heard, was alarmed by a heated argument as he passed along the corridors on his duties. The vicar here, wandering about on his own as is his wont, also heard the commotion. Now Nate, being a disciplined soldier, understood instantly the import of the voices, and he took it upon himself to enter the room without permission."

"Terrible it was," Nate offered with a slow shake of his head. "Took the breath right from me lungs."

"Shocking," the vicar volunteered.

"Of course it was," Flint said. "There, lying on the floor and expiring rapidly, was the master of the house. And there, standing over him"—and he reached out suddenly and grabbed Caitlin's wrist, twisting her palm to the light—"with blood on her hands was his wife. It's no secret, of course, she despised him for the way he lorded it over her family estate. I expect there was a great deal more, secrets of the bedchamber, to which we will never become privy. A sad state of affairs. But then, murder always is."

"I will see you in hell, James Flint," she hissed. But though Flint tensed, she made no move to attack him. Her limbs had turned to ice as she now saw the full contours of the perfect trap into which she'd fallen, and which numbed her mind into the most basic of reactions. "You bastard," she hissed, though she'd no strength to give the epithet weight.

"Be that as it may." He continued his pacing. "Mr. Birwyn, in one of the most curious of life's little byplays, has suddenly and most astutely realized he was quite mistaken from the start. Isn't that correct, Mr. Birwyn?"

This isn't happening, Caitlin thought wildly; I'm just losing my mind, that's all. This really isn't happening.

"Aye," Birwyn said solemnly, though he was incapable of holding back a grin at Flint's toying game. "Seems I heard this fightin' goin' on in here, see, and I says to the vicar here we oughta do somethin' about it 'cause it sounds like the major's gotten hisself into a spot of bad trouble."

"Exactly," said the vicar, nodding like a puppet.

"So," Birwyn continued in a montone born of obvious re-hearsal, "we comes in all sudden like, and saw that drunken sot Mike Phobis standin' over the major, puffin' and pantin' like he'd just done hisself a hell of a fight. Blood all over him, there was, a terrible mess. Fair turned me stomach, it did."

Again Lynne agreed, his expression so somber he looked almost comical.

"Well, it took a bit of doin', but it turns out Phobis heard about all that pretty gold the major was pourin' at the party, so he decides he wants a bit of it for hisself. Greedy little bastard. Always was. From Northumberland he comes from. Queer lot up there, very hot-headed. Good riddance, if you asks me. He don't fight good nohow."

Caitlin's desire to scream had been replaced by an over-whelming urge to laugh. It started as a slight giggle in the midst of Birwyn's practiced testimony, and finally exploded beyond her control at the man's gall in assessing Phobis's character. The three men were taken by surprise: Lynne was startled, Birwyn glaring, Flint had slightly lifted a brow.

Caitlin saw none of it. With hands clamped hard over her face she rocked and laughed hysterically, her feet kicked out blindly, her eyes spilled tears and stained her white gloves. It wasn't until Flint had had his fill of her outburst and cracked a glancing fist against her head that she gasped, choked, and stopped laughing. Rage replaced her mirth. Heedless of the danger she was in, she launched herself from her chair toward Flint, but when his fist caught her in the chest and sent her back to her seat, she yelped and found herself gulping for breath.

"Cor," Birwyn muttered, half in admiration.

At that moment a stream of curses poured from Caitlin's lips, invective coated with acid that filled the room until Flint raised a hand to strike her again. She clamped her mouth shut, feeling the heat of her anger and desperation redden her body from her cheeks to her bosom.

"You will be silent," Flint ordered her quietly. "You will be silent, and you will listen."

Birwyn nudged the vicar with an elbow, and Lynne shrank against the door.

"I think I've heard quite enough, thank you," Caitlin said coldly.

"Ah, but you haven't told me which tale you prefer."

Mad, she judged; the man is completely mad, and there's nothing I can do about it.

"Vicar," Flint said then, "you'd best be on your way. I'll have a man reach you before dawn to clue you in on what our lady has decided."

Lynne hesitated, licking at his lips, but a faint grunt from Birwyn sent him out the door before Caitlin could blink.

Flint settled himself again, clasping his hands in front of him. "Caitlin, perhaps we'd better be more direct, since there's not much time left before we're discovered."

She glared, hoping for a miracle that would make her hatred tangible, her gaze lethal.

"You see, if we come to the conclusion that it was, in fact, you who did the major in, then there are a number of things that will happen." He held up one finger. "The first is your incarceration. Since we are not quite as barbaric as the French, we will spare both your head and your pretty neck. But I suspect you will spend the rest of your days in a cell half this room's size, with nothing but straw for a bed, rats and lice for companions. You will grow old in there, Caitlin, and you will die forgotten. Meanwhile, Seacliff will pass into the hands of the man who can afford its upkeep. I think it need not be said who that man will be."

She looked down at her fingers, held limp in her lap.

"However, the second choice is rather pleasant, if I do say so myself. Here, you have come upon the assailant immediately after the vicar and my lieutenant. He will, of course, be hanged. But you . . . you, my dear, shall survive admirably."

"As what?" she said flatly.

Flint looked at her, surprised she hadn't joined him in his game. "As the mistress of Seacliff, what else?"

"Will I really?" she said, making it evident she doubted the generosity he displayed.

"I give you my word, Lady Morgan."

She scoffed, and he sighed in exasperation.

"It will work this way and no other, my lady: you will keep your rooms, all your staff, all those marvelous luxuries to which you have grown so devoted." A thought occurred to him, and he snapped his fingers in delight. "Naturally, you'll also inherit the major's lands in Eton. Judging from your rather boldly proclaimed lack of interest in England, however, I expect you'll wish to sell them as soon as is proper."

"Why should I?" she challenged.

"Well, Caitlin, you're really not up to traveling these days, are you? I mean, your illness, your bereavement . . . It will be quite some time before you take to horse again, isn't that right?"

She looked up in a panic, her heart frozen, her eyes wide. "What . . . what do you mean?"

"I mean, Caitlin," he said sternly, "what I say. You will survive. I give you my word you shall. But on my terms, my lady. On my terms alone."

She was almost too terrified to ask: "Which are?"

"Except for a very occasional stroll around the grounds, and an appearance now and then before the locals to be sure they don't stampede like the herds they guard, you will remain within these walls. You will live, but you will not leave."

She gripped the armrests tightly, fighting off the temptation to swoon.

"Though," he added thoughtfully, "I imagine you'll try to escape now and then. You wouldn't be Caitlin if you didn't, I suppose."

As if seared by a brand she straightened, her hands now in fists that strained the seams of her gloves.

"As a matter of fact," he said, smiling, "I'm sure you've done so in the past. I would be very disappointed indeed, my lady, if you hadn't at least planned to escape your confinement, perhaps even made a futile attempt at it now and again. And you'll continue to do so, I'm sure." His lips parted in a decidedly feral grin, and she could have sworn the scar at the corner of his mouth fairly glowed with anticipation. "You don't contradict me, my lady. Am I to assume that I've hit near the mark?"

"It occurs to me," she answered as brittlely as she could, "that someone like Morag Burton is much too good for you. She probably feels as if she's been wallowing with swine."

Flint ignored her jibe with a disdainful wave at the air. "It's obvious we have no martyr here," he explained to Birwyn. "You will waste no time seeing to Mr. Phobis. I myself shall alert the staff to our little tragedy as soon as Lady Morgan has composed herself." He gestured, and Birwyn left them alone.

And once the door was closed Caitlin was on her feet. She made no move toward Flint, nor did she look at her husband's body. Instead, she turned and began fussing with the scattered papers still lying on the desk. None of the words on them made much sense; none of the figures seemed familiar to her. Perspiration ran in torrents along her spine and down her sides, and once again she had to struggle to keep from feeling nauseated.

Madness. It was all madness, and she had no alternative but to acquiesce to Flint's demands.

But it wasn't the thought of life imprisonment that made her shoulders droop and her knees refuse to lock. It was the idea that her escape had been stymied by her own inaction. Had she moved sooner, had she not waited until virtually the last minute to leave, she could have avoided all this. She would have been well on her way, and though Oliver might have been killed in any case, she would have had at least a fighting chance to prove her innocence before a friendly court in London. But not here. Here she would be considered guilty no matter which road she took; the only saving grace was the chance to choose between seeing another sunrise and suffering eternal darkness.

She placed her hands gently on her bare shoulders and closed her eyes tightly.

"Caitlin," Flint whispered, "it won't be all that bad, I promise you. You shall have free run of the house and grounds as before, and I will see to it that you come to no harm."

She looked at the shelves in front of her, at the ledgers and books. "And what happens to your army, Mr. Flint?"

"Ah, they'll be waiting for their arms. That frigate from Glasgow has a deeper hold than most suspect."

"And then? Are you going to sell yourself to the king to fight in the colonies?"

He laughed softly, half turned her, and trailed a finger along the line of her jaw. She jerked her head away. But he as quickly grabbed her chin and held it while he stared, then released her and let his finger move across her upper chest.

"Caitlin, Caitlin, how little you understand," he whispered.

"How little I was told," she countered, keeping her gaze on the books, and her mind from the touch of him, now caressing the tops of her breasts.

"That was the major's notion, to serve the king. I, on the other hand, recall telling you once that I would place my loyalty at the feet of the highest bidder. And in this case, I do believe King Louis has claim to my soul."

She whirled on him, astounded. "Louis? You mean, you intend to fight for France?"

Clearly he was growing impatient, yet he could tear neither

his gaze nor his hand away from the cushion of her bosom.

"I mean exactly that, Caitlin. The fighting has already started in America—and it will last dreadfully long, I can assure you. Louis will waste little time seeing which way the winds of war are blowing. It would mean a great deal to him to have insurrections erupting to distract the British just before his armies and navy are launched. I expect such rebellions will take a fair number of troops from an already badly depleted field."

"You will hang," she spat, shoving him away.

"No," he said. "Drunken Mike Phobis will hang. In the morning, if I'm not mistaken."

Her eyes narrowed. "You regard no life as sacred, do you? A man killed to drive off Griffin; a man killed to be sure you still hold Seacliff. There's no shame in you, is there? No shame at all."

"What shame I have," he said, "is for those who refuse to fight for what they want. I admired your husband, my lady. For all his faults and stupidities he knew what he wanted and he did not stop until he achieved it. Unfortunately, I got there before he did."

She wanted to say more, to prolong the time in the room before she would have to face the staff with the news of Oliver's death—and before she would have to begin her own sentence of imprisonment within these walls. In effect, then, save that she'd now become a widow, nothing had changed. She was back to where she had started, with no idea what the next move would be.

She put the back of one hand to her brow. "I . . . I feel rather faint, Mr. Flint."

He was by her side again, and before she could comprehend what was happening his lips were on her neck, her shoulders, slipping down to her breasts where she could feel his steaming breath slipping below her neckline. She gasped, but could not wrench away. Like a steel vise his fingers took hold of her breast and pinched the skin between them, making her whimper. She twisted, which only seemed to inflame him. He cupped a breast in one hand while the other began tugging at the lace bindings of her bodice.

"Bastard!" she whispered harshly. "They'll be back—"

He bit her, and she cried out. Then finally she broke his hold and spun away. The flimsy material of her gown parted with a single tear, and she crossed her hands in front of her exposed breasts, backing to the wall while he grinned without mirth and rubbed his palms together.

"It seems," he said as he came slowly nearer, "that our Mr. Phobis turned on you before he was subdued by Mr. Birwyn. The drink had gone to his head."

She could not help stealing a glance at Oliver's covered body, at the clean soles of his boots poking out from beneath the drapery. And in the sullen light she caught the lust sparking in Flint's eyes, his tongue moistening his lips. Like a wolf before a meal, she thought as she reached behind her and grabbed a ledger from the shelf.

The movement bared her breasts and tumbled them into the light. Flint stared at them fixedly, and she wondered suddenly if she might take advantage of his all too evident desire. If she could maneuver him into the proper position, using her body as a weapon, there was still a chance she could get into the south tower and explain her predicament before she was pursued. The staff would rally around her, she was sure; they could do naught else if they wanted to save their skins.

But she'd taken too long to make her decision. By the time she'd lowered the ledger back to its place, Flint had regained control and was smiling again.

"Ah, my lady," he said, "there'll be other times more appropriate."

"I doubt it," she said, masking her bitter disappointment.

"Don't," he said. "All will go well for me, I'm sure, and by summer there'll be the perfect opportunity to complete my conquests."

In spite of herself her puzzlement showed. "I don't understand."

"But Caitlin," he said, spreading his arms wide. "By the end of this summer, you'll be my wife."

25

ORIN DANIELS stood alone in the churchyard. In his hands he held a black cup, and about his shoulders hung a patched cloak of earthen brown. A breeze coasted down the hillside from the east and tousled his close-cropped hair, and every few minutes he would scratch at the mass of scar tissue that had once been an eyebrow. His attitude was one of respectful meditation, and those who walked past him on the road refrained from disturbing his mood. He sensed their gaze, however, boring into his back with silent recriminations. In many minds he knew he was a traitor; he had remained at Seacliff after others had left. The villagers' opinion bothered him, but not to the point of distressing him. What he was doing was right, he was sure of it. Otherwise he would have gone like the rest of them—either been sacked outright by Flint, or escaped in the middle of the night to relatives or friends in villages beyond the valley.

Of course, he thought staring at his father's headstone, that was before the possibility of escape had been closed off. Now there were men stationed everywhere, sitting high on the boulders and checking each wagon, each cart as it passed through Seacliff's gates to distant markets. And in each cart and wagon were more of Flint's men, silent and watching, hiding beneath their billowing shirts and cloaks weapons at the ready in case someone was foolish enough to attempt flight.

A wondrous sad thing, Dad, he thought; a wondrous sad thing.

He lifted his gaze to the rear wall, and to the pastureland and fields beyond. New greenery was bursting through the rich, dark ground, and with the lambing and calving already started, dozens of tiny, stumbling additions to the small herds and flocks now frolicked on the grass. Their bleats and hungry cries filled the air to rival the cries of returning birds. The thaws had already passed, but the streams and rills were still swollen, still rushing, and in many places the ground was sodden from the overflow. Flowers wild and cultivated brought rainbows to the earth, and in the morning silence he could hear the hum of the bees from Tom Johnson's hives rising noisily on the breeze.

He sighed and twisted the cap in his hands.

It was time for a decision, and he wasn't sure he had the courage to make it.

He was not so full of himself that he believed the world would stop without him; on the other hand, if he was caught, his mistress would have only Gwen left to care for her. And if he was caught, he wasn't entirely sure Lady Morgan would be able to survive the coming season.

The focus of his vision changed, and he was staring at the mountains, willing them to come alive with men brandishing weapons, with men whose hatred for the English equaled his own and who were willing to lay down their lives to rid the valley of these British vermin. But there was nothing to be seen. And there had been nothing since the turn of the year. Oh, a few of the younger men had managed to slip away now and again: Johnson's youngest son, Willy, and Randall's cousin, Terry, a few of the farmhands and just last week all the men of one family that had been working Falconrest land. That, however, was the exception rather than the rule; most of the night flights had occurred before Flint posted men around the valley.

Did he have the courage to join the outlaws?

He slapped the cap angrily on his head and stalked away, knowing that the courage he needed to remain with Lady Morgan was at least equal to that needed for fleeing to the glens.

At the gate he stopped to watch a wagon rumble by, on the bench sat the widow Sharnac's only son, Edward. There were rumors he, too, was about to take the chance, but nothing in the younger man's demeanor suggested anything but compliance with Seacliff's new regime. They exchanged wary glances. Orin nodded, gnawed thoughtfully on the inside of one cheek and nodded again. Instead of turning around toward Seacliff, he veered left toward the commons. He needed someone to talk to. Martin Randall would give him the advice he required.

On the way he passed Ellis Lynne, and the vicar gave him his best smile, then walked on a few paces before turning and staring. The reverend didn't trust the farrier; not a whit, not a mile. Every Sunday he took the back pew and glared at the minister, his lips mouthing the prayers and little else. And he always left the moment the service was done. Lynne suspected the man of giving aid to the rebels, but without substantial proof he could only mutter veiled insinuations and hope Flint would get the message.

So far, however, he hadn't.

And he was forced to admit to himself that he was growing increasingly afraid. From the day that man—whatever his name was—had been hanged for the major's murder, Flint had inaugurated a stealthy campaign of terror to solidify his position. Taxes had been doubled under the guise of support for the king's military mobilization; the men Morgan had assembled had been withdrawn from the village and housed in long huts in the grove beyond the estate's north wall, where they were easier to control. Flint would send them down into the village en masse, like wolves upon helpless sheep in the night. Three men had been flogged for attempting to join the rebels, and immediately afterward the posting had started. Finally the staff at Seacliff had been reduced to almost nothing. One morning, like a bolt of invisible lightning, the Courder sisters had turned up at Sharnac's requesting shelter. That afternoon all the maids were at the church demanding sanctuary. Some had been accommodated; the rest were permitted to seek out relatives in other towns. As far as Lynne could ascertain, only the old man, Bradford; the scullery wench, Mary, and Orin Daniels; Gwen Thomas and her lover, Orin's brother, remained inside Seacliff's walls.

The logic of staying escaped him; the logic, but not the fear.

He crossed the commons and stood in its center, shaded by an oak said to have been planted there by Lady Morgan's great-grandfather. A quick glance around the streets revealed only the houses and shops. He might as well have been in a community of ghosts, for all the life that he saw. Men were at the forges and the plows, women at the spinning wheels and hearthstones, but their faces reflected nothing. Any number of them had discovered compliance the easiest, safest road to travel, and the handful whose hearts were bitter kept their tirades to themselves.

He sighed. They were fools, of course. All they had to do was see the beauty of the situation, and they would be as happy as they'd always been. Flint was not a carelessly cruel man; he attacked his enemies and left the others alone. Why couldn't they see that? Why in hell's name couldn't they be less Welsh, less goddamned stubborn?

A shrug. It didn't matter. The gold beneath the flooring under his bed was multiplying nicely. Let them walk around as though their necks were in a noose if they wished; he wasn't quite so saturnine. He knew the value of dealing with men who had no hearts to speak of and—considering the size of his payments—who valued his service rather highly.

In the distance a coach approached, and Lynne watched as it slowed to make its way around the green. He nodded politely when Davy Daniels glanced down at him from the high seat. Nice boy, he thought; quiet now, but nice. The coach passed on.

Davy Daniels scowled to himself when he saw the vicar. He was barely able to refrain himself from taking out his disgust on the team. The coach was empty. He'd just returned from taking Birwyn to Chetwyndon, on Bristol Bay. Davy hadn't asked why, and he hadn't been offered a reason. Which was good enough for him; the fewer questions he posed, the longer he would live. And the longer he lived the closer to retribution James Flint would get.

But he could not help thinking of a June just the year before, a June when he'd brought his mistress back to her home and into the maelstrom that had finally engulfed her. Though he knew none of it was any fault of his, he couldn't stop the guilt from keeping him awake at night, from taking perhaps too much gin in the solitude of his bed, from wandering at midnight around Seacliff and wishing the walls would crash down on his head.

He took the rise and directed the team to the carriage house, his face suddenly breaking into a broad smile when he saw Lady Morgan standing at the cliff wall.

She turned at the sound of the coach, saw Davy, and smiled, then waved and waited for him to respond before turning back to the sea. It spoke to her, thundering and whispering, beckoning and promising, but she repulsed its siren lure with a glare that would have stayed the tide had it felt the power of her anger.

The winter had passed with years substituting for days. When spring arrived, it was as if the green had sprung overnight, so suddenly had it swept down from the hills and covered the land. When April crept into May, she finally left her apartments and tested Flint's patience by taking walks on the back lawn and singing loudly in Welsh. But he did not pull the reins. In fact, she countered herself exceedingly lucky that she'd seen him only a handful of times since the night of Oliver's murder. And that was more her doing than his. Once resigned to the sincerity of his threats, she'd decided she would be her own jailer for the time being. All her meals, all her meager recreations, all her brief conversations with Gwen were held in her rooms. Not once during the winter did she leave them. Not even when she learned of the staff's virtual elimination or when she heard of the defections from the village. In her spare time she read, began a journal, and had Gwen teach her the intricacies of embroidery and lace-making.

She survived, as Flint had said she would.

And as Flint had predicted, she plotted and schemed and prayed for the day when she would hold the sword that pierced his blackguard's heart.

She knew no better, more constructive way to sustain herself. She had done her share of weeping, of ranting, of railing against the forces enlisted against her. Yet none of it had helped. None of it had brought her one inch closer to the day Flint would lower his guard and let her slip through.

Yet her hatred of him grew.

She pried at a loose stone in the wall, lifted it when it came away, then threw it as hard as she could. The tide was out, and the stones landed on the rocky beach, bounced up and fell away, lost among its fellows. She threw another and was working on a third when a rustling in the new grass made her turn.

Flint had paled somewhat through the winter, but his bearing had lost none of its arrogance. He had his hands clasped behind his back, his eyes squinting in the bright morning light. When he reached the wall he leaned an elbow on it and regarded the bay thoughtfully.

"A terrible thing, all that water," he said without looking to her. "Such power down there, and we're helpless to harness it for our own use."

"You're doing well enough on land," she said. "I should think you'd be satisfied."

An eyebrow rose in mild surprise. "Do I detect a biblical admonition, my lady?"

"You may detect all you wish, Mr. Flint. I have nothing more to say to you."

"On the contrary," he told her as she walked away toward the house. "We have a great deal to talk about today, Caitlin. I don't believe your memory is so frail that you cannot imagine the content of my upcoming sermon."

She studied the gentle blue of the sky, the delicate shapes of isolated clouds, and she was more relieved than afraid that this moment had finally arrived. She set her chin, fixed her lips tautly, and permitted him a view of her profile, waiting for him to commence. She would be every inch the lady. She would not give him the satisfaction of knowing her heart beat a military tattoo and her blood roared through her temples. And she held the pose gamely, her eyes fixed on the barracks hunched together near the far wall, her mind drifting to the sense of emptiness she'd felt since the staff had been forced to leave; to the interminable evenings alone in her bed, to the stories Gwen passed along to her of the increasing number of villagers who, when she'd not ousted Flint immediately, believed she concurred with most, if not all, of his behavior. That lack of faith, more than anything, sliced her to the quick.

And yet . . . and yet even in that blackest of all times she'd also been able to discover a perverse feeling of gratitude not only to her late husband, but also to her captor. Because of them she was not the same woman she'd been in Eton. She had learned on peril of her life to think before speaking; she had found within her a reservoir of strength she thought had fled on the death of her father. But she kept that strength hidden as best she could. Her only salvation now lay in Flint's continuing underestimation of her character.

She only prayed she wasn't deluding herself.

Flint pushed away from the wall and strode toward her, stopping a few feet distant and regarding her thoughtfully. She did not look at him. She kept her hands at her sides, and her eyes straight ahead.

"I've been thinking about Falconrest," he said as if remarking on the weather.

A dog barked in the stables. The blows of Orin's hammer rang out clearly through the early May air.

"It seems to me, don't you think, that Master Radnor has forfeited his property since the sentence was passed upon him."

Her hair, which she had not restrained with ribbons, was

blown languidly by the breeze. She reached up and pulled its mass over one shoulder, stroking it there idly. This was not the first time he'd mentioned this topic. Each visit by the circuit court traveling from Bangor to Cardiff found the king's judge faced with a petition demanding the property be handed over to the mistress of Seacliff, and after each visit the judge declined to rule because no charge had been made before the bench. And when he looked to Flint for such a charge, Flint only scowled and took back the petition. There was no charge, he knew, because local sentencing had already been handed down, and it was not the policy of the king's men to interfere in local matters so long as they did not contravene the king's law.

That, Caitlin knew, had been Flint's first mistake.

His second was not having killed her when he had the chance.

"Did you hear me, my lady?"

"I did," she said, her voice sounding strange—aloof, and somewhat hard. "And I also know the law, Mr. Flint."

"Ah, yes, the law." He nodded and put a finger to his chin. "But the law says nothing about purchasing the land outright, does it? And by his absence, it seems to me that Radnor has allowed Mr. Jones to become his estate agent. In that capacity, I believe Mr. Jones will see the wisdom of the offer I will make to him before the week is done."

"He will never accept."

Flint smiled. "I believe he will. He's not a stupid man, my lady. Not a stupid man at all."

She looked at him for the first time, coldly. "What will you threaten him with? A flogging? Maiming? Or will it be hanging? I think you will discover that Richard is not easily cowed, least of all by the likes of you."

Flint clucked and shook his head. "I thought you knew me better than that, my dear. I am not an unreasonable man, when other men are willing to be reasonable. And women, too."

She steeled herself. It was coming at last.

"And speaking of women—which I find the most delightful of topics—I should like to know when you will consent to be my wife."

Expecting it and actually hearing it were two different matters; it came like a blow, and she had all she could do to keep from lunging for his throat. Her answer, however, was far less complex than her emotions: "Never."

"My dear, let me remind you there is always the possibility of a terrible miscarriage of justice. It could very well be that certain papers will come into my shocked possession, papers which prove beyond a doubt that I was horribly wrong in passing hasty sentence on that poor Northumberland lad." He waited, toeing the ground with his boot. "Do you think I have made such an error, my lady?"

"I think," she said, "you are a foul, disgusting, merciless swine."

He was in front of her before she knew he'd moved, grabbing her soft shoulders and pulling her hard against his thighs. "Do not push me, my lady," he said quietly. "In case you had not noticed, you are no longer needed around here. As a figure-head your role is done. There is no question who is in control, who holds the purse strings, who holds the keys to people's lives. Me, Caitlin, not you. If you should die this instant, nothing would change."

She leaned away from him and his vehemence, and when finally he released her from his licentious grip, she gasped and stood back to catch her breath.

"That house was built by men we'll never know of," he said. "Its original owners were conquered by those who came after. And your forebears conquered them in turn. I, my lady, am the latest conqueror. Seacliff is mine now, and I don't need you to hold it."

With a visible effort she held her silence. Venting her anger now would accomplish nothing but further misery. She walked stiffly away from him, into the center hall through the rear entrance and directly to her rooms. There she stood in front of the fireplace and stared at her father's bust on the mantel. Tears of frustration spilled down her cheeks, and her chest heaved with the sobs she would not permit to reach her lips.

She wished Gwen would come to her now, though she knew that was unlikely. Since the others had been dismissed, Gwen had been charged with maintaining the whole of the household, including the preparation of meals. Though Mary and Bradford would lend Gwen a hand now and again, and Davy sneaked in from the stables once in a while, she was on her own for the most part. From dawn until well past sunset, she had so little time to herself that Caitlin was lucky to exchange a dozen words with her once a week—less often since spring had arrived. Flint, by unspoken command and with his silent lieutenants, had slowly, steadily decreased the areas of the house in which Caitlin might move unchallenged until she was restricted to her rooms, the hall, and the back lawn.

And with her refusal of Flint's marriage proposal, she knew with a certainty that she would be refused permission to leave the room in which she now stood.

She was right.

Later that evening, hungering for Gwen's company, she made for the door, only to find a laconic Yorkshire trooper outside. He merely showed her his musket and gestured her back inside. His replacement the following morning did the same, after handing her a tray of bread and telling her she would receive nothing more until supper. She blustered, swore, but the man would not be moved into even passing a message to Flint.

She seethed over the next few days, once even considered not eating as a protest. But reason prevailed. Though she was confined to her apartment—obviously until she consented to marry her jailer—the basic situation had remained unchanged. The man was not perfect. He would err eventually. And she spent many of her daylight hours standing on the balcony, watching the sea blend into sky at the horizon and searching for a way to turn things to her advantage.

And it was on just such a day, during a moment when she hovered between depression and determination, that Gwen appeared for the first time in days with her supper tray. A full ten minutes was taken in silent embrace, ten more while Caitlin ranted over Gwen's loss of weight, the rags she wore, the condition of her hands and complexion. When she calmed down, however, and with a suspicious glance at the guard who had stationed himself in the vanity room outside the bedroom, she brought Gwen to the balcony and together they watched the sun setting over the water.

Briefly, she told Gwen of Flint's condition for release, and reaffirmed her own position. "I could play the sham with Oliver," she said, "because he never wanted me. That won't work with James. And I would sooner slit my throat than have to be his wife in all things."

Gwen looked at her sideways. "Perhaps," she said, "you won't have to."

26

THOUGH THE day was warm, the air was biting enough to send Gwen back into the room to fetch a shawl for her mistress. Caitlin did not complain about the delay. She knew that Gwen was merely checking on the guard to make sure he wasn't eavesdropping, and that the importance of what she wanted to relay was great enough for her to risk the terrors of crossing the balcony. Gwen was frightened of heights, and since the balcony was very high, the drop had always seemed fathomless to her. Caitlin waited, then smiled when her friend reappeared and placed the fringed, thin garment of wool over her shoulders. She took the edges and held them over her breast and put her free hand on Gwen's arm to give her some small measure of comfort.

"I feel like I'm flyin' sometimes," the younger woman said, her teeth chattering.

The ground lay far below, the sea farther still. On the horizon the specks of white and brown marked a passing ship. And the sky was low as scudding clouds signaled the approach of a storm from the direction of Ireland.

"Griff's come back," Gwen said then.

Caitlin almost lost her balance, she spun around so rapidly. She had to get hold of herself before the guard noticed her agitation. "What do you mean, returned? Is he here, in the valley?"

Gwen nodded toward the horizon. "From Ireland," she said. "There was, I'm told, a fair number of soldiers in the mountains just before the snows, and Griffin took his men across the channel to hide. No love was lost between him and the English, and he wintered there."

"How do you know this?" she asked anxiously.

Gwen shook her head. "I cannot tell. You should not know,

Cat, because . . ." Her voice trailed off, and Caitlin nodded her understanding. "But he's back, and it won't be long before he knows what's happened here, if he doesn't already."

Caitlin stood at one of the gaps in the wall and gripped the cold stone as if it were a sanctified relic. It was several minutes before she dared speak again. "He can't come here."

"He will. He'll try."

"He cannot. He must not." Fearfully, she looked at Gwen. "The one who told you this must warn Griff that returning here would be too dangerous. There are too many of Flint's men here. Griff would never get close enough to do either of us any good."

"I know," Gwen said. "But you haven't been out, Cat. Flint has increased the numbers of his people in the fields. A fly can't travel without his knowing it. No message will get out."

She brought a fist down on the wall. "It *must!*"

"What do you plan to do, then? Sprout wings and fly over the heads of those creatures? We'll have to trust Griffin, Cat. He's not so foolish that he'll come down here like the flood without checking the banks first."

"And if he doesn't?"

The implication lay heavy between them. Caitlin paced the length of the balcony, looking up to the tower's serrated crown, looking down to the lawn that might as well have been as distant as a star.

"How long has he been back?"

Gwen shrugged.

"And there's no way a message can be sent?"

"Only if whoever takes it plans not to return. Assuming," she added sourly, "he makes it at all."

"He'll be back at me soon," she said, referring to Flint. "You've seen him. He's waiting for something; I don't know what. But it's going to force him into some kind of action. Is there any news from France?"

"Only what I hear from the old fart, who thinks Flint tells him everything under the sun." She bridled at the thought of Bradford's smugness, then let it pass when she saw Caitlin's uncompromising expression. "He says the fighting's been worse in the colonies. There's to be a full war there, he says, no getting around that. King Louis is doing nothing. He makes noises like a stuck pig, but he does nothing. Bradford says he'll wait to see how the Americans do. If German George looks like he's going to lose . . ."

Caitlin nodded thoughtfully. She also suspected that Philip in Spain would not let an opportunity pass to tweak the British lion's tail. Such a situation would be tailor-made for Flint's private little army—an army, she guessed, that would not remain very little for very long.

"Cat, this news troubles you?"

"Some," she admitted. "And I have the horrid feeling I should be bothered more than I am." Again she paced, shaking her head and grunting meaninglessly. Then, as if a barrier had been sprung up before her, she stopped.

Gwen watched her carefully. Cloud shadows and sunlight passed rapidly over her face. Her eyes narrowed and widened and her mouth formed a grim line.

"Does Bradford say anything about where all these swine are posted?" Caitlin finally asked.

"No, Cat. You'd think he was a great general himself the way he struts around and pretends to have great secrets."

"At the gap, surely," she muttered as if she were alone. "I've seen them on the cliffs. Probably at the reaches, too." She looked up. "Do you know if any are at the reaches, Gwen, at the north end fields?" A fleeting gesture told Gwen not to bother replying, and she squinted as though attempting to focus on something at a greater distance than she could see. Then she settled back against the wall with a loud, heavy sigh and nodded once.

Gwen instantly knew what was coming, and turned away.

"That won't do, Gwen Thomas," she said softly. "It will still be there when you turn around again."

"You can't do it," Gwen told her, and stepped across the threshold into the room.

Caitlin followed slowly, glancing once toward the doorway. The guard was not in sight. "What do you think I do up here all day, count dust motes?"

"I know, I know," Gwen admitted with an impotent wave. "But there's no one now to help you."

"There is," she said. "You, Davy, and Orin."

"How? When?"

"The *how* I will tell you when the time comes and no sooner. The *when* shall be . . ." She looked over her shoulder at the clouds. "When hell comes to Seacliff."

Gwen's face formed a mask of bewilderment, but Caitlin only kissed her cheek and allowed at the top of her voice how the supper on her tray was worse than fodder for a dying horse. She ate, however, and chatted about the weather, the reading she had done, the lives of the villagers, as if her father were still master of the estate. Gwen did her best to hold her end of the conversation, but there were moments when she lapsed into puzzled silence and clearly doubted the stability of her mistress's mind. And the more concerned she grew, the more Caitlin laughed aloud until the hour just after dark passed as if the good times had returned and there was no man in their lives named James Patrick Flint.

Then, just before Gwen left, Caitlin took her wrist and peered deep into her eyes. "You will tell Orin it's my birthday," she said.

Gwen opened her mouth, but Caitlin raised a hand to quiet her.

"Tell him," she said firmly. "And tell him the tether must be long enough to reach the sky."

Gwen left shaking her head and muttering to herself, not even bothering to stop a second and swear at the guard. Once the door had closed behind her, Caitlin busied herself by laying a fire and as she knelt before the hearth, she felt the eyes of her father staring down at her from the mantel. She looked up, and grinned. Shadows played across the stone face, so that the eyes seemed to blink, the mouth to twitch, and the brow to crease in approval. The comfort of the illusion was enough to keep her steady when, four days later, the outer door slammed open while she was preparing for bed, and Flint strode in.

She was sitting at her mirror, a pearl-handled brush in her hand, and had been marveling at the way the luster remained in her hair after so long a confinement. She remembered an evening when, as a child, she'd sat at her mother's feet and watched hypnotically as her mother brushed through similar strands, releasing the firelight in soft starbursts, darting across the mirror as if fireflies had been trapped within. The woman, whose face had grown slightly blurred as Caitlin grew older, had hummed to herself and smiled dreamily. Caitlin had taken to praying for whatever happiness had brought her mother such contentment.

She'd been remembering and had just sighed, a smile on her lips, when Flint strode in.

She was wearing little more than a flimsy nightgown over which she had thrown a robe whose cuffs were furred, the neck feathered, and the hem encrusted with semiprecious stones. Flint was taken aback by his reception and stopped in his tracks, the thought striking him that perhaps the woman had something up those elegant and voluminous sleeves of hers. It was not like her to greet him in such a fashion; the best he expected was wintery indifference, and the worst a sharp tongue honed by months of incarceration.

He himself was in a dressing gown of black and silver, his shirt opened to the waist and black slippers on his feet. A split second was all it took to realize she had not yet recognized him, that she was still in a dream world from which she was returning by slow stages. He waited. Having guarded his patience this long, a few more moments would make no difference.

And when she started as if dashed with cold water, he smiled.

"Your answer," he said as she gathered her wits about her. "I'm afraid, my dear, I have little time left to play your foolish games."

"I do not play games with my life," she told him. And her left hand fluttered to her chest when she saw the frank direction of his gaze. A flush of anger and embarrassment only increased the tension, and to break it, she looked back to the mirror, picked up the brush and pulled it harshly through her hair. His reflection appeared behind hers, and she was barely able to prevent herself from shuddering when his hands grasped her shoulders and began kneading them.

"Nevertheless, Caitlin, I must know what to do with you."

"You have done quite enough, I should think."

"Not nearly enough, Caitlin. Not by half." He leaned down and pressed his lips to the top of her head. In a soft voice he said: "Has it ever occurred to you that in some mysterious and, I admit, rather unnerving way you have taken my heart."

"Then I shall give it back," she said instantly. "I have no use for it."

His right hand slipped around to the base of her throat, and thrust aside the robe to touch her bare skin. "But I have use for yours."

"You can't have it."

"I shall take it if I have to," he said. "One way or another."

Her smile was sardonic. "You have a queer way of courting a woman, Mr. Flint. Soft words couched in threats. It must be hard to fill your bed, I shouldn't wonder."

She lowered the brush as his hand eased back and forth, raising a heat she tried to dispel by reminding herself of all the evil he had done. Yet, when his fingertips brushed over the tops of her breasts, the shudder that racked her was not due to revulsion.

His smile, always slightly crooked because of the scar, widened into almost a grimace. "I do not wish to see you in prison, Caitlin. You can believe that, if you believe nothing else."

She did. For whatever reasons, she believed it.

"And neither do I wish to see your lovely body lowered into a grave."

"Another threat?"

"A prediction," he qualified. "I've been rather successful with predictions, you know. Were Sir Oliver still with us, he would confirm that I long ago predicted the troubles in the colonies, and I could not help but see the king's own problems." He tapped his temple significantly. "His sanity's leaving him, I think."

"A pity."

"For the country, yes. Had you been to London with me some months ago you would have heard the merchants complaining angrily about the American war. The colonies are their prime market. Lose them, and a great many enterprises will turn to dust." He kissed her hair again. "Not a history lesson, my dear, and not idle chatter. If markets shrivel, this valley will go with them."

"This valley was here before the English came, Mr. Flint, and it will be here when they leave."

He raised an eyebrow. "Surely you're not referring to me?"

She glared in response.

He clucked his tongue, his hand slipping even lower. He would have cradled her breast had she not stopped him with an angry gesture. A moment later, his left hand cupped her chin gently, lifted her face and turned it to study her profile.

"Marvelous. Absolutely marvelous."

"From anyone else, that would be a compliment."

She thought she'd pushed him too far when a flash of anger crossed his brow, but it was gone when he replaced the frown with a smile that had no depth, held no emotion, was no more sincere than those she'd seen on the face of her late husband.

"An answer," he insisted.

"You've had it for months."

"Are you sure, Caitlin? Are you absolutely sure life would be so bad with me?" His voice dropped to a husky whisper. "We did have a time, you know. One short, marvelous time back there in Eton. Did . . . did that repel you so?"

"It does now."

"Ah," he said quickly, "but it did not then, did it?" His hands dropped away, back to her shoulders. "And if it did not once, it may not again."

"You beguile yourself, Mr. Flint."

"I know myself, Lady Morgan."

She turned without warning on the stool, forcing him back a step. "Mr. Flint, you have come to learn if I will marry you or not. I will not. You have heard my answer, you know I will not change my mind, and you know I understand full well what I am letting myself into. Now, if you would be so kind as to leave me . . ."

Flint stared for a moment she thought unbearably long, then took hold of her arms and pulled her to her feet. She held her head back, but he did not try to kiss her. Instead, he pulled her out of the room, through the vanity and into the reception room where a small window faced the valley. He dragged her to it, his strides so long she had to run to keep her balance. Then he virtually threw her against the sill and pointed.

"There!" he said. "What do you see there?"

She looked through the panes only briefly, not wanting to turn away from him. "Night," she said, simply.

"Look again, Caitlin. There's a sun out there of my own creation."

She stiffened against his body, but did as she was bidden. At first she saw nothing but the vague contours of the village below. The moon was hidden in a bank of low clouds, and since a fine mist filled the air, the lanternlight from the village homes burned only faintly. Then, slowly, her gaze was drawn upward to a wavering glare on the opposite hillside. It was a fire, and a large one. Smoke billowed upward as flames writhed toward the low cloud ceiling; though the distance was great, she could just make out tiny figures racing about madly.

She did not need to hear him whispering in her ear. After a second's thought, she knew she was watching the funeral pyre of Falconrest.

"You couldn't have it," she said throatily, "so you have destroyed it."

"The fortunes of war, my dear, the fortunes of war," he said, watching the fire hypnotically. "I will regret it in years to come, perhaps. But for now it gives me a great deal of satisfaction."

She hardly knew what she was doing. One moment she could not take her horrified gaze from the conflagration lighting the hills like some foul demon's torch, the next she had turned on Flint and had brought her fist across his cheek. It was a punch, not a slap, and it came as such a surprise that it rocked him into the wall. He put a hand to his aching jaw and glared at her.

Caitlin ran.

She knew it was fruitless—that there was no place to hide—but instinct had taken over, and she hoped to reach the bedroom before Flint could recover.

She almost made it.

Just as she slammed the door and was fumbling with the latch, he kicked at it and flung it wide open, the edge catching her shoulder and tumbling her to the floor. He stood over her, fists at his sides, breathing heavily and swallowing. Then he reached down and took a fistful of her robe. She tried to snare his wrist, but he was too fast. He pulled once, pulled again, and when her arm would not slip through the sleeve the material finally gave. She rolled over and out of the robe, staring around the room wildly in search of a weapon and only at the last moment spied her father's bust. She leaped for it, but Flint was beside her in one stride, the back of his hand catching her chest and flinging her to the bed.

She crawled backwards frantically, wanting but not daring to pull the hem of her nightgown down over her legs. But before she reached the other side of the mattress he reached out again, caught the neckline of the gown and yanked. Her head snapped forward, and she felt a burning lash across the nape of her neck. He yanked again, and the center seam gave a few inches. The sound made him grin, made her gasp, then dig her nails into the back of his hand. He yelled and released her, and she spun off the mattress to her feet.

Her arms had turned to lead, and something had coated her mouth and throat so she couldn't scream. Perspiration washed over her, and the gown's material soaked it up. The damp fabric clung to her like a second skin and revealed to Flint far more than it concealed. She didn't care. What mattered to her was that he not touch her again.

Slowly, silently, he inched sideways around to the footboard. Before he could move, she was on the mattress again, flinging aside the pillows and pressing herself against the headboard. Her hair covered one side of her face and veiled her exposed breasts. The only light in the room was from the fire in the grate, and it turned his face into a satanic crimson mask that made her dizzy when she watched him closely. He tilted his head and moved on; she sidled away, dropping to the floor when he reached the other side of the bed.

"I am quicker than you," he said.

She would not speak. While one part of her mind was trying to anticipate his next move, the other was trying to locate a weapon close at hand. If she turned to the mantel he would be on her; if she headed for the door he would have her in two steps; and there was nothing at all near or on the bed that she could use.

"Caitlin, Caitlin, how foolish you are."

As she backed toward the edge of the bed platform her foot caught on the hem of her gown. She almost fell flat on her face and in that paralyzing moment of helplessness he rounded the corner and, with one hand gripping the bedpost, snared her again. This time she did not move. She stood there, immobile, as he tore the cloth from her body. Then he sat on the edge of the mattress holding the crumpled gown in his hands.

"Yes," he said, nodding. "Yes."

She made no attempt to cover herself. Instead, she stepped to the floor and backed away until she reached the hearth. The firelight rippled across the swells of her breasts, the firm plane of her stomach, and added a golden sheen to the perspiration on her flesh. At grave risk to herself—slowly, without taking her eyes from his—she knelt beside the hearth and lowered her head submissively.

"Caitlin, what is it?" Flint said, rising and tossing the shreds of the gown to one side.

"If you want me, there's nothing I can do to stop you."

He knelt in front of her and stroked the satin slope of her shoulder, touched her breasts, her abdomen, put his hands firmly on her flanks and turned his face to kiss her. She did not respond. She remained as a statue, neither accepting nor resisting, and though her heart recoiled at the fondling of her breasts, at the callous probing between her thighs, she did nothing but stare at him.

It did not take long for frustration to overtake him. He grabbed her shoulders and shook her. "I thought you said I could have you!" he shouted. "What in hell are you playing at now?"

"You can have me," she said without raising her voice, "but nothing more. Nothing more, Mr. Flint."

He slapped her, but her head was rigid and did not recoil. "Nothing more."

He slapped her again, three and four times before clubbing her with a fist and jumping to his feet. "You're not human," he hissed. "None of you Welsh are." He raised his arm to strike her again.

She stared. "Nothing more."

And it was easier than she'd hoped; for the most part all she had to do was remember the ashes of Falconrest, and not even his blows could pierce her armor.

"You will die!" he vowed as he stalked from the room. "Damn you, woman, you will not live out the week!"

The door slammed, the mirrors trembled, and Caitlin remained on the hearth, not moving until dawn a few hours later. And when first light slanted into the room she rose, took another robe from the closet and asked the guard at the door to fetch Gwen Thomas. There was a message to be delivered, and she wanted her breakfast.

27

THE RAIN had begun the afternoon before as a gray blanket that descended over the valley from the reaches of Cardigan Bay. Mist crowned the treetops, gathered in the mouths of burrows, filled the land's depressions until the outlines of objects blurred and appeared otherworldly. Tendrils of white fog snaked across the surface of the streams, swirling, shredding, rejoining in a rush to bury the shallows under a deceptively thick cover. Then the air chilled as the invisible sun dropped below the horizon, and the mist became a drizzle, and the drizzle a light rain, that softened the ruts in lanes, slickened the crushed stone of the main roads, and dripped from leaves and eaves into empty, fat rain barrels.

It was a spring rain, a nourishing rain, and Caitlin stood at the balcony door and watched it render the bay invisible. She hugged herself for warmth despite the blazing hearth; she looked hopelessly at the cloud cover and wished she could locate some sign of lightning, some indication of turbulence beyond the gentle rainfall. It had been two days since Gwen had told her that she'd passed Caitlin's message on to Orin; two days of praying for the heavens to stop their taunting and give her what she demanded.

And during those two days, Gwen had told her, Flint had begun behaving like a man who had lost all his senses. He prowled the corridors cursing and muttering to himself, barking incomprehensible orders at Nate Birwyn. Once he took his chestnut gelding for a ride that lasted nearly the entire day, returning only for supper, drenched and sneezing and forcing even Birwyn to keep a safe distance.

He's working up to it, Caitlin decided. In his own dark way he probably really did love her, and unless he carried out his threat to see her dead, he would be granting her a power over

him no person had ever exercised before. He could never live
that way, and she knew it. How long it would take before he
convinced himself to kill her, she could only guess.

Two men walked across the back lawn. With their heads
covered by floppy-brimmed hats and their cloaks darkly sodden, they looked like gnomes just out of their burrows. She
could see no weapons, but she sensed they were there just the
same. Pistols or muskets, tucked just out of reach of the rain.
The men passed from view, and she bit her lower lip lightly,
frowned, and returned to her secretary, staring at, without seeing,
the blank page of her journal. The temptation to put down
everything that crossed her mind was immense, but she had
restrained herself in case of prying eyes: Mary, whenever she
flitted into the room with her feather duster and inane chatter;
Bradford, when he brought her one of her meals; and Flint
himself, whose curiosity would not be thwarted by a simple
lock and a thin strap of burnished leather.

She pushed aside the inkwell and quill. She had no intention
of signing her own death warrant.

Another day passed. The rain subsided, and there were small
breaks in the clouds. She almost wept when she saw the streams
of sunlight funneled down from them. The evening before,
long after she had finished eating, she had heard Flint stalking
the gallery and screaming imprecations at the walls. At first
she'd decided Gwen had been right, that the man had gone
mad; later, however, when the house had quieted down, she
understood in a flash that his madness was only a pretense. He
was a man too much in control of himself to allow her rejection
to drive him insane. Was he trying to break her resistance by
gnawing at her fears? What better way to convince her to marry
him than by pretending he was losing his mind at the thought
of having to kill her?

Which meant, she prayed, there was still some faint hope
he would not kill her as he had vowed.

She was strong, and she withstood the pressure, but she was
not strong enough to face the next morning when the clouds
scattered, the blue skies returned in force, and the temperature
climbed to warn of coming summer.

She wept, and allowed the tears to flow unhindered.

And in weeping, she understood there was more than the
weather's betrayal working at her mind. After realizing that

Flint was feigning madness, she'd formed a decision, quite without her realizing it: to die would be to abandon much more than her life. She would be leaving behind too many helpless people, too many memories, and too much history to the whims of James Patrick Flint and his ghostly band of men.

By permitting him to kill her she would commit a safe form of suicide, giving herself over to the consequences of foolish stubbornness and blinding pride.

And if she did that, she would receive and deserve all the approbation her people would heap upon her; and if she turned her back now on all she had come to believe she stood for, her consignment to hell would be the most lenient of punishments.

She turned away from the sun and the blue sky.

She stripped and bathed in cold water, not bothering to lace the bath with scent. Then she sat naked at the vanity, brushing her hair two hundred strokes, until its texture and color were almost spectral in their beauty. Choosing the simplest gown she owned—a high-necked brown dress without a single gracing of lace—she walked to the outer door and opened it. The guard, startled, wheeled around and stared.

"You will please inform Mr. Flint that I have reconsidered," she said, after taking a deep, shuddering breath that did not stem the chill that coursed through her blood.

"M'lady?"

"Never mind trying to understand what I'm talking about," she said quietly, but firmly. "Just deliver the message at once, please. And tell him I shall be waiting."

The day passed without a response.

The following morning taunted her cruelly with billowing white clouds that lined the horizon, but reached Seacliff in a few trailing wisps.

On the morning of the third day Gwen burst into her chambers, her face crimson with outrage and her hands raking the air or pulling harshly at her hair as she searched for words.

"I've heard," she finally said, practically shouting.

Caitlin was in the same plain dress, and sat in an armchair she had dragged before the open French doors. A vagrant breeze toyed with strands of her hair, and at times blew them in front of her eyes, making her push them back in annoyance. She did not turn around, so Gwen rounded the chair and stood in front of her, hands now at her hips and her chest pumping for breath.

"I've heard what you're planning to do."

Caitlin slowly lifted her gaze. "I have no choice," she said flatly.

"What? You could die!"

She refused to be baited. "And what good would that do, Gwen? What earthly good would my dying do for anyone?"

Gwen's disgust bleached all beauty from her face. "The word's already in the village, you know," she said scornfully. "La, you should hear what they're saying now." She flicked out a hand toward Caitlin's unmoving head. "Your ears surely must be burning all this while." She stalked away and kicked at the bed dais. "You must sleep well, then."

"I don't sleep at all."

Gwen froze, her spine rigid and her head held high. Then she looked over her shoulder. "God willing, you'll never sleep another night in your life."

"Gwen, please—"

"Gwen, please," she mocked. "Gwen, please. You were dying, and I nursed you back. You were to run on your birthday, and I was going with you. That . . . that *man* put his hands on me, and I took it because I feared for your life. And now . . . now you're going to take him as a husband just because you don't want to die?" She drew in a deep breath, and the room took on a frigid silence. "He's taken it all from you, hasn't he? You've nothing left, am I right?"

"You don't understand, Gwen."

Gwen's shoulders sagged, and though she shed no tears, her voice was filled with the weeping she must have been doing since she'd gotten the news. "I do. I really do. I had just hoped you could be Cat awhile longer, just until—"

The sound of Gwen's fleeing footsteps lingered on long after she had gone; Caitlin was alone again. Still waiting. Still seated in front of the balcony doors and watching the undulations of the sea. Mary brought all her meals. Bradford twice requested she prepare a wedding guest list—and twice Caitlin informed him she would have none of it, that Flint could invite King George for all she gave a damn. Nate Birwyn poked his one-eyed head in one morning and asked if she wouldn't care to take a short ride in the cart. She shook her head without looking at him, and he left with a careless shrug.

He's still playing his secret games, she thought when May slipped into June with the sun high overhead and the sea turned a deep shifting blue; now he's waiting for me to send him a plea to end the suspense.

But she was still alive. And though she was still alone, she knew that he had finally made his third mistake: if the first had been in not taking Griffin, and the second in not killing her shortly afterward, then the third was in permitting her all this time to think.

And think she did.

And in thinking found something she didn't dare yet call hope.

One afternoon she asked Bradford if he had any word from Gwen, anything at all. The old retainer, his face more deeply lined than ever and his few wisps of graying hair brittle and stiff, sniffed and informed her that the Thomas woman had thrown all her belongings into a sack and had taken a bed in the Daniels cottage. Mr. Flint did not seem to mind. He never mentioned her at all.

Caitlin did not permit herself to despair. Sooner or later, Gwen would forgive her.

In the middle of June Mary woke her shortly after dawn and told her she was to prepare herself. Mr. Flint would call on her after supper, and he left explicit instructions that she be well fed and well groomed.

She took the brown dress out again, and set the pearl-backed brush to her hair.

When at the stroke of seven, Flint opened the door, she was waiting in the center of the room, composed but not smiling.

He said nothing at first. He merely walked around her as if inspecting a possible livestock purchase. He nodded, he grunted, he reached out and sifted her hair through his fingers. She held herself still, her hands clasped demurely at her waist and her eyes fixed on a point midway between Flint and herself. She did not focus her gaze until he'd stopped his perusal and nodded his approval.

"I'm glad you're pleased," she said, her voice hollow.

"I am well pleased indeed," he told her formally. Then a hint of mischief sparked his eyes. "But you don't fool me for

a minute, Caitlin Morgan. Be aware of that fact—you don't
fool me for a minute. The only reason you're doing this is to
save your lovely neck."

"I do not deny it."

He applauded her silently. "Well done, Caitlin, well done.
I would not have it any other way. It is," he said, rubbing his
hands together, "rather like a campaign, don't you think? I
have all the armies at my command, ready and eager to do
battle, and you are the fortress. The first defenses have been
breached, so to speak, and now I move on to the next." Then
he frowned and shook his head. "No, that's a poor way of
putting it. I apologize. You must know by now that I think
more highly of you than that."

Caitlin smiled, thinking all the while how apt the military
analogy really was. The man would have to break down many
lines of defense before conquering her, and if she had anything
to say about it, that moment would never come.

"There's some activity in the hills," he said then, eyeing
her shrewdly. "It appears a few of your wayward lambs are
determined to return to their flock."

"You've taken care of that, I'm sure," she said dryly.

"Oh, I have, my dear. I have. They've seen a little more
than they bargained for, I think." He paused. "I just thought
you'd like to know."

She faced him squarely. "Thank you."

He laughed, a rich and rolling laugh that forced him to reach
for her shoulder for support. She did not move or sway under
his pressure. Neither did her lips break their solemn taut line
when he invited her with a gesture to join in his delight. Feigning regret when she declined, he sobered, caught his breath
with a gasp, and took her elbow.

"We will go downstairs now and inform the staff of the
date, if you don't mind."

"You have set one, then?"

"Indeed, my dear." He grinned.

"If I'm to be part of this, don't you think I should know?"

Another laugh, quick and grating. "Caitlin, you are truly a
wonder. How does three days hence suit you?"

Three days suited her not at all, but her nod encouraged
him to break into a genuine smile that lasted all the way to the
front room. She glanced around slowly as he guided her to the
couch by the massive hearth. It had been so long since she had

seen the blackened stoves; it was as if she were viewing them for the first time. And nothing had changed. The tapestries and portraits were still in their places; the bookshelves were still lined with volumes and ledgers; and the sideboards and chairs were still in their usual places. There was a faint gray layer of dust on the wood, to be sure, and it did not take more than a quick glance to see that the draperies had not been taken down for shaking since last fall—but other than that, nothing had changed.

And she felt somehow cheated.

After all she had been through, after the lives that had been lost over the past year, the room should have looked as if it had suffered a cataclysm.

They stood on the hearth, and as if at an unseen signal Bradford entered from the side corridor, Mary shuffling in at his heels. Flint nodded graciously to them and slipped an arm around Caitlin's waist. When he began speaking, she was startled and almost demanded he wait for the others; but then she remembered that all the "others"—the staff—were gone.

"For the next three days," Flint told Bradford, "you will need some assistance from Mr. Birwyn's men to help you around the place. I will see to it they follow whatever instructions you choose to give them. If there is any trouble, any grumbling, you will come to me at once, and I shall determine the punishment. Mary," he said to the young wench gaping at him, "I will fetch some of the ladies from the village to lend you a hand cleaning the rooms. All of them must be absolutely perfect, from the floors to the walls. See to it, please, that you also prepare a list of foodstuffs for the banquet following the ceremony. None of it must come from outside the valley. This will be a windfall for our people in more ways than one." Then he turned on Bradford. "Send Davy down for the vicar straightaway. Lady Morgan and I will want to see him as soon as possible."

Mary curtsied clumsily and hurried from the room at Flint's offhanded dismissal. Caitlin was astonished, however, to see Bradford hesitate before leaving. Such reluctance wasn't like him at all, and she could not help thinking that perhaps his lifelong allegiance to the major had not been completely transferred to the major's former steward. If that was true, however, it was such a small thing it was not worth considering. Certainly it was no cause for hope.

As soon as they were alone again, Flint took his arm away from her waist and stared at the ashes piled against the firewall. "Bradford is getting old," he said.

Caitlin held her breath, praying the man hadn't managed to read her mind—though there was no small satisfaction in knowing she'd been right about Bradford's wavering loyalty.

"He tells me . . . he has been telling me for days that I should choose another time for the wedding. He claims that by sniffing the air like some misbegotten hound he can tell when it will rain, even if there are no clouds in the sky. And he fears our first day as man and wife will be spoiled by the weather." He looked back at her. "Do you think that foolish or wise?"

"If you are really asking for my opinion, Mr. Flint, then no, I don't think it foolish in the least. There is, in fact, a certain smell to the air before a storm arrives. I believe there's rain in a fine mist that we neither see nor feel, but which can be smelled just the same."

"You think so?"

She smiled tightly. "I know so."

He considered, and dismissed her words. "It makes no difference, for all of that, my lady. Rain or shine or Bradford's infernal mothering, we will proceed just the same."

"As you will, Mr. Flint."

"Indeed," he said. "As I will."

He strode swiftly across the room, and Caitlin waited until he'd reached the doorway before calling his name. He turned, just as Nate Birwyn appeared at his side.

"Mr. Flint," she said loudly, hoping volume would hide the trembling of her voice, "if I'm to be married in three days' time there are things I must do."

"Then do them, my lady."

Hold, she told her temper; hold.

"I should like very much to visit my father's grave. And my late husband's."

His eyes narrowed slightly, but he granted the request with an offhanded wave.

"And I should like to pay a call on Master Randall."

"Oh?" Flint exchanged glances with Birwyn.

"It is customary," she said, "for the wife to present the husband with a gift, is it not?"

Flint's grin was feral. "I should think Seacliff would be gift enough, Caitlin."

"Perhaps," she agreed, biting down a sudden wave of revulsion, "but would you deny me the opportunity to add something to the occasion?"

Birwyn's expression was doubtful, but she was positive Flint would not be able to resist the lure, especially since he believed he had already hooked the catch.

"Very well," he said. And then, with a low bow, "If you'll excuse me . . ."

Caitlin waited until the two men had left, then sank onto the couch and covered her face with her hands. They were clammy, and they twitched as her tension was slowly released. She wanted desperately to scream, or to grab hold of the heaviest object she could lift and heave it through the window, but at the moment the most important thing was to maintain her control. If she slipped now, in front of Flint or anyone else, it would be all over.

Ten minutes passed before she felt steady enough to rise. Then she made her way directly to her rooms where she sat at her desk and wrote hastily in the light of a wavering candle. When she was finished she tore the page from her journal and, lifting a candle, walked to the fireplace where she knelt on the hearth and placed the journal sheet on the ashes. Holding the flame to the bottom edge she watched her last words begin to curl and turn brown. Then she blew out the glowing wick and lay on her bed, staring at the ceiling while the tiny blue flame flickered, blazed, and died, having devoured her words:

It is done, and now that it is done there is no turning away. I am alone and friendless, which is of my own doing. I dare not involve others until I know what I'm doing will succeed. It is better this way. There is much pain, and there is much darkness around me, but with God's help I shall be able to find the light that will free me and the balm to ease the pain.

If I do not, if failure is cast into my path, then Gwen, dear Gwen, will have her wish.

If I fail, I will be dead.

And if I fail, Griffin will never hear from my lips how much I have truly loved him, and love him now. A little late in the coming, perhaps, but late in coming rather than never understanding at all is a far better course.

Would that I had the prophetic powers to lead me. Father,
I do not want to die.

She sighed loudly, and by slow degrees. Writing the words
had been a way to make a compact with herself. Once before
she had attempted to throw off her shackles; now she would
try again. And this time there would be nothing to thwart her.
One way or another it would end.

And the end would begin tomorrow.

"Tomorrow," she whispered, both a vow and a shudder of
fear. "Tomorrow."

28

THE GRASS IN THE cemetery had been recently
scythed, and a few of the graves had been freshened with
flowers. The old birch overhanging the mausoleum had weath-
ered still another winter, its foliage thick and cool and sheltering
the gamboling of several frisky squirrels. Caitlin stood beneath
the branches for several minutes, listening to their play and
smiling thoughtfully. Occasionally she would be showered with
broken twigs and torn leaves or the shells of acorns. When her
hand rose to brush at her hair and shoulders, her movement
was languid, almost as though she was reluctant, or was listening instead to the muted voices of the boys' choir practicing
in the nearby church. They would be singing for her the day
after tomorrow, and the dulcet tones of the hymn carried more
than a little melancholy and regret.

She sighed, and picked her way through the maze of knobby
roots poking through the ground until she reached the bronze
door of the crypt. A glance over her shoulder revealed Birwyn
standing patiently at the gates. She pushed the door open,
stepped in, and closed herself off from the village, and from
the world.

The total darkness did not disturb her. Within moments she

had struck a flint, set it to a wick, and held the candle by its holder at eye level. There was her father, the plaque tarnished already, and below him, closest to the floor, was Sir Oliver. Not exactly, she thought with mordant humor, the position he would have chosen for himself.

Carefully, so as not to agitate the flame, she placed the holder on the floor and sat beside it, adjusting her skirts about her ankles and pulling off her white gloves. It was her guess that she remain undisturbed for at least fifteen minutes. Then Birwyn would grow anxious and summon the courage he needed to come through the gates and see if she hadn't discovered some way to flee. During that time Caitlin would be trying to call forth her own courage, for her next stop was Martin Randall's shop, assuming he would greet her at all.

The air grew close.

She felt no fear about sitting among the dead; at present they provided her with more company than did most of the living. Ironic, she thought. Although she had spent most of her life in pursuit of amusement and recreation, she was now drawing comfort from those who would never dance or laugh again.

"Father," she whispered then, "do you remember the time Oliver first came to you to ask for my hand? I could see, later, how you had struggled with your pride as you gave it, and how annoyed you were with me for fussing so about it. But neither of us was to blame for what happened later. We couldn't know. *I* couldn't have known. If I hadn't been so addlepated, perhaps I might have seen. But I was, and I didn't. And I hope you will forgive me now, for what I'm about to do."

Stiffly she rose to her feet, wincing at the pain in her knees as she reached down for the candle and extinguished the flame. She fumbled for a moment before finding the door and, pulling it open, blinking at the bright sunlight. She stepped over the threshold just as Birwyn put his hand on the gate latch. She nodded to him, he nodded back, and she turned away, staring into the misty darkness of the crypt until she could feel her guard's eyes boring into the back of her neck.

Inhaling deeply, her lips forming a grim line, she rejoined him, allowing him to open the gate and hold her elbow as she climbed into the cart and took her seat. Davy had volunteered to drive her, but she had refused to let him, steeling herself against the hurt in his eyes. She needed the one-eyed man now to remind herself not to commit a folly. Davy would give her false courage; Birwyn extra caution.

Around the commons they rode, the midafternoon sun slightly paled by a dim haze that had taken hold of the valley just after dawn. The bay, too, she noted, was restless; the swells were erratic, some large and some regular-sized, and the color was changing in spite of the sky's constant blue. They seemed to grow darker, then, angry, and once in a while a stiff gust broke whitecaps into spray. The tension she'd felt since awakening seemed to have been transmitted to the air, which was unmoving, stifling, like the air in a room that had been sealed shut for centuries.

There were a few people in their gardens, a few more standing in the Stag's Head yard, and all of them turned their heads boldly when she left the cart and walked through the gap in Randall's wall. On a post near the door hung a sign: *M. Randall, Esq. Fine Work in Gold and Tin*. There was an oversized window to her right, and it displayed kettles and pots, utensils and sconces, all of which circled a large oval plate of elaborately hammered gold. The gold plate had been there as long as she could remember; her father had once tried to purchase it, but the goldsmith had refused, saying he had worked for three years to get the floral and stag designs right, and once accomplished he was unable to part with the plate at any price.

It was a wonder, she thought, that Flint hadn't found a way to take it for himself.

The shop door was ajar.

There was no sound within.

She checked first to see if Birwyn was still on the wagon perch before pushing open the door and stepping into a dimly lit room. A low display case stood on her right just in front of the window, a table and two high-backed chairs sat on her left for waiting customers, and directly ahead was a long table covered with a white linen cloth on which had been arranged more than a dozen candelabra of varying sizes and shapes.

As she stepped toward them, aware of how very warm it was inside despite the cooling thatched roof, a door in the back wall opened and Martin Randall stepped inside. He was clearly not expecting her. He pulled the door to, turned, and his square jaw nearly dropped to his chest. His flustered reaction lasted only a second; then he was around the table in a hurry, wiping his large scarred hands on his apron.

"Lady Morgan," he said in bewildered greeting.

She smiled at him and held out her hand.

Randall hesitated, casting a surreptitious glance sideways toward the large window to make sure they were unobserved. Then he took her hand, but released it suddenly, as if she were on fire. Though she was hurt, Caitlin could not blame him. She was lucky, considering his reputation for daring, that he didn't throw her out on her ear.

"I expect you've come about the wedding and such?" he said, measuring the words carefully in English.

"I certainly have," she said, quite deliberately in Welsh and delighting at the amazement that broke across his face. He had expected her to converse in English. Hadn't she gone English as everyone was saying? "And other things."

"Other things?"

She passed around him and made an elaborate show of examining the candelabra. "I am told, Master Randall, that you are quite knowledgeable about things other than your craft."

"M'lady?" he said, puzzled.

"I have heard, for example," she said casually, "that you have a great skill at wrestling, that there is no one in or out of the valley who dares challenge you."

"I have never been thrown, m'lady," he said, a faint note of pride entering his voice and blending with his bewilderment. "But I—"

She turned on him, still smiling. "Master Randall," she scolded playfully, "from what I hear, that isn't strictly true."

He drew himself up, his forearms visible beneath his rolled-up sleeves, the muscles bulging under a thick matting of black hair. "You have heard wrong, m'lady, if you'll pardon me for saying so."

"Well, now." She eased around him again, deliberately allowing her skirts to brush against his trouser leg, stopping when she reached the display case and, when he did not follow, motioning him behind it. He hesitated, and she pointed while she stared out the window at Birwyn, who was eyeing the cottage under his broad-brimmed dark hat.

She stared down through the glass top of the case and spoke without looking up. "I hear that there is one who manages to best you each time you try."

A silence followed, and she watched his reflection as he stepped between her and the window. He was frowning.

"I believe it is Griffin Radnor who has the key to your skill."

Silence again. The frown had turned to a deep, wary scowl.

Then: "If you turn around, Master Randall, you will see waiting in the trap a friend of James Flint's. He will be in here in a very few minutes, wondering if perhaps you haven't done something horrid to me."

"M'lady—"

"He is not very nice, to put it mildly," she went on, ignoring his interruption. "We do not get along, Mr. Birwyn and I."

Now Randall's silence was clearly quizzical. When he turned, and Birwyn straightened slightly, he knew the two of them could be observed through the window. He fussed a bit with some of the items, then grunted as he lifted the gold plate from its shelf. A flare of sunlight reflecting from its center made Caitlin turn away, but not before she caught a glimpse of Randall smiling.

"The man has one eye," the goldsmith said, lowering the plate slowly to the struts atop the case.

"He sees nevertheless."

She put a finger to her chin and cocked her head as if studying the designs.

"You've not been down in a while and some, m'lady." The voice was neutral.

"I've had little choice in the matter," she answered bluntly, the finger folding into her fist.

"And now you're to marry?"

"Perhaps."

An eyebrow rose, but Randall said nothing.

"As I recall," she continued, biting nervously at her lips and praying she wasn't mistaken, "there was talk, aside from your exploits in wrestling, that you managed, from time to time, to slip a chest of supplies or two to the men living outside the valley. Our men," she amended quickly. And held her breath. It was done. If he denied it, if he suspected her of being an agent of Flint's, she would have to find some other way to contact Griffin Radnor. But by then, it might be too late.

"People do talk," he said suspiciously.

"And people do, from time to time, manage to slip away to the men, don't they?"

"I've heard it's been done."

She looked up at him, locking gazes with him in earnest

appeal. "It will be done again, Master Randall. It must be done again, or the Evans family will vanish from Wales as if it had never existed."

There was nothing readable in his expression. Instead, he picked up the plate again and replaced it in the window, dusted it with the corner of his apron and shook his head slowly. Then he snapped his head around as Birwyn, finally rid of his patience, swung down from his seat and walked purposefully toward the shop.

"Do you hunt much, m'lady?"

She blinked, confused.

"There's a perfect place for deer, in case you've a mind for venison on your wedding day. If you ken Alan Carver's farm at the north end, there's a trail they follow so the hunt won't find them."

The door opened, and Birwyn stood on the threshold.

"I do indeed enjoy hunting," she said, stepping away from the case. "But I'm sorry to say there's little enough time left for the work you say you'll have to do." She turned to Birwyn and smiled sadly. "I'm afraid James will have to be disappointed, Nate."

"Sorry, m'lady," Randall said abjectly. "I do the best I can."

"I'm sure you do," she told him.

"M'lady," Birwyn said, his tone shaded in menace, "it's time I was takin' you back."

She brushed past him without a backward glance, and had just seated herself in the cart when Randall broke from the shop and ran up to her, panting. Birwyn started to whip the pony into motion anyway, but Caitlin stopped him by poking his back.

"M'lady," Randall said, "I've been thinkin' about the order you've given."

"Yes?" A swift prayer, then, that Birwyn would not hear the pounding of her heart.

"There are some hereabouts who wouldn't even make the effort."

She looked down the road through the village, at the sullen stares that confronted her, and her throat felt dry. "I know, I know. But I truly do wish that very thing, Master Randall. It would mean a lot. A great deal, in fact." Then she gambled on Birwyn's continued confusion over the cryptic conversation and looked Randall straight in the eye. "But I am determined to make this wedding a memorable one, no matter what people may think of me. It may come as a surprise, but I am still my father's daughter."

Randall stepped back as if a great weight had been lifted suddenly from his chest. "I shall do my best, m'lady," he said, bowing, touching his hand to his brow.

She wanted to weep, with joy and relief. "I know you will, Martin." Then she poked Birwyn again. "I think it's time we moved on, don't you, Nate? Mr. Flint will be waiting."

The whip cracked, and the cart turned around in the narrow street, and as they swung around the commons' verdant square, she dared not look again at Martin Randall. She found herself drenched in perspiration, but not from the sun's heat. A chill worked its way along her spine, but not from the cool breeze blowing soothingly over her skin. And there was a churning in her stomach, but she hoped it was not from having misplaced her trust.

Birwyn whistled tunelessly; the pony's hooves on the road laid centuries ago by the Romans sounded loudly, like musketfire; and when they reached the top of the rise, Caitlin stayed in the cart all the way to the stables, instead of hopping out and walking the rest of the way to Seacliff, as was her custom. Though her guardian looked at her strangely, she did not head directly for the house. Instead she moved on to Orin Daniels's cottage, saw Gwen at the well and before the surprised woman could protest, grabbed firm hold of her arm and pulled her toward the cliff wall.

"I have nothin' to say," Gwen muttered several times as they walked. But she did not try to pull away.

"You don't have to say anything," Caitlin told her as though she were scolding a child. "All you have to do is listen, and then you can leave."

"With pleasure."

At the wall, Caitlin released her, and she stepped hurriedly away, as if Caitlin had the plague. She rubbed at her arm gingerly and spat once against the wind.

"I want you in my rooms tomorrow night," Caitlin told her, staring out at the water.

"I'd sooner die."

"You will if you do not."

Gwen spun on her, eyes flashing hatred. "So that's how it is, is it? He's not only turned you coward; he's turned you English at last."

"He's done nothing of the sort. I just won't have Mary's hands on me while I dress."

"And I'll not have my hands on that dress. What do you take me for, Cat?"

"I take you for someone who has been through hell, as I have," she said simply. "And if you truly despised me, you would have tried to get away from here long before now." Her smile was rueful. "You see, I know you too well, Gwen Thomas. I know you all too well."

"Well, I don't know you at all," Gwen said less forcefully.

"You know me better than you think."

"Do I?"

A voice from the house interrupted them, and Caitlin turned to see Flint standing in the doorway of the rear sitting room. He was dressed for riding, and in his left hand he held the coiled whip she knew all too well. He called her again and beckoned angrily, impatiently.

"Tomorrow night, gone seven," she said, and did not give Gwen an opportunity to argue further; she walked away with her chin high and her hands buried in her skirts. When she reached Flint, he stepped aside and gestured her into the room.

"Birwyn tells me you spent some time with the goldsmith," he said accusingly.

Her expression was blank. "Am I to assume you are jealous?"

"You are to assume nothing. I want to know what you found so interesting in that grubby little shop of his."

Haughtily she drew herself up. "I was, if you must know, hoping Mr. Randall would be able to fashion a gift for you, as I believe I've already mentioned."

"And?"

"And there was too little time. He was much more interested in the coming days' hunting than he was in our nuptials."

Flint leaned close to her face, and she could smell wine on his breath as well as see the tiny veins inflamed across his eyes. "If you are lying to me, Caitlin . . ." and the whip uncoiled and snaked toward the floor.

"What would it profit me?" she asked indignantly. "Do you

think I've asked Mr. Randall to gather the farmers together and storm this house and spirit me away? And do you really think he would even try if I had? Really, Mr. Flint. Really."

He wavered between suspicion and trust, and finally chose the latter by kissing her quickly on the cheek. "You do want to live, don't you?"

"I would not be doing this thing if I did not."

"You may go, then," he said. "But mind," he cautioned before she left the room. "Mind you do not give me cause to change my tune."

"Never," she said sweetly, and with a swish of her skirts vanished into the corridor. Flint waited, thinking she might return for a parting word, then headed outside where he met Birwyn. Together they walked toward the barracks, heads down, Flint's whip trailing behind.

"I don't trust her," he said.

"Ye've a right not to," Birwyn agreed.

"I want men around this place, starting sunset tomorrow. They will not leave until I give the word, is that understood?"

Birwyn faltered, dropped several paces behind, and had to hurry to catch up with his master. "But the frigate—"

"Will not beach for another week. We've plenty of time for business. I'm expecting that man from London tomorrow. He will have the gold, and the instructions. I do not, my dear friend, expect to wait much longer before we begin stirring the pot to a boil."

When they reached the northern arm of the wall, they passed through a ragged gap into the barracks yard. Men who had been lounging beneath the trees jumped quickly to their feet, saluted, and focused their eyes straight ahead of them. Within moments, word had passed to those inside, and the yard filled with all those who were not on duty around the valley. Flint examined them critically, but did not smile until he was satisfied with their appearance.

"Gentlemen," he finally said, "I'm inviting you to a wedding."

From her balcony Caitlin watched Flint and Birwyn climb through the wall and disappear into the gathering shadows beneath the trees. She knew where they were headed, and she suspected what Flint would do when he arrived. But it did not matter. One man or a thousand, she had gone too far now to turn back. And it astonished her to discover that, since sparring with him in this very room so many months before, she felt for the first time a tingling, rushing excitement. Much of it was due to the first positive action she had taken since winter; the rest to the inevitability of it all, as if her trials and humiliations were only preparations for a test that would determine once and for all the true strength of her convictions.

There would be no more posturing, no more tantrums or rants; no more postponements, no reasons for altering her plans. It was now or never, since she'd given Randall a strong clue to her aims, and by doing this, she'd forced herself to move.

With relief, she found herself humming before her mirror as she undressed. She slipped into her nightgown and robe, then sat before the mirror. Humming as she brushed her hair, every few minutes she broke into a laugh more genuine than anything she'd felt since the beginning of the year.

She wondered if this was how Griffin felt whenever he flaunted the English standards, or whenever he "tweaked the nose of the British lion," as her father used to say both in admiration, and criticism of Griffin Radnor. If it was, she forgave him all his excesses, and all his shortcomings. The feeling was rather like having drunk an overabundance of wine— giddy and lightheaded, spurring the blood and heightening the senses. She had no illusions about the danger involved. Indeed the danger excited her, almost as much as what lay beyond— freedom.

And there was a beyond even farther away than that, a final goal—returning Seacliff into the hands of its true caretakers. The people who cared.

One day, she thought, one day things will be decided . . . and this time I will be the one to make the decision, myself.

29

IT WAS more an autumn wind than one appropriate
for June. Streaking across the water from the southwest and
making a ghostly mist from the spray it peeled off the waves,
the wind bellowed and howled over the mouths of chimneys,
rattled panes and punished the trees that clung desperately to
the cliffsides. The weather brought to Caitlin's mind the de-
liciously chilling stories old Daniels used to tell as they huddled
around the hearth and watched his fleshy hands make shadow-
monsters on the walls. That had been an innocent time. A
younger time. And even now, as she paced the length of her
room, the excitement of the hours to come added extra tension
to her already highly strung nerves. The voice of the wind was
beautiful in its fury, and it filled her with a hope she once
believed she'd never feel again.

On impulse, she threw open the balcony doors and stepped
outside. Her dress was instantly flatted against her figure, and
her hair was blown to one side. It was long past seven, long
past Gwen's appointed hour, but Caitlin was not worried. Instead, she lifted her face to the night sky and let the wind soothe
her eyes, her cheeks, her arms, like cool fingers, then took a
deep breath and luxuriated in the bracing chill that confirmed
her in her purpose.

Seacliff. Well named, she thought, gripping the wall and
leaning into the swiftly moving air. Here was where nature's
power struck first, and where it left last before turning out to
sea. In the days of her father and grandfather there were always
ruby red standards flying from the tops of both massive towers,
and the valley's inhabitants would check them every morning
and night to learn the direction of the wind. They served as a
harbinger of the storms and the calm times to come. The poles
were empty now. Oliver had thought the practice frivolous—

and a poor excuse for reminding the villagers the Evans family still lived safely within these walls.

She looked up. Here and there, as invisible clouds drifted over the landscape, she could see islands of stars and the faint glow of an unseen moon. A faint smile creased her lips. Bradford was right; there would be rain tomorrow, whether the wind calmed down or not. She didn't mind that at all. Rain would lend a solemn, gloomy cast to the occasion, much more appropriate than bright skies and balmy breezes.

For an hour or more she let the turmoil play around her, comfort her, before returning inside and reluctantly bolting the doors. Then she poked at the hearth fire, stood before the mirror, and finally left the room.

There was no guard.

With her arms crossed over her chest, hands gripping her upper arms, she walked the gallery's circumference, listening to the wind slipping through the cracks in the walls, listening to the beams creak and groan as they supported the massive weight of centuries-old stone. Dust eddied in corners. The standards in the center hall fluttered from their poles. She descended to the ground floor and walked slowly through the pageant of rooms, stopping first at each threshold to be sure she was alone. It was more than a way of killing time until dawn; it was a journey through the whole of her life, a voyage of bright lights and laughter, scoldings and punishments, learning and weeping, and games well and poorly played.

And the longer she walked the more attuned to the house she became. Every shadow was familiar, every nook and cranny held a memory. She could see the subtle differences between her family's additions and those of their ancestors. She could taste the air, reminding her of parties she'd long since forgotten; and she could catch the scent of polished wood, smooth stone, tapestries freshly cleaned, and the few patches of overlooked mold. Perfumes and perspiration, tobacco and wine, wool and silk and cotton and flesh all blended and gave Seacliff its distinctive air.

By the time she had returned to the center hall she finally knew in every fiber of her soul what she'd already decided in her mind: that Seacliff was hers and there was no escaping it, and she would never lose it to James Flint. Not without a fight.

She laughed aloud and headed for the staircase. There was

one thing left to do, and then she would have to sleep.

"Madam."

She grabbed the banister and felt her heart in her throat. She turned slowly and saw Bradford standing in the entrance of the side corridor. Only a few chimneyed candles were lighted, and his face was in partial shadow.

"Yes?" she said, thinking Flint had sent him to her. Then she realized he seemed somewhat nervous. His shoulders were more rounded than ever, and he seemed incapable of keeping his head from turning slightly from side to side. "Yes?" she repeated.

"About tomorrow, m'lady." His voice quavered.

She waited, puzzled by his demeanor.

"It appears that it will rain."

"It does," she said.

"I . . . I suppose Mr. Flint has no plans to postpone the ceremony."

"Because of the weather?" She started to laugh, caught herself and wondered what the old man was driving at. "Bradford, Mr. Flint has said nothing to me about a postponement. As far as I'm concerned, the wedding will be held."

"The major," he began, and stopped himself. "Pardon me, m'lady. I'm sorry to bother you."

He turned on his heels and hurried down the hall. Caitlin, frowning, made her way slowly up the stairs. She suspected he was disturbed over her refusal to mourn for her late husband, in spite of the manner of his death, and he was probably trying to express his nervous displeasure at her remarrying so soon. Convention dictated that she wait a year at least; she was remarrying in less than six months.

It was possible that this was why Bradford was agitated, she thought as she reached the gallery, but somehow she didn't think it very likely. There was something more, something he hadn't told her. But with a shake of her head she dismissed it; there were weightier matters to worry about. Matters that, when all things were considered, would please the old retainer no end at the last.

A stairwell, narrow and unlighted, opened in the wall just before the door to her apartments. It led to only one place—the third floor of the south tower: her father's rooms. Though all the other Evanses had lived in the main building, her mother had taken a liking to the magnificent view from the tower, and he had bowed to her wishes. No one had visited there since his death, and as she climbed the stone steps and stopped before his door, she noticed that the air was stale, musty.

She took a deep breath and she moistened her lips nervously.

The door opened stiffly, its hinges squealing so loudly she thought surely someone would hear it. But she did not hesitate; she squeezed inside and closed the door behind her. She needed no light for what she was about to do. All she needed was another ration of courage to prevent her from disgracing her family spirits.

The interior of the Daniels's cottage was brightened by the golden light from candles and a fire blazing in the hearth. A partition had been constructed on the left side of the house to provide privacy for Gwen and Davy; old Les's pallet had long since been removed. The two brothers were seated in tall, narrow chairs flanking the fireplace, and Gwen occupied a bench facing the flames as she worked on a quilt spread over her lap.

"Imagine her thinking I'd come at her call, like I was a dog or worse," she muttered, stabbing at a patch with her needle.

"Cor," Davy sighed, leaning back and closing his eyes. "There she goes again."

"Well, damn your eyes, I got a right, don't I?" she said.

"You have cause," Orin rumbled around the stem of his clay pipe. "You have cause."

The wind stirred the fire and the ashes eddied under the logs stacked on the andirons. Then Orin took the pipe from his mouth and examined the contents of its bowl. Gwen glanced up at him without lifting her head, and she could see by his expression that the evening's lecture was about to begin. She groaned silently, but there was no getting around it. Every night, or so it seemed, he asked quietly when she and his young brother would be seeing the vicar. It wasn't right, he would say, the way they were living together. As if people didn't have enough to talk about, what with all the goings on in the main house, he didn't think it proper they should add fuel to the fires of gossip.

But, though she and Davy had spoken of it often, neither of them felt comfortable with the idea of marriage. It wasn't their love, which seemed to have increased in strength and purpose; it was their mistress. Their marrying now, Davy ar-

gued, might somehow be construed as a slap in her face, showing her what true happiness could be if only the right people
were involved in the relationship. Though more often than not
Gwen tended to agree with Orin, Davy would not budge from
his position. And a stubborn Davy was five times worse than
a deep-rooted stump in a cornfield.

But Orin surprised her.

"We'll be havin' a visitor soon enough," he said, without
meeting either of their startled gazes.

Davy made a loud, disgusted noise and reached for the green
bottle of gin next to his chair. But he never completed his
motion. In no time, Orin was out of his chair and had grabbed
the bottle by its neck. With little more than a glare, he reduced
his brother to a small child.

"Who?" Gwen asked, before Davy recovered his courage
and made a grab for the gin.

"You'll—"

A faint knocking at the door froze them all. The sound was
barely heard over the battering of the wind, but it filled the
small room with ominous tension. Gwen slowly folded the quilt
and put aside her needles and patches; Davy straightened, and
folded his legs under the chair in case he had to stand in a
hurry. Orin, however, only set his pipe on the rough-hewn
mantel and stepped around Gwen's bench to the door. When
it opened the wind gusted through, whipping the fire to a frenzy
and making Gwen gasp at the night's cold breath. But it wasn't
until their visitor had moved into the light that she recognized
him.

"Martin," she said to the goldsmith, "what in heaven's name
are you doin' up here?"

Randall accepted Orin's assistance in removing his large
hat and voluminous cloak. Then he stood in front of the fire
to warm his hands and back. Once done, he took Orin's chair
and stretched out his legs.

"You're here," he said to her, nodding his pleasure.

She blinked. "Well, of course I am! Where'd you think I'd
be on a hellish night like this? Walkin' the cliffs, waitin' for
a ship?"

"Gwen," Davy cautioned.

"Well, it was a silly question, wasn't it?" she said, making
room for Orin on the bench. Then, with a frown, she under-

stood. "You knew he was comin', didn't you, Davy?"

Davy nodded, blushing at the guilty secret.

She looked at Orin, who was watching the fire, then at Randall, who was looking straight at her. "How'd you know I'd be here?" she demanded.

"The mistress spoke with you today."

Astonished, she half rose, and would have stood up had not Orin taken her arm lightly and pressed her back into the chair. "What's going on? What does Cat have to do with any of this? Talk to me, David! Orin! What does—" She stopped, and her eyes widened.

"She gave you an order," Randall said quietly.

"Damn right," Gwen snapped. "It could've been Flint talkin' she was so damned high and mighty. La, you'd think she was one of them ladies we was always seein' at Eton."

"You disobeyed her," Randall said, his full lips quivering now in a faint, amused smile.

"Damn right again I did. Nobody talks to me like that and gets away with it. Who does she think I am anyway, that little slut Mary?"

Randall roared, his head knocking against the back of his chair, while Orin chuckled deeply in his throat and Davy covered a laugh with the back of his hand. Gwen, enraged, leaped to her feet and stood with her back to the fire, where she ignored the heat on her spine.

"Enough!" she shouted. "Enough of this, you hear me?"

"Davy," Randall said once his composure returned, "you were right."

"Right?" she yelped. "Right about what, David Daniels?"

Davy's face seemed ready to split in half with his grin. "That if the mistress talked to you proper and stuffy, you'd do just the opposite, just to spite her."

It took awhile for the words to sink in, awhile longer before she confessed to bewilderment and took her place again. "Please," she said then, "please stop this and tell me."

Randall nodded once, sharply, and gave her a quick narration of Caitlin's visit to his shop. He had not mistaken any of the messages she had sent him beneath her words and had, shortly afterward, contrived a reason to visit the farrier and convey her plan.

As soon as he was finished, Gwen started to her feet but

Orin stopped her again. "No," he said gently. "You must stay here, out of the way. It was obviously the mistress's wish you not be in the house tonight."

"But why?"

Randall fell silent, and neither Orin nor Davy would give her a clue. Panic rose in her breast, and her heart began a wild pounding. "She's doin' something foolish, isn't she?" she said. "She's—"

Davy immediately squeezed onto the bench beside her and put his arms around her shoulders. She leaned into him, suddenly cold.

"I thought she'd gone English," she whispered.

"So did we all, to our shame," Randall said. "But that's changed now. Now we must be ready when the mistress is. We cannot fail her. All hell is breaking loose at Seacliff tonight."

Gwen slowly lifted her head, her eyes wide again. "She . . . I've heard that before." She looked to Orin. "I've said that to you before." She snapped her fingers. "On her birthday!"

Orin nodded, then cocked his head to listen to the wind. "It didn't happen then," he said. "But it's happening now. It's happening now."

Caitlin slipped down the staircase with a bundle tucked under one arm. At the bottom she scanned the gallery furtively before darting into her apartment and stuffing the bundle into the chest at the footboard of her bed. A sigh of relief escaped her as she slumped onto the chest and lowered her head. Her breathing was shallow and ragged, and her hands trembled. Then she glanced up at her reflection in the full-length mirror and groaned. If ever guilt was written across a woman's features, it was written across hers. Boldly. In blood red. For all the world and James Flint to see.

She stood up and wrung her hands. She had no idea how she was going to make it through the night. Sleep was out of the question. So was pacing the floor; she'd be exhausted by morning. She walked to the side window and looked down at the staff cottages, then at the wavering dim light that marked the Daniels's home. By straining, she thought she was able to see figures before the fire through the window, but she knew it had to be only her imagination. Thank God Gwen had not lost any of her spirit or her independence. She would have been in great danger had she, through a resurgence of loyalty, sought out her mistress and stayed with her the last night before Caitlin's disastrous union. She had hated ordering her friend about this afternoon, but it was the only way she could ensure the safety of them both.

A bath was the next thing, she decided a few minutes later. A bath to calm her nerves, and perhaps soothe her to sleep. She yanked the bellpull by the door and paced impatiently around the room until Mary arrived, sullen and red-eyed, and almost balking when she was told to fetch hot water for the tub.

But she did. And within the hour Caitlin was immersed in a cloud of comforting steam. She might have drifted off had not the outer door slammed open and Flint strolled into her chamber as though walking through a garden.

Caitlin did not bother to cover herself. "You have heard of knocking, I presume?" she said coldly.

Flint, in his velvet dressing gown, his dark hair brushed down to his shoulders, smiled broadly. "Even on the night before our nuptials you insist on playing the scold."

"I am doing nothing of the sort."

He bowed to her correction. "It appears our guests will be somewhat damp tomorrow," he said, walking to the French doors and peering out at the night.

"I don't think anyone will come."

"Now, Caitlin," he said without turning around, "I believe there will be more here than you suspect."

She thought of his men camped in their barracks, and shuddered. "Perhaps."

"No perhaps about it. Just before I came up here a wagon-load of assistants came to the door. The Courders, I believe, for the cooking, and some of the younger men for the cleaning. I trust they will not disturb your sleep."

"I will make the best of it."

A sudden turn, a long stride, and he was kneeling by the iron tub, where he dangled the fingers of one hand in the water near her breasts. "You will not regret this, Caitlin."

"I doubt it."

His smile grew strained, and she was forced to admire the way he kept his temper in check.

"I was thinking," he said, swirling a finger around one of her nipples, "that these rooms may very well prove to be inadequate for our purposes. What would you say to using your father's apartments above us?"

She almost choked on her fury, but when he looked at her questioningly, she only shrugged, not daring to speak.

"You disappoint me, Caitlin. I had hoped for some display of righteousness."

"Your hopes," she told him, "are not always achieved, are they, Mr. Flint?"

He slapped the water with a palm, and she wiped the moisture from her face quickly. "My lady," he said sternly, "if nothing else, tomorrow you will cease to call me Mr. Flint. I will be James to you, or I will be nothing!"

"Very well. James." She shifted. "I would like to get out."

He rose and backed away. "Then get out, my lady."

"Alone, if you please."

Again his temper flared and flushed his cheeks, but this time he lost control. Before she could stop him, he had grabbed her arms and yanked her from the water. He dragged her halfway across the room and threw her to the bed. She rolled away from him, but not swiftly enough. He was on her in no time, flipping her onto her back and pinning down her shoulders, his legs straddling her hips. Fear paralyzed her, and she was unable to stop him when he moved his hands from her shoulders to her wrists and brought her arms over her head. Her flesh gleamed in the bronze firelight, and the shade of her hair caught sparks that seemed to take on a life of their own.

"No," he said, gazing into her widening eyes. "No, my dear, I shall not have you tonight. That would be unseemly." Then his voice lowered to a hissing. "But tomorrow, Caitlin, you shall be mine. Every inch of you, every shadow, every curve. You shall be mine, and there is nothing you can do to stop me. Nothing! I am in command, and your last defense has crumbled."

He kissed her then, harshly and long, bringing the salty taste of blood to her mouth before he pulled away brusquely and left her trembling on the bed. She lay there for over an hour, unseeing, not hearing, until the room's chill set her limbs to quaking. As if in a dream, she rose and stumbled to the wardrobe, pulled out a nightgown and slipped it over her head. To the fire she went for warmth. To the blankets, for protection.

Then, exhausted, she stared at the open doorway until sleep engulfed her.

30

MARY MOVED about the room quietly, opening the curtains, scraping candle wax from the floor with a long-handled scoop, pouring fresh water into the mistress's basin. She didn't care whether she woke Caitlin or not. She had her work to do, and the mistress be damned. She'd started down in the staff quarters, where already Flint was up and poking at the food laid out on the preparation tables, sticking his nose into the pots simmering over the hearth, ordering the staff around. Twice he'd pinched Mary, and twice she'd made a playful grab for his legs, but he did nothing more, nor had he signaled his desire to continue their liaison after his marriage. If he didn't, she had already decided she would slip out of the valley and make her way back to England. No point staying around. She didn't like these people. Whenever she was around they spoke in their native tongue, laughing and pointing in her direction. They spat at her and kicked at her shins at the slightest excuse, and they excluded her from gossip and general conversation. If it hadn't been for Flint, she would have left long ago. She slapped her duster down hard against the vanity table.

Caitlin stirred, murmuring in her sleep.

Mary glanced around the room to be sure all was in order, then left hurriedly, pausing at the outer door to smile, then slam it shut as hard as she could.

Caitlin sat bolt upright, her hands clawing the covers and her eyes fearful and wide. The dream she'd just had was lost the moment she realized where she was, but its aftereffects left her cold, and she rubbed her arms vigorously until she felt the circulation start again.

Today, she thought then; today was the day.

Her mouth felt dry. The hand that reached for the water pitcher on the nightstand shook so violently that she had to grab her wrist to steady it. The water was fresh, cold, and

when she checked the room from her bed she saw that Mary
had been there already. Thank goodness she wouldn't have to
face Flint's mistress first thing. Without bothering to take her
robe from the foot of the bed, Caitlin raced to the balcony
doors and flung them open.

Then she laughed. She felt almost free.

The sky was still dark; the wind had slowed to a lull but
was forceful enough to stir the waves. The scent of rain was
strong. She raked her hands through her hair, letting it cascade
down over her chest, and she reveled in the thought that one
portion of her lengthy prayer had been answered. But only one.
There was still so much to do before the day was out, before
the vicar and the villagers arrived, and so much could go wrong
before then.

Time, then. She needed to preserve as much of it as she
could. To rush now would make her suspect, or would make
Flint eager. And if he grew eager, there was no telling what
might strike his mind. He excelled under stress.

A long moment staring into her father's sculptured eyes,
and a longer one with her eyes closed and memories crowding
all thought out, and she took a deep breath. Suddenly the door
cracked open, but it was only Mary bustling in with buckets
of hot water. She was sniffling and sneezing, and her red hair
was a tangle, her bodice partly unlaced. Caitlin faced her
expressionlessly, waiting till the woman was gone. And when
she finally left, Caitlin sprinkled the water with lavender, piled
her hair atop her head, and slipped into the tub.

An hour later, when the water had cooled and was no longer
comfortable, Caitlin climbed awkwardly out of the tub, wrapped
herself in a thick, quilted robe, and dried herself as best she
could.

Trying to pace herself, she moved as slowly as she could
as she reviewed every aspect of her plan, searching for pitfalls,
prodding for weaknesses that would be her undoing.

And there were many. So many *ifs*. *If* the storm did not
return; *if* Randall ignored what she'd told him; *if* Flint refused
to allow her out of his sight; *if* her courage failed her at the
last moment; *if* . . . *if* . . . *if* . . . She bunched her hands into fists
and shut her eyes tightly, forcing herself to rein in the panic
that had rooted itself in the pit of her stomach. Too soon, she
told herself; it's much too soon to grow fainthearted. What

would your father think? What would Griffin think?

Griff.

She sat in front of her mirror and stared at her reflection. Behind her she could see a vague image of Griffin as she remembered him, but it was only a vague image. Flint's men had effectively prevented him from entering the valley or sending her a message. And, she thought, what if Gwen had been mistaken and he had not, in fact, returned from Ireland at all? Or what if he had been seriously injured and was unable to assist her?

Oh, my God . . . what if he's dead?

"No!" her mind cried. A pulse throbbed in the hollow of her throat.

A gentle knock at the door startled her, and her overreaction made her smile, roll her eyes toward the ceiling, and chide herself for jumping at shadows. It was too soon to be so skittish, too soon, though when Bradford entered with her luncheon tray she realized she'd overslept and the morning had passed quickly.

"The wind is up," Bradford said as he placed the tray on a low square table in front of the hearth. Then he clucked at Mary's forgetfulness and busied himself with kindling and logs. The room was chilly. "The wind is up," he said again, rising.

"It will not be a pleasant day," she said, taking a chair and allowing him to push it forward.

"Shall I send Mary up to assist you in dressing?"

"No," she said quickly. "I can manage by myself, thank you, Bradford."

"As you wish, m'lady." He bowed and moved toward the door.

"Bradford?"

He stopped.

"Last night, Bradford. Were you . . . that is, is there something you wish to tell me?"

"No, m'lady. Except that I trust you and Mr. Flint will be most happy this day."

When he was gone she grabbed a piece of cold beef and chewed on it angrily. She shouldn't have spoken to him that way, inviting confidences like that. He was a man's man, and he had no part in her life except to drift through it as the head of the household staff. She was grasping at straws, hoping she might find an ally within the walls as well as outside them.

But she reminded herself sternly she was alone in this, and had been from the beginning. And not even a miraculous change in Bradford's old heart was going to change that.

The lid of the chest was up, the once neatly folded clothes were now in a jumble.

Caitlin stood in front of the mirror and fussed with her gown, first frowning, then glaring, then stepping away from the glass to be sure nothing was out of place. She was wearing a shimmering pale blue gown laced with strands and tiny bows of black and gold. The neckline was fashionably low, but she had covered the exposed portion of her breasts with a veil of nearly transparent cotton and lace, which she hoped the guests and Flint would think a concession to the sobriety of the ceremony and the day. Without Gwen to help her, there was very little she could do with her hair, except painstakingly braid it—at the cost of aching shoulders and back—and then pin it snugly to the back of her head. The style accentuated her high forehead and the lean lines of her face, but the uncomeliness couldn't be helped. There would be no time later to do anything with it.

Hands on hips, she turned slowly, watching herself, and finally deciding that unless she'd seriously miscalculated there was nothing more she could do. The gown was flowing and bulky, her figure full, and her hair...

"All right, all right," she said, laughing at her own refusal to believe the evidence of her eyes. "It's near time, Cat, and you're not done yet."

Bradford stood alone in the cavernous front hall. Twice in the last ten minutes he'd been summoned to the door to admit first the vicar, then Martin Randall and that hideous Broary woman. Despite the rising wind and the threat of heavy rain they were all coming, it appeared. There was nothing more he could do now to stop the wedding from taking place. The major's memory had been shortlived by all except himself; he only hoped he would be forgiven for taking part in this sacrilegious affair.

The knocker sounded again.

He brushed at his spotless livery and touched the sides of his wig to be sure it was straight. A swift check down the hall, to the rooms on either side, and he stepped forward.

"Good afternoon, Mistress Sharnac. We are pleased you could attend."

Nate Birwyn stood outside the door to Flint's room in the north tower and rocked impatiently on his heels. He was in livery despite his protests, and the bastard had even made him wash his patch and shave the stubble on his pointed chin. Now the only thing he had to do was wait, as he'd been doing since dawn. If the gold Flint paid him didn't fill his purse so nicely, he'd have been over the hills and back to England in a trice. As it was, he'd had to post all the men around the house, station a few inside, make sure they were armed, with their weapons concealed, and send a half-dozen men back to the barracks for another wash because they smelled like a pig sty.

A nursemaid, that's what he was. A bloody damned nursemaid.

From somewhere in the house a clock chimed one.

He took a deep breath. One hour, and it would be done. They would drink a little wine, stand around chatting as if they hadn't seen each other in years. The vicar would say his few words, and Nate would be on his way to the kitchen to coax Mary out of her stockings. He grinned to himself and licked his coarse lips. Ah, wouldn't Flint be a hornet if he knew what Mary did after she left his rooms at night!

A muffled footstep sounded behind him. He came instantly to attention. A minute later the door swung open, and Flint stepped out.

Flint was unaccountably nervous, but was determined not to let a single one of them see through his facade. He squared his shoulders and looked at Birwyn.

"Well?" he demanded. "Well, do you think the woman will be pleased?"

"Should be hanged if she ain't," Birwyn replied.

Flint nodded his satisfaction and pulled the door shut.

He was wearing a deep velvet jacket cut away in back and falling to mid-thigh. Silver buttons marched in rows down his chest, and gold thread wove through his cuffs and hem. His shirt was blinding white, and the lace jabot cascaded from his throat in fluffed layers that added inches to his size. His breeches were of velvet and the same midnight hue; his boots, gold-buckled and gold-topped, reached to his knees and were polished to a mirror finish. Rather than wear his hair in a simple queue, he'd had Mary use the brush and iron to fashion it in gentle waves that covered his ears and fell to his shoulders. He was clean-shaven, darkly tanned, and his appearance was marred only by the dead white scar that ran from the corner of his mouth to the side of his nose.

"Yes," he agreed. "She will be very pleased indeed. If she knows what's good for her."

Birwyn chuckled and fell into step beside him as he marched along the corridor to the central hall, crossed it, then started down the opposite corridor to the staff quarters.

"It will be immensely warm in there," he said, tugging fitfully at his blown lace cuffs. "Be a good man and see to it those two old cows haven't ruined the feast, will you?"

Birwyn saluted him. "Whatever you say, m'lord."

Flint laughed and clapped his shoulder. "Not yet, Nate. Not quite yet. But you can be sure I'm working on it with all due haste."

Birwyn vanished on his errand, and Flint turned, hearing voices in the front room. Already it starts, he thought, and looked up to the ceiling, as if he could see through the massive beams and stone to Caitlin's rooms above. A momentary frown darkened his expression, then passed. And when it did, he broke into a great smile and flung open the corridor doors, his hand extended to greet the vicar while his tongue formed a compliment for the Mistresses Sharnac and Broary.

Caitlin heard the clock chime and knew she could no longer remain safely in her room. She hurried to the desk, and from a pigeonhole pulled an emerald-colored sheath; within was a slim dagger she'd spent part of the morning sharpening on a whetstone she'd taken from the kitchen. She laid it on the chest, the scabbard beside it.

Then she walked over to the sculpture on the mantel and cupped her hands around her father's face. A tear glistened in the corner of her eye, and she banished it with a brush of her finger.

"Good-bye, Father," she whispered. "There won't be time later, God willing. Please don't worry. I'll be back, one way or another."

She emitted a deep, prolonged sigh for things past and gone, gathered her skirts in one hand, and strode through the apartment to the gallery in the blink of an eye. The last time she had dressed this way was on the day a candle tree had been lit in the hall below to celebrate her birthday. Now there was only Bradford, waiting patiently by the door. He saw her as she made her way regally down the staircase, and to her surprise, he rushed over to offer his hand as she reached the bottom step.

"Why . . . thank you, Bradford," she said.

"You're welcome, m'lady," he said, and escorted her to the front room.

It took her less than a minute to realize that virtually everyone in the valley had come. It was difficult to maintain her composure in the face of the scene's similarity to her last birthday. But she managed graciously, accepting murmured congratulations with a brief nod and stilted smile. Then Flint stepped into the middle of the room and reached for her hands.

"My dear," he said quietly, before turning to the others. "I must say, friends, this is undoubtedly the most beautiful bride in the kingdom."

A spattering of applause, then a general movement toward a long table set up before the hearth where Mary, ludicrously bedecked in a white and brown dress, flowers pinned in her hair, ladled out generous portions of a wine punch which, Caitlin was informed, had been mixed by Orin Daniels.

When all the glasses were filled, Reverend Lynne stepped over to Flint's side and turned to face his congregation.

"My dear, dear friends," he said in English, "I am moved to propose a toast to this couple."

"Here, here," said a voice Caitlin recognized as Davy's.

The vicar beamed. "To the Widow Morgan, and to James Patrick Flint. May their sojourn on this earth, and at Seacliff, be strewn with life's treasures and devoid of life's dangers. May they, by God's grace, fill this mansion and our lives with cheer, joy, and children. And may none of us ever forget whose children we really are. To the bride and groom!"

Everyone cried, "To the bride and groom," and quaffed their cups.

The vicar drank quickly, and turned to offer his glass again to Mary. The others were not so quick to drink or to seek a second round, but Flint could not help draining his glass in a single gulp.

"Gads!" he said when he could catch his breath again. "My

God, Master Daniels, you've outdone yourself."

Orin, hovering just behind the first rank of guests, tugged at his forelock in embarrassment. Caitlin, however, set her own glass aside; she knew Orin had probably loaded the punch with every kind of liquor he could think of; and even if it was not as potent as Flint suggested, she probably would have lost it all in an explosion of laughter on spotting Orin's face, and the comically sour look on it.

"It's a shame we don't have music," she said to Flint when, his glass refilled, he took her elbow and led her to the windows.

"Not enough time," he said. "But there will be music in your heart before this day is done." He leaned over and kissed her cheek, and she was just barely able to conceal her distaste.

She was saved, too, from further conversation when the villagers began crowding around her, making small talk in Welsh and apologizing to Flint in English for using their language. Soon enough he scowled and headed back for another drink. And, while no one said anything directly to her, Caitlin was positive Randall had spread a few discreet words here and there, for her Welsh guests were polite, cheerful, and behaving as if they saw nothing untoward about her upcoming marriage.

And somewhere in the midst of it all, she heard the deep-throated clamor of thunder rolling down from the hills.

Flint laughed loudly.

A pattering at the panes behind her told Caitlin the rain had finally come.

Flint lifted his glass high overhead and tossed it into the fireplace. Within seconds most of the men did likewise, and the shattering crystal sounded like a volley of musketfire.

Then, before she was ready, the vicar was standing before her. "M'lady," he said unctuously, "I believe Mr. Flint is ready."

A space had been cleared in front of the hearth, the table dragged away, and a white cloth placed over the floor. She allowed herself to be taken forward by the hand, her eyes partly closed and a scream locked behind her tightly clamped lips. The vicar instantly stepped onto a low platform, reached inside his black coat, and extracted a Bible.

He smiled, and with a nod to Caitlin and Flint, indicated they should move closer together. When they had, the vicar opened the holy book, leafed through it briefly, and placed a finger on a crisp page. Flint cleared his throat, while Caitlin struggled not to faint.

Lynne looked out over the assembly and swallowed. Then his smile broadened as he began, "Dearly beloved, we are gathered—"

"You sod!"

A gasp rose from the crowd, and an oath from Flint as he whirled around, glaring.

"You damned drunken sod, how *dare* you touch her in the face of God!"

It was Martin Randall, shoving Quinn Broary behind him, away from Orin Daniels.

"She's mine, you damned ass!" Daniels bellowed.

"Drunk," Randall repeated. "Drunk, and a blasphemer!"

"Quiet!" Flint roared, but the command came too late. Orin had formed a fist at Randall's insult, and had already slammed it into Randall's chest. The goldsmith staggered back into Broary, knocking her to the floor. A woman screamed, followed by another, and another, and Reverend Lynne waved his arms wildly in a feeble effort to restore order, his face blanched from the effort.

Randall recovered quickly and flung himself at Daniels, his teeth snapping at the farrier's ear as they toppled to the floor at the crowd's feet. Flint, screaming imprecations, bullied his way through the crowd, but before he could reach the brawlers Davy had jumped on Randall's back and was pummeling his head. A hand took his shoulder and dragged him off. He swung wildly, and was instantly caught in a wrestling match that forced the crowd back against the walls where they watched in horror.

"Damn you!" Flint was bellowing. He reached for Randall's hair and was knocked off balance when Quinn Broary found herself in a tussle with Mistress Sharnac.

"Madness," he screamed. "Nate! Nate! Get in here and stop this at once!"

Someone lifted the punch bowl and flung it against the wall by the side door just as Birwyn plunged into the turmoil. He had to crouch to get through the mass of onlookers, his brace of pistols suddenly large in his hands. He had no chance to use them, however. From out of nowhere, Gwen tripped and fell on top of him, her skirts covering his head while she shrieked and flailed her arms.

"M'lady," the vicar implored. "Please do something, m'lady."

Caitlin turned around and glared at the trembling cleric. "Go to hell," she said. She then reached out and shoved him off the platform and into the fireplace. Then she pushed her way through the milling, shouting, brawling crowd. She could not see Flint, but she knew there was little time left before his men would come to his aid and restore a semblance of order. She gasped when an elbow caught her in the ribs, gasped again in surprise when an unseen hand pressed into the small of her back and shoved her toward the hall.

Buffeted and propelled, then, she wove her way across the room, broke free like a cork from a bottle, and headed for the staircase. There was no one around, but she could hear footsteps in the corridor leading to the north tower. The soldiers were coming. She hesitated, then fled upward, her mouth gasping for air, her hands pulling her skirts high above her ankles— to expose a pair of boots she had washed with white paint so they would pass, at a glance, for slippers when her feet were exposed.

A shout, and Flint sprawled into the hall.

She took no time to do more than glance at him before redoubling her speed, only vaguely hearing more shouts from the front room, then the onrush of racing feet and breaking glass.

"Caitlin!"

Three-quarters of the way there she saw Bradford waiting at the head of the staircase. She did not stop to think. She moved on, hearing Flint taking the steps two at a time behind her, hearing his ragged breathing and the oaths he hurled along the way.

"Bradford, your life if you don't stop her!" he commanded.

She reached the top only two steps ahead of Flint, almost falling when Bradford stepped nimbly aside, while making it appear as if she'd shoved him off-balance. She ran, heard an anguished shout, and turned just as Bradford toppled off the step and into Flint's path. The sound of the two of them plummeting down the stairs brought a cry to her lips and almost stopped her in her purpose. But deciding she must go on, she kicked open her door at a dead run, ran into the bedchamber, and snatched up the dagger she'd left on the chest. There was no time to fuss with laces and stays; she slashed at the front of her gown until it lay in tatters at her feet. Then she rolled down the sleeves and trouser legs of her father's clothes, tucked the trousers into the boots, and grabbed a hooded cloak and floppy hat from the wardrobe. The hat fit perfectly over her trussed-up hair, and the cloak concealed her sex instantly.

There was no time to think.

Only a brief moment to pray that Orin had remembered. Then she threw back the balcony doors and stepped into the teeth of the storm.

Lightning flared blue-white over the bay, cracking in jagged lines over the trees in the grove that hid the barracks. She stumbled forward and saw with a shout of delight the four-pronged grappling hook clutching a gap in the wall. She looked out, looked down, wiped the lashing cold rain from her face and climbed through the gap. Grabbing the attached rope, she lowered herself from the balcony. The wind slammed her against the stone; the rope, slick with rain, burned her palms as she descended more rapidly than she wanted. Her elbows bled, her knees bled, and a gash opened on her cheek when the wind, spinning her like a top, smashed her against the tower.

It seemed like ages, eons, later that her hands gave way and she fell, landing in the muddy grass with such force that she knocked the wind from her lungs.

No, she thought as she struggled to her feet, gasping. No, my dear God, please no!

Hands grabbed her arms and she screamed, the scream instantly was lost in the fury of the storm. She lashed out, was held tighter and pulled to the tower's base where a lantern was resting, protected from the wind by its storm panes. It was lifted, and she saw the roan saddled and ready in the circle of its light.

Then she saw Gwen, weeping.

There was no time for words. They embraced quickly, and she mounted the roan, riding astride like a man hell-bent for the trail Martin Randall had described to her. She looked back only once, and saw all the windows in Seacliff ablaze with angry light. Gwen and the stranger who'd helped Caitlin into the saddle had long fled, their tiny lantern against Seacliff's great walls, gone from view. Then she was riding on, across the fields, across the valley, the storm thundering at her heels and driving all thought from her mind. She didn't even have time to realize she'd at last escaped.

PART FOUR

Conqueror

Wales, 1776

31

THE SHADOW shaped itself into a creature straight out of Old Les's most hideous night tale: tall, lean, with blue-black claws that glowed evilly in the darkness as they reached for Caitlin's throat. Its face was that of a beast she couldn't name but whose rapacious countenance sneered the seven deadly sins, particularly lust. It was marked by greed and an insane satisfaction at having cornered its prey at last. Its red-glowing eyes pinned her to the ground as surely as if they were flaming lances; the deep, dead-skin scar that pulled at the edge of its fanged and grinning lips rippled obscenely; and to its massive hairy chest was strapped a thick black whip sheathed in the skin of hell's most venomous serpent. She scrambled backward on her haunches, her mouth open in a silent, agonizing scream that echoed helplessly through her mind. She had no weapons, and when she looked down for an instant she realized the creature had somehow managed to shred all her clothing while she'd been sleeping. She was naked. Defenseless. And in seconds backed up against a stone wall. In response, she drew her knees to her chest, whimpered, and finally flung out a futile hand in an effort to stay the beast's relentless advance. But the creature only laughed and snapped its fangs at her hand. She shrieked, reaching desperately around her in the dark until her fingers closed over a triangular stone. She threatened the thing with it, but the creature laughed again, and with little warning, lunged toward her. Caitlin jumped back, forgetting the wall, and cracking her skull against it, the impact of which ignited pinwheels of brilliant red fire behind her eyes. She cried out . . . cried out again and flailed her arms wildly until she realized she was alone. Still alone in the cave.

A brief, violent bout of trembling overtook her, and she waited until it was over, then pushed herself to a sitting position and gingerly rubbed the back of her head. She must have tossed and turned uncontrollably during the nightmare, because the ache in her head was real. She grimaced, pulled the cloak protectively around her, and stared at the glowing embers of the fire she'd built just inside the cave's mouth. Those, she thought, were the creature's eyes. And the scar she had seen indicated Flint as surely as if his name had been branded on the creature's forehead.

The sky outside had turned a dismal gray, and water dripped through the tangled vines partially obscuring the cave's entrance, collecting in a shallow basin worn in the smooth rock. Though it was not the most pleasant sight or sound she'd ever experienced, the cave was somehow comforting. She felt safe, which helped to drive off the nightmare and bring her back to where she was.

And that, she thought sourly, was . . . lost.

She had ridden like a madwoman across the valley floor, the roan stretching and striding as it had never done before, catching the fear, the excitement, and the urgency in her voice as she exhorted it onward. By the time she'd reached the foothills to the north the cannonade of thunder had subsided somewhat and left her with a steady, chilling, driving rain. Through Carver's farm she pounded, through the thick underbrush beyond, and onto what she hoped was the trail Randall had told her about. But it must have been the wrong one. Or he had been mistaken. She rode for hours, until well past dawn, the roan tiring, stumbling, and nearly throwing her off several times until she dismounted and walked alongside it. She stopped only once, to eat a large piece of bread she had taken from the kitchen and hidden in a pocket of her cloak. She sat on a boulder and gnawed on it nervously, seeing in the rain shadows lurking over her, hearing between peals of thunder and cracks of lightning the hoofbeats of frenzied pursuit.

It was then that she began to laugh. Giggling at first, then sprawling on the broad-topped stone and lifting her face toward the sky as she laughed with abandon. Pursuit there very well may be, even in this hellish storm, but the sight of the villagers brawling in the front room, the vicar sprawled legs akimbo and eyes popping with astonishment, Flint and Bradford—dear, dear miraculous Bradford—pitching off that first step . . . all of it was too wonderfully delightful not to laugh at.

She had done it. She had actually escaped! As she struggled

to her feet and onto the roan's back, she thought, God help the man who tries to stop me now.

The road ahead of her rose gently, skirting the summits shrouded in thick cloud, crossing white frothing streams on wooden bridges that swayed alarmingly in the wind. By sunset she could barely grip the reins and lead the horse to a relatively sheltered plot beneath a thick stand of evergreens. There, with the cloak wrapped snugly around her and a clump of moss for a pillow, she slept until daybreak. When she awoke she felt like a deer at bay. Sleep left her in a rush, and she was on her feet, positive she was surrounded by a hundred of Flint's men, all waiting for her to move before they put their swords to her. But she was alone, and the worst of the storm had apparently passed. She spent another day riding, climbing higher and higher into the mountains, the trail narrowing at times to almost nothing, so little used was it. Fog filled the tiny valleys below her, and the heavy mist clung to her face like a clammy woolen veil.

By then she was less afraid that Flint's men might be riding hellbent behind her than she was of missing any signs that would lead her in the right direction—to the outlaws.

By the end of the second full day her meager supply of food was gone.

Early the third morning the roan was panicked by something moving in the thick underbrush flanking the trail. The horse bolted, and Caitlin barely had time to twist her hands into its mane to avoid being tossed off its back into the mud and undergrowth. The ride was precarious, branches whipping overhead and tugging at her hood, scratching her back, lashing across her face, and raising fierce welts on her cheeks. It was odd, riding astride like a man, but she quickly adjusted, jamming her knees into the horse's sides and letting it have its head, hoping it would tire itself out before speeding into a killing run.

Alongside an engorged stream they raced, Caitlin wrestling to keep the spooked horse from attempting to ford. A sudden, open field proved tempting, and it swerved, nearly toppling her from her perch as it leaped over a low copse of brier and headed toward the dark wall of forest on the opposite side.

She saw what was coming long before it happened, but with a curious sense of inevitability, she could think of nothing swiftly enough to prevent the onrush of events. The roan plunged into the woodland, a low-hanging branch lashed Caitlin across the chest, and she was swept from the saddle with a short, piercing cry. Unconsciousness immediately engulfed her, and when she finally came to, she was alone. The roan had fled. Her breasts ached as she gulped for air, and when she sat up she realized she'd fallen on a bed of pine needles, which had protected her against broken bones, though not against scratches. Recovering somewhat, she beat her thighs with her fists in frustration. Scrambling to her feet, she looked around at the field. The mist had enshrouded it, but she was positive she saw darker shadows plunging through the tall grass toward her.

There was no time to hunt for the mount or to do anything more than check to be sure she still had the slender dagger. Then she moved into the trees as quickly as her dull aches and scratches would permit her, and felt the ground rise beneath her feet. Every so often she dropped down on a boulder to rest and to check the trail below.

Night fell. The mist was swept away by a wind far warmer than that which had driven her to this point, and when she looked up she could see patches of stars through the sodden foliage. They were small comfort. Stars, to her mind, also meant the possibility of a moon. And moonlight would mean keeping to shadows, and slowing her already curtailed pace.

She judged the time to be shortly before midnight when she rounded a sharp bend in a narrow deer trail and saw the cave. Initially, she was wary. Though the prospect of dry ground and the protection of the mountain, however brief, was extraordinarily tempting, there was also Flint's pursuit to consider. She seldom thought actively about her pursuers, knowing that Flint himself would have caught her long before this; someone else must be out searching for her, and it had only been by the sheerest of luck that she'd gotten this far without capture. Perhaps, she thought wryly, getting lost had actually been a help instead of a hindrance. If any of Flint's men knew about the hunting trail, they would more than likely search it. Since she'd not been on this other trail for two days, she might very well be in no immediate danger at all.

But danger was danger, immediate or not.

The cave might well serve as her prison as well as a temporary resting place.

She heard the faint, haunting cries of a pack of wolves somewhere off in the forest. Instinctively she knew they were miles away, but the very thought of rounding a bend and coming up on a wolf was enough to send her scrambling up the slope. She fought her way through the screen of dangling vines and slipped into the darkness.

There she built the fire.

There she had the nightmare.

There she awoke on the fourth morning after leaving Seacliff to see the gray morning promising more rain.

Slowly, she stood and walked to the mouth of the cave, parted the vines, and looked out. The hill sloped sharply downward beyond the trail, dropping off into a thick profusion of trees. She could see across their gently swaying tops, to the land that leveled into a funnel-shaped valley and climbed almost instantly to a much larger hill. Crags and cottage-sized boulders marked its summit; fog curled around its dark face; and the distant shadows of hawks on the wing crisscrossed its peak.

When she stepped outside and looked to her right, toward home, the view was the same as when she looked left.

And in the presence of the awesome beauty surrounding her she felt the first stirrings of despair.

It was all very well to say that she had evaded her pursuers, that her life would be spared, at least for a while. But what good was that when she was utterly and completely lost? There were no familiar landmarks. She could have been in the middle of Prussia for all she knew. And though she had prided and praised herself, on the daring of her flight, she'd also managed to forget to ask Randall one vital thing—how to make contact with the outlaws. Naively, she had just assumed that if she ventured into their domain, they would find her and all would be taken care of. And maybe, if the storm hadn't been so fierce and so long-lasting, her scheme might have worked.

And maybe, she thought glumly, King George will come down the trail on his fat white horse and show me the way himself.

A sigh, and she reminded herself that recriminations were not going to get her where she wanted to go. Choosing a direction, she slipped and slid down the slope to the trail, foraged through some brush for berries to eat now, and berries to pack into her cloak, and moved on. Northward. At least she might stumble into England again.

Right now, however, she was in the middle of a land that seldom, if ever, saw the trace of a human footprint. And the longer she walked the more she felt at the same time gently humbled and strangely excited. It was an exploration, a discovery, and she found herself attempting to memorize the lay of the land just in case she should ever come here again.

Midday saw the gray considerably lightened, the temperature warm as spring, and the soles of her feet aching in her boots. More and more often she rested by a silvery stream, or in the shade of an oak or hickory hundred of years older than she. She no longer had the feeling she would be recaptured at any moment; and once she recognized that fact, she also felt disturbingly alone. Woodlore, she admitted somewhat glumly to herself, was not her forte. She'd never learned to make a snare from sapling and vine; she had no idea how to fashion a bow from a branch—or for that matter, even what tree one should take the branch from in the first place. When she saw a family of deer in a meadow on an opposite hillside, she pulled out her small dagger and stared at it angrily.

"What good are you going to do me now?" she muttered at it, and almost flung it away.

The cloak, which had dried out overnight, provided scant protection against the immensity of the wilderness she found before her. The trail was long since gone, vanished by degrees into low grasses and a series of connecting glens the beauty of which, on any other occasion, would have brought tears of joy to her eyes.

A waterfall spilling what looked to be diamonds into a rainbow-hued pool stopped her for an hour. She sat on the bank and watched the swirling water, mesmerizing herself until she had to force herself to get to her feet and move on.

Northward. She at least knew how to orient herself by using the sun's position in the sky as her compass.

Deeper into the mountains she moved, where the forest hid even the dimmest glow of the sun above the clouds, where the shadows beneath the closely spaced trees seemed darker, more forbidding, more fearful.

As what little light there was began to fade, Caitlin searched for a place to spend the night. Until now she had been walking as if in her sleep, numbing her mind against the thousand tiny aches and pains that had settled in her calves and thighs, in the small of her back and between her hunched shoulders. By refusing to permit herself to think she was able to pass the day without noting the passage of time, to move from place to place without measuring how far she had gone each hour.

But once she brought herself back to the present, she had to bite her lips against exhaustion and pain. One step more, she told herself; one step more is one step farther away from Flint. You can't stop now. After coming all this way, you can't stop. Griffin is there, you see, just on the other side of that hill, through that stand of maple and hickory, in the shadows there on the other side of that stream. He's there. He's waiting. If you stop now he'll think you aren't coming and he'll move on, and you'll never meet him, and you'll wander forever and a day and never be found.

There. There, by that boulder. See? I told you, Cat. I told you he'd be waiting!

She blinked and rubbed a weary hand over her eyes. Now her mind was playing tricks on her. Now it was telling her there was a man standing in the shadow of a boulder nearly as tall as a young tree, by the side of the trail. She didn't ask herself where or when she had picked up the trail; she was just on it again. Just as that man standing by the boulder and watching her was just there. It happened, that's all, and she should count herself lucky that . . .

She stopped, suddenly realizing that what she was thinking and what she was seeing weren't part of a walking dream.

The forest she had entered was mostly evergreen, the lowest branches waving high above her head. Slants of light cut through the gloom, outlining pockets of ground mist, adding a shimmering silver to the bark and to the raindrops still caught in low holly shrubs. One of those spears of light reached over the top of a convoluted brown boulder, creating beneath it a wedge of shadow in which stood a man. She had no idea how long he had been watching her, but there was no question that he could see her. He was wearing over his narrow shoulders a dark cloak much like her own, the hood over her head, the hem just barely above the damp, soft ground. Boots, breeches, and shirt were streaked with new and old mud, and beneath a wide-brimmed brown hat—again, much like her own—she could discern a stern, rugged face framed by a heavy black beard.

As far as she knew, there were no villages nearby.

The man, then, either had to be one of those she was seeking, or one of Flint's men who had somehow circled ahead of her.

The notion of running fled as fast as it came. She was too

tired, and she had no idea where she could run if a chase began.

Then he lowered his arms which he had folded over his chest, and stepped fully into the dim light. His attitude indicated that he expected her to come forward, and after several moment's indecision, she did. Just close enough to be able to talk to him without having to shout.

And when she stopped again her eyes widened in surprise, her legs almost sagged with relief.

The man was not as old as he appeared to be from a distance, though there was age in his deep blue eyes, which belonged to a man a decade or more older. He was taller than she remembered—though her memory of him was dim—yet he bore a distinct family resemblance to his cousin Martin Randall.

"Terry?" she said, not daring yet to believe it. "Is that you, Terry Wyndym?"

Wyndym frowned and leaned closer. There was ten feet between them, but it might as well have been ten miles. "Who wants to know?"

She laughed quickly, relieved, and tossed back her hood so he might see her face. "It's me!" she cried. "Terry it's me, Caitlin Evans."

He frowned again, examining her, studying her, until finally he nodded. The smile he gave her, however, was neither welcoming nor pleasant. "Aye," he said with a smile that was almost a smirk. "Aye, so it is. But it's Lady Morgan now, ain't that right?"

She had leaned into a step that would have sent her running to him, but she stopped at the tone of his voice—harsh, insolent, so much a reminder of Oliver's manner that she turned her head to look at him obliquely, a finger thoughtfully to her chin. "My husband is dead," she said.

"And the man with him?" He took a step toward her, the grip of a pistol poking up from his waistband.

"Flint?"

Wyndym nodded.

"He is."

"You tired of him, did you?"

"Now listen, Terry Wyndym," she said, her exhaustion and hunger robbing her of her patience. "I don't see what all this has to do with anything." She gestured behind her, around her. "You can see I'm alone. My horse ran off, and I've been walking for days. I need rest. I need food. My God, Terry, can't you see—"

"I see the lady what thinks she's English," he answered flatly, closing the distance again between them.

"Eng—what in God's name are you talking about?"

"Oh," he said, "you goin' t'tell me you ain't had nothin' to do with Lam Johns? With Davy Daniels? With—"

She spun away from him, fist to her mouth and despair clouding her face. *All this way,* she thought. *I've come all this way, and they think I've been working with Oliver, with Flint. All this way, and for what?*

A hand clamped hard on her shoulder and whirled her around. She lost her balance, and Wyndym took hold of her arms and half carried her off the road, then released her so suddenly she fell backward, her arms stretched out behind her to prevent her from falling prone. Then he tossed his cloak back over both shoulders and pulled out his pistol. She uttered a muffled gasp, closed her eyes in relief when she saw him lay it carefully beside him.

"Terry, you're mistaken," she pleaded when she saw his hands reach for his belt. "Terry, please!"

"Bitch," he said, eyes narrowed, tongue licking slowly at his lips. "Ye has a lot of nerve, I'll say that much."

"Dammit, Terry," she flared, anger momentarily overshadowing her fear. "Dammit, it's not what you think at all! I came to see Griffin. I need his help!"

He paused, buckle in one hand. Then he glanced suspiciously down the trail she'd followed blindly. "Alone, are ye?"

"Alone?" She almost yelled the word. "Of course I'm alone! You think I brought the king himself with me?"

"Wouldn't put it past you. Heard a lot of things since I left last year. Lot of things." He shook his head, partly in sorrow, partly in anger. Then he flung himself at her before she could roll away, one knee jammed between her thighs while he leaned over her, his breath hot and harsh on her face. She turned away, and he laughed. "You fight like this for Flint, do you?"

She spat at him, but he only laughed louder. And when she tried to scream he instantly clamped a palm over her mouth.

"Now you listen, Lady Bloody Morgan," he whispered angrily. "I don't know why you come out here, how you come by us, but it don't matter. Ye ain't welcome, not a bit, and I'm goin' to give you a little partin' present to remember me by."

She shouted at him under his hand, her eyes wide as she strained to make him understand what a terrible mistake he was making. It was to no avail. The more she struggled, the harder he pressed her into the ground, finally rising slightly to plant a knee firmly in her stomach. Air left her lungs in a rush, and a swarm of dark spots passed through her vision. All she could think of was the injustice of it all; all she could do was wriggle and squirm as he pawed at her, snapping open the shirt and exposing her breasts in the gray light. Then he reached for her waistband, and in doing so lifted his hand from her mouth and his knee from her abdomen. Immediately, she brought her own knee into his groin and screamed as he did, pushed him over and crawled back into the prickly protection of a bush.

Wyndym curled up on the ground, groaning, swearing. Then he rolled into a kneeling position and glared at her.

"Ye'll pay," he warned.

She tried to close the shirt and stand at the same time. "Terry—"

"Ye'll pay," he repeated, standing and swaying.

Then a loud thud made Caitlin blink, sent Wyndym sprawling onto his face as a cloud of dust rose from his back. A small, well-fashioned club lay on the forest floor, and as she stared at it a man stepped out from behind a massive black oak and shook his head.

"Every time I see you you're fightin' a man," he said, reaching for the club.

"Damn you," she said, without much force. "Damn you, Griffin Radnor."

32

THERE WERE nearly a dozen huts in the small clearing of the pine forest. Most of them were crudely thatched, with small stones painstakingly set in a mosaiclike pattern to form the walls. Over and around them bowers of fresh branches had been thrown to camouflage the huts from passersby. Cooking fires burned in the deep pits only from dawn to sunset;

they wanted no intruders attracted to their camp. There were no horses, no dogs. At any given time half the forty men who lived in the village were gone. Some hunted stag in the hills; others sought grouse in the meadows; the rest prowled the coastal roads for signs of British troops. An eerie aura—caused by the lack of women, animals, and foot traffic—surrounded the place. So Caitlin felt.

"Just before the New Year a patrol found our tracks," Griffin was saying. "There were only a dozen of them, from a ship set sail out of Bangor. We were sure, when they didn't return, we would have to find some other place. But no one else came. Those men might not have existed at all."

He was lying on a pallet covered with deerskin and pelts taken from winter wolves, the fur intact and soft. Caitlin lay beside him, one hand trailing across the scarred flesh of his chest, the other on her thigh beneath a crude woolen blanket. It was night. A stiff hide covering had been drawn over the door and single window, and a low flame burned in the rough fireplace.

Remembering Wyndym's reaction, and that of some of the others when Griffin brought her into the camp, she felt as if she, too, were English. Griffin had reassured her that all would be well, but she was not quite so confident. Too many tales from Seacliff had obviously made their way here, and it would take more than a good-natured scolding and a few promises from Radnor before she would be accepted.

Now, however, as she nestled in the comfort of his arms, feeling the warmth of his flesh against hers, the past eight months had been reduced to the scattered fragments of a night-mare.

At his insistence, and in the presence of Wyndym and six others who were apparently the leaders of the band, she had told her story. It had been difficult at first, remembering the pain, the betrayals, and the physical abuses, but as she saw the time pass before her eyes, saw the blood running from Davy's lashed back, saw the tired and strained Gwen her voice grew solemn, then impassioned, then outraged. She told them of Oliver's deceit, of his plan for the mercenaries who were even now turning the valley into a fortress; she spoke with venom in her voice about Flint's machinations not only against her but against her murdered husband. Then, with a plea for for-giveness unspoken but present she confessed to her unwitting complicity, her blindness, and blamed it on youth, on glittering gold, and on her awareness, which came all too late, that she was more her father's daughter than she had ever imagined.

"You were rather hard on yourself out there," Griffin told her, caressing the underside of her chin with one finger.

"Not half as hard as I've been inside."

His smile was tender as he kissed the top of her head. "You've come a long way, Cat, since we swam together in the bay."

She giggled. "I didn't know what a man was, then."

"And now?"

She punched his chest playfully.

"And you?" she asked after a silence that lasted for several long, peaceful minutes.

"Me?" he said innocently. "What about me?"

"I heard you spent your winter with the Irish."

He snorted. "True. I did indeed, Cat. I certainly did indeed."

"And?"

"My lord, woman," he said, half lifting himself on one elbow, "you've been through hell and have returned full of fire. Don't you intend to sleep at all tonight?"

"I must know," she told him seriously. "I have to know that the tales I heard weren't just stories told out of court. Please. Tell me."

He settled again, idly stroking her breasts. "There's not much, Cat. I told you what I'd learned in London, and what you've said today has confirmed it. But I'd hoped a case would have been presented to the circuit court when it passed through. It would have been the best way, all in all."

"I don't see how."

"Cat, the English will let us alone when they understand once and for all that we are not the barbarians they've been led to believe. My God, they strip our mines of coal for their infernal new factories, they take our children into English schools and make them forget their native tongue, and they take our men into their armies because they fight as well as any ten of their own. But for all that, we mean nothing to them. They think we're worse than the Irish, not much better than the Scots.

"But if we show them we respect a just law as much, if not more, than they . . ." He shrugged. "A battle won, and rather a significant one, I might add."

"But you didn't," she said, snuggling closer, her mouth against his chest.

"No. No, I did not, m'love. Mr. Flint, it seems, had other plans. The accusation of murder drove me out, and I found my way here easily enough. Those rumors you heard, that I was sending these men food and gold—all true. I confess it."

"And I knew it," she whispered. "If not in my mind, then somewhere in my heart."

He laughed heartily. "No, Cat, not quite. I was not helping murderers and thieves. Every man here, every man I have taken with me, has been exiled because of some unjust accusation by the English. Oh, a few brigands turn up, I admit, but we cast them out just as swiftly as do the English. I want no part of that lot, believe me.

"I came here, and told them all I knew, and we were only half our present number at the time. Half, Cat. The others, the new ones, you recognize them already from your home."

She sighed heavily. "I don't know, Griff. I don't think they really believe we're from the same place. I don't think they believe we are at all."

"Ah, now," he soothed, running a hand through her hair, "most of them do. I would say, all in all, you did very well by yourself this day. Considering what you'd been through just before, I don't think I could've made a better stand against Flint myself."

Then he fell into a thoughtful silence, and she was nearly lulled to sleep when he began speaking again, in bursts of anger, in spurts of frustration. Foot patrols had hounded them from the start—from their first encampments near the valley to ones deeper in the mountains—patrols initially from the British army, then deadlier ones sent by James Flint. When she interrupted to explain briefly about the growing fighting in the colonies, he understood at once why no replacement had been sent. The army was gearing up for something it considered far more important than a ragged band of outlaws who knew the hills too well to be trapped in a day. It also explained why they were able to build this village in the glen without any molestation. The lobsterbacks had been routed to another place.

But that stroke of good fortune was canceled out by a hard winter. Storms of the sort not seen since Griffin's youth drove most of the game away and into the English lowlands. With food in short supply, coupled with the continuing harsh weather, it had been only a matter of time before illness struck the band. And when it did, it struck with a vengeance. Men died coughing in their sleep, and others were so weak they were unable to do more than raise themselves from their pallets to take weak broth from their fellows.

Some of the less confident ones deserted.

Two more killed themselves in a knife fight over a burned hare's carcass.

And Flint never seemed to rest.

Once he had secured the valley to his liking, and was unable to cajole, coerce, or lie his way into ownership of Falconrest and Radnor land, he began sending small patrols into the hills. Flint's men scoured every slope, every cavern, every stream. They hunted the so-called outlaws as if they were vermin, or mad dogs, or marauding wolves. Every so often they would find themselves lucky; they would come upon a man or two who had found the strength to forage for food, and kill them without thinking. A few here and there were spared only long enough to be tortured into delivering answers before they died.

"Ambush," Griffin said, his voice almost a growl. "Every time it happened, it was the coward's way, not the man's. And once, because Flint knew I was nearby, he had one of those boys hanged from a tree and done as you would a stag. Like an animal."

He closed his eyes tightly and took a long, deep breath.

There were other groups of outlaws or rebels in the hills, but too many of them had their own axes to grind, and they simply weren't interested in joining Griffin and his force. Some were maimed or crippled and wanted only death as revenge; others couldn't understand dying for a valley most of them had never heard of, not comprehending that if Flint was left unpunished, his madness would increase, and he would attempt to subdue other places. Chaos would reign, and London's wrath would fall heavily on all of them, so swiftly and so mercilessly that Wales would never recover.

It was just Griffin then, and a handful of men who were fighting Flint, fighting the weather—fighting with the knowledge that they were outnumbered and doomed to failure. Their only saving grace was the valley spread out before them, acting as a kind of beacon to light the way, to remind them they had a crusade, a mission, a reason to go on.

News from the valley and from Seacliff had been coming in through Davy and Orin, but recently it had become scarce— since Flint's men had finished sealing off the valley from the outside world. Randall and the Daniels brothers risked their lives trying to get supplies through—food, bits of clothing, a pauper's share of ammunition—but heroic though the effort was, the supplies weren't nearly sufficient.

They had reluctantly decided then to flee for the winter. If the blizzards didn't get them, their lack of vital supplies would render them helpless in their battle against Flint. Their first thought was Scotland, but that was quickly ruled out when they realized they'd have to trek through a portion of England itself. They would also find themselves first in the Lowlands, where royalists wouldn't hesitate to turn them in for gold. Ireland, then, was finally their only hope of survival.

"We lived like dogs," he said, his voice soft with fury as he remembered the humiliations. "We weren't of the church, and we weren't there to deliver our souls, so most of them ignored us. Hatred of the English was common, but the villages were too afraid of the English guns and swords to shelter us. We hunted as best we could, lived in barns, in sheds . . . Once I spent a week on a fishing boat. It had been docked for the season, I suppose, and I discovered it quite by accident. A week smelling like cod!"

He nearly spat in a corner, and Caitlin laughed.

The vagrant Welsh had scattered at Griffin's insistence. The two score men then in the band were too great in number to pass unnoticed. But even then, when they scattered, they met disaster. A few were lost to the harsh winter, several to irate Irishmen who saw death in Welsh shadows, and two—Griff winced and shuddered—fell in love and stayed behind to become farmers.

"Is falling in love so terrible, then?" she asked in feigned reaction to an insult.

"Well," he said, "it would be if it were with the women I saw over there."

"Those men were frightened, Griff, and they saw beauty where you have no eyes." She waited for a retort. There was none, and she leaned forward to kiss his cheek. "You heard about Falconrest."

"I did."

"I saw it burning, Griff. Flint made me watch it burn to the ground. And he laughed."

"At our best we were fifty," he said as if he hadn't heard.

When she frowned he told her by way of explanation that they had tried to ferret out Flint's weak points once they'd returned to Wales and the snow had thawed. There were, however, far more of the enemy in the valley than when they had left. And they were more deadly. One man did get through—Terry Wyndym—and his report of the villagers' fear and isolation had disheartened them.

"Even you?" she said, disbelieving.

"Cat, a wise man knows when not to bell the cat—when the cat has fangs that outreach a man's arm."

"He's not a cat!" she snapped, sitting up and slapping his shoulder, hard. "He's a man. A foul, disgusting, evil man, to be sure, but he's a man nonetheless. And he made one mistake after another throughout the winter. His last was in not sending his whole army after me."

"Why should he? He knows where you were going. And he knows that he's no reason to fear a woman being added to this motley group we have here."

She scowled. "Pardon me, Mr. Radnor, but I believe I did rather well on my own account."

"You did that," he admitted. "But what does it get you, Cat? Seacliff is still his, and I wouldn't be surprised if by now he has false papers to prove it's his, all pretty and ribboned and signed and legal. We still can't get in without losing too many men. We have food now that the game is back, but what does that gain us, eh? A roll of fat around the belly and precious little more."

"Well, for one thing," she said, "it gets me you, doesn't it?"

"Oh, does it, now?" he challenged, raising his clefted chin to her.

She nodded once.

"And what makes you say that, Caitlin Morgan?"

"Evans," she said. "Oliver is dead, and I am Caitlin Evans again."

"All right. Evans. So?"

She squirmed until she was leaning over him, her breasts brushing his chest, one leg entwined with his. "Griff," she said solemnly, "I have been after you for half a decade, and I was too blind-sided to know it. And when I did know it, you left me. Not deliberately, and for reasons I didn't know until now. But when you came to me that night—"

"You saved my life then, Cat."

"—I understood a great deal more than I ever had. I'm not

one with words, but I know. I know."

She kissed him then. Gently, long, as the shadows of the low fire rippled across them. As the soft summer night wind shook the door's covering. As a night thrush trilled in the forest around them. She kissed him—his lips, his forehead, the heat of his copper hair, the lids of his closed eyes, his cheeks, his chin, the side and hollow of his neck. She touched each of the scars he had received in his fighting, unable to stop a tear from being shed for each one. It was a crude bed they were in, a rude hut with a dying fire, but for all the jewels she saw glinting in his eyes, the perfume of his love, the elegance of his desire, it could have been Windsor Castle, and she could have been the queen.

He touched her—cheeks, back, breasts, thighs—and she was lying in a shallow, swift-running stream whose movement was like that of quicksilver, her skin straining to receive every caress, every movement. It was cool and it was warm; it was cold and it was hot.

He kissed her and slipped his hands into her hair, and she was moving with the stream now, the foliage glittering overhead like a flock of emerald birds, the ground beneath her back a bed of down and silk, cloud and sun. Lying atop him she was floating; on her side, and she was dreaming; on her back, and she gripped the bunched muscles of his shoulders and wedded her lips to his.

When he groaned, she answered; when he smiled, she was radiant; when he paused and mouthed "I love you, Cat," she felt a release of tears and made no attempt to wipe them away.

And when he joined with her in a gentle coupling that brought a soft cry to her throat, the scars of his flesh and the scars of her soul faded in a flash of heat that made her gasp, made her laugh, made her sink her teeth gently into his shoulder to keep from screaming her release to the others. It was not embarrassment, however, nor was it shame. This moment, more than their first and more than in her dreams, was shared only by Griffin and herself. Intense. Private. As different from her liaison with James Flint as clear water is from pond water.

The fire, the hut, and the forest were gone; what remained was a carpet of stars and a moon for a lantern and the smoldering look in his eyes as he leaned down, caressing her breasts almost reverently before kissing her lips, softly, hotly, whispering "Caitlin" before the final moment.

They moved, and neither guided; they raced, and neither pushed; they expanded and they climbed, and when they fell it was together.

She wept, and dried her cheeks.

He held her to him and caressed her languidly, filled her ears with promises of caverns of gold; she held him, and she caressed him, and she accepted the promises with a lazy satisfied grin. And when they slept, her head was in the crook of his arm, her leg over his knees, and her heart so filled with laughter that she kept smiling in her sleep.

When they awoke, he wondered aloud after a kiss what they might do with their day.

"Well," she said, "this is rather pleasant, I must say, but the others will get jealous."

"Not as jealous as I if you so much as look at them, my dear."

Regretfully, she leaned away from his embrace. "Do you really want to know what's going to happen?"

A wary look narrowed his eyes. "Caitlin Evans, dammit, have you seduced me?"

A playful look touched her face. "And haven't you ever been seduced, Mr. Radnor?"

"Never as thoroughly as this."

"Then you'll want to know what I think."

The wary expression grew bemused. "I think . . . well, sooner shot for a sheep as a lamb. All right, Cat, what am I going to do?"

"You," she said, "are going to help take back Seacliff."

He waited, thinking, then sighed with melancholy. "Cat, I've told you—"

"No." She hushed him, closing his lips with a finger. "I heard very well, thank you, what you told me last night. But you didn't hear what I had to say."

"As I recall, lass, you didn't give me much of a chance to."

"Then listen now, and I'll tell you how we'll do it."

And he did. First grinning, then laughing, then jumping from the pallet and wrapping a cloak over his nakedness to pace the floor and consider. Caitlin watched him with eyes brightly excited, admiring, waiting. She knew the idea would intrigue him, knew too it would lure him because he would be using Flint's own plans against him. It was an irony, and a fitting reward. He'd be unable to refuse.

When his thinking was done, he knelt on the floor and took her hands tightly in his. "Cat, you have thought on this, haven't you? I mean, rather, this isn't something you've decided at the same time you were telling me."

"Are you asking if I thought before I spoke?"

Reluctantly, and somewhat shamefacedly, he nodded.

She laughed, grabbed his face and kissed him soundly, then leaned back out of the way when he reached for her boldly. "Sir!" she said.

"Oh, Caitlin, please!"

"All right, then," she said, composing herself and nodding. "I spent days wandering around these damned hills. I've spent months as a prisoner in my own house. And the more I heard about Flint's sealing off the valley and the patrols he boldly sent even to the marketplace, the more I knew beyond doubt this was the only way I was going to get back my home."

Griffin scratched at his jaw. "The others'll take some convincing."

"I'll convince them."

He rose and walked away, rubbing nervously at the back of his neck. "You seem sure, Cat."

"I have to. It's the only way."

"Some may die."

"Men have died before, for their homes. Lam Johns, for one."

He turned and looked at her significantly. "And women, Cat? Do women die, too?"

She straightened. "I will say this once, Griff, and I will not say it again: I could have chosen death at least twice over this past year. Twice! I chose to live, not because I was afraid of dying, but because my death would have meant little to this valley or to Seacliff. Certainly it would not have delivered my domain free of that bastard's hands. I do not intend to die now, either. I intend to leave this place as soon as I am able, and go home. You and your men may come with me or not, as you choose. But before this month is over, Griffin Radnor, I will be in Seacliff. And I will be there as its mistress once again."

She waited patiently, watching doubt, then admiration sweep across his features. Then he reached out his hand. She took it without hesitation and allowed him to pull her gently from the bed, not into his arms but into a handclasp of allegiance.

"You're not the same, are you?" he said quietly. "You're not the woman I talked to at the ringstones at all."

"No, I'm not." And it was neither an apology nor a confession; it was a bold declaration.

"Good," he said with a forceful nod of his head. "In that case, Cat, I've got nothing to lose."

33

GWEN WINCED as she lifted the bucket from the well's rim and placed it on the ground. Twinges from lacerations on her back still bothered her from time to time, but she endured them gratefully. A small price to pay, she thought, for the pleasure of seeing Cat flee Seacliff that night. She looked up. The sky was a perfect blue, as deep as the bay's low swelling water, as vast as all the earth. Then she glanced toward the house, toward the stables, toward the cottages, most of which were still deserted. Everything seemed normal. Chickens were in the yard, scratching for the meal; dogs were sniffing about the trees and carriage yard, one of them lying in the shade of a lightning-scarred hickory feeding her litter of mud-yellow pups; Davy was walking the horses; Orin was working at his forge; and Mary was near the cliff wall with a large washtub, scrubbing linen clean.

All so normal, and yet not normal at all.

After Cat had fled into the storm, Birwyn and a dozen men had galloped after her. They were gone for two days, returning only the evening before, bedraggled, disgruntled, and bringing with them Caitlin's roan. Gwen had fainted when she heard the news, but Orin had assured her that since the animal's mistress had not been found there was still hope she was alive, somewhere, perhaps even with Griffin.

Gwen chose to believe this version. To consider the alternative would have been too much for her to bear.

Davy waved when he saw her looking on, patted one of the

grays fondly on its haunch, and trotted over to help her carry the water buckets into the cottage.

"Your back?" he said, kicking open the door with his foot.

"A bother," she replied, "but not a loss."

After Gwen had thrown herself atop Birwyn during the melee in the front room, he'd finally managed to extricate himself by tossing her against the paneled wall. At the same time someone had thrown a cushion from one of the chairs, striking a sconce above her and shattering the chimney. When she hit the wall she scraped several shards of glass against her back, and they'd made some minor but painful cuts along her spine. Davy himself, and Orin, were still sporting bruises and a black eye each as a result of the staged brawl, and both carried them as badges of honor, refusing even the simplest of medications to ease the stiffness or the occasional lancing pain.

"Have ye seen the man?" he said, while she dumped the water into a large wooden barrel they would use for drinking and cooking later in the warm day.

"Not since yesterday."

He grinned and, when she turned around, grasped her in a loose embrace. "He hobbles about like a one-legged chicken. With the walking stick he looks like an old man."

They chuckled, but they did not laugh. Flint's left ankle had been severely sprained from the fall down the stairs, and there was something wrong, too, with his right arm. Davy had raced to the hall in time to see the last moments of the fall, and it was he who had run to Flint's assistance, and then to Bradford's.

But for Bradford, it was too late.

"He was a fair odd man," he said as Gwen kissed the point of his chin. "I'd've thought he'd be Flint's man for sure."

"No," she said. "He was the major's, and no one else's. And he was no fool. He didn't believe for a minute that that poor Northumberland lad had done the killing. You could see it workin' at him from the inside. We'd fought too much, he and I, for him to talk to me. And he was never sure he could talk to the mistress."

"But he was a good man at the last," Davy told her gently. "Without him, the mistress never could've done it."

Gwen gave a quick, rueful laugh. "I hate to say this, Davy, but I'm going to miss the old fart. He may have been a sod, but . . ." She shrugged. "Spilled milk, Davy. Spilled milk."

The rest of her thought went unspoken. They both knew that all they could do now was wait. Wait to see if Caitlin had survived; and if she had, to see what she would do to get back what was rightfully hers. Meanwhile, they had to live with James Flint.

Never in Gwen's life had she seen such fury, such absolute rage in a man as she saw in Flint when he realized he'd been bested. He began screaming at the top of his lungs at the foot of the stairs, and Lordy! She'd never heard such a string of oaths or incomprehensible sentences strung together at once. He must have been in pain, but his yells were forceful enough to stop the staged brawl. It was as if the king himself had strolled through the door. After that, there was much confusion and embarrassment, men running helter-skelter through the house and out into the storm, while the villagers themselves quietly slunk off to their homes. Three days had passed—as had the storm—before anyone saw Flint again. And when he appeared in the kitchen early one morning Gwen's first thought was that he was a dead man. His face was drawn, unshaven, badly bruised; his hair was unkempt, and his clothes looked as if he had slept in them. He grumbled about having something decent to eat for a change and left. Shortly afterward, she and Mary were summoned to the front room where he sat on the couch, staring into the hearth.

"She planned it all, you know," he said without looking at them. "Everything was planned."

His voice was quiet, and all the more dangerous for it.

"Nobody leaves this place until she is returned, do you understand me?" Still the quiet, still the threat. "You will do what you have to so I do not starve or lack for my comforts, but no one leaves. No one."

Mary shrugged as if it didn't make a bit of difference to her one way or the other, but Gwen as she left couldn't help feeling as if a ghost had walked over her grave. She expected Flint's men to make reprisals on the village; there were none. And the people she spoke to, those who ventured on occasion up a back, hidden path to Orin's cottage, said they wished he would do something to relieve the tension.

No one knew who would suffer first. But sooner or later Flint would have his revenge.

A week passed, and the only excitement occurred the day Ellis Lynne attempted to leave. Shortly after dawn, a cart piled high with trunks and sacks rolled out of the vicar's yard. Lynne was driving. And he was alone. He might have made it had not Morag Burton run screaming from the vicarage before he'd circled the commons, shrieking imprecations and waking all those who hadn't risen with the sun. Lynne tried to whip his pony to greater speed, but the cart was too heavy, too unwieldy, and before he was halfway up the road toward the gap it toppled him and his belongings into a ditch.

One of the trunks burst open and, as the people gaped in amazement, hundreds of gold coins spilled into the grass.

A shout rose up, and the villagers charged—not for the vicar, who was groaning and rolling on the ground, but for the gold. Within moments it had vanished, and Lynne was left to right the cart, repack his gear, and return sheepishly to his home. He said nothing about the stolen money. And the following Sunday there was no one in the pews when he ascended the pulpit for his sermon.

"We wait," Orin said stolidly on the eighth night, after Gwen had wondered aloud if they shouldn't at least be trying to contact someone in the hills. "Martin can do nothing with Flint's men about. Neither can we. We will do the mistress no good by being dead when she returns."

"No!" Wyndym shouted, one hand slashing viciously through the air. "I cannot understand you, Griffin. The woman ain't got her reason, surely ye can see that much. She thinks we're the whole bloody Brit army!"

Griffin said nothing, waiting patiently until Wyndym had finished his tirade. He, Caitlin, and eighteen others were in the clearing formed by the rough circle of huts. Many were seated on crude benches, and the rest were either lying on the ground or leaning against the boles of the surrounding trees. They were half the number Caitlin had seen when she'd arrived. The rest had left. They had not deserted, and they were genuinely apologetic. But they had no immediate stake in the deliverance of Seacliff, and so they moved on, deeper into the mountains where they could await either a pardon or some other fate.

"My God, it's madness."

Caitlin, seated primly on a stump and still in her father's clothes, stifled an impulse to lose her temper and be done with it. The day after she and Griff had sealed their lives, she had fallen into a three-day cycle of sleeping, eating, sleeping again. Exhaustion had caught up with her in an untimely fashion, and now that she was ready to move, Wyndym and his bristling beard had stepped in her way.

He was, it appeared, the only one who still did not trust her.

"Listen," the young man said, his voice breaking. "I'll say it for the last time, and you all must listen to me! We are *not* an army. Twenty if we're countin' the lady. Would you have the grace to tell me how nineteen men and one woman are goin' to attack a valley, stand off nearly one hundred trained men, and take the big house all in one fight?" He threw up his hands in disgust. "Lor', Griffin, it ain't possible. We can't do it!"

Griffin's clothes were loose, shades of green, and the copper in his hair flared like fire. He walked the width of the circle and stood before Terry, one hand smoothing the front of his shirt.

"In the first place, Terry, no one said we were going to attack the valley."

Wyndym's hand pointed at Caitlin. "But she—"

Griffin slapped the hand down, gently. "She said nothing of the sort. Nor has she said anything about taking on all of Flint's bloody soldiers. We don't have to! For what has to be done, we have all the men we need right here."

A grumbling from one of the others brought Caitlin's face around. She couldn't tell if they were agreeing or if they were having second thoughts.

"M'lady," one of them said—Willy Jonson, a farmer whose wife had been murdered by Flint's men after they'd raped her— "ain't there no other way? Can't...God help me, can't the Brits give us a hand?"

Caitlin smiled at the long-armed, bald man. "The Brits would sooner see us kill each other off. Then they'd have that much less to worry about among the barbarians."

A round of quiet laughter, and Terry's face was dark. He knew when he was beaten, but he still couldn't help resisting to the last. "I still don't like it."

Caitlin stood, grabbing her cloak from the ground and tossing it carelessly over one arm. Griffin turned to intercept her, but she pushed him aside and glared at Wyndym.

"Don't like it, then," she snapped. "Don't like it. But we've wasted enough time arguing here. The longer we bicker, the more time Flint will have to catch on to our game. We must move now, or we're done." Her eyes narrowed, and her voice lowered. "And hear me, Terrance Wyndym—if I have to do it alone, I shall."

She looked to Griffin suddenly, then walked into the hut and threw her cloak into a corner. Reaching under the pallet she pulled out a rucksack crammed with rations. She grunted as she lifted it to her shoulders, smiled without mirth as she slid her sheath and dagger into her waistband. Then she stepped outside again.

"I am going to the sea. Now. The rest of you can do what you bloody well please."

Without meeting a single startled gaze she marched from the clearing, looking up only once to check the sun's position. Five minutes later she could hear footsteps behind her, but she would not glance back. It was a monumental effort she was asking of these men—first to trust her after all they believed she had done to them, then to follow her into the bastions of hell itself.

But she hadn't been bluffing.

If need be, she would indeed do it all herself—or die in the attempt.

"It was a grand show you put on back there," Griffin said as he fell in step beside her. "But Cat, you were taking a bloody great risk."

"Did I have a choice?"

He grinned. "Not much of a one, no."

Worry then creased her forehead. "Do you think I'm being foolish? Stupid?"

They walked on for several minutes, the sounds of footsteps behind them growing louder, more numerous.

"Not stupid, no," he said finally. "I'm the one who's been stupid." He waved off an interruption. "I should have come back at once instead of running off to Ireland. I could have used the storms to my advantage, instead of letting them beat me." His grin was somewhat abashed. "I'm not used to being on the losing end, you know. I don't think I like the taste of it."

"No one does," she said.

"But me less than others. I've been fighting all my life, it seems. In the army, with the seasons to keep my people alive . . . with you."

She glanced sideways at him, but kept silent.

"And I'm too damned proud; that's my problem. I don't want Randall and the others to think I've run out on them."

"They don't think that, Griff."

"They will, if I don't do something."

The determination in his voice startled her, and for a moment the ragged edge of fear sliced through her mind. She wanted suddenly to caution him against the temptation to play the hero. She knew it was in him. She had seen it all her life, in their games, in their love play. The only time it had failed him was when her engagement to Sir Oliver had been announced; and then his pride and his profound sense of honor had prevented him from taking what neither of them at the time had really known was his.

Instead of speaking, she laid a hand briefly on his arm and he covered it, just as briefly, with his own.

Lovers they might be for all the obstacles that had been thrown at them, but for the time being they were also comrades in arms. The coming conflict was frightening to think about, and she shuddered. And though she firmly believed what she had told him that first night—that she had no intention of dying—she could not help feeling a twinge of apprehension.

This was no game she was playing now.

The stakes were not counters; they were the sum of her life.

Two days later they reached an inlet of Cardigan Bay. At its base was a tiny fishing village, with a few scattered farms climbing the mountains' steep slopes. They had seen no one in their march south, no signs of the army or of Flint's patrols. Nevertheless, as they dropped wearily to the ground above the village and passed goatskins of water around, they understood they could not necessarily count on every Welshman to be sympathetic to their cause. They'd already seen the phenomenon once, in the halving of their band.

Griffin sat with his hands gripping his drawn-up knees. He scanned the area below, then fiercely nodded to bring Wyndym to his side. "You know boats, Terry. Can you see anything down there to help us?"

Wyndym, who had said less than a dozen words to anyone throughout the journey, squatted on his haunches and peered through the waning sun's glare at the few skiffs and boats docked at water's edge or drawn up on the stony beach.

"'Tis a poor place," he said. "We take even two boats, they'll be hurting."

"We've no time to go farther north," Griffin reminded him. "And there's nothing south of here but Seacliff."

"Do it matter if the boat be big?" Willy Jonson asked.

Wyndym grunted. "Nope. We ain't goin' to sea. We're just takin' the coast, nice and easy like." He pointed his chin toward the stone and wood homes below, then to the shoreline beyond them. "Most any one o'them will do."

"When?" Caitlin asked suddenly, not liking the way Wyndym ignored her.

Wyndym's reply was laced with venom: "After sunset, m'lady. 'Less, of course, ye want to walk down there now, have a few words with the folks and tell 'em we're goin' to steal their livelihood but not to worry."

"Careful," Griffin said without shifting his gaze from the bay.

An uneasy silence marked an equally uneasy truce as they drifted back into the trees to await sunset. Caitlin, however, could not emulate the others, who had sprawled where they could find meager comfort and were attempting to sleep for the long night's work ahead. She walked instead out to the slope, then back into the forest, her fingers tingling and her feet restless with the demand to move on.

And she was worried about Terry.

Like the others, he had his family to return to, and thus just as much reason to take part in this as any; but she couldn't help recalling the harsh, victorious look in his eyes when he'd pinned her to the ground that first day and pawed at her. It had been childish of her to believe all Welshmen were saints and all the English demons; she should have known that even among her own people there were those who could not see beyond their own concerns and lives. They had their own lives, and nothing else mattered. Terry Wyndym, she thought, was like that. And in this situation, where he would put himself before all others, he could be just as dangerous as James Flint or Nate Birwyn.

The idea disturbed her. It had her looking over her shoulder at every shadow that flickered beneath a bough, or behind a bush. It made her breathing shallow, and had her walking through the grass as if on eggshells filled with knives.

A hand touched her shoulder. She jumped back and gasped.

It was Griffin, smiling.

"It's time, Cat," he said.

She blinked stupidly, then realized she had been walking

the last hour through almost total darkness. My Lord, she thought, if this is the way I'm going to be, we're lost.

"Are you afraid?" she asked, just to hear the sound of her voice over the night sounds of the forest.

He nodded. "Of course I am. A man would be a fool not to feel fear when he's going into something like this. Knowing this is the difference between a man, and a coward."

"Have . . . have you ever been a coward, Griff?"

A hesitation, and he looked toward the bay and its brilliant silver carpet sparkling beneath the moon. "Only once." He paused. "When Sir Oliver took you that first time to England, I left Falconrest. I went to Cardiff, to London, almost crossed the Channel to Calais. I wanted no part of Morgan, of Seacliff, even of my own land. I decided I was going to be a world traveler. I would see Cathay and India, Florence and Milan, and return someday dressed in gold and silk and dripping with silver. I even thought of returning to the army, but we didn't get along the first time, as I recall, and I saw no reason to believe this time would be any different."

"Griff—"

He placed a hand on the side of her neck and drew her to him. Kissed her and then tenderly pushed her away. "We'll not have any time together from now on, you understand."

It was a statement.

She nodded, swallowing hard against a lump that had grown large in her throat.

"But you must promise me you'll have a care. This will do none of us any good if you end up like your father. Or, God help us, like your husband."

She tried to speak, and had to clear her throat so she wouldn't sound as if she were weeping. "I will. But mind you this, Griffin Radnor: I do not intend to find a corner to hide in."

"If you do, I'll drag you out."

They kissed again, this time holding desperately to each other until a warning hiss from the shadows broke them apart.

"Are you comin' or no?" Wyndym asked them.

"We're coming," Caitlin said before Griffin could speak. "If I stand here much longer, I'll turn into a tree."

34

AT A SIGNAL from Griffin they broke from the protection of the trees and fanned out stealthily down a slope along the village's southern flank. Eight men broke into a dead run for the beach while the others moved less hurriedly but no less cautiously. Shadows against the moon-touched grass, they increased their speed as the danger from alerted dogs grew; they raced now on their toes, trying not to make a sound, their clubs in their hands at the ready. They had agreed beforehand that, should there be a fight, no man was to lash out with a killing blow; thus, knives, daggers, and the one short sword they possessed were kept sheathed.

They neared the cottages, smoke curling lazily from several chimneys despite the warmth of the night. From behind pitted and patched glass the dim glow of cooking fires could be seen, flickering as figures passed in front of them. A song drifted from an open doorway, a mother crooning to her child. From another house came the welcome sound of a loud, boisterous argument punctuated by muffled blows and ribald laughter.

The first eight, led by Wyndym, negotiated the stony beach in almost perfect silence. Wyndym then made his way along the row of boats and jabbed at those to be dragged into the surf. The waves here were low, lapping rather than breaking against pilings and worn pebbles. Within moments three boats rather than two had been chosen, and at a grunted command from Wyndym the men half-lifted, half-shoved the vessels into the water.

Caitlin heard the scraping as she ran behind Griff, and she winced. Surely they were loud enough to wake the dead. Yet there was no stirring within the cottages, and before she knew it she was wading in the cold water, her arms outstretched for balance. A hand grabbed her wrist. Another took her waist and someone lifted her into the first boat, a long vessel with a single mast and the sail folded at its base. It smelled of brine and fish, but Caitlin was more concerned with the thumping of boots on the planks, with the creak of oarlocks as men scurried about in the darkness trying to find places for themselves without pitching over the side.

A dog barked furiously, and a man bawled at it to be silent if it wanted to live to see the dawn.

The waves grew to breakers as the oars dipped into the water, splashing over the wedge-shaped bow and drenching everyone within. Caitlin huddled on the stern thwart, drawing her legs as close as she could to keep out of the way. Except for the pinpricks of lights from the fishing village, the land rose blackly all around them; the moon had retreated behind a bank of thick, silver-edged clouds.

A curse, muffled and harsh, broke the silence. Someone in her own boat asked if anyone knew how to hoist the bloody sail, and swore a disgusted oath when the response was negative.

Gripping the gunwales as hard as she could, Caitlin braced herself against the violent pitch and yaw, closing her eyes at one point when she was sure the craft would capsize under the blow of a white-foamed wave. Then she was lifted, held up for an eternity, as the boat plunged into the trough. A nervous laugh from her right—Willy Jonson—she was perversely pleased to note, indicated someone was just as frightened as she.

Then, as if a curtain had been drawn back, they were out of the inlet and into the open sea. The swells cradled them darkly, but once they had established a rhythm at the oars, the nauseating roll of the boat settled into a rocking motion that was almost soothing. They released their long-held breath and attempted a few jokes. The laughter was forced but grateful. On their left as the boats moved in single file southward, the cliffs loomed like an unbroken black wall, topped by a few shrubs and a handful of straggly trees.

The sea breeze was chilling, and Caitlin wished she'd not made such a show of leaving the camp. She could have at least brought her cloak along.

The moon broke clear again, briefly, and she could see someone in the boat ahead signaling to them. A circular motion, repeated over and over until Jonson, who had somehow managed to assume temporary command, whispered to the oarsmen to bring their craft alongside the other boats. It took several attempts before the men were able to maneuver all three vessels together, gunwale to gunwale, but when it was accomplished, Caitlin crawled forward and spoke softly.

"The tide will be in when we get there," she said, listening as the word was passed to those who couldn't hear. "Griffin will bring his in just north of the Norse wall, below the barracks. There's a path. Slippery from the tide, but it will have to serve. Terry will go south of the wall to another. That one is set rather deeply in and should be no trouble. Those men will go directly to the village and find Randall and anyone else you can think of whom you can trust."

"And what about you, lady?" Wyndym sneered out of the darkness. "What will ye be doin' all this time?"

"I'll go on to Seacliff," she said.

"M'lady," Jonson asked behind her left shoulder, "there are so many men . . ."

"But they have only a handful of leaders," she said, suddenly tired of explaining, but knowing how much these farmers and craftsmen needed the assurance yet another time. "Remember, the soldiers are doing this for pay, not out of loyalty and not for glory. Take away the source of their livelihood and they'll not give us very much trouble."

"So say you," Wyndym muttered.

"I *do* say," she retorted.

"Ye ken a great bit about them, lady."

"I lived with them a great bit, mister."

Wyndym continued his grumbling, but he was hushed angrily by several of his men, and further conversation was broken off when a series of large swells finally floated the boats apart. Caitlin moved slowly back to her place, smiling at the eight men with her though she knew they probably could not see her face clearly. Griffin had said nothing during the entire exchange, and she missed the reassuring sound of his deep voice, the touch—just one touch—of his hand on her cheek. It had been his idea to come to Seacliff through the bivouac of barracks, not hers. He had claimed that a few bolts thrown and a fire or two lit would create confusion enough to sufficiently isolate those soldiers who were not already scattered throughout the valley. She'd balked at first, but his insistence was too great, and she had at last given in.

Now, despite Jonson's pleasant murmuring and the few quiet attempts at humor drifting back to her from the others, she felt depressingly alone.

A wave rocked the boat precariously, and she bit down hard on her lower lip.

Faint echoes of the oars returned to her from the face of the cliffs, and she could not help imagining a horde of English troops or several dozen of Flint's men gauging the three boats' painful progress, sniggering at such a pitiful armada while they loaded their muskets and sharpened their swords. Ludicrous, she thought in a moment of sudden self-doubt; the entire venture was ludicrous. Here was a woman no more used to fighting than Griffin was to running, a woman coddled and cradled most of her life, who was now embarked on a campaign that could almost be considered military.

A grin came to her lips unbidden. Though she knew her father would be proud of her for what she was doing, he would also probably fall into a chair laughing. Not at her, but at the thought of her carrying a standard.

"M'lady?" It was Willy, his bald scalp giving him a curiously innocent look. "M'lady, the lads and I, we was talkin', and we wants ye t'know we be right sorry for all them bad words that was said against you."

She took his callused hand and squeezed it, smiled, and tossed her head to keep her hair from blinding her. It had not been braided since her night alone with Griffin, and without a hat, it had grown tangled and dirty, yet still capable of catching the shimmering lances of moonlight that escaped wherever breaks in the clouds formed.

"It's all right," she said quietly. "When all is said and done, Willy, I probably deserved them."

He didn't know how to respond, so he ducked his head and crawled away to take his turn at one of the four oars. The shifting of the men caused the skiff to heel dangerously, and it shipped water from one side. Automatically, Caitlin pulled up her legs, then realized with a self-conscious grin that she couldn't get much wetter than she already was. It seemed to be her lot these days to travel through her country drenched to the skin as if something were reminding her that her return to the easy life was not going to transpire astride a mythic stallion.

They rowed throughout most of the night, just outside the breakers that crashed against the cliffs. When, however, the boulders at the top were outlined in a dim dawn and the stars began fading on the western horizon, they started searching for a place to pull in for a rest. Backs were aching, arms throbbing, and the crust of sea salt on their faces made them feel as if skin was cracking with every smile and grimace.

A cove was discovered just before full light, hidden from view by massive boulders jutting out from the cliff wall, and bounded by a natural jetty that angled into the bay to form a broad pool of quiet amid the turmoil of the bay. With fair skill they maneuvered around the outer rocks into the peaceful water, and saw there was a narrow sand beach hard against the base. Without speaking they made for it, landed, and sprawled out on either dry sand or rock as they waited for the sun to warm and dry them.

Caitlin watched as Griffin walked toward her, and noticed that his face was lined with weariness. They did not speak. Arm in arm they moved among the men and spoke to them, reviewing the plan and bolstering their spirits. Only Wyndym would not converse; when he saw them approaching he rolled away onto his side and closed his eyes. Caitlin looked at Griffin, who only shrugged and stepped carefully around the man's feet. A few minutes later they were sitting on a natural table at the land end of the jetty.

"I should say something to him," she said, nodding toward the sleeping Wyndym.

"Nothing you can say, Cat, will change his mind. Not only are you a woman, but you've gone English as well, or so he believes. He came only because he wanted to go home. I put Jack Cullough in the same boat to keep an eye on Terry. He'll do us no harm."

Caitlin wasn't sure, but when she looked at Griff's profile against the steadily brightening blue of the sky, at the hair that swept in waves to his shoulders, and at the wry smile that had returned to his lips, she thought, He's enjoying this. The man's actually enjoying this!

An inexplicable sadness came over her for an instant; she suddenly understood Griffin far more thoroughly than she had before. It wasn't the battle he was looking forward to—though that was part of it, being as he was a brawler disguised as a man of means and land—it was the excitement that came with it. The taunting of death, of pain; the sheer physical and mental exhilaration of it all. She had experienced that emotion only once before, on the morning of her escape, and it hadn't been until now that she realized how addictive it could be. To spend one's life standing up to danger, beckoning it, laughing in its face, and then . . . and then *besting it!*

Marvelous . . . and sad.

Sad, because she wondered then if he would ever really be happy living among the gentry, running a valley and a vast landed estate the way her father had done. She laid her cheek against his arm and closed her eyes, listening to the sound of his breathing; it matched the rhythm of the waves breaking against the jetty's pointed finger and along its slick, rocky sides.

He must have sensed her melancholy, for he put his arm around her shoulders and hugged her once, tightly, before shifting slightly so her head would be on his shoulder.

"Sleep," he whispered. "Unless we run into the Royal Navy, we'll be at Seacliff before midnight."

This time the tide had ebbed and had left a trail of hard-packed sand, shells and dark strands of kelp in its wake. A few of the men woke before midafternoon and explored the rocks as far as they dared climb. They returned to sharpen and clean their weapons, using whetstones on their daggers and shirttails on their muskets. Their armory was hardly overwhelming, but their skill was great. They saw very little difference between braining a hog for slaughter and a man for revenge; it was all the same to them, and they were beginning to feel restless.

Terry Wyndym had a nightmare. In it a massive wave rose out of the bay and thundered across the valley, sweeping all before it, leaving only him and Caitlin Evans behind—and Caitlin held a dagger that shone like polished diamonds and was pointed at his gut.

Griffin dozed but did not sleep. The cries of sea birds wheeling from their cliff nests spoke to him of freedom, and of capture; a play of large fish beyond the breakers made him wonder what it would be like to spend one's entire life in a world colored in shades of green, blue, and cold, relentless black; and staring at the slimy sides of the boulders and at the stark blacks and browns made him conjure up an image of the ruins of Falconrest. Not one of the handful of messages he'd received since the fire mentioned the fate of his steward, Richard Jones. But he knew. He knew beyond doubt that Jones was dead. The man would have stayed to fight either the torchers or the blaze, and since he most likely encountered the former, he probably wasn't allowed to leave the scene alive.

Griffin was sitting with his back against a rock, Caitlin still snuggled softly under his arm. Every few minutes he would stroke her arm or hair absently, and for a considerable length of time speculated on a life shared with her. It certainly wouldn't be easy. Such a volatile mind as hers was constantly shifting from one decision to another at a dizzying pace. He smiled to himself. It would not be easy, but it certainly wouldn't be dull.

He shifted slightly and lifted his right hand to shade his eyes against the reddening glare of the sun. Clouds. He was sure there were clouds building across the horizon. He blinked, and they were gone. He closed his eyes and dozed, awakening only when he felt a twilight breeze caressing his cheek, a breeze that carried with it the decided scent of rain.

Caitlin sighed when she felt herself shaken, rubbed the heels of her hands over her eyes to drive off sleep. When she sat up, however, she groaned as she encountered the stiffness of her hip and the tingling of her right leg. She stretched, kissed Griffin's cheek quickly and would have asked him if he had rested at all, but the ominously thoughtful look in his eyes stopped her.

"What is it?" she said.

He lifted his face toward the sky.

She looked, and her lips tightened.

The sun was already down, the day's blue now indigo and black. Instead of stars she saw only mountains of clouds slipping down from the north with dark gray summits and blackened bases. And at the horizon, where there was still some light, she saw tendrils of rain fall toward the water. The swells were already high, the tide coming in fast, and the lullaby of the breakers had turned to a low grumbling.

"The rain will overtake us," Griffin said, climbing awkwardly to his feet and pulling her up with him.

"We still daren't travel by land," she said. "At the first alarm we'd be lost."

"If we can't reach the trails up the rocks, we'll be lost just as well."

She wavered as she followed him back down to the beach, frowning when she saw the others already waiting by the boats.

They had seen the approaching storm and had already made their decision; not even Terry Wyndym would suggest attacking a rifleman with a club.

"Hard rowin'," said Willy Jonson with a smile that was mostly bravado.

Another slapped the side of his craft and laughed. "Never knew what it'd be like to drown sittin' 'stead of swimmin'."

"Can you swim, Danny?" a third asked with a laugh.

"Like a bloody fish, lad, like a bloody beautiful fish."

"Well, gentlemen," Caitlin said into the general laughter, "let us pray we won't have to test Danny's word."

She knew then that they were not afraid. At every other step of the way they had always had alternatives. They could run. They could hide. They could stand and fight. Not now. They had broken from their safe cover in the mountains, had stolen from their own kind, and were less than four hours' traveling time to homes from which they'd been exiled for months. Some of them would not live to see their families again. Yet they were eager to enter the foray.

Griffin cleared his throat, ready to give the order, when suddenly Caitlin stayed him with a look and hurried down the beach to the first boat. There, to the startled and pleased amazement of all watching, she hugged the first man she came to and planted a kiss solidly on his mouth. He was flustered, and the men teased him, but by the time she had reached the second boat the other men had formed a ragged line and were waiting, brushing at their ragtag clothes, smoothing down their hair, wiping their lips on their sleeves. They said nothing. They kissed and hugged her in return, and not a few turned away with a glint of tears in their eyes.

Terry Wyndym she saved for last.

"Well, Terry," she said neutrally.

"M'lady," he offered, his eyes downcast.

"You'll give me a chance to prove myself, then."

His blunt-toed boot scuffed the sand. "It's crossed my mind."

"Did anything in particular change it?"

"Martin told ye how to find us, didn't he?"

She nodded.

"He's been wrong afore, y'know."

"He has," she admitted. "But he's also taken a great lot of chances for you, and for the others. He's taken a chance with me."

"Aye, I thought as much." His chest heaved as he inhaled and released his breath. "I might as well, too." The grin she saw in the dimming light was sheepish. "'Sides, if ye leave me here I'll be stranded; I can't swim."

A split second passed that filled her heart with hope; then she flung her arms around him and hugged him, held him, and whispered, "God be with you, Terrance Wyndym."

An embrace for Griffin, several minutes long and a lifetime too short, and she punched at the air. Immediately, they scrambled the boats into the rising water and leaped in, disdaining the sails in favor of the strength of their backs.

It was a simple matter to break out of the jetty's protection, but once in open water again they found some of the swells rising higher than their heads, the whitecaps showing sooner than before, and the wind picking up as the clouds plummeted toward them. The oarlocks protested, the keels groaned, and she was forced to hold the gunwales in a white-knuckled grip to keep from lurching over into the bay.

The sky continued to darken, turning for several minutes at a time a shade of green laced with black. Gulls streaked over their heads, heading for the protection of the woodland or their cliffside nests. Spouts of foam rose into the air like spectral hands and were shattered like glass when the wind gusted. Caitlin found she could no longer look at either cliff or horizon; their rising and falling motion made her stomach queasy. So she watched the faces of the men pulling the oars: grim, hard-set, dripping with sea spray and flushed dark with exertion. Her own hands clenched and opened in her lap, as if they wanted to take an oar themselves. Her hair whipped across her face, stinging her cheeks until finally she grabbed it and made a hasty braid that blew in the wind.

"How bad will it be, Willy?" she said to the farmer when she saw him anxiously scanning the clouds.

"How t'say, mistress," he said, sitting beside her to grip the tiller. "Don't hear no thunder, so lightning is a fair distance. But the wind . . ." He gave an exaggerated shudder she understood all too well. A strong wind would make their proposed landing all the more precarious.

The minutes passed in hour-long spurts.

Once the clouds had massed overhead, they rowed in almost total darkness, their only guide the sound of the waves against the rocks on their left.

Caitlin was at the tiller now, both hands holding its slippery arm so hard her forearms trembled. Her eyes squinted as she sought the rocks, and signs of Seacliff, her head ached in the wind's constant keening, and she felt more than once as if her shoulders would be pulled apart as a wave lifted them almost clear of the surface. She had to clench her jaw to keep from screaming.

The first spatter of rain came just before midnight.

The first squall spun them dangerously off course.

But after it passed there was relative calm, and Jonson left an oar to give her a breathing spell. She nodded her thanks and cupped her hands around his ear: "Willy, we're going to have to come in straight on."

He nodded his understanding.

"Do you think we can do it?"

The wind rose again, and when he jerked his head toward the tiller she grabbed it, gasping at the power of the sea as it rushed against the rudder. After regaining control, she tilted her head down while he cupped his hands around her ear. "If we don't," he shouted and still she barely heard him, "we'll have to take a swim. I don't fancy swimmin', mistress, if ye don't mind."

She laughed and mouthed him a kiss, shouted a warning to take care when several men from the bow exchanged places with the oarsmen. The boat heeled, righted itself, and was struck broadside by a wave no one saw coming. The world tilted crazily, water gushed whitely over the sides, and when the rudder lost its bite in the water, the sudden release threw Caitlin to the deck. She gasped and swallowed a mouthful of the sea, scrambled back to her place when the boat passed the wave's crest and miraculously landed upright.

A second swell battered them, and when that, too, had subsided, she stifled a horrified shout when she saw one oar swinging wildly in its lock. The man using it had been washed overboard. Silently. Without warning. And the sea had closed over him as if he'd never been.

The black cliffs and the black sky, the black water and the black rain swirled around them.

Wearily, she gave the tiller over to Jonson and slumped forward, her hands dangling over her knees and her mouth gasping for air. Incongruously, she remembered a fall afternoon when she was little more than seven. Her father had taken her to the teeming port of Cardiff where she had seen more ships, more sailors, more outright chaos than she'd ever imagined possible. A captain friend of her father's offered to take them up the Bristol Channel when he sailed for London, leaving them off on a spit of rock opposite Land's End in Cornwall. Though the vessel had moved slowly, the villages sliding past them on either side seeming to pass at little more than the speed of a fast walk, she had been so excited that she'd climbed onto a high coil of hawser and waved frantically at the few souls she saw on the shore.

She'd nearly fallen overboard, and would have had it not been for a quick-thinking first mate.

"Lass," he'd said, "ye've got to remember there's more to fallin' than just hittin' the water."

And even at that age she'd known what he'd meant—that there was all that turmoil and unfathomable depth beneath the surface, all the way to the bottom. She hadn't known how to swim then, and the lesson was well learned.

A jolt on the rudder forced her mind back to her job, and she beckoned to Jonson quickly. Pointing, she waited until he'd taken the tiller in his own hands before easing herself off the thwart and weaving her way to the naked mast in the center. There she stood, her arms wrapped tightly around the perilously thin post, staring into the darkness.

Waiting.

It seemed to her she had spent her entire life waiting.

The wind lashed her, the rain increased and she felt nothing, and suddenly she stiffened.

"There!" she screamed. And screamed, "There! There!" again.

The oars paused and every head turned.

Through the wind-driven rain, through the spray that splattered them, they could see lights shimmering atop the cliffs. And even in the darkness Caitlin could discern the brooding outline of Seacliff—like her . . . waiting.

35

THEY TURNED about at Caitlin's insistence.

With Seacliff towering so close above her, she suddenly felt the need to think, to worry, to take some valuable time and see where she might go wrong. And that could too easily be done, she thought as they breasted the relentlessly rolling swells and came about when they were only a mile from shore. She should have arranged for signals between the boats to be exchanged when they were positioned; she should have planned for alternate landing sites in case the tide was too high and the currents too powerful; she should have done a great many things, she knew, but it was too late to worry about it now. The other boats were invisible in the dark, perhaps even now making their way as close to the cliffs as they dared, seeking to land near those paths that wound all the way to the top.

"M'lady," Jonson said, puzzled.

She motioned him silent as she stared up at the windows ablaze with lights and wondered what had been happening behind those walls.

"M'lady, I beg you . . ."

She unwrapped her arms slowly from the mast and braced her feet on the deck. The men stared up at her, wondering what next she wanted done. She said nothing to them. She only searched each face seen clearly or not, looking for the weakest link, the strongest, for the one who would panic at precisely the wrong moment. And when she failed, as she knew she would, she pulled the hastily fashioned braid over her shoulder and unplaited it. When her hair was free and streaming in the wind, she took hold of the mast again and nodded.

"Now, Mr. Jonson," she said firmly. "We go now."

The sea was far less taxing as they came about once again and headed in. The swells gave them momentum, and the oars served now as brakes to prevent them from spinning helplessly or being dashed murderously against the rocks. Bobbing, diving, climbing again, they rode the back of the sea toward the cliffs, Caitlin straining with those at the bow to spot the trail carved into the rock by the Norsemen who had built Seacliff's wall centuries ago.

She saw it then.

As they sped down the face of a wave into a deep trough she saw a slight pale streak running up the face of the rock. When the boat rose, she lost it, then searched in panic and found it again, pointing it out to the men. A fair portion of it was under the water's surface, and it was evident by the force of the tide against the stone that she had made a costly, stupid error. She had hoped to be able to come under the path, or alongside it, with the boat; but the only possible way they would be able to make it in was to bring the boat as close as they dared, and swim for shore. The stairs carved into the stone were wide and deep, and there were wooden railings lashed onto thin iron posts driven into the bedrock. These she could see more clearly as they approached the cliff. But how to get to them without being dashed to death?

Jonson gave over the tiller to the man called Danny and came to stand beside her. His expression told her he saw the predicament at once, and they were silent for several minutes.

"Well," he said, "leastways, we ain't got the rain."

Her nod was desultory. The rain had indeed stopped, and there were occasional narrow gaps in the clouds; but the wind stayed with them. The wind, and the breakers.

"If we get too close, it'll be like hammer and anvil and us between," he said finally, a depth of sorrow in his voice that made her want to weep.

"A few moments," she said through her teeth. "Damn, if we only had a few moments we could..."

She stopped, her voice trailing into the night wind.

"M'lady?" Jonson peered closely at her, thinking she had reached the end of her tether. "M'lady?"

"Willy," she said, looking around the mast straight at him, "do you think we could leave this boat in less than a minute?"

Jonson frowned. "Less than a minute?"

"A minute. One minute. Less than half that, in fact."

He glanced around and shrugged. "If it means livin' or gettin' bashed, I'd say we could."

"Then grab hold, Mr. Jonson!" And she took the mast in

both hands and began pulling, pushing, laughing when he saw
her purpose and took hold of it, too.

Nearer they moved; and the rocks took on definite shape.

Nearer they got; and the lower floors of Seacliff above them
vanished from view.

Three men and Caitlin struggled with the mast, and though
the others strained and shouted to keep the oars deep in the
water and slow their progress, they moved inevitably, inex-
orably . . . nearer.

A crackling noise like a thousand bolts of lightning shattered
the air around them and the mast gave way sharply, spilling
them all into the bottom of the boat. Jonson was calling out
orders even before he got to his feet, and Caitlin was rushing
toward the bow, the masthead in her grip, the rest of it held
by those who came behind. It reminded her of nothing so much
as a whaler's harpoon, and their quarry towered above their
heads implacably silent, while the sea demonically thundered
around them.

An oar splintered.

Another oar snapped in half and Danny lost control of the
rudder for a heart-stopping moment.

Nearer they crept.

They could hear now the roaring of the tide in the several
caves that pocked the wall, the waves smashing in and swirling
around them, returning in time to whip the small craft in another
assault. Seacliff was then completely out of sight.

Nearer they came.

Twenty yards remained, and Caitlin could feel the tension
grow around her, a palpable force that weighed down her shoulders and dried out her mouth.

The word was passed: Immediately the masthead touched
the wall, they were to make their way forward and jump for
the steps. The railings were slippery, dripping spray and clumps
of kelp, and it was understood there would be little help for
them if they slipped and went under. They were to hit the step,
grab the railing, and start running as best they could until they
were far enough up so all the others had room and there was
no danger of a rogue wave taking them back again.

Ten yards, and she heard someone praying, heard the rest
of them responding.

Five yards, and she braced herself.

A touch in the small of her back, but she did not turn her

head. She knew Jonson was asking if she wanted to go first, and she shook her head.

The waves swelled and dragged. They drew to within five feet and slipped back five more. The men on the oars swore into the wind at the top of their voices as they, and Danny at the rudder, tried desperately to keep the bow near their target.

The masthead scraped rock, pulled away, rammed into it with such force that a sudden brace of fire raced along her arms to her shoulders. She gasped, and shouted, and the first two men vaulted off the bow. Time stopped, the wind howled defiance, and when a curtain of spray receded she could see them on hands and knees making their way upward. Their ragged cheering was short-lived; the bow and mast struck the wall again and the second pair made their leap. Then Jonson scrambled back through the deepening water in the bottom and waved Danny forward. He protested, but the farmer yanked him to his feet with one powerful hand and shoved him past Caitlin. She called good luck after him, braced herself again, and the last pair but one left the bow in a sudden explosion of white, cold water.

It wasn't until they were safely off that she realized she alone was holding the mast. The end weight was too much. She lowered it, turned in a panic and braced it against its own stump. One time, she thought; this would work one time, and it would be over. Then she looked up at Willy, who was grinning at her and nodding.

"No!" she shouted, and pointed a command.

Jonson refused, still grinning.

"Damn you, Jonson, this is your mistress, not some barmaid. Do as you're told!"

Jonson, trained by generations of subservience to the Evans family, took a deep breath while Caitlin knelt on the skiff's bottom and took hold of the mast near the stump. She waited. The boat rose, moving more swiftly now that the oars weren't being used as brakes. When the mast speared the wall a third time he was past her on the dead run, leaping long before he reached the bow, his arms out, his mouth open in a cry, and his figure immediately cut off from her sight by the untimely blast of a wave less than five feet below him.

At the same time, the mast finally gave way. Slammed backward by the collision and out of Caitlin's grip, then gouged through the blunt stern, shattering into pieces as it went. The boat spun wildly about, and she was thrown to her stomach. Nearly a foot of water filled the boat now, and as the craft slipped forward and back in the sequence of waves it also dropped lower, until each movement of the water sent gallons spilling over its sides. Caitlin flailed and spat, thinking she could hear someone screaming at her over the wind. But whatever the instructions were, they came too late. The boat capsized, and the raging sea closed over her, engulfing her in a maelstrom of black water.

Martin Randall stood in the back room of his cottage and looked out the rear window. The wind had abated somewhat, yet the tiny panes still trembled at its passing, and an occasional flurry of rain blurred his vision. He turned around with a sigh and strode to a small table in the middle of the room. A brown and red crock and a glazed goblet beckoned, and he resisted for only a moment before pouring himself the gin and emptying the glass in a single gulp.

The fire made him gasp; the tears in his eyes lingered before he brushed them angrily away.

He poured a second ration, and he sat on a rickety chair and stared at the cloudy liquid, wishing it were wine, wishing it were poison. But poison, he decided, was too good for him. He should be banished into the mountains without a stitch of clothing on him, forced to suffer the same fate to which he had condemned Lady Morgan. He snarled and gripped the goblet more tightly. No, he thought; even that was too good for him. He should be flailed. Every inch of skin on his back peeled off an inch at a time. He should bleed to death, slowly. It was only fitting, only just.

He lifted the goblet to his lips, and his arm froze.

He listened intently, his heart suddenly filling his throat.

A minute passed, and another before he relaxed. The wind, Martin told himself; you're hearing voices on the wind now.

And why not? Hadn't he been hearing Caitlin's voice in his dreams for over a week now? Hadn't his nightmares driven Quinn from his bed to one of her own, back there on the other side of that curtain? She had tried mightily to console him and assuage his rampant guilt, but not even her vast love for him enabled his mind to work clearly. He heard her now, tossing in her sleep, and wanted desperately to go to her. To have her hold him, give him comfort.

He held the thought and nursed it, finally set down the untouched goblet and rose to his feet. He swayed, then grabbed the edge of the table and started for the curtain . . . and froze again, his head cocked and his eyes narrowed.

There! Damn his eyes, there was something moving out there.

Keeping well away from the window, he inched toward the back door. It could be a deer, a fox, one of Sharnac's confounded dogs, but he didn't really think so. The sounds he'd heard were quiet enough, but not carrying an animal's stealth. The muscles across his stomach tightened, and he reached for a stout walking stick propped against the wall. If not a fox, then maybe it was a weasel—one of Flint's men finally coming for him. The reign of silent terror was over, and he would be the first victim of the new era.

A muffled thump sounded as something heavy fell against the door. Randall jumped back in surprise, the stick poised over his shoulder like a club.

Another sound, and before he could react the door flew open and into his astonished arms fell the sodden, half-drowned form of Terry Wyndym.

"My . . . God!" Randall exclaimed.

"No," Terry gasped with a grateful weak smile. "Just me and the lady."

There were no guards posted around the perimeter of the barracks, and only a handful of lanterns burned outside the buildings' single doors. Griffin nodded bitterly to himself, wondering why he should be surprised. Flint, after all, was a supremely confident man and would probably try to enlist any man who managed to penetrate the valley this deeply.

There were eight low buildings, four on either side of a narrow grassy lane that was littered with benches, wine sacks, and scattered articles of clothing—not all of them men's. As far as he could tell, no one was outside. Two of the seven men with him had already slipped around to the other side, and an owl's weak call told him they were in place.

The man standing next to him in the shadow of the trees grunted. Griffin laid a restraining hand on his shoulder. "In a few minutes, Peter," he said to the man, who had once lived on Radnor land. "We must be sure Wyndym and Mistress Evans have reached their places safely."

"And how do we do that?" came the gravelly voiced answer. "Do we fly over there?"

"We wait," he said, "and we listen. If we hear nothing in the next hour, we'll begin and pray they've done their work quietly."

Peter made a wet noise of disgust and crouched down on his haunches. Griffin did the same, taking from his belt a long hunting knife that he scraped over the toes of his boots absently, keeping his mind a blank, watching for signs of movement at the eight doorways, listening for a signal from Caitlin.

And when he judged the hour had indeed slipped by, he was tempted to wait another. Tempted, but no more. Instead, he rose and flexed the muscles of his legs to loosen them, nodded to Peter, who disappeared into the woodland to warn the others, then filled his lungs with air and allowed himself a grin.

He stepped out from under the tree and walked boldly toward the nearest door. The lantern affixed to the frame hung only from a loop of wire that was twisted around a nail. Deftly and soundlessly he unfastened the wire, possessed himself of the lantern, then turned his back to the building, and walked to the center of the open area. At the same time the rest of his men did the same.

It was an odd sight: eight men standing in a strong wind, their shirts rippling hard about them, their hair flailing around their eyes, and their mouths working at extraordinary grins. It was incredible, many of them were thinking, how a man such as Flint could be so arrogantly confident that he did not protect his own back yard. Yet it was also typical. And somewhat sobering that they should be here, here at Seacliff after all this time.

Griffin lifted his lantern.

The others did the same.

Then in a flurry of comets, they flung the lanterns against the walls where they shattered in sharp explosions, the oil running down the planks in ribbons of blue-gold flame that momentarily covered the windows. Griffin did not expect the barracks to burn to the ground, not after all the rain and not in the high wind, but he hoped the fires would last long enough to cause panic.

They did.

Shouts and hysterical screams split the night air, and the

outlaws raced to stand by the doors, clubs in hand. The doors soon enough flew open as Flint's mercenaries tumbled outside, struggling into their clothes or cloaks, several of them tripping over their own feet and spilling ignominiously to the ground.

It was, Griffin thought later, almost pathetically easy. Those who escaped the well-placed outlaws' clubs were either too drunk or too confused to offer much resistance. In addition, most of his men were quick-witted enough to exchange their clubs and staffs for the muskets Flint's soldiers carried. After that, it was only a matter of a few minutes before three dozen mercenaries were herded into the first building and jammed against the rear wall. And when he was positive there was no one else in the other barracks, Griffin faced his prisoners, hands on his hips, his hunting knife exposed so that the blade glinted in the lanternlight.

"'Ere, 'oo the 'ell are you?" one of the men demanded.

"Does it really matter?" Griff said, facing the stunned, sullen men. "What does matter, it seems to me, is that you are all in here, and I'm the one who has you."

"Not for long," someone else offered. "We'll be due on post in a while."

"My friend," Griffin said, bowing mockingly, "in a while you'll not have any posts to be due on." He paused, letting his words penetrate before dropping his casual manner. "Now listen to me, the lot of you. We're not out to harm anyone, but should you try for the door we'll not stop to ask your reason. You'll be shot down, simple as that. And while we're waiting for a message I'm expecting, you would do well, I should think, to consider the method of your employment. You may discover it will be healthier to take your gold from me."

"'Ave you got it?" a wary voice asked.

"I have what it takes," Griff told him without hesitation. "I have what it takes," he repeated, chuckling.

It was so cold beneath the surface of the water that Caitlin nearly lost consciousness, but she held on grimly, her cheeks puffed with air as she pushed down and away from the sinking boat. She did not swim far, however. Her sense of direction was thoroughly befuddled, and she needed to return to the surface as quickly as she could before she was either dragged out to sea, or smashed against the base of the cliff.

Though her eyes were open she could see nothing, hear

nothing but the roaring of her blood in her ears, and her limbs were growing numb startlingly fast. She struck out blindly once her tumbling had been controlled, reaching with long strokes and pulling herself along to where she remembered the steps were last seen, praying and hoping her direction was right. Not far away she could faintly hear the crash of the breakers. It terrified her. She almost panicked. Her lungs began to burn, and bubbles of air sifted between her lips.

Up, she told herself; damn you, Caitlin, up!

It seemed that she fought the boiling surf for hours before her hand struck rock just as the last of her air exploded from her chest. No, she thought, it wasn't rock at all. It was wood. A long piece of wood. But it was too late. Even as her hands closed around it and pulled weakly, her mind was losing its spark. Clouds of soft, gentle black velvet drifted over her, enticing her, coaxing her to abandon the struggle and give herself up to the sea. It was tempting. It was remarkably tempting, considering all she had vowed, all she had been through. All she had to do—the undertow snaring her legs while the shove of the water slammed her hard against the wall—all she had to do was let go. First the right hand, then the left hand, and she would belong to Neptune for eternity. And she would be with her parents. She could hear them calling to her. Urging her to flee the land of mortals and come into the shade of heavenly warmth. Warmth. That's what she wanted now— pulling, banging, pulling without feeling—that's what she needed. A fire and a warm embrace and the voice of her father scolding her for nearly toppling over the side into Bristol Channel.

Pulling. Her lungs were afire, her throat scorched.

Her parents were shouting at her now, demanding she forget her foolish notions and leave all behind her. Her soul was all that mattered. And the wood. The wood. Hang on to the wood.

"The wood, mistress! Damn you . . ."

Jonson, his legs held by Danny, whose legs in turn were being held by another, ducked his head beneath the sea's foam and grasped Caitlin's wrist. She came without a struggle, and as he broke the surface, gasping and snorting, he feared he'd been too late. She was dead; at the last, she had died to allow him to live.

Tugging, squirming, as the sea grasped for them greedily, they hauled her up laboriously, swearing at her, swearing at each other until they were above the surf at last, huddling against the slick stone wall on a broad step.

"Be she alive?" Danny asked anxiously. The others looked over his shoulder at the woman lying in Jonson's lap.

"Don't know," Willy said, a catch in his voice. "Don't know."

They talked incessantly to each other while they tried to push the water from her lungs, drive the blue from her lips and bring back her color. They talked . . .

. . . and Caitlin heard the voices.

"No," she murmured. "I don't want to go. I don't want to go. Not now. Not . . . not . . . now."

A shouting above the thunderous breakers puzzled her. Why were her parents yelling like that? Why were they so gleeful? Hadn't she told them she didn't want to go with them? Weren't they listening to her? Weren't they?

She opened her eyes to confront them and saw a bold man peering at her, water from sea spray dripping from his face as if he were crying. She closed her eyes again, reopened them, and remembered where she was.

"Thank God," Jonson said prayerfully, falling back in relief. "Thank God."

36

DAWN SLIPPED closer by an hour before Caitlin was able to stand and breathe freely again. But once she was on her feet she wasted no time leading Jonson and the others up the path, the surf growling below them, the clouds racing overhead, their edges lined with shining gray. The wind had abated for the time being, reduced to a deceptive whispering through the treetops. Caitlin listened to it for a moment as she pulled herself along the slick, rattling railing. The wind had no message for her, however, and she moved onward, upward, until the wall was within reach. Then she dropped to her knees and lowered her head.

The others gathered as closely as they could about her. The

scrape of their weapons leaving their sheaths and scabbards
was lost in the roar of the breakers. Their own gasping and
panting matched hers, and when she finally looked up she saw
a motley collection of bedraggled, trembling men fighting off
the cold of both sea and air. It was a wonder no more of them
had been lost in their travels, she thought, and forced herself
to give them a smile to prove she'd not left them.

Then, puffing her cheeks and releasing the air in a long,
meaningful sigh, she poked at four chests and signaled them
to make their way around to the front of Seacliff by way of
the south tower. One, she directed in mime, should detour to
the second staff cottage, just in case Wyndym or his followers
had not made it. As far as she knew these men were the only
ones left. Since she'd heard no fighting or sounds of struggle,
she told herself she had to assume she was on her own for the
time being.

The scrape of a boot against a stone sounded not far away.

The men pushed as close as they could to the stone face
just below the wall, listening, holding their breath. The snap
of a twig breaking in two could next be heard. Caitlin, putting
a finger to her lips, eased herself up to the last step and put
her shoulder against the wall. Slowly, infinitely slowly, she
raised her head to the top and saw a man standing not ten feet
away, his face upturned toward the sky. She was puzzled until
she saw in the wash of light from the house a flask in his hand.
When he'd finished his tippling, he secured the flask somewhere in the folds of his cloak, and turned toward the water.
She ducked just in time, held her breath and waited. Then they
heard him walk past and stop.

A second set of footsteps neared, and stopped, and a man
with a heavy Yorkshire accent said, "Not much time now, is
it? They'll be comin' to relieve us."

"Ach, if they wake up. Christ, man, y'know, if it weren't
for the gold I'd be on the first coach out of here."

"Ye'd best not let the old man hear ye say that."

"Or One-Eye."

They laughed, and she heard one thump the other's shoulder
companionably. A moment's more chatter, and the first man
was alone again, muttering to himself about the weather and
the country and why he had to listen to talk of damned Welsh
women when the only one worth having that he'd seen since
coming was long since gone, and wasn't that the devil's promise.

Caitlin grinned at the lefthanded compliment, then drew her dagger from its sheath and cupped one hand around her mouth. She coughed lightly. Though he was out of sight, she could sense the man turn sharply, could see him frown, could feel him question the soundness of his hearing. She coughed again, and waved a hushing hand at the stirring below her.

He was coming. Though he was trying to be silent she was able to pick out the swish of his cloak, the rub of his trousers, the irregular slap of his musket's stock against his arm. Her lips suddenly went dry, and she licked them. Her legs began to cramp, and she ignored the dull pain as she kept her gaze upward, waiting.

The light from the house spread out in a series of golden bars across the lawn, those from the upper stories slanting gently downward and casting shadows all the way to the wall. She had no problem sorting out his shadow. His capped head almost immediately afterward came into view directly above her. He was staring perplexedly at the water. Then, just as he was about to turn around, he changed his mind and leaned forward, peering through the darkness at a spot just in front of Caitlin. When she judged he wouldn't bend any farther, she moved—her right hand whipping up and grabbing the front of his shirt, pulling sharply outward and down. Her left hand followed the right instantly, driving the dagger into his throat. With a cry and a gurgling noise, he fell past her like a giant night creature whose wings had failed. When he tumbled, his musket tumbled with him, and the only sign that he'd fallen into the water was a brief and sudden explosion of white in the writhing black maelstrom.

Swiftly, then, she pulled herself up and over the wall, the others right behind her. The second guard was walking aimlessly in the opposite direction, and they kept to the wall as they ran, breaking for the house only when they were opposite the south tower. Caitlin took the lead, waving the four men on when she reached the door to the staff quarters and fell against the tower wall. Jonson, crouched beneath the single window, inched his way up and peered in, dropped down again and held up one finger. Caitlin pointed to her breast. Jonson, after a moment, nodded. She breathed deeply, stepped away from the tower and took hold of the door.

A dog barked in the stables.

The door opened and she raced in, running across the floor and throwing herself on Mary and knocking her to the floor before the chambermaid could utter a single cry. But her eyes, when she recognized Caitlin, widened, and she paled; she groaned beneath Caitlin's palm and would have fainted had not Caitlin slapped her with the daggered hand.

"Flint," she whispered in the woman's ear. "Flint!"

Mary struggled to break free, and Caitlin shifted until she was sitting on her stomach, the dagger's point pressed into her throat.

"Flint, damn you," she repeated.

"Mistress!" Jonson warned suddenly in a whisper, pointing at the door to the tower's lower hall. "Someone be comin'."

"Bradford?" Caitlin asked.

Mary shook her head.

"Gwen?"

Mary whimpered, and the dagger jabbed her skin once.

Jonson and Danny, with clubs in their hands raised and at the ready, stood on either side of the door. Now she could hear the footsteps, a man's by the sound of them and not stopping at any of the rooms along the way. She held her breath, glaring at Mary to keep her silent, then turned to face whoever entered.

The door opened, and Nate Birwyn came through. He was four paces into the common room before he realized something was wrong. By that time, Jonson had closed the door behind him, and Danny had drawn his own knife from his belt. The others stepped into the light, but Nate saw only Caitlin straddling Mary on the floor.

His good eye bulged. "My God!"

Caitlin slapped Mary once to warn her, then rose, letting Jonson take her place, push Mary into a chair, and stand threateningly over her. "Mr. Birwyn," she said, "how nice of you to welcome me home."

Birwyn tensed, but a quick appraisal of the force ranged against him made him see the futility of attempting to escape. He shrugged acquiescence and perched on a corner of the long table.

"Didn't expect you," he said.

Time, she thought; I can't waste time.

"Where's Flint?"

"How'd you manage it, m'lady?" Birywn asked innocently. "Didn't think you had the army."

"The bay," Danny told him, moving nearer to show him the glint of his blade.

"Ah." Birwyn nodded. "James, y'see, didn't think you'd try anythin' in a storm like out there."

"Flint!" she demanded.

"You heard the mistress," Danny growled. "Where's Mr. Flint?"

Birwyn shrugged maddeningly, and Caitlin lost her patience. She walked up to him and showed him her blade, still marked with the blood of the guard. His eye narrowed, and his mouth grew taut. She suspected he was thinking it hadn't been she who'd done the killing, and though she had not allowed herself to think about her action, it seemed to her, too, that someone else had held the dagger and plunged it into the guard's throat. Someone else had used his weight and surprise to cast the soldier down into the sea.

"Flint—for the last time!" she said harshly, and held the point of the dagger close to his eye.

"Well," he said without flinching, "there's a story in that, y'know."

Griffin paced the length of the barracks yard and back again, glancing in the door to see if his men still watched their charges. He was worried. Something should have happened by now, and he blamed himself for allowing Caitlin to take such complete charge without offering some advice of his own, or at least suggesting a system of warning and victory signals. As it was, he'd sent Peter to search the grounds around the house, to see what he could learn. And he realized that soon enough his prisoners were going to realize that a concerted rush on the outlaws would overwhelm them handily.

He walked, and stared toward Seacliff as if the sheer force of his will would allow him to penetrate the darkness and determine Caitlin's whereabouts. And as he stared, he became aware of a light dancing at the corner of his vision. With his weapon at the ready he spun around just as a wall of flame roared up the front of the barracks across the green. He whirled to snap an order to his men, but he knew it was too late. A guard materialized out of the darkness to his left, saw the fire raging, saw Griffin standing in the full light, and vanished again.

Courage, he told himself as he hurried inside; have courage, lad, or we're done for.

The mercenaries were milling about in their cramped corner,

and Griffin, with a stern glance at his men, faced them as he studied the sleek blade his right hand held high. "Gentlemen," he said calmly, "it appears the wind is up. You're in no mortal danger, of course, if you stay here. I doubt the fire will jump in your laps. But," he added, slightly louder, using his left hand to wave his men from the building, "I do suspect you will lose something of your lives if you try to leave very soon." He smiled. "And please, do remember what I told you before. The man who fills your purses will fill them no more." He moved backward to the door, reached out and took hold of its edge, the heat of the fire nearly scorching his back.

Two of the mercenaries broke into a run, and stopped as if hitting an invisible wall when Griffin showed them the gleam of his dagger.

"Hasty," he scolded. "Very hasty. You're not thinking, gentlemen, not thinking at all. Of course, I could be wrong, couldn't I? You could be feeling a profound loyalty to Mr. Flint, and in that case you'll want to fight for him—to the death, mind—simply because you love him. If that's the case, then good hunting."

He jumped out and slammed the door, throwing the bolt down and stepping aside while his men propped benches against it, using large stones to brace its base. Then he picked three men to stay behind, to watch the window and the door—and to release those inside should the sparks that now filled the air make a torch of the building.

A muttered word of encouragement, and he turned on his heels and ran, heedless of the mercenaries' pleading shouts.

"Story!" Caitlin exclaimed, seething with disgust and impatience. But Nate spread his arms wide to indicate that he had no other choice, that what she wanted to know would not be forthcoming unless she heard him out. She shifted her gaze to the point of her blade and saw in it the distorted reflection of her face. She concentrated on it for several long moments while she wrestled with her temper. When it was done—she had no idea where she'd found the strength to do it—she looked up again and nodded.

Birwyn combed his fingers through his hair and was about to begin his tale when Danny uttered a terrified, startled oath. Caitlin snapped her gaze to the window and gasped when she saw a hideously deformed visage staring in at her. It was but the space of a few seconds before she recognized Griffin's man, Peter, his face contorted by the raindrops clinging to the panes. Instantly taking advantage of the interruption, Birwyn threw himself off the table, at once shoving Caitlin backward and flinging out his arm to catch Danny in a vicious blow to the chest. Danny grunted, staggered, as Birwyn snatched his dagger away and sprinted for the door. When Jonson moved to pursue him, Mary rammed her knee between his legs and brought him crashing to the floor.

Caitlin recovered just as the tower door slammed, shouting an instruction before she took up the chase.

Her men followed as she sprinted down the short hall, into the main house in time to see Birwyn reach the end of the corridor and disappear to the right. Before she was halfway there she heard the front door thunder to a close. She slowed, and by the time she'd reached the center hall, she was walking, her men nervously trailing behind her.

"Flint," she ordered then. "We'll take care of Birwyn later. I want this house searched. Every room. Every closet. I want to know where James Flint is!"

The men scattered, except for the two she had instructed to drag chairs from the dining room as braces against the north tower door in case mercenaries tried to come through those apartments. Then she raced up the steps to the gallery and began her own search. Room by room. Kicking open doors and leaping over the threshold with her dagger held in front of her. She could hear footsteps below her, shouts, directions, but no cries of discovery.

She saved her own room for last, and was glad she had.

The reception room was a shambles, furniture tipped over and tapestries yanked down from the walls. The vanity, too, had been savaged. But the bedchamber stopped her and brought a anguished moan to her lips.

All the windows had been broken, the draperies shredded and strewn on the floor. The wardrobe was pitted, splintered and tipped over, its back having snapped in half. Mirrors were shattered, chairs gouged and turned to matchwood, and her bed—from canopy to mattress—looked as if an enraged, monstrous lion had clawed it to shreds until nothing was left but the frame, and the posts broken in two. In the center of this chaos lay the grappling hook and rope she'd used for her escape, and it took her no time at all to conclude that Flint, at some time returning here to seek a clue to her whereabouts, had found the device and in an eruption of temper used it to wreak the destruction she now stumbled through.

Her arms hung limply at her sides as she walked to the fireplace. Her knees gave way and she dropped to the hearth when she saw the bust of her father lying in pieces against the firewall. The dagger dropped from her hand. One by one she pulled the shards of stone from the ashes and laid them in a mound at her knees. She wept, not with sorrow but with impotent rage, a furious red flush crossing her cheeks until, with a strangled scream, she leaped to her feet and raced for the stairs.

And stopped, suddenly, to listen.

There was fighting downstairs. She could hear the clash of swords, the crack of blows landing on bone, the crackle of musketfire, and the crashing of chairs against the paneling and stone. Warily, she trotted to the gallery and looked down, her eyes large and her mouth agape.

The double front doors were flung open, one of them hanging precariously from a single hinge. Outside she could see wavering images struggling beneath torches held high, and though it lasted but a moment she was positive she saw Orin Daniels rush by with a club in his hand, his shirt torn from the shoulder.

In the hall, too, men were fighting, though the conflict was contained and considerably more vicious. It was easy to tell the outlaws by their green vestments, and the mercenaries by their catchall uniforms and bedraggled civilian clothing. And as she watched, stunned into immobility, Griffin sprang from the side corridor at the foot of the staircase, laughing wildly, his hair loose and his left hand brandishing a staff six feet long.

He waded into the battle almost casually, thumping skulls, grabbing the back of a shirt and flinging a man aside as if he were weightless. He dropped the staff at one point when a band of Flint's men rushed in from the outside. Picking up the nearest mercenary by his collar and belt Griffin tossed him into the charging men, scattering and rendering them helpless.

Caitlin's blood raced, and she called out to him without thinking.

He turned, and the smile that flashed on his lips made her forget for a moment the dismay she'd felt in her rooms.

Then she cried out a warning, and Griffin spun around in

a crouch just as a club whistled over his head. The man froze in astonishment, just long enough for Griffin to land a blow in his stomach, another to his jaw, and turn to deliver the same combination to a man charging him with an outstretched dagger.

Davy Daniels stood framed in the doorway, his left arm bleeding. He took one enemy from behind with his staff, then stopped another who was attempting to flee into the dining room.

Caitlin leaned over the gallery railing and looked toward the back and saw more of the same. It was evident, however, that the few mercenaries who had chosen to hold Seacliff for Flint were losing, and losing badly. Within the space of a few minutes she saw only villagers run out of the corridors, the rooms, through the front doors.

And then she saw Gwen.

And Nate Birwyn.

They came out of the corridor at the foot of the staircase, Gwen trembling violently, her head held back by Birwyn's hand clamped under her chin, her back arched to strain away from the dagger he held snugly against her spine. When Griffin saw them, he instinctively raised his staff, but Birwyn shook his head, a great evil smile creasing his lips. One by one the others stopped their fighting, and in less than a minute there were only the sounds of the injured groaning, and a few scattered shouts from the men still fighting on the front lawn.

"Ye'll let me and the gel pass," Birwyn said as if he were discussing the weather.

Davy and Orin stood in the doorway, their friends ranged on either side, unmoving.

Griffin was alone in the center of the hall, unconscious men lying in clumps all around him. He shook his head, slowly, and Gwen whimpered.

"All right, then," Birwyn said unconcernedly. "There are other ways, man."

He moved to the stairs and begin backing up them, pulling Gwen with him. Griffin dropped his staff and reached into his belt to pull out a pistol. It was cocked, but though he moved along the hall, following the two up the steps with the banister between them, Caitlin could see from the frustration in his eyes he could not get a clear shot at Birwyn without striking Gwen as well.

Caitlin moved.

Without a definite idea of what she could do, she inched along the railing to the top step.

Griffin's gaze flicked to her and away. "Birwyn!" he said loudly. "Birwyn, this is madness."

Birwyn only tightened his grip on Gwen's jaw and laughed softly at her cry. "We'll see, Welshman. We'll see. I been in worse straits afore."

"Have you, now?"

Caitlin took one step down, then another. Her left hand was on the banister, her right hand extended for balance . . . and to signal the men to be silent.

"Indeed, Welshman. Indeed."

When Birwyn started to turn around to see how far he had to go, Griffin called his name again, sharply, and Caitlin held her breath. "Flint," Griff said. "Where the hell is Flint?"

"I do believe that little fire out there gave him pause, Welshman. I do believe it did. To tell the truth, I ain't seen him in quite a while."

"He's a coward," Griffin sneered, still moving along the hall.

"Who's to say?" Birwyn told him. "He lives to fight another day, don't he?"

Suddenly, Griffin shouted again, this time flinging the pistol into the air. Birwyn froze and half turned. Caitlin jumped down a step and reached over the banister, caught the pistol, and dropped to a crouch, her finger fumbling for the trigger. The delay was disastrous. Birwyn's arm stabbed forward and Gwen screamed, threw up her hands and slumped to the steps, a dark red stain spreading rapidly across her waist. Birwyn ignored her. Instead, he took a step up, grinning at Caitlin.

"M'lady," he said, "that's a dangerous thing ye have there."

Caitlin gritted her teeth. "I'll use it, believe me."

"But I'm without arms now," he said, opening his hands to show her the knife was gone. "You wouldn't shoot a man without arms, would you?"

She blocked out his voice as best she could, but she did not retreat. Instead, she rose slowly and stretched out her arms, gripping the pistol tightly and praying none of the powder had fallen from the pan in its flight.

Birwyn took another step, grinning.

"Would ye like t'see somethin', m'lady?" he asked innocently.

She blinked. He was only eight steps down. One more and he would be close enough to lunge.

Then, in a movement too swift for her to follow, he snatched off his patch and showed her the black hole where his eye had once been. At the same time he leaned into a running stance, hoping the sight would immobilize her just enough.

Caitlin gasped.

Birwyn lunged.

And she pulled the trigger to send the ball through his heart.

37

CAITLIN STOOD wearily on the front lawn, her arms and legs leaden, attempting to fill her lungs with fresh air. The sky over the eastern hills was graying, the ridges soft and the shadows creeping down the slopes toward the farms. All about her there was subdued but joyful activity. Carts were being drawn up to haul off the dead; the surviving mercenaries had been gathered into a herd and, at her instructions, were being driven from the valley. She wanted no part of them now. All she wanted was to get them out of her home, and out of her country. What they did once they reached England was their affair, not hers. But her concluding message to them had been clear: she would spread the word through every shire in Wales, and if any one of them showed his face across the border again he would be summarily killed. And from the look in her eyes they knew it was no idle threat.

Gwen was in Orin's cottage. The wound she had received was not deep, only bloody. Caitlin had bound it herself and had given the woman a tonic to allow her surcease from pain and some escape in slumber. Afterward, she learned of Bradford's death and mourned his loss.

Behind her, in the house, she could hear parties of men who were led by Mrs. Courder and her sister as they cleaned up. They were laughing, not a few of them singing, but in spite of it all, Caitlin felt the victory was hollow.

Two hours of intensive, frantic searching had not uncovered the hiding place of James Flint.

She had sighed, looked down at herself and grinned sardonically. Seacliff was hers at last, and here she stood still in her father's clothes—bloodied, soaked through with rain, and ill-fitting—a wonderful sight she was sure the villagers would spin into tales for their granchildren to hear in years to come. The mistress of Seacliff, garbed in man's clothes, laying siege to her own manor.

Griffin's hand lay against the small of her back, and she pressed her cheek to his shoulder.

"Fair night's work," he said.

"But all that dying," she said despairingly, "all that blood, and it's still not over."

"He's long gone, Cat," he assured her quietly. "He's out of the valley forever."

"I wish I could believe that."

"You must," he insisted, turning to face her. "Cat, you've done more than any hundred men could have done. You've given these people back their lives, and their laughter." He cocked his head as if listening. "They'll face hell for you now. Even poor Terry."

She smiled wanly, and accepted his kiss gratefully. But when it was done she asked him for a moment to be alone with her father. He nodded his understanding, kissed her again, and took hold of her shoulders before she left him.

"Cat," he said, "I don't believe I've mentioned this to you before, but you do have my heart, you know. I do love you, Caitlin Evans. I'm mad, but I love you."

Then he was gone, into the house for a tankard of beer with the men. She watched his broad back until it was swallowed by darkness, then turned and made her way around the house to the pine at the corner of the wall. The skies were clear, the first light reaching nearly to the horizon. She put her hand on the rough tree bole and closed her eyes briefly. A breeze wafted through her hair and ruffled her shirtfront. A gull called. Cattle began lowing in the pastures.

"I've killed two men, Father," she whispered. "Many more have died, both theirs and ours. But he said it, you know. James said it himself. This house belongs to its conquerors. And this time I'm the victor. I hope I did it right."

She waited, not really expecting an answer, then pushed

away from the tree and leaned over the wall. The tide was turning, but the sea was still high from the storm's all-night battering. A grin creased her soft features as she remembered with a chill and delight the harrowing leap from the boat now splintered at the bottom, the near-drowning she'd experienced, and the way the cliffs had called to her from the mouths of caves high up in the sea wall.

She would probably have nightmares, but she would have stories, too. And she supposed that in the Welsh tradition they would be embroidered and gilded and made heroic in their proportions.

She moved along the wall until she was above the path, and she wondered how long it had taken those now forgotten Norsemen to chisel the steps out, how many of their dragon-headed longboats had landed on the beach. She supposed that was true heroism. And when the Romans came, did they hide in the caves until nightfall, waiting for their chance to escape? Or were they gone by first light? Which of those races reached this place first?

A call from the house sent her spinning around. It was Alice Courder, asking petulantly if she and her sister were expected to feed all these people.

"Who gave you that idea?" she called back, laughing.

"Master Griffin!" the woman shouted.

Caitlin sobered, then laughed again. "Please, Alice, do as he asks. It's little enough we can do for our friends."

Alice, however, didn't seem to think so. She scowled and vanished back inside, muttering to herself.

It was a fine moment, and one that should have lasted. Caitlin, however, was trying to decide if she should sit with Gwen for a while before sleeping herself when a dark voice whispered at the back of her mind. She stood like a statue facing the house for almost a full minute, fearing that the nightmare had another scene to play. Then, slowly, she turned to the wall and looked down.

Below were the ridges of rock that overhung the caves.

As if in a dream she climbed over the wall and lowered herself to the first step, noting almost absently that a year's battering from the sea had weakened the thin posts lashed between the iron spikes. If anyone the night before had leaned too heavily against one it surely would have split and sent him plunging into the water.

She made her way down cautiously, leaning out as far as she dared to spot each of the cave mouths just beyond reach of the steps. It could have been done, she thought. He could have climbed down this far, then used the rocks and cracks to make his way over to one of the caves. It would have been extremely dangerous—one slip and he would have been gone— but not too dangerous for a man fleeing for his life.

She prayed she was wrong.

Flint, from what she'd heard from Orin, had injured his arm and his leg in the fall that had killed Bradford. It would have been agony for him to—

She stopped, one hand brushing impatiently at the spray that covered her like intermittent mist.

She stared, and her heart slowed as if it had taken one shock too many.

She spotted a small cave some thirty yards across the cliff wall. There was a movement. A flash of white, of dark, and a hand reached out around the edge to grip, to pull . . . and the head of James Flint appeared in the faint light. A wave broke against the stone and raced up the wall; when it cleared, dripping and sliding down and leaving blossoms of foam in its wake, he was in full view, and staring at her dumbly. He recovered swiftly enough, however, and nodded. With the wind coming down from the north his voice carried easily.

"Well, Caitlin, I assume it's over."

It took her some time to find her voice, and when she did she was startled by the cold hatred that filled it. "It's over, yes," she said.

He shrugged. "Mr. Birwyn?"

"Dead. By my hand," she added.

The scar distorted his lip hideously as he broke into a rueful grin. "From the beginning I underestimated you, my lady. Right from the beginning."

"It seems you did."

He looked down at the sea, then turned around and lowered his legs to an outcropping just below the cave. A grimace of pain crossed his face, but he was too busy searching for handholds, looking for places to plant his feet firmly, to give in to it. As she watched him move like a crab toward her, she was amazed that he had managed to do the same in pitch darkness.

"I guess," he said, grunting, "we'll not meet again."

"Only if I join you in hell, James, only in hell."

A man's voice called to her from above, distantly, and Flint held his place, craning his neck to see if anyone had spotted him. Then, reminding her now of a spider stalking its prey, he moved again, slightly downward now, toward the nearest broad step.

Caitlin held her breath, and found she was unable to move. It would be simple, she told herself, so simple to climb below him and wait. And once he was near enough to reach, grab his ankle and cause him to fall. If he did not reach the water, he would be stunned long enough for her to scream for help, for Griffin to come and take him prisoner. Then she frowned at herself. It *was* simple, and she *should* be screaming now, but something checked her. Something impinged on the impulse to do what was necessary.

He climbed lower, and closer. His clothes were torn, and she could see dried blood caked on the side of his neck.

When she glanced up, she knew what it was. Over the edge of the wall hung the twisted, needled branch of her father's pine. She knew instinctively it marked the place where Flint had fought with David Evans and had thrown him over the edge. When she returned her gaze to Flint, the midnight of her eyes had turned to obsidian.

He slipped once, and she held her breath.

He climbed, and slipped again, this time losing his hold and dropping to the steps. He landed on hands and knees, and his head was bowed as she came down to meet him. When he looked up, he was smiling.

"You would jail me?" he asked mockingly.

"No," she said. "I'm not strong enough for that."

He rose unsteadily to his feet, wary puzzlement in his eyes when she stopped on the step above, within reach yet unafraid. The sea boiled fifty feet below them, the tide far enough out to expose jagged boulders lining the cliff's base, yet not far enough out to uncover the beach.

He shook his head regretfully. "We could have been quite the couple, Caitlin, you and I. A fair traveling pair we could have been."

"Never," she said.

"A dream of mine, that's all," he answered, and before she could jump away he had closed the space between them and had his arms around her. His lips brushed her cheek as she struggled, and his familiar laugh filled her ears. When she kicked his shins, he slapped her hard and grabbed her again.

"I don't lose," he told her. "And if you won't go with me now, I'll just have to go alone, won't I?"

Her hands had worked their way up to his chest, and her answer was a shove that broke the embrace and made him stagger backward. His buttocks struck the railing while his arms stretched out to balance him. But it was too late. The crack of splintering wood was musket-loud, and as he began to fall over the edge his eyes widened in utter amazement.

Then he fell, and Caitlin stepped close to the broken railing and watched his body plunge silently into the surf. She watched for nearly an hour, and when he did not surface again she turned and made her way back home.

The following day she was at the wall again. Gwen was doing well, and complaining, and Caitlin had ordered her to marry Davy without delay. Davy had laughed, but Gwen had bristled.

"So," she'd said from her bed, "you're taking over now, are you?"

Caitlin grinned at her. "I am that, yes."

"And you think you can order me about like a simple maid?"

"A maid, no; simple, yes."

"Cat!"

"I don't envy you," she said to Davy, who couldn't stop grinning. "She's going to be hell to live with."

"Cat, dammit!"

"I can manage," Davy said. "But if you don't mind, mistress, I'd just as soon not have the vicar say the words."

Caitlin nodded her agreement. "You won't have to worry, Davy. Randall found him hiding in his cellar, and he's been allowed three days to leave Wales. There'll be a replacement from Cardiff soon enough. I should think, by that time, Gwen will be much better."

"Not if you're going to speak to me like that," Gwen said in a huff, and Caitlin left the cottage laughing, listening to the bantering filling the room behind her. She hurried to the kitchen to arrange deliveries for the Courders, then strode into the front room where she'd had all her father's ledgers brought. She'd decided to waste no time in getting the estate running as smoothly as possible. It was almost time for dinner when Griffin entered the room.

She looked up, saw him, and rose. "You don't knock?"

"I was asked," he said, grinning as he approached her. But when he tried to embrace her, she held him at bay.

"Asked? By whom?"

"Gwen," he said. "She said something about tit for tat, whatever that means."

"Oh, dear," Caitlin said, then broke into a laugh as she leaned against his chest, feeling his strength, feeling her own strength as well. When she told him what she'd told Gwen that morning, he stared at her askance.

"You're not willing, then?"

"I didn't say that," she corrected. "But you must understand one thing. If we're to be married, we must be equals. I'll not have it the way it was with Oliver."

He lifted her off the floor suddenly and kissed her solidly on the lips. When she squealed and wriggled, he only held her tighter. "Equals, you say."

"Griff Radnor, put me down!"

"Equals." He half closed his eyes, as if he were considering a rather dubious offer. "Equals."

She yanked at his hair, and he put her down in a hurry, stepping back while she smoothed her blouse and skirts primly and fixed him with a stare. They held the pose for nearly a full minute before she put a hand to her mouth and smothered a quick laugh.

"Equals," she insisted.

"All right," he sighed in mock defeat. "If that's the only way I'm to have you, then equals it will be."

"And something else."

Wary now, he stroked his chin. "Yes?" he said cautiously.

"No more adventures, Griffin. I won't have you leaving me just because your boot itches."

He crossed his heart and lifted his gaze toward the heavens. "I swear, Cat. No more adventures. I'll stay by you, no matter what. This is my home now, too, and I won't want to jeopardize it."

But when he took her into his arms and she laid her head on his shoulder, he could not see the smile that parted her lips, the love that sparked her eyes, and the expression on her face that said Caitlin Evans, of Seacliff, was not a woman to be fooled.

After all, she thought as the smile broadened to a grin, it was not some false gentry but Griffin Radnor whom she loved. She must hope he wouldn't mind when he discovered she'd never leave his side.

Sweeping Stories of Historical Romance

Bestselling Books

☐ 21889-X	**EXPANDED UNIVERSE,** Robert A. Heinlein	$3.95
☐ 47809-3	**THE LEFT HAND OF DARKNESS,** Ursala K. LeGuin	$2.95
☐ 48519-7	**LIVE LONGER NOW,** Jon. N. Leonard, J. L. Hofer and N. Pritikin	$3.50
☐ 80581-7	**THIEVE'S WORLD,** Robert Lynn Asprin, Ed.	$2.95
☐ 02884-5	**ARCHANGEL,** Gerald Seymour	$3.50
☐ 08933-X	**BUSHIDO,** Beresford Osborne	$3.50
☐ 08950-X	**THE BUTCHER'S BOY,** Thomas Perry	$3.50
☐ 09231-4	**CASHING IN,** Antonia Gowar	$3.50
☐ 78035-0	**STAR COLONY,** Keith Laumer	$2.95
☐ 11503-9	**A COLD BLUE LIGHT,** Marvin Kay and Parke Godwin	$3.50
☐ 24097-6	**THE FLOATING ADMIRAL,** Agatha Christie, Dorothy Sayers, G.K. Chesterton & others	$2.95
☐ 21599-8	**ESCAPE VELOCITY,** Christopher Stasheff	$2.95
☐ 37154-X	**INVASION: EARTH,** Harry Harrison	$2.75

Prices may be slightly higher in Canada.

Available at your local bookstore or return this form to:

CHARTER BOOKS
Book Mailing Service
P.O. Box 690, Rockville Centre, NY 11571

Please send me the titles checked above. I enclose _____. Include 75¢ for postage and handling if one book is ordered; 25¢ per book for two or more not to exceed $1.75. California, Illinois, New York and Tennessee residents please add sales tax.

NAME_____

ADDRESS_____

CITY_____STATE/ZIP_____

(allow six weeks for delivery)   A-9